ENSHADOWED

Also by Kelly Creagh

NEVERMORE

Enshadowed

A NEVERMORE Book

KELLY CREAGH

Atheneum Books for Young Readers
NEW YORK LONDON TORONTO SYDNEY NEW DELHI

ATHENEUM BOOKS FOR YOUNG READERS
An imprint of Simon & Schuster Children's Publishing Division
1230 Avenue of the Americas, New York, New York 10020

Copyright © 2012 by Kelly Creagh
This book contains excerpts from "Annabel Lee," "Berenice," "The Sleeper," "The Raven," and "The Fall of the House of Usher" by Edgar Allan Poe.
ATHENEUM BOOKS FOR YOUNG READERS is a registered trademark of Simon & Schuster, Inc.
Atheneum logo is a trademark of Simon & Schuster, Inc.
For information about special discounts for bulk purchases, please contact Simon & Schuster Special Sales at 1-866-506-1949 or business@simonandschuster.com.
The Simon & Schuster Speakers Bureau can bring authors to your live event. For more information or to book an event, contact the Simon & Schuster Speakers Bureau at 1-866-248-3049 or visit our website at www.simonspeakers.com.
The text for this book is set in Stempel Garamond LT.
Manufactured in the United States of America
First Edition
2 4 6 8 10 9 7 5 3 1
Library of Congress Cataloging-in-Publication Data
Creagh, Kelly.
Enshadowed / Kelly Creagh. — 1st ed.
p. cm. — (A Nevermore book)
Summary: Isobel, haunted by the memory of Varen, goes to Baltimore where she confronts the dark figure known as the Poe Toaster, succeeds in interrupting his ritual, and discovers a way to return to the dreamworld, where she must face a new adversary.
ISBN 978-1-4424-0204-1 (hardcover)
ISBN 978-1-4424-0207-2 (eBook)
[1. Horror stories. 2. Poe, Edgar Allan, 1809–1849—Fiction. 3. High schools—Fiction. 4. Schools—Fiction.] I. Title.
PZ7.C85983Ens 2012
[Fic]—dc22   2012001292

FOR MOM,

my bestie

Contents

*   *   *

The realities of the world affected me as visions, and as visions only, while the wild ideas of the land of dreams became, in turn—not the material of my every-day existence—but in very deed that existence utterly and solely in itself.

—Edgar Allan Poe, "Berenice"

Oh, lady bright! Can it be right—
This window open to the night?
The wanton airs, from the tree-top,
Laughingly through the lattice drop—
The bodiless airs, a wizard rout,
Flit through thy chamber in and out,
And wave the curtain canopy
So fitfully—so fearfully—
Above the closed and fringed lid
'Neath which thy slumb'ring soul lies hid,
That, o'er the floor and down the wall,
Like ghosts the shadows rise and fall!
Oh, lady dear, hast thou no fear?

—Edgar Allan Poe, "The Sleeper"

*   *   *

Prologue
Washington University Hospital
Baltimore
October 7, 1849

"Edgar?"

Speaking softly, Dr. Moran leaned over his patient. His eyes traced the wan and pallid countenance of the famous poet, Edgar Poe. But the man who lay on the hospital bed before him now, bathed in the dim yellow lamplight, bore little resemblance to his dignified portraits. He seemed, instead, more like a ghostly shell of that man, a wasted imposter, his cheeks shadow-sunken, his skin waxen, white as the sheets beneath him. Dark lashes fringed his bruise-purple lids, serving to blacken the deep crescent-shaped hollows beneath each eye. Sweat glistened on his broad brow, less from fever and more, the doctor knew, from exertion.

Rain pattered against the vaulted Gothic windows, glittering crystal beads that quivered into long streaks against the backdrop of darkness.

Though morning approached, the shadows of night pervaded the otherwise empty room.

Outside, the wind moaned, while the clop of horses'

hooves and the rattle of carriage wheels echoed from the alley below.

"Edgar," Moran spoke again, "can you hear me?"

Poe's eyes drifted lazily open, glassy and distant, like the sightless eyes of a child's doll, black as inkwells. He stared at the ceiling.

Moran checked his patient's pulse, his thumb and finger clasping the clammy skin of the poet's wrist. There, a racing throb marked the seconds.

The doctor hesitated. He did not wish to send his patient into a frenzy yet again. Still, he could not help but press for another moment of lucidity, another brief glimmer of the man locked within the mania. Another clue to the puzzle of what had happened four days ago, when Poe had been brought into his care, delirious, covered from head to foot in ashen grit, insensible, dressed in another man's clothing and unable to relate a single coherent detail as to where he had been—or who he had been with, for that matter.

"Do you remember where you are?" Moran asked. The doctor shifted in his seat, and the old wooden chair creaked beneath him.

Suddenly Poe's arm shot out. He grasped for the doctor, locking his wrist in a grip that held all the strength of rigor mortis. "Who is it?" Edgar gasped, a rattle sounding in his chest, his voice husky, raw from the hours of screaming. "Who is here?"

"Be calm," Moran urged. He allowed Edgar's clammy grip to remain, hoping that the physical contact would somehow ground him, that it could bring him back, tether him to reality.

"Reynolds?" Poe whispered. His hand tightened around Moran's wrist with unbelievable strength, quivering with urgency. "Reynolds . . . tell me that you've come at last."

The doctor swallowed. He wet his lips, which fought to form words before he knew what to say. "It is Dr. Moran, Edgar. Your physician. As I'm sure you remember."

Poe's face contorted. His eyes squeezed shut. His mouth opened, the corners collapsing in silent anguish. He released the doctor, his grip falling limp. "I should have known," he moaned, every syllable dripping the blackest despair, "that you would leave me here. Like this."

"Edgar," Moran whispered, "I wish only to help. Can you tell me what happened? Can you tell me how you came to be in Baltimore?"

"But I am not," Poe said, rocking his head back and forth against the damp pillow. With these words, his breathing turned shallow and quick. A shudder ran through him, causing the bed itself to tremble.

Moran frowned at his patient and groped for what next to say, for whatever words might keep Poe's mind present, distracted from hallucination, from the entities he claimed he saw slipping through the walls in swirls of black smoke. "Mr. Poe, you mentioned yesterday that you had a wife. In Richmond. Can you tell me—"

"Almost," Poe whispered. "Almost. But then, Reynolds, I *have* a wife." With these words, he traced his fingertips lightly across his chest, over a place where a portion of his shirt lay open. "Here. All the while," he murmured. "Locked within this feverish heart. All the while."

"Who is this Reynolds you speak of?" Moran asked. "A friend, perhaps?"

"Perhaps," Poe replied, his hand falling away as he fixated on the ceiling. "We shall see. The shadows gather. Can you hear them whispering? *She* is coming. And so we shall see."

Poe's eyes grew wider then, their centers expanding, black as pitch.

Moran watched, transfixed. He had treated delirium many times before. But what was it about this man's condition that made him want to steal a glance at the barren walls that encircled them, to be certain that there was truly nothing there?

Edgar gasped. His body went rigid. Arching his spine, he threw his head to one side and howled. Writhing, he gripped the bed beneath him, twisting the fabric of the matted bedclothes, crying out, "REYNOLDS!"

Moran shot to his feet.

"REYNOLDS!" Poe screamed again, renewing the cry that had carried him through the night, his voice now raw and ragged.

"Edgar!" Moran shouted, grasping for his patient's hand. "Edgar, you are *safe*."

"REYNOLDS!"

"There is nothing here that can harm you. Edgar, listen to me! It's over. Do you hear me? Whatever has happened, it is over!"

Poe froze in that moment, his teeth gritted, his face fraught with agony, beads of sweat sliding down his temples.

Then something in him changed. He seemed to return to himself all at once, like the flickering flame of a candle that had managed to steady itself after a gust of cold wind. His body began to relax and he sank slowly into the bed.

For the first time, his gaze turned to lock with Moran's.

The doctor stared, unblinking, stricken as he watched the blackened centers of Poe's eyes recede, like clouds from a storm-ravaged sea, revealing the bright rims of two blue-gray irises.

Poe stared at him with sudden intensity and intelligence, present for the first time. "Is it?" he asked.

As he exhaled, Poe's hand grew limp in the doctor's grip. "Lord help my poor soul," he breathed, even as the glow within those bright and glittering eyes dimmed, fading as fast as it had come.

"Edgar," Moran called.

But it was too late, for the eyes that stared up at him now, wide and sightless, held their strange light no more.

1
Deep into That Darkness

"Okay, Hawks," Coach Anne said. "That's a wrap. We can officially call that our last run before Nationals. At least until we hit Dallas."

Isobel released a sigh, her shoulders slumping in relief.

Around her, tired whoops and clapping echoed through the gym, everyone breaking off to find their water bottles and towels.

A dull ache spread its way slowly through her as she allowed her muscles to unclench. Her whole body felt like a twisted rope unwinding.

Already, Coach had drilled the routine at least twenty times. Even if Coach *had* wanted them to go again, Isobel didn't think she could have managed another pike basket toss, let alone landed one more full.

She knew she wasn't the only one running on fumes either.

She'd felt the entire squad's energy draining away little by little, like a machine operating on a single dying battery.

Coach must have felt it too. Isobel had no doubt that she would have drilled them until midnight if she hadn't sensed her squad preparing for mutiny.

Then again, it wasn't unusual for Coach to pull this kind of boot-camp, cheer-till-you-drop drillathon, especially right before a big competition. And this was *the* competition, after all. But her motivation for killing them like this lay less, Isobel knew, in ironing out any last-minute kinks and more in sending everyone home too tired to do anything but crash.

"I want you all to get some *rest* tonight," Coach shouted above a sudden burst of laughing and talking, her words confirming Isobel's suspicions. "That means no late-night Facebook updates, no texting, no two a.m. phone calls with Mr. or Miss Flavor of the Week, and *no* last-minute stunting in the living room—I'm talking to you, Miss Dorbon. I want everybody here in one piece and ready to go at five a.m. *sharp*. Got that?" Coach lifted one thick arm over her frizzy poof of brown hair and pointed at her wristwatch. "Bus leaves at *six* on the dot, so set your alarms. No hitting the snooze button forty times. No 'I forgot my uniform.' No excuses. I know I don't have to tell any of you that we won't wait if you're late."

Speaking of late, Isobel wondered what time it was. It felt like they'd been there for hours.

She glanced above the gym doors to the white-faced clock secured behind the protective metal grate designed to shield it from foul balls.

At the sight of the dark, familiar figure standing in the doorway, however, all thoughts of time flew from her mind.

Hands stuffed into the pockets of his black jeans, he watched her from behind reflective sunglasses, his expression calm, blank.

A panicked stirring arose inside her, coupled with a nagging sensation that tugged at the back of her mind, like a child pulling on the hem of her mother's dress. It was as though some deeper part of her was trying desperately to get her attention.

Behind her, Isobel could hear Coach Anne's continued tirade as she rattled off reminders about their uniforms and which colored tennis shoe inserts to wear. Blue bows for hair this time, she droned, not yellow. A-line skirts, *not* pleated.

The longer Isobel stared at the figure standing in the open doorway, though, the more distant Coach's voice began to grow. The walls of the gymnasium, the squad, and the floor, too—they all blurred out of her vision until there was only him.

Isobel walked toward the figure and reached for the glasses, the urge to strip them from his face and look into his eyes nothing short of a compulsion.

He stopped her hand with his. The contact made her pause, and the nameless dread inside her melted away as his fingers intertwined with hers.

His hand felt so warm.

"Ready to go?" he asked.

His voice rippled through her, low, soft, and a little husky—like the hushed crackling of an old-fashioned record player just before the music starts. Quieting the tangled mesh of her thoughts, it numbed her like a drug.

Her eyes flicked down from his glasses to the slight smile that tugged at one corner of his mouth. A glint of light caught on his lip ring, causing the silver to flash.

Suddenly it was too hard to breathe. She wanted to feel that tiny slip of metal against her own lips, to kiss him. As if that would somehow help her catch her breath.

But she couldn't escape the feeling that there was something about the moment, something about his very *presence* that she wasn't grasping. It was as if her mind had misplaced some vital bit of information. Or lost it entirely.

"What—what are you doing here?" she asked him, because it was the one question that kept pushing all the others out of the way.

One of his eyebrows drifted above the top edge of his sunglasses. His half smile remained in place. "I came to pick you up," he said. "You're my girlfriend. I do that now, remember?"

Girlfriend.

The word felt like a switchblade to her heart. The pain it evoked was more tender than sharp, though, the kind that comes along with saying good-bye to a friend you know you'll never see again.

"C'mon," he said before she could ask any more questions. He began to turn away and she felt his hand tighten around hers, squeezing, tugging her after him. "We should go."

Isobel found herself following him, her steps falling in stride with his.

She wanted to look back, to see who'd been watching and who had noticed. Certainly Coach had seen her go. Isobel couldn't understand why Coach wasn't yelling at her right that very second, shouting for her to come back and that practice wasn't over until after cooldown. But she didn't have time to turn around. She and Varen had already reached the double doors that led out into the school's rear parking lot.

They pushed through, greeted by a cascade of snow that poured from above, the gray-purple clouds all but blotting out the sky, leaving no room for the cold winter sun.

Varen's black 1967 Cougar sat alone in the empty parking lot, a dark inkblot surrounded by a sea of vacant whiteness.

Isobel frowned. Where were all the other cars? Where was the line of minivans and SUVs waiting to pick up the rest of the squad? Where was Coach's hulking, rust-red Suburban?

"I need to show you something," she heard Varen say, though he didn't turn around.

Isobel's focus narrowed in on the nape of his neck, the place where his hair, black and silken, jagged as crows' feathers, brushed the collar of his T-shirt.

Had she only just noticed how long it had grown?

A breeze whipped past them, and his bare arms made her wonder why he hadn't worn his jacket.

"Varen, where are we going?"

"You'll see," was his only response as he hurried her through the parking lot. Beneath their feet, the snow, still fresh and powdery, made no sound.

Reaching the Cougar, he opened and held the passenger-side door for her, the cab light illuminating the familiar burgundy interior.

She hesitated and glanced back to Varen. Shifting his weight from one foot to the other, he gestured to the upholstery.

"Yeah," he said, "sorry about that. Still waiting on those mink seat covers."

Isobel shot him a wry smile. Before she could return his trademark sarcasm with her own dry quip, though, something about his appearance made her pause.

There was something missing. Something off . . .

She realized that even though she was looking straight at him, she could not see herself in the mirrored lenses of his glasses, only the reflection of blackened trees standing in rows behind her, their thin prison-bar trunks still visible through the thickening screen of falling snow.

In the reflection, a large ebony bird lifted off from one of the twisted branches, and the sound of its beating wings caused her to flinch and whirl. But when she looked, there were no trees. No bird. Only the rigid outline of Trenton High's neo-Gothic facade.

From here, Isobel could just make out the four spires of the school's main entrance tower peeking up over the roof's ledge. The countless windowpanes glared white, refracting the overcast light like a thousand dead eyes. Even though she'd just left the squad in the gym, the entire building now appeared deserted—except for the top floor, where Isobel thought she saw the silhouette of someone standing in one of the windows, watching them.

"Get in," Varen said. "Now."

Isobel turned and sank into the car, spurred by the urgency in his voice.

She shut the door behind her and, glancing to the driver's

side, was shocked to find him already there, one hand on the steering wheel, the other locked around the stick shift, the bulky onyx gem of his class ring shining like oil in the stark light.

The car hummed. Isobel felt her seat vibrate beneath her as the engine rumbled, though she couldn't recall his turning the key. The smell of exhaust fumes filtered into her awareness while the windshield wipers jumped into action, slashing back and forth to cast off the gathering snow. By now, the cascade of whiteness had grown so heavy that the world outside had all but vanished.

Beside her on the seat, the ratty old Discman Varen had rigged up to the Cougar's dashboard radio sprang to life. Through the tiny rectangular window, Isobel saw the disc inside whir. A woman's soft voice erupted through a hiss of static. Her humming, unaccompanied by any instrumentals, filled the car. Soft and sweet, sad but beautiful, the naked melody was one Isobel had never heard before. The voice, too, was unfamiliar, possessing an airy quality, wispy and almost shy.

Without warning, Varen snatched the Discman, yanking it free from the wires that connected it to the dashboard, instantly silencing the static and the humming. With a hard scowl, he tossed the CD player into the backseat. Grabbing the stick shift again, he threw the car into gear.

His foot hit the gas pedal and they began to move, accelerating to top speed. Isobel opened her mouth to speak, but Varen cut her off, turning the wheel sharply.

Pressed to the passenger-side door, she groped for something to hold on to, instantly reminded of that night he'd driven her home, careening down the road while ignoring her desperate pleas for him to stop. Fear erupted inside her like a match striking. She gripped the seat beneath her, able only to see endless white through the windows.

"Varen! You can't even see where you're going!"

"I don't have to," he said.

Isobel felt her muscles tighten again, coiling up, tensing in preparation for the impact that would surely kill them both any second.

"Varen! Ple—" Isobel stopped, her words evaporating in her mouth as she caught sight of the small clock embedded into the dashboard.

The hands of the clock looped opposite each other and spun lazily around and around, never stopping. She watched the needle of the speedometer tip to and fro like the pendulum of a metronome.

The gas gauge read empty, but she could *hear* the engine growling, guzzling fuel.

"Wait," she whispered, more to herself than to him. "This isn't . . . This is a dr—"

"*Don't,*" he snapped, silencing her. "Not yet."

His foot slammed on the brake. Isobel pitched forward in her seat as the car skidded to a halt, its tires shrieking.

Like sand being blown from a relic, the snow coating the windshield began to erode.

Or rather, Isobel thought, the *ash*.

Tiny blots of bright crimson now fluttered down all around them, lighting on the windshield.

The car jerked to a final stop, causing Isobel to fly back again. Frantic, she turned toward the driver's side, only to find the car door flung open and Varen gone.

Outside, countless red roses bobbed their heads, their waxy leaves rustling in a sudden gust of wind that sent even more blood-colored petals raining over the car.

Thick and heady, the aroma of the blossoms weighed down the air.

Isobel fumbled for the handle on her door, which popped open as soon as she touched the latch. Jerking her arm with it, the door swung out wide over the jagged edge of a black cliff.

Far below, milky waters churned amid toothy rocks while the waves clamored one over the other, snapping like white wolves before smashing against the flat face of the cliff.

Isobel gave a silent shriek. She backpedaled for the driver's side. Twisting, she grabbed hold of the steering wheel, using it to pull herself out on the other side.

She spilled hard onto the ground. Rolling onto her back, she hiked one knee up and kicked, sending the door of the Cougar slamming shut.

The echoing clap caused the car to disperse into ashes.

Isobel raised her arms to shield her face from the spray of grit. Through the settling dust, she saw that the cliffs had vanished, leaving only the surrounding walls of ruby blossoms.

In the midst of what appeared to be an enormous rose

garden, a familiar structure became discernible through the screen of the settling powder.

Isobel recognized the structure as the fountain from Varen's neighborhood. It now stood in the center of a circular dome-shaped room enclosed by scarlet blooms.

Without the curtain of crystal water pouring from the ledge of its rounded green basin, the fountain was a silent and eerie monument.

Isobel pulled herself to her feet, her practice sneakers caked with ash, chalk white against a carpet of ruby petals.

Her eyes locked on the statue of the woman that stood at the top of the fountain, her stiff stone veil clutched in her hands, the fabric arcing out behind her nearly nude figure in a backward C.

Isobel turned in a circle. All around her, buds and blossoms in various states of unfurling dotted the trellised walls. High over the statue's head, thick vines met at a circular opening at the top of the domed ceiling. Through the porthole, she could see a tangled webwork of black tree limbs.

What was this place?

And where was—?

"Varen!"

"Here."

Isobel started, nearly yelping as she found him standing right in front of her.

She peered up into eyes no longer shielded by sunglasses. Their centers were black, swept clean of color and light.

She searched through their darkness, desperate to find

some irrefutable evidence in their depths that could prove it was really him.

"Is—is any of this real?" she asked. "Are *you* real?"

He lifted a hand to her cheek, his fingers brushing her jaw.

"Even if this is a dream," he whispered, "I'm not."

Isobel's eyes widened, recognizing those words as her own, the same ones she had once uttered to him. She reached for him, her arms twining around his neck, drawing him to her so that his scent poured over her, that combination of incense, citrus, and dried leaves overriding the funeral smell of the crowding flowers.

He lowered his forehead to hers, his hair draping around their faces, the smooth strands tickling her skin.

"Don't leave," she breathed.

"I'm here," he whispered. "Right here. Waiting."

He leaned in.

Isobel tilted her chin up, ready for the press of his lips.

She wanted to let her eyes fall shut, but something, a sensation of being watched, stopped her. Her glance slid past his shoulder, her focus drawn to the statue atop the fountain.

Between the inky strands of Varen's hair, Isobel watched its eyes slide open. She stared, transfixed, as the statue turned its head toward them, aiming those two empty pits of blackness straight at her.

2

Sorrow for the Lost

Isobel awoke with a start. She sucked in a sharp gasp of air, and her gaze met with the blank surface of her bedroom ceiling.

She blinked as a swirl of images shuttered through her brain like snapshots in a broken reel of film. Closing her eyes, she tried to find one frame to latch on to, one fleeting symbol or shadow that would trigger the memory of what it was she'd been dreaming about.

But the pictures slid by too quickly, growing dimmer and more uncertain the faster her consciousness swam toward the surface of reality.

Isobel groaned. She didn't want to wake up. She wanted to slip under again. She wanted to go back.

Rolling onto her side, she peered groggily through the narrow slice of window visible between her twin white-lace curtains.

It was still dark outside, still early.

If she threw the covers over her head and tried to sleep again, Isobel wondered if she would be able to return to whatever dream she'd been having. Even if she couldn't recall where she had been or what had been happening, she knew that the dream had not had a chance to end where it should have. There had been something left unsaid. No, she thought, there had been something left undone. What was it?

Isobel sighed. It was no use straining. The thread was broken.

She turned to glance at her digital clock.

6:30, it read in cool blue numbers.

She froze.

Oh my God. Six freaking thirty?

An ice bomb exploded somewhere in the pit of her stomach, set off by the sudden realization that she was supposed to be on a bus right that very moment, a bus that had probably reached the county line by now, filled with every member of Trenton High's varsity cheerleading squad. Every member except *her.*

"Daaaad!" Her voice scraped raw from the back of her throat. Isobel tossed off her covers, her legs prickling with gooseflesh as she staggered out of bed, hurtling toward her bedroom door. She threw it open and rushed out and onto the landing that overlooked the foyer and downstairs hallway.

Darkness bathed the house, quietness filling every corner.

At the end of the hall, Danny's bedroom door stood ajar, and Isobel could just make out her little brother's snores emanating from within.

She hurried to the stairs, not caring if she woke him, her bare feet thundering down the carpet-covered steps. "Da—"

Isobel jerked to a halt midway down, surprised to see her father enter the foyer, his upturned face clean-shaven, his expression questioning. He held his briefcase in one hand, a travel mug of coffee in the other. He wore black slacks and a clean white button-down shirt, the silver pin-striped tie she'd given him last Father's Day laced through the collar.

He raised his eyebrows at her.

"Miss the bus again, kiddo?" he asked, a slightly bemused look on his face.

Isobel stood motionless on the stairs, her thoughts racing. As the blank spaces of all the current whens and wheres refilled, the frantic beating of her heart began to slow. Spotting the darkened Christmas tree through the living room archway, she felt a warm gush of relief wash through her.

Nationals. The competition. It had all already happened. She'd been home from Dallas for a week now. She hadn't missed the bus, either. In fact, she'd been early.

They had won, too. Trenton High Spirit Squad now held the all-too-rare title of three-time NCA champions.

Isobel could still hear the squad's piercing screams of victory echo through her head. In her mind's eye, she pictured them all huddled together, a squealing, teary mob of blue and yellow, everyone clamoring to lay a hand on the gleaming golden trophy.

"Third time this week," her father said, drawing Isobel's attention back to his presence in the foyer.

With glazed eyes, she followed his movements as he set his briefcase down next to the umbrella stand. He stepped forward, grabbing his gray wool peacoat from where he'd hung it on the banister post. Juggling the coffee mug between his hands, he kept his gaze steady on her while he shrugged the coat on one sleeve at a time.

"Think I'm going to have to talk to Coach about this," he said. "Tell her to cool it a little next time on all those extra practices. I'm just waiting for the day you wake up from the nightmare where you think you *lost*."

Isobel grasped the stairway banister. She clutched the wood hard, her fingernails digging into the cherry finish. Slowly she lowered herself to sit on the edge of one step while fragments from her dream began to resurface, bobbing up like driftwood from a shipwreck. Amid the tangle of familiar and unfamiliar, mundane and frightening, one quiet face floated forward to occupy the forefront of her mind.

She was beginning to wonder if she would ever again be able to picture his eyes the way they'd been before . . . before . . .

"Hey. Relax, Izzy," her father said, leaning forward to nudge her knee with a fist. "Trophy's in the bag, champ."

The dream—it always started out with her being at final practice. And though she'd had it a handful of times now, it had never lasted so long. Every time before this, every *single* time, she'd awoken as soon as she saw him—as soon as she realized that his being there wasn't possible and that she had to be dreaming. In other words, as soon as she became lucid.

This time had been different, though. Somehow she'd managed to forget about reality long enough to remain within the dream. Long enough for him to show her what he'd wanted her to see.

But what *had* he wanted her to see?

"Sooo," her dad said. "I know it's Christmas Eve, but as you can probably guess, I've got to head into the office for a couple hours. Very Bob Cratchit of me, I know." He checked his wristwatch. "I should be back early, though. Noon at the latest. You and I are still on for our last-minute mall trip, right? I still have to pick up your mother's gift from the jeweler. Orange Julius on me?"

Isobel nodded at him. She'd have agreed to anything in that moment so long as it would make him go away, so long as it would let her be alone again so she could concentrate on salvaging the bits and pieces of time spent with Varen, even if she couldn't be 100 percent certain if those moments had been real.

They *had* to have been real, though. It only made sense that he would try to reach her this way. He had seemed so solid, so there. Her hand still tingled from where he'd held it, her skin alive with the memory of his warmth.

"Oooo-kay," Isobel heard her dad say, "then I'll call when I'm on my way to pick you up. In the meantime, Izzy, why don't you try going back to bed? I think you're still a little worn out from the all the competition stuff. I mean, they call it winter *break* for a reason."

Again, Isobel nodded. Nod, nod, nod. It was what she did best these days.

Concern flashed across his features, and his smile faltered.

Quickly she found her voice. "You're probably right," she said.

He continued to watch her, frowning, like there was still

something else he wanted to say. Instead of saying it, though, he pushed his smile into place again. Turning, he opened the front door and let in a burst of frigid winter air.

Even though the sudden brush of cold wind should have sent a shiver rattling through her, it didn't.

Outside, Isobel could see that the deep blue darkness had since lightened, evidence that the dawn was doing its best to push back the curtain of night.

Her father remained only a moment longer before bending, at last, to pick up his briefcase.

"I'll call you, okay?" he said. He raised his coffee mug to the side of his head as though it were a cell phone, like he thought she needed sign language.

"Yeah," she said, "sounds good."

He gave a half wave, then shuffled out, poking his head back in at the last moment to say, "Grab the door for me?"

Isobel pushed herself up from the stairs. She pressed the door closed behind him while her father shouldered his way past the outer storm door.

She leaned her forehead against the wood, listening to his shoes click against the sidewalk as his footsteps grew distant.

With her hand still gripping the knob, she caught herself wishing she could run after him and call him back. Time and again she'd had to fight the urge to tell him everything, even though she knew he would never believe any of it.

A moment longer, though, and she might have confessed that actually, she *had* had the nightmare he'd mentioned—the one where she'd lost. But unlike the recurring dream about practice, it hadn't concerned Nationals at all.

It had concerned everything else. The *only* thing else.

But it hadn't been a dream.

These days, it was getting harder and harder to tell what was.

She spun, putting her back to the door, listening to the quiet hum of the sedan's engine as her father backed the car out of the driveway and onto their street.

The twin beams of the headlights flashed through the living room window, casting a host of misshapen shadows along the floors and walls, making Isobel feel suddenly less alone.

A chill climbed up her spine, receding only when dimness and silence settled over the house once more.

She glanced up to the darkened doorway of her bedroom.

Her dad had told her to try to go back to sleep. Now that she was wide awake, though, Isobel began to doubt if she would ever know true rest again.

3
Bleak December

Her father's "no later than noon" call lit up Isobel's cell closer to four. Something had come up, he said, which had essentially turned his quick Christmas Eve trip to the office into another full workday. So it wasn't until after five that they were finally able to wrestle their way through traffic and into the mall. Amazingly, they managed to extract themselves from the mad bustle, bags in tow, appendages intact, by seven. They were even able to locate the sedan before the first semi-frozen droplets of the weatherman's projected "wintry mix" began to pepper the pavement.

Isobel stared out the passenger-side window as her father maneuvered the car through the congested parking lot. Slushy rain streaked the glass, turning the whole view mottled. Christmas lights blurred into glowing smudges, while the bright holiday window displays melded into shapeless meshes of color.

As the sedan edged toward the main road, a sifting of white snow slowly began to replace the sleet. It collected on the windshield in fluffy specks between wiper-blade swipes, the downy flecks bringing Isobel's thoughts back, yet again, to her dream.

"Awfully quiet over there," Isobel's dad said. "How about some music?"

He didn't wait for an answer. Instead he flipped on the radio, and through a scratch of fuzz that made Isobel flinch, Bing Crosby's voice broke, crooning about a white Christmas.

They turned, emerging from the bottleneck squeeze to join with the steady flow of traffic. Rows of trees swished past on the left, clumps of wild mistletoe clinging to their barren branches like tangled knots in petrified hair.

Despite her father's attempt to spark conversation, Isobel's thoughts remained lost in a world that existed between here and forever. A world that still held *him*.

For the entire day, the brief flashes of Varen's face, both torturous and comforting, had been the only thing she could concentrate on.

The dream itself still felt loose in her head, more distant than a childhood memory.

More than anything, she remembered being close to Varen. She just couldn't recall where they'd been or what he had said.

And as the day had dragged on, she wondered if her subconscious could somehow be the culprit behind the repeated dreams, doing its best to provide her with the one thing—the one person—that it hurt too much to be without.

"If this keeps up," her dad said, putting on his turn signal, "we might just get one of those."

Isobel stirred from her thoughts. "One of those what?"

"A white Christmas, Iz," he said, his eyes never leaving

the road. "What are you thinking so hard about over there, anyway?"

As they switched lanes, her dad offered a wave of thanks to the lady in the kid-packed SUV who had let them over. Isobel glanced down at her hands in her lap.

"Oh." She summoned her best semblance of a smile. "Just thinking about . . . Nationals," she lied, and touched the thin golden band on the ring finger of her right hand. She twisted the ring, turning it around and around. NATIONAL CHAMPION it read in bold capital letters that framed a smooth, glinting, Trenton-blue gemstone.

"Seems like you've been thinking about that an awful lot lately," he said. "Or worrying about it, I should say. I mean, to the point where you're dreaming that it didn't happen." He paused, looking away from the road to glance in her direction. Isobel knew he was waiting for her to speak, but she couldn't think of what to say. She didn't know what it was he wanted to hear. It was better, she thought, to remain silent and let him draw his own conclusions. At least it was easier to hide the truth that way.

"You know, Izzy," he said, returning his attention to the road, "you were really great out there this year. I mean, better than ever. And I'm not just saying that. I have to admit, I was a little nervous when I saw Heywood do their routine, but you guys smoked them. You know that, don't you? I mean . . . I can't help but get this feeling that, for whatever reason, you keep asking yourself if you really deserved to win. It's like you feel guilty about it, when I don't think I've ever seen you more focused. The squad was great, but you, Izzy, it's like you were on another plane of existence. I mean, you were totally *zoned*. You should be proud of yourself."

"I am," she said, giving the ring a final twist as the sedan rolled into their subdivision, past the triple-tiered fountain, which now stood as still and silent as a cemetery monument, collecting snow in its empty basins.

Isobel sensed her dad glancing her way again, so she looked up and squeezed out yet another false smile. She tried her best to hold the expression, even when he looked away, but keeping up the game was starting to take its toll.

At the very least, she'd tried to make it seem like Nationals had mattered to her in the way it once had, before that day at school when she'd been paired to work with a certain jade-eyed goth boy named Varen Nethers. Before she'd known a single thing about him or the ominous subject he'd chosen for their English project—the man who was Edgar Allan Poe.

But Isobel was a bad actress. When it came down to it, there was only so much "I'm okay—*really*" smiling she could muster when she wasn't out on the floor cheering, when she didn't have any choreography or chants to prop up the new cardboard-cutout version of herself. Without a distraction that took all her mind and body, it was just too hard to pretend that she wasn't empty on the inside. Or that she didn't know far more about what had happened on Halloween than what she had told her parents.

The events of that night came back to her in flashes. The Grim Facade. The dreamworld masquerade. The falling ash and the woodlands. The sky ripped into shreds by bleeding strips of violet. And his eyes. Always those eyes. Again and again she saw the blackness overtake them. She watched it spiral out, consuming her reflection, leaving behind a stranger.

"You think Mom will like the locket?"

"What?" Isobel blinked. "Yeah," she said, recovering quickly, realizing that he must have meant the gift he'd picked up that afternoon, the one the store clerk had had to retrieve from the special-orders case. "Of course she will."

The sedan slowed as it neared the stop sign just before their street. Isobel raised her thumb to her lips and bit down on her nail. "Hey, Dad," she said, speaking around her thumbnail, "have you thought any more about, you know, us going up to take a look at U of M?"

Instead of rolling through the stop sign the way he usually did, the car gave a sudden slight jerk as he pressed the brake. At the same moment, Isobel saw his lips flatten into a thin, tight line.

"I have," he said, his voice taking on that strained sternness she had grown more and more accustomed to during the past two months.

From Halloween on, as the weather had grown colder, so, it seemed, had her father's temperament, his fuse snipped shorter than the days themselves.

Isobel had become so used to tiptoeing around him, filtering her words and monitoring her requests, that it was getting harder to remember a time when things hadn't been so tense between them, so guarded.

It made her wonder if he would ever forgive her for lying to him. For sneaking off.

For falling in love with the wrong boy.

"And?" she prompted.

He sighed. Loosening his grip on the wheel, he made the turn onto their street. "And I think it's great that you're thinking about college, Izzy, I do. But we don't have to go look at a school right away, you know. You're still only a junior. There's plenty of time. We can even go this summer if you're still thinking about Maryland. Dallas and Nationals set us back a bit in the way of travel funds, kiddo. I just don't think it's feasible right now. Besides, you don't really want to travel in *January*, do you?"

"But," Isobel started. She clutched the door handle tight, trying to keep herself in check. She couldn't seem too eager. She couldn't seem too desperate, or he would see straight through her.

Taking a breath, she began again. "Dad, Martin Luther King weekend is the only time we don't have practice or a game. And this summer will be my last chance for cheer camp."

Her dad turned the steering wheel again, pulling the sedan into the driveway. In the same motion, he reached up to his visor and pressed the remote for the garage door. Snow filtered down in large clumps now, creating a rushing screen between the grille of the car and the yawning mouth of the garage as it opened with a low, grinding noise. A gray shadow slid over them as the sedan rolled into the dimly lit space.

"There's always spring break, Izzy. Maybe we can go for your birthday. That way we could spend a little time there. Maybe see the Inner Harbor. I hear they've got a great aquarium." He put the car into park and sat back, both hands resting on the top of the steering wheel, arms rigid. "But you know, I've talked to your mother about it, and I can't say she's exactly thrilled with the idea of your going so far away for school."

"Because of what happened on Halloween."

Immediately, Isobel regretted blurting these words. She pulled her hands into her lap, curling them into fists. Looking down again, she glared at the Nationals ring she had thought would solve the problem of her parents' doubts and bit her bottom lip, waiting for the rebuff.

Her dad turned off the car, killing the Christmas music. He pulled the keys from the ignition and the cab light sprang on. Isobel stole a glance in his direction. In the stark light, his features looked harder than they had in the months before. The lines around his mouth seemed deeper than she remembered, and maybe that was because these days she did her best to avoid looking either of her parents directly in the eye. Not just because of the guilt that had come from the lying and the sneaking off, or from the boundless worry she had caused them both that night, but because she had grown to fear her own transparency, to fear how much of the truth they would see. Especially her dad.

He waited until the car grew cold to answer.

"Halloween is part of it," he said, a hint of fogged breath

escaping his lips. "And you can't blame her for that, Izzy. You can't blame either of us."

Isobel felt her insides sink.

She turned away from him and, releasing the catch on her seat belt, grabbed the door handle and slid out. Winter air closed in around her, causing her own breath to appear in small white puffs. She felt a surge of gratitude for the cold. It helped her regain her composure. It kept her from cracking.

"Grab the bags out of the back, would you, Iz?"

Isobel obeyed, acting on autopilot as she did her best to resume an air of nonchalance. She opened the rear passenger-side door and withdrew their shopping bags full of boxes and packages, Christmas presents wrapped hurriedly in bright paper by harried clerks behind bustling customer service counters.

Isobel shut the car door, not daring to say anything else about Maryland. What else *could* she say? She knew better than to try and push the subject any further. She couldn't risk it. If either of her parents so much as suspected that she had other reasons for wanting to go, reasons beyond looking at a university cheer squad, then the entire plan, if it could even be called a plan at this point, would unravel. Her somewhat wishy-washy status of house arrest, she had no doubt, would elevate to an all-out code-red lockdown.

With that thought, Isobel made a solemn oath to herself not to mention Maryland again. After tomorrow, after Christmas, she would need to cut her losses and start figuring out a way to get there on her own.

A twisty sensation, like a python unwinding from a branch, unfurled through her gut. The thought of traveling to such a huge city alone sent a jolt of panic through her. Not to mention the fact that she would have to steal from her parents in order to afford a plane ticket or even bus fare. And then there was the added problem that she'd have to sneak out, and lie. Again.

But Baltimore was her last hope. Her *only* hope. There, in a cemetery, during the early morning hours of January 19, Edgar Allan Poe's birthday, a man could be observed every year visiting the poet's grave. A man in a cloak and a hat. A man who hid his face behind a white scarf.

A coward, Isobel thought, her hands tightening into fists around the shopping bag handles.

Known the world over as the "Poe Toaster," he had been appearing at Poe's grave for decades. Materializing out of nowhere, he would place three red roses there and then vanish.

Only a single photograph of him existed. Taken sometime back in the nineties for *Life* magazine, the scratchy black-and-white print showed a night-vision image, pixelated and indefinite.

Either luck or fate had caused the photo to fall into Isobel's hands.

After grading her and Varen's paper and project on Poe, Isobel's English teacher, Mr. Swanson, had handed back the assignment with an article detailing the Poe Toaster's rite. Also included in the article had been the infamous image.

A shock had run through Isobel the moment she had set eyes on it. She could not have mistaken the kneeling man in the photograph. It was the same man who had once appeared to her in her dreams, calling himself "Reynolds." The same man who had warned her from the beginning, who had fought by her side and had even saved her life.

In the very end, though, he had lied to her.

Isobel felt a stab of bitter coldness at the memory of how he had betrayed her, cruelly playing her own hope against her.

Before she discovered that he'd tricked her into thinking that, like her, Varen had returned safely to the real world, Reynolds had promised Isobel that the two of them would never meet again. But Isobel knew he would never count on her discovering his identity as the Poe Toaster.

Why would he, when he'd never counted on her doing anything but blindly playing along with his own plans?

Her resolve deepening, Isobel headed for the kitchen door and shouldered her way in, her dad following close behind.

As she crossed the threshold, the aroma of baked turkey and mashed potatoes rushed her, the rich scent accompanied by a wave of warmth.

Her mom stood at the stove dressed in worn dark-wash jeans and an oversize gray sweatshirt. Stirring a saucepan of gravy with one hand, she held open a thin paperback novel in the other. Isobel recognized the book as one of the trashy thrillers she liked to read between her brick-thick classics.

Her mom turned her head when she heard the door, though it took a second longer for her eyes to part from the page. At last she lowered the book, flashing Isobel one of her distracted "I'm still somewhere else" smiles.

"Back already?" she asked. "That was quick for a Christmas Eve venture to the mall."

Isobel pulled off her white knit hat. A loud growl rumbled through her stomach, even though she didn't feel the gnawing hunger it implied.

She set the bags down and peeled off her gloves. Shedding her coat, she hung it on one of the hooks behind the door.

From the living room, she could hear the familiar sound of video-game music punctuated by the slashing twang of swords and the anguished cries of fallen undead. *Danny,* she thought. Still in front of the TV. *Always* in front of the TV.

Isobel's mom laid her book aside, open and facedown on the countertop to hold her place. "I started dinner late because I thought you two would be gone at least another half hour," she said.

"You know me," Isobel's dad chimed in, shutting the door. He shed his coat and hung it next to Isobel's. "Quick and simple. That's the way we roll, right, Izzy?"

Isobel shot him an incredulous stare. Had he really just said "roll"?

Snatching up the bags again, Isobel headed for the archway that led out into the hall but stopped when she felt two sets of eyes boring into her back. She glanced over her shoulder to find her suspicions confirmed.

"What?" she asked.

On the stove, the saucepan of gravy started to burble and

slurp. Her mom, as though snapping from a trance, turned away and switched off the burner.

Hands shoved into his pockets, her dad continued to stare at her.

She already knew what he must be thinking. He was probably wondering to himself if things would ever go back to being normal. If she would ever be the same again. If *they* would ever be the same.

In turn, Isobel wondered how long it would take for him to realize the obvious answer to that.

She gave the bags a shake. "So I think I'll go try to find a place to stash this stuff." Without waiting for a response, she ducked into the hall.

"Yeah," she heard him call after her. "Good thinking."

As Isobel made her way into the hallway, she thought she could hear her mother whispering, asking her father, "What happened?" and she knew he would cave and tell her that she'd brought up the Maryland trip. Again.

Isobel cringed. She switched the shopping bags to one hand and grabbed her scarf with the other, pulling the itchy woolen fabric free from her throat. Stalking down the hall, she passed the archway that led into the living room, where both the TV and the Christmas tree glowed with soft silvery light. Isobel stopped long enough to squint at the television screen, which displayed a spreadsheet of video-game statistics, weapon lists, and blinking vital signs.

That the game had been paused could have been an indication of only two things: Either her little brother had had to pee so bad that he couldn't hold it any longer, or he'd been abducted by aliens.

Isobel snorted at the abandoned controller and empty spot in front of the TV, sure that *she* had never been so epically lame at twelve years old.

Reaching the end of the hallway, she rounded the banister to face the stairway and started with a yelp.

Danny, who had apparently *not* ascended to the mother ship, stood at the bottom of the stairs, his chubby arms open wide, blocking her path. While one hand clasped the banister post, he pressed the other flat to the opposite wall, creating a barricade with his body.

"Season's greetings, sister," he said.

Isobel eyed her little brother. It always made her wary whenever he addressed her as anything other than the usual "cheer troll" or "nerf herder."

"What do you want?"

He tossed his head to one side to clear away the lengthening bangs of his dark mud-brown hair from his sharp blue eyes. A smirk pulled at one corner of his mouth, giving him an impish look. "Only to inform you of a recent transaction in which you were an integral element," he said, pug nose thrust into the air.

Isobel felt a twitch in her left eye. "Danny, just spit it out and move already."

"If it makes it *easier* for you to understand," he said with a sigh, adopting a tone one of his computer screen characters might use with any nameless underling, "I shall hereafter employ the usage of smaller words more digestible to your limited heathen mortal palate."

"You drink milk straight out of the carton and you're calling *me* a heathen? Danny, tell me what you want and then get out of my way. I'm not in the mood."

"Fine," he said, his expression collapsing into a deadpan stare. "So you know that weird friend of yours Dad hates? Bracelets. Talks funny. Too much hair?"

"Gwen?" Isobel asked, eyes narrowing. She knew her brother could hardly mean anyone else. Aside from being pretty much her only friend these days, Gwen Daniels had been Isobel's one accomplice in sneaking out on Halloween night. And Isobel's dad had never forgotten that it had been Gwen who had lied to him outright, telling him that she and Isobel would be going to a parent-supervised all-girl karaoke sleepover at her house—not meeting Varen at an underground goth party.

"She's up in your room," Danny said, and jerked his head toward the stretch of stairs behind him.

Isobel's eyes flew wide. "Gwen's *here*?"

"Gave me ten bucks to let her in."

"*What?*" Isobel glanced up to where her door stood slightly ajar. Inside, a long shadow drifted across, momentarily blocking the light coming from within. She mounted the stairs, but Danny backpedaled in front of her, snapping his arms wide again. She halted, shooting him an icy glare of warning.

"Ten bucks to *let her in*," he said. "*But*," he added, finger lifted, eyebrows rising to vanish beneath his mop of hair, "you and I both know that such a nominal fee hardly covers my silence." With that, he held out one chubby hand, palm up.

Isobel gaped at her brother. "I'm not paying you!" she nearly shouted, and swatted his hand aside. She hurtled forward, shouldering past him, shopping bags in tow.

To her surprise, Danny fell to one side, where he lounged against the wall, arms folded. "Think Dad won't ground you for the rest of Christmas break?" he called after her.

Isobel halted midway up the stairs. She turned to glare back at him.

He beamed at her.

Isobel imagined how good it would feel to reach out and snatch free a patch of his mussed hair. Growling, she slammed the bags down.

It wasn't so much that she feared being grounded. Especially when she couldn't be certain that she'd ever officially been *un*grounded. Or, for that matter, if she ever would be. But she didn't want her mom or dad finding out about Gwen all the same. Not when Gwen was the one person besides herself who knew what had *really* happened Halloween night.

She had been there.

Gwen had told Isobel that she'd known it was all real. And contrary to what everyone else believed, including the police, Gwen knew that Varen had not simply run away.

Isobel yanked her purse from her shoulder and rifled through the middle pocket. "You're such a freaking snot-monger," she snarled. Locating a ten, the last of her Christmas allowance, she crumpled the bill and flung it at him. It bounced off his shoulder and landed on the stairs. Danny, taking on an air of reserved dignity, bent to retrieve the money. He smoothed the crumpled paper by rubbing it back and forth on the banister. Next, he held the bill up to the light as though checking for authenticity.

Finally he pocketed the money and, smiling, made a show of gesturing toward the stairs, his arm sweeping out Vanna White–style. "Your party awaits you up the steps and in the room to the left. As you make your way up, please remember to keep all hands, arms, tentacles, pincers, and mandibles inside the railings at all times and — "

"Just so you know," Isobel snapped, all but spitting her words over her shoulder as she hauled up the bags again and climbed to the top of the landing, "I muted the TV and took your stupid game off pause."

Danny dropped the scam act like a hot plate. He scampered down the stairs and bolted for the living room, belly wobbling, socked feet thundering. Isobel could practically *hear* him dive-bomb into his usual spot in front of the television, a swatch of beige carpeting that she could swear was taking on the contours of his butt.

Muttering, she trudged to her bedroom door, which was cracked an inch.

The knife-blade slice of frost-colored light that streamed out into the hallway flickered suddenly, as though someone inside had darted past.

"Gwen?" she whispered. Placing a hand flat against the door, she pushed her way in.

4

Into the Night

Isobel craned her neck inside her room, surprised to find her friend reclined in the middle of the full-size bed, her back propped against the cubbyhole headboard, supported by a stack of pillows. In one hand, Gwen held a folded-over magazine; her entire head was obscured behind the glossy image of a pouting, airbrushed Maybelline model. Her skinny legs lay stretched out in front of her, her blue-and-white-striped stockinged feet wagging beneath the hem of a long, bluish-green broom skirt.

Isobel couldn't help but smile. Even in the middle of winter it seemed as though Gwen was unwilling to forgo her usual skirt-over-spandex-leggings look for a more practical (not to mention warmer) pair of jeans or corduroys.

Over one shoulder, Gwen's forever long and straight mouse-brown hair lay draped in a ropelike braid. Her free hand rummaged through Isobel's emergency stash bag of chocolate-covered pretzels. Seemingly oblivious to Isobel's presence, Gwen continued to graze, the sound of crunching issuing loudly from behind the magazine.

"Helloooo," Isobel said as she slipped inside. She paused, glancing first left and then right, still trying to determine the

source of the shadow she thought she had seen only a moment before. Confused, she shut her bedroom door behind her. It clicked quietly into place, but Gwen still didn't look up. Isobel frowned. She set the shopping bags down, approached her bed, and placed one hand on the magazine to lower it.

Gwen's attention snapped upward. She froze in mid-chew, brows arched in surprise. She blinked chestnut eyes at Isobel from behind her oval-framed glasses until recognition settled in. Then, the tension in her frame easing, she dropped the magazine to her lap, swallowed, and plucked free a pair of white earbuds.

"Home at last," she quipped in her dry Brooklyn accent. "If I'd known they were letting you out of the house, I'd have brought along a book. Honestly, how do you read this schlock?" Gwen gestured to the magazine in her lap. "I mean, who cares if it's better to wax your eyebrows or tweeze them? As long as you're not shaving them off and drawing them back on in brown Sharpie like my aunt Clarice. By the way, next time do me a favor and warn me when there's going to be a cover charge, would you?"

Isobel winced. "Sorry about that. Listen, I'll pay you back."

Gwen waved her off, her array of thin metal bracelets clinking like chimes. "Eh, I'd settle for giving your brother a swirly." With nimble fingers, she wound her earbud cord around her lime-green iPod before stuffing them into the hand-sewn patchwork purse at her side. "Believe me," she added, palm raised, "normally, I'm the kind of person who prefers the nontactile approach when it comes to retribution, but if you decide you want to dunk your brother's head in the toilet and you need help, I won't think that's asking too much. As long as you're the one doing the heavy lifting, I think I can manage to press the flush."

Isobel grinned in spite of herself. She had not seen Gwen since school had let out for Christmas break the previous week. Even before that, with practice every day because of Nationals, they'd only been able to talk briefly between class breaks, at lunch, and over Facebook. But with Isobel's dad still griping over Gwen's involvement in Halloween night, they'd both agreed to lie low on phone calls and texting. Especially with Isobel's dad checking her cell like a nurse with a heart monitor.

"I see you found my pretzels," Isobel said. She tossed her own purse onto the bed next to Gwen's.

Gwen sat up. She brushed her hands off, dusting Isobel's pink bedspread with crumbs. "They called to me from your top dresser drawer. What can I say? I got a case of the munchies from smelling whatever it is your mom's cooking down there," she prattled on. "And there was no telling how long you were gonna be gone, so what was I supposed to do? Starve myself? They're a little stale, though—Whoa!" Gwen halted, her eyes bugging. Without warning, she swiped at Isobel, snatching her hand and bringing it to her nose. "Talk about bling," she said, eyeing Isobel's championship ring. "That where you've been all this time? Deep-sea diving with the *Titanic* wreckage?"

Isobel pried her hand gently from Gwen's. Shrugging,

she tucked a stray lock of hair behind her ear, then turned and sank down on the edge of her bed next to Gwen. She stuffed both hands between her knees to hide the ring from view. "Coach's idea," she said. "The squad voted on ordering them, since this was our third win in a row. I wasn't going to get one, but when Dad found out about it, he insisted."

Gwen grunted. Leaning back again, she folded her arms behind her head and crossed her bony legs at the ankles. "How *is* the warden anyway? That who you've been out with?"

"Last-minute Christmas shopping," Isobel said.

Gwen perked up at the word "shopping." Seeming to notice the small cluster of bags for the first time, she all but catapulted off the bed. "You shouldn't have," she said, situating herself in a cross-legged position on Isobel's rose-colored carpeting, hiking up her skirt and exposing the dark-brown stirrup leggings beneath. She dipped an arm into a gold bag accented with green and red holly designs. "Especially since I'm Jewish."

Isobel smiled. "That one's for Dad," she said, watching as Gwen removed and shook a sleek rectangular box wrapped in green-and-gold paper. The object inside thudded heavily against the cardboard.

"Let me guess," Gwen said. "Padlock to add to his collection?"

Isobel rolled her eyes. "Cologne."

"Let's hope it helps," Gwen muttered, and went back to foraging, the tissue paper rustling noisily as she retrieved a small, flat parcel wrapped in glittery red.

"Ooh," she said, plucking at the gauzy green bow. "This one looks fancy." She weighed the box in one hand, then lifted it to her ear, giving it a shake. A quiet whispering sound came from within. "Tennis bracelet?" she guessed.

"Close. Snowflake locket. Dad's gift to Mom."

"Humph." Gwen placed the box on the floor next to the other. "What else you got in here?" she asked over the crinkling of bags.

Isobel glanced away, her attention caught by the popcorn-size flecks of white collecting on the sill outside her window. Pushing off from the bed, she went to open her lace curtains.

"Jeez," she murmured, "it's really starting to come down."

"What? That?" Gwen scoffed. "That's cotton candy snow. All fluff and empty calories. It'll be gone first thing in the morning, just wait."

Staring at the roof ledge, Isobel zeroed in on one of the tiles near the middle of the downward slope, one with an upturned edge, curled like a beckoning finger.

It made her think of that night Varen had climbed onto her roof. In his effort to make a peace offering in the form of cooler-packed cartons of ice cream, he'd somehow lost his footing. Isobel recalled her sense of utter helplessness as she'd watched him sail backward, nearly shooting straight over the edge, only to catch himself at the last second.

It had been the one and only time she'd ever seen him falter.

Before that night, he'd always been so sure-footed, so controlled. Not only in his movements and stride, but in his manners and words, too. Every syllable he spoke had a purpose. Every pointed glance held a hidden meaning or an underlying message. It was as if he had his own secret language, one she'd only just begun to understand.

"Hey, what's this?"

"Huh?" Isobel turned just in time to see Gwen pull free a long brown-and-cream-colored scarf from a mint-green bag made from recycled paper. A pair of fingerless gloves, crocheted from the same material as the scarf and accented with two woolly, wide-eyed owls, dangled from one end, attached by a tag.

"Oh," Isobel said. "Those are for you. I know it's a little belated, but happy Hanukkah."

"For *me*?" Grinning, Gwen ducked her head to loop the scarf around her neck. Next, she tugged on the gloves, fingers flexing. "I love the owls. Oh, and they're warm."

She tilted her chin up and tossed the end of her new scarf over one shoulder, fighter-pilot-style. After that, she grabbed the remaining bags and relocated to Isobel's bed.

"Let me guess," Gwen said as she drew out Isobel's still unwrapped gift to Danny—a pair of heavy-duty black headphones accented with green skull designs. "These are for the little gonif, am I right? I don't think it's unfair to assume that I'm a shareholder in these, do you? I vote we let him try them on, plug them in, and *then* we do the swirly."

"I just hope he wears them," Isobel muttered, returning her attention to the window. "So I don't have to listen to that video-game garbage anymore. Since school's been out, he's been staying up all night playing on his computer. I can't sleep." Her focus switched from the cascade of falling snow to her image reflected in the darkened glass. Arms crossed, she studied the outline of her straight blond hair and wan features. Her gaze lingered on the faint dark half-circles etched beneath each eye.

For a moment, it was as though she couldn't place her own face. A stranger, too thin and too pale, stared back at her, withered-looking, like a plant in need of sunlight.

Behind her, the rustling of bags and papers ceased.

"But you and I both know that's not the real reason," Gwen said.

Isobel's gaze shifted from her own reflection to Gwen's.

A beat of silence radiated between them.

Again Isobel smiled, but it was the rueful kind this time. She knew this was Gwen's way of ending the easy banter, of cutting to the chase and getting down to the real reason she'd come.

Her arms still folded, Isobel turned to face Gwen, though without meeting her eyes.

For a moment, she contemplated telling Gwen about last night's dream. She stopped herself short, however, reeling in the urge to do so as soon as she opened her mouth.

There was something still so vaporous about the vision. As if it might dissolve the second she tried to put the experience into actual words. That, and she wanted to keep on believing that it had been real. If she told someone else, even if that someone happened to be her best friend, would she then run the risk of having all her doubts confirmed?

"No," Isobel said at last. "I guess it's not."

Gwen swiveled where she sat to face Isobel.

"What's the verdict on Baltimore, anyway?" she asked. "Are you going?"

And just like that, playtime was over.

Isobel drew in a shuddering breath. "Dad says no."

Gwen's mouth twitched at one corner, as though she wasn't certain how to react. At the very least, Isobel's answer hadn't seemed to surprise her. "Did you use the excuse of going to look at a school like I told you?"

Isobel nodded.

"And that didn't work?" Gwen leaned back, looking stumped. "Sheeze. You'd think your parents would throw a parade."

Isobel shot her a glare.

"I mean . . . you'd be cheering for a university squad!" Gwen waggled her fists as though she held a pair of invisible pom-poms. "I hear the trophies get bigger in college?" she said, her voice turning up at the end like she couldn't be sure.

This time, Isobel didn't smile. Her mood for joking had dissipated.

"I'll just have to find another way," she said, crossing to kneel beside the bags Gwen had left on the floor. One at a time, she repacked the presents.

"Isobel . . . ," Gwen began. She took a long time before continuing, which made Isobel worry, since filtering wasn't one of Gwen's regular talents. "I've been doing a lot of thinking," she said at last. "And in all honesty, how can you be sure this Poe Toaster guy is even going to show up this year?"

Isobel scowled. "He *has* to show up," she snapped. "The article says that the Toaster comes every single year. What would make this year any different?"

In the corner of her vision, Isobel marked Gwen's measured and slow approach. She kept her eyes downcast, even as the hem of Gwen's skirt and the toes of her striped socks stopped within a foot of where Isobel knelt.

"The article also says that nobody knows how this guy gets into the graveyard," Gwen said. "Or out, for that matter."

Isobel said nothing.

"What I don't understand," Gwen went on, "is what happens once you're there. Let's say, for instance, that we actually get you to Baltimore. Then you manage to sneak into the *locked* graveyard without getting arrested for trespassing, grabbed off the street, shoved into a van, or shot. Next, this guy shows up, and then what?"

"He knows where Varen is. *That's* what. What else is there?"

There came the sharp clank of bracelets as Gwen lowered herself to kneel beside Isobel. "So . . . are you saying that you *don't* know where he is?" she asked.

Isobel stopped repacking the presents, able to feel Gwen's searching gaze.

Up until this point, she had managed to dodge Gwen's gentle prods concerning the details of that night. And for her part, Gwen had refrained from asking *too* much during the short spurts of time in which they'd seen each other at school. Isobel had no doubt that Gwen's effort to restrain herself from bombarding her with questions must have been nothing short of agonizing. And Isobel could now sense that the time for evasion, along with Gwen's patience, had reached its end.

"Are you *ever* going to tell me what happened that night?" Gwen asked. "What *really* happened? If you're going to do this, Isobel, if you're going to go to Baltimore, then you're going to need help. And you're going to need a *plan*."

Isobel already knew that Gwen was right. As much as she wanted to think otherwise, she doubted she could do it all alone. Cornered at last, she looked up.

"There's so much. I barely understand it myself. I don't even know where to start."

"The beginning is good," Gwen prompted.

The beginning? Isobel wanted to laugh, mostly because it sounded so logical. But there was nothing logical about it.

Isobel thought about the day she and Varen had first met, that day when Mr. Swanson had paired them together for the project. She remembered the way Varen had looked, sitting slouched in his chair, all darkness and quiet brooding, his black book pinned between his arm and the desk.

"It all started because of his writing," Isobel murmured, aware that this was the first time she'd divulged this to anyone. "He was writing about . . . another world."

"Another world?" Gwen made a face, as though the words didn't taste right in her mouth.

But Gwen had seen Reynolds fight that night at the Grim

Facade after all, had known that his opponent, the specter
swathed in crimson robes, awash in blood, had not been
an illusion. She had known, too, unlike the rest of those in
attendance, that the battle with the Red Death had not been
a staged performance.

"Is it . . . safe to assume that that's where Varen is now? In
this other world?" she asked, each word like a timid step into
a pitch-black room.

Isobel nodded slowly, relieved to have Gwen connect
the dots on her own. It helped not having to put things into
words herself.

Words.

Hadn't Reynolds once warned her about the power of
words? What had he said? That they could conjure, that they
could bring things into being.

"Before any of it started," Isobel said, taking in a gulp
of air, "before everything unraveled, before I started to see
things, to hear things, Varen was writing. Remember that
black sketchbook he always carried with him? It all had
something to do with Poe. I think that's why Varen chose
him for the project. He was reading Poe."

"Did you ever read any of what Varen wrote?"

Isobel nodded. "Once. And . . . again. Later."

"And?"

Isobel shook her head. "He was always writing about
the same thing," she whispered. "About a woman. She came
to him in his dreams, appearing every night. Calling to him
for . . . something."

"You mean it was like a dream journal?" Gwen asked, eyes narrowing.

"No," Isobel murmured, then corrected herself. "It was a *kind* of dream journal. But it was also a story. She . . . this woman, she wanted him to write. It . . . I think it gave her power."

"Do you still have it?"

"Varen's journal?" Isobel shook her head once more. "No. I burned it. I had to. It was the only way to . . . to close the link."

"Link?" Gwen asked.

"Varen created a link with the story he wrote," Isobel explained, "between this world and . . . and a dreamworld. But then everything started to leak together. That's what happened at the Grim Facade. Then, when I destroyed the journal, I broke the link. I only did it because I thought Varen was here. Back in this world. Safe. I thought he had come back. But . . ."

Gwen eyed her with uncertainty. Up until this moment, she had been eager to learn about the details of that night, the strange and seemingly unexplainable events that had led to Varen's vanishing. Now, though, with her upper lip crimped into a squiggly line of unease, she looked as though she couldn't be sure of what Isobel was telling her.

"Gwen, I know you must think that I'm crazy, that I'm making this up, but I was there."

"I was there too, remember?"

"No, Gwen. I mean, I was *there*. On the other side. In the

dreamworld. I went looking for him there. *That's* where I went when you couldn't find me."

Gwen frowned, her eyes darting to one side. "About this woman," she began. "The one you said Varen was writing about?"

Isobel could sense Gwen's growing apprehension. She felt nervous tension radiating from her friend's tiny frame, as palpable as an electric current.

Isobel kept her eyes steady on Gwen, waiting, finally ready for whatever she might ask.

"What did she look like?"

The simplicity of the question surprised Isobel. She thought about it for a moment, once again envisioning the woman who had appeared to her in the inverted dream version of the bookstore attic, luminous in swaths of white gossamer and tumbling veils. "She was . . . well, she was beautiful," she admitted. "And at first, that's all I could think when I saw her. She had white skin, like marble. And long, thick black hair. Tons of it." As she spoke, Isobel traced her fingers through the air around her own hair, her hands gliding down past her shoulders and, before she knew it, all the way to the floor. "She wore layers of white veils that wound down to her feet. And her eyes . . ." Isobel shook her head. She would never in her life forget those eyes. "They were black. Completely black."

She glanced up, realizing that she'd been lost in thought. She focused on the distraught expression that her friend now wore. It was so unfamiliar to her that Isobel had to backtrack mentally through her words, wondering what she had said that Gwen had found so disturbing. Then again, hadn't Gwen already witnessed the worst for herself at the Grim Facade? Like Pinfeathers and the Nocs—those hollow demons, shape-shifting monsters with shattered faces and razor claws, that had followed Isobel from their world to this one.

Maybe, Isobel reasoned, Gwen was still trying to wrap her head around the concept of there being another dimension. Though, given everything that had happened, Isobel knew there weren't too many other conclusions left for Gwen to draw.

"Did she tell you her name?" Gwen asked, her words slow, her voice laden with such dead seriousness that it made Isobel pause before answering.

"Varen called her Bess, I think," Isobel said, still trying to gauge the source of Gwen's sudden trepidation. "But then, when I asked her, she said her name was Ligeia, which was weird because I knew that was a character from one of Poe's stories. Then she said that she had many names. She called herself—"

"*Lilith,*" Gwen whispered, her face white.

Isobel's mouth popped open in shock.

Quickly Gwen stood. Dashing to the bed, she snatched up her purse and coat. Then, stooping to gather her shoes, she stuffed everything under one arm, opened Isobel's door, and darted out into the hall.

"Gwen!" Isobel leaped to her feet. She rushed out of

her room, only to find her friend already halfway down the stairs. She resisted the urge to call out, not wanting to alert her parents, who were still in the kitchen, and barreled after her.

Gwen did not pause when she reached the foyer. Opening the front door, she shoved her way through the outer storm door and vanished into the darkness with a swirl of skirts.

Isobel caught the storm door just as it latched.

"No," she rasped, and fumbled to turn the handle. Outside, she could see Gwen hurrying through the winter bluster toward the old 1990s navy-blue Cadillac parked across the street.

Managing at last to twist the handle, Isobel pushed the door open. She stumbled into the cold, down from the porch and through the darkened yard, only realizing she didn't have shoes on when the snow soaked through the thin layer of her socks. She ran despite the bitter sting.

"Gwen!" she shouted, no longer caring who heard. "Stop!" Her voice echoed, reverberating through her silent, still neighborhood.

Ahead of her, Gwen faltered, tripping over the now snow-caked hem of her skirt before colliding with the driver's-side door of the Cadillac.

Isobel heard the jangle of car keys. She ran faster.

"Gwen!"

"I can't talk to you!" Gwen shouted, whirling to face Isobel, who skittered to a halt. "Ever again."

Isobel gaped at her. Gwen, in turn, swiveled away and,

pulling the car door open, sank inside the Cadillac, shoving her things into the vacant passenger seat.

Isobel forced herself to move and caught the door before Gwen could pull it shut. "Why are you doing this?" she demanded. "How did you know—?"

Gwen put her key into the ignition and twisted it. The Cadillac rumbled to life, cutting Isobel off. Its headlights sprang on, illuminating the curtain of cascading snow.

"May God protect you," was Gwen's only answer before she tugged the door free from Isobel's grip. It slammed shut with an echoing clap.

"Wait!" Isobel shouted, staring into the driver's-side window through her own distraught reflection at Gwen as she shifted the car into gear.

"Open the door!" Isobel slammed her palm against the glass. "Gwen, if you know something, you have to tell me! *Gwen!*"

Isobel heard the engine rev. The rear tires spun before gaining traction.

"You can't just leave like this!" Isobel screamed. She latched onto the handle of the driver's-side door and pulled, only to find it locked. "Gwen! You're the only one I have. You're the only one who knows the truth! Please!"

The car lumbered forward, snow groaning as it compressed beneath the tires, the frozen handle tearing free from Isobel's grip.

"Gwen!"

Whining, the Cadillac gave a grating screech as it swung

around her in a wide arc. Isobel turned where she stood, her hair whipping in her face as the car sped past her with a guttural growl, its headlights slashing through the darkness.

The crimson taillights flared. Isobel stared after them as Gwen swerved, fishtailing around the stop sign at the end of the street and speeding out of sight.

5

Shadow of a Shade

The wind tugged at the sleeves of Isobel's T-shirt. It pulled at her hair and clung to her bare arms. But she no longer felt the cold. Only the sandlike sting of the snow as it raked her chapped face.

She stood statue straight in the diffuse lamplight, her gaze locked on the set of tire tracks that snaked their way through the inch-thick layer of snow.

Her throat felt tight, crammed with so many unspoken questions.

She forced herself to swallow them while she waited for car lights to reappear, for the Cadillac to turn the corner. For Gwen to come back.

But nothing happened.

Gradually the frigid knife-edge cold crept back into her awareness, and a shudder racked her frame.

How long could she stand out here like this, waiting?

Never long enough, she thought, because Gwen wasn't going to come back.

Isobel looked up. She stared at the countless specks that rained down around her, each white flake highlighted against the black backdrop of night, like a thousand falling stars in a dead sky.

She had to wonder if this sensation of being shredded and left to the wind, of being left behind, could even touch what *he* must have felt the moment he'd realized she wasn't coming back for him. That he was alone. Utterly and completely alone.

"Hey!"

Isobel glanced over her shoulder toward her house.

Danny stood in the doorway, washed in a glow of warm light. Squinting at her and leaning out, he looked like a plump bird poking its head out of a cuckoo clock.

"What are you *doing*?" he shouted.

Isobel hugged herself tightly against a sudden whip-snap of frozen wind and forced herself to move, stalking back toward her house with hunched shoulders. By the time she reached her front yard, her feet had gone completely numb. So much so that she could only feel the downy softness of the snow itself along with the frozen grass blades as they crunched beneath her heels.

Danny stepped back when she reached the porch. He gawked at her, actually holding the storm door open to allow her room to enter. His eyes grew even wider as she stepped inside.

"You went out there without *shoes*?" he asked. "Are you *crazy*?"

She didn't answer. Against the warm inside air, her skin flared fire hot. Her feet prickled, the numbness slipping quickly away, replaced by the sensation that the Oriental rug she stood on had been transformed into a bed of burning coals.

"Mom's been calling for you," Danny said. He watched

her with wary uncertainty, as though he couldn't be sure she
was even listening. "It's . . . time to eat."

"Tell them I'm not hungry."

"Uh . . . it's Christmas Eve."

"Then tell them I'm sick."

He arched a questioning brow at her.

She pushed past him and made a beeline for the stairs.

To his credit, he didn't try to stop her, and it was his
silence that told Isobel he would do what she'd said.

When she reached the top landing, she slipped into the
bathroom.

Shutting the door behind her, she made certain to lock it.

It wasn't long after Isobel climbed into the steaming bath-
water that the knock came. She could tell by the faint triple
tap that it was her mother who stood outside the door.

Soaking in the hot water, her bare knees tucked against
her chest, Isobel pictured her dad and little brother sitting
at the dining room table, her mother's holiday china empty
before them while the turkey cooled on its platter.

In this house, missing a family meal (let alone Christmas
Eve supper) was like missing a military roll call. If you were
absent without leave, a member of the troops would invari-
ably be dispatched to seek you out.

"Isobel?" Her mother's voice came muffled through the
door. "Everything okay in there?"

Isobel set her chin on her knees. "Just . . . my stomach,"
she lied.

"Izzy," her mom tried again, "Danny said that he saw you standing outside in the street just now. Is everything all right? Did something happen?"

Isobel narrowed her puffy eyes, glaring at her distorted reflection in the tub faucet. Her face looked curved and muddled, like the image in a funhouse mirror.

"Izzy?"

"I just . . . wanted to see the snow."

"In your socks, honey?"

Isobel scowled. Couldn't Danny keep his mouth shut about anything? At the very least, she hoped her ten bucks had actually bought his silence about Gwen having been there. She doubted he'd said anything, though. It would have been difficult for him to mention without incriminating himself in some way. Besides that, Isobel knew that her mother wouldn't have hesitated to bring up an unannounced visitor first thing. Especially if that visitor happened to be the nefarious Gwen Daniels, bad influence extraordinaire.

Deserter extraordinaire, Isobel thought.

Until that moment, she hadn't allowed herself to get angry at Gwen. She'd been too confused, too lost in the aftershock. Her brain couldn't seem to sort through, let alone comprehend, the sequence of that evening's events.

Worst of all, Isobel kept telling herself that Gwen hadn't really meant it, that she'd be back. As soon as she got out of the bathtub, Isobel would go to her room and find ten texts and at least three voice mails waiting for her on her cell phone.

Deep down, though, she knew better than to hope for that.

KELLY CREAGH — 61

Gwen's fear had been too real, her words of warning too final. She had known the name Lilith. It had meant something to her. Something terrible. Bad enough to send her literally fleeing.

Isobel bit her bottom lip, an endless stream of questions ping-ponging back and forth in her head. How could Gwen have known that name? Why had it terrified her so much?

"He's worried about you, you know."

Isobel's eyes shot toward the bathroom door again. She'd almost forgotten that her mother was still there.

She knew that by "he," her mom must have been referring to Danny, though she hardly thought such a statement could be true. The only reason he pretended to care about her right now probably had more to do with the great opportunity it provided to keep their parents distracted and his pathway to the TV unobstructed.

"We're all worried about you," her mother went on. "You've been so distant. It's like living with a stranger. It's scaring us, Izzy."

At these words, Isobel felt a gentle shift take place inside her, like a set of scales tipping. Her brow softened as she recalled the anxious expression on her little brother's face when he'd stepped back to let her in from the cold. Her dad's numerous attempts to extract some kind of meaningful conversation out of her also came to mind. And now her mother was standing just outside the door, doing her best to lure Isobel back from the ledge everyone thought she must be teetering on.

Her mom's voice came again, less muffled than before, as though she was standing as close to the jamb as possible. "It's been this way ever since . . ."

Her mother's hesitation made Isobel tense.

"As much as you've been trying to hide it, Izzy," she went on, "I *know* what this is about. This all has something to do with that boy, doesn't it?"

At the barest mention of Varen, the nodule of fear within Isobel exploded. *"No,"* she snapped before she could stop herself. "It doesn't have *anything* to do with him."

Even to her own ears her words sounded pale, unconvincing.

"Isobel. I know—"

"You *don't* know." Fresh tears filled her eyes, causing the room to swim. Isobel blinked and the tears fell, searing the skin of her already raw cheeks.

After all her effort to hide the truth, her mother had still seen right through her. Her whole family had.

And now, with Gwen gone and her mother and father tuned to her every move, how would she ever get to Baltimore?

Isobel drew in a shaky breath. The prospect that she would miss her one and only chance to find him, to bring him back home—it was too much to even conceive. Shutting her eyes tight, she willed the tide of despair welling up within her to subside. It filled her anyway, leaving her to wonder if the battle for Varen's return, for his *soul*, was one she could never win because it was one she had already lost.

"Izzy." She heard the doorknob rattle. Her mother's voice,

louder and more insistent now, sliced through her thoughts. "Why don't you get dressed? Come downstairs to dinner. Then I'll make us some tea and we'll talk. Just you and me."

Isobel shook her head, trying to get a grip. "This isn't what you think."

"Isobel, you can't tell me . . . From the moment you and he—"

"You're wrong!" Isobel shouted, her voice rising over her mother's. "This isn't about *him*. I don't *care* about him, okay? I wish I'd never even met him. So just drop it!"

Isobel clamped quaking hands over her mouth.

A sob rose up from her depths, but she caught it before it could escape. She swallowed hard, forcing it down again.

It felt like drowning.

Torn between hoping her mom would go away and wanting her to knock again, Isobel grew still, listening.

She heard only a soft sigh, followed by feet shuffling on the carpet.

A moment later, she caught the sound of the stairs creaking and then her mother's voice calling for her father.

"Sam? Sam . . ."

The water had not yet grown cold, but Isobel knew she couldn't sit there while her parents took turns conducting tag-team damage control.

Isobel climbed out of the tub, wiping the drying tears from her face with both hands. She wrapped herself in her pink robe and, tilting her head to one side, pulled her hair free from its ponytail holder. She paused, though, startled by the sight of someone's shadow visible beneath the door.

Had her mother only pretended to leave?

"Mom?"

No answer.

She continued to watch the shadow, waiting for it to move or shift, but it didn't budge. Instead it seemed planted, as though cast by a statue rather than a person.

"Dad?"

Again, no answer.

That left only one person. But Isobel couldn't understand why she hadn't heard Danny's clunky footfall on the stairs or his loud mouth-breathing. Despite all his ninja sentiments and Boy Scout "training," Isobel's little brother had never earned a badge for stealth.

"What is it, Danny? What do you want?"

Silence.

Isobel's gaze remained focused on the space beneath the door. At last the shadow shifted, and she watched it drift backward one step at a time before fading from view.

Scowling, she hurried to unlock and yank the door open.

Brisk air seized her damp skin.

A coldness too stagnant to be a draft permeated the empty space. She saw no one on the landing or the stairs. And there was no one in the hall, either.

To her left, Danny's door stood ajar, his room dark.

Isobel padded to stand at the banister overlooking the downstairs hallway. She scanned the empty foyer as, outside, a snowplow lumbered by. Its headlights cast a wash of white light through the house windows, sending sheets of gray shadows sliding down the walls.

"Let's let her cool off for a bit, okay?" she heard her father say, his voice drifting from the kitchen. "She probably just needs a little space."

A sudden trill of electronic music erupted from the living room, and a burst of zombie screams from Danny's game muffled her mother's reply.

Isobel stepped back from the banister, surprised by her dad's words but also thankful.

She didn't think she could have fielded any more questions that night.

The cold seeping through her robe, she turned and made her way toward her bedroom.

She stopped just outside the door, though, arrested by the sound of soft piano music coming from within. Slow and sad, the notes drifted to her through a filter of static.

Isobel pushed her door gently open.

Clear shafts of icy moonlight streamed through her curtains, throwing floral lace patterns onto her carpet and casting her surroundings into different shades of frost blue.

She slipped inside and her attention turned immediately to her digital clock radio.

The numbers on the clock glowed 8:49 in electric blue while the song, composed of overlapping notes and delayed timing, flowed forth from its tiny speakers. In the background, Isobel thought she could detect a woman's voice humming along, but there was too much interference to be certain.

For a moment, Isobel thought she recognized the tune. She listened hard, the urge to place the refrain so overpowering that it outweighed the more immediate question of who had turned her radio on to begin with.

Isobel shut her door softly behind her. She strode over to where the clock sat on her headboard, hoping that when the song ended, the radio station announcer would mention its title. As she drew closer, however, the song faded out, the speakers sputtering static while another station struggled to take over.

She swiveled the radio's dial back and forth, but the channel had vanished. Then a fast-paced pop song from one of her usual stations broke through the static, making her jump.

She clicked the radio off. Glowering at the now silent clock, Isobel struggled to grasp the time and the place in which she'd heard that song.

Maybe it was an instrumental number from one of the old-school musicals her mom liked to listen to while she cleaned.

Did that mean her mom had come into her room while she'd been in the bath?

One glance toward her closet door told Isobel that was exactly what had happened.

Varen's green mechanic's jacket hung on the outside of the white slatted folding door, the collar looped around the small knob.

The sight of it hanging there, so exposed, jolted Isobel's heart into hyperspeed.

She had not laid eyes on the jacket since the night she had stowed it away nearly two months ago, the same night she had found and read the note Varen had left for her in one of the pockets.

Oh no. *The note.*

Isobel rushed to grab the jacket, her hands fumbling through the coarse folds, searching for the pocket that crinkled. Reaching inside, her fingers brushed the piece of stiff paper, and her shoulders sagged with relief.

Had her mom found the note, Isobel knew she would have taken it for the accumulating evidence file. Worse, she might even have shown it to her father.

Isobel knew the act of turning on the radio and hanging the jacket in plain sight had been her mother's way of making a statement.

Unable to resist, Isobel hugged the jacket close, rewarded with a scent that seized her heart like a clenched fist.

It smelled like him. God. It *still* smelled like him.

Isobel carried the jacket back to her bed, where she laid it out flat. She stared down at the image of the dead crow etched in black against the white patch of fabric safety-pinned to the back. Letting her fingers trail down one sleeve, she then turned toward her dresser and went to open the top drawer. Pulling out a worn pair of pajama shorts and a loose-fitting T-shirt, she tossed her robe to the floor and got dressed in the dark.

She picked up the jacket again, carefully threading her arms through the sleeves. It slid onto her shoulders with a hushing sound.

Somehow, its stiff weight managed to ground her. She came back to herself, scarcely realizing how far away she had really been.

Not bothering to peel back the covers, Isobel climbed onto her bed. She lay down on her side, facing the window, Varen's note to her crinkling inside the right pocket.

She gripped the collar of the jacket and tucked it around her chin. She didn't need to take the note out to know what it said. She'd already memorized the words written there.

Over and over again, she repeated the last line in her head.

I will see you again.

It was something she knew she would have to believe if she wanted to keep from losing her mind.

If she was even going to entertain the idea of leaving for Baltimore on her own, if she was going to try and formulate a plan, a *new* plan, she would need all her sanity.

Downstairs, she heard the furnace shut off, allowing a more concentrated silence to close in around her.

Isobel shut her eyes, even though she wasn't sleepy.

Her mind circled back to the previous night's dream. By now, though, the only thing that remained untarnished by layers of wishful thinking and fogginess was the core feeling it had left her with. It lay buried deep within her, like a piece of grit worried into a pearl.

In the end, it was the only thing she really needed in order to keep going.

Hope.

6

Some Late Visitor

Cold wind swept over her.

Isobel shivered; loose strands of her hair tickled her cheek in spiderweb wisps. She pulled the jacket more tightly around her, curling into herself.

Though the draft died away, dissipating like a sigh, it left the room frigid in its wake. Thin and sharp, the air stung her nose as she inhaled.

Isobel stirred. Through half-mast eyelids, she saw her breath puff out before her in the dim wash of filmy moonlight that still shone through her bedroom window.

Her open window.

She scowled, squinting at the gaping foot-wide gap as another breeze, harsher than the first, surged through, causing her lace curtains to swell.

Smoothing her hair back, she pushed herself up onto her elbows, wondering who had opened the window. More important, why?

When a blast of arctic air brought with it a spray of snow, Isobel sat upright. Shuddering uncontrollably, her teeth chattering, she pushed her confusion aside and scooted toward the edge of her bed.

She froze, though, a clangor of silent alarms triggering within as her focus was drawn to the outer fringe of her vision. To the dark figure standing at the foot of her bed.

Her hands gripped the covers beneath her. Slowly she turned her head to look.

Motionless, he stood watching her, his thin, angular form little more than a black outline in the darkness.

When he moved, sliding one black-clad knee onto the edge of her bed, she heard the soft clink of chains.

Her gaze dropped to the place where the mattress sank beneath his weight, where one slender white hand splayed itself against her pale comforter, the onyx square of his class ring glinting behind the silver *V* set in its center.

Isobel remained still, making no move either toward him or away.

She could only mark his steady approach with her eyes, following his spindly frame as he climbed onto her bed, moving toward her. *Over* her.

She felt herself tip backward beneath him. Looking up, she scoured those shadow-swathed features, seeking his eyes through the forest of his dark hair, the only things that could tell her for certain whether or not this was another dream.

But what else could it be?

His face drifted to hover within an inch of hers. She felt his breath against her cheek.

Isobel parted her lips, prepared to speak, but he stopped her mouth with his.

Her eyes fluttered shut. Smooth and velvet soft, his kiss

ignited her from the inside, sending a flash-fire coursing through her, surging to engulf all rationality, all question or doubt.

An involuntary moan escaped her as the slim curve of his lip ring, tempered by the frigid air, pressed against her mouth. She sought it out, warming it with her own lips as he pressed down on her.

Fastening one hand to the nape of his neck, she pulled him to her, her fingers intertwining with the dark, feather-soft wisps of his hair.

The moment felt so real. *He* felt real.

Isobel pulled him closer still, suddenly afraid that he would slip through her grasp, or that at any moment she would wake up and he would be gone again.

She felt his hands fall to trace her sides, sliding past the jacket to burrow beneath the thin barrier of her T-shirt. They glided upward, gathering material as they went, pushing back the fabric to expose her stomach.

Her pulse quickened, causing her thoughts to disconnect.

A burst of winter wind rushed around them.

She arched beneath him, her own hands seeking to bury themselves under his shirt.

But she found no heat in his skin.

Isobel frowned as her palms followed the corded knitting of strong muscles.

He felt strange to her somehow. His skin was too smooth, his body too light.

He lifted away from her long enough to strip his shirt

off over his head, long enough for her to glimpse the jagged line of an angry white scar etched like a curved lightning bolt along one side of his torso.

"*Varen?*"

He descended once again, his mouth locking with hers, silencing her.

The urgency in his kiss grew, climbing toward ferocity. She struggled to keep up, to catch her breath.

She pressed her palms flat to his bare chest . . . and felt no heartbeat.

His grip on her tightened.

With a whimper, Isobel tried pulling away. She wanted him to slow down, to stop. She needed to understand what was happening.

Both of her hands rushed to cup his face, to push him back. But her fingers fell through on one side, curling to hook onto the jagged cut-glass socket in his cheek.

She stiffened.

Against her mouth, she felt his lips curve into a slow smile.

He drew back, angling to grin at her, displaying two rows of sharp crimson teeth visible through the gaping void in the side of his face.

"I've missed you, too, *cheerleader*," hissed a familiar voice.

7

Unrest

Isobel screamed.

Her howl, primal and fierce, pierced the nighttime silence.

She strained against her bed, her hair whipping at her face. Twisting and writhing, she finally yanked free from the hands that grasped for her wrists. Scrambling back, she slammed into her headboard, banging her skull on the wooden frame.

"—sobel!"

Her eyes sprang open. The room swirled into focus.

She blinked rapidly at the artificial light that radiated from her ceiling fixture, her heart thundering in her chest, manic as a captured bird.

"Isobel, wake up. Wake up, baby."

She gasped, heaving, and swallowed the air in gulps.

Someone patted her cheek. She seized the large, warm hand between both of hers, her attention narrowing on the thick golden band that encircled one finger and the slim dark hairs that poked out from beneath the drooping cuff of a familiar navy fleece robe.

Isobel looked into the face of her father. He stared at her hard, eyes searching, his dark brows knitted together.

She glanced from him to her window. Closed. Against

the backdrop of snow and night, her lace curtains hung motionless.

She felt a hand brush her cheek, and she flinched. She turned back to her father, whose eyes strove to make contact with hers.

"Isobel, look at me. You were dreaming, kiddo. Dreaming."

She heard herself whimper as she scooted to sit up. Her empty stomach churned, and she swallowed in an effort to repress a wave of nausea.

Her dad grasped her by the shoulders, and Isobel collapsed into his arms. She pressed her face into his neck and released one long, choking sob.

"Shhh," he hushed. "Just a bad dream. That's all."

Over his shoulder, she caught sight of her mother hovering close by, her face anxious, etched with delicate lines of worry. She drew near and sank onto the bed next to them, placing a cool palm to Isobel's brow. That was when Isobel saw Danny standing in the open doorway.

Disheveled and groggy, he wore a pair of baggy black sweatpants. His belly strained against a too-tight Batman T-shirt, while his dark hair stuck up in tufts around his head. He sent a squinting glare around the room.

"Jeez," he muttered, turning in a slow circle, as though still half expecting to find some evidence of an ax murderer's presence. "I mean, were you *trying* to break the sound barrier?"

Isobel quaked in her father's arms while the adrenaline made its final rounds through her system. Fingers twitching, she curled them into the collar of his robe.

"It's okay," her dad said as he rocked her, his voice firm, commanding, as though his saying so held the power to make it true. He stroked her back, and she could feel his hand bumping over the safety pins on Varen's jacket.

Pretending not to notice the meaning-filled glance shared by her parents, Isobel shut her eyes and tried to slow her breathing, to bring her heart to normal speed and return her mind to reality.

While her father rubbed her back, her mother smoothed her hair, nimble fingertips tucking flyaway strands behind her ears.

All the attention made her feel so small, so helpless, like she'd somehow reverted to being five years old again.

Only now her parents couldn't tell her that nightmares weren't real.

Because she knew better.

No one brought up the nightmare the next morning while unwrapping presents. Not even Danny, who Isobel thought would have been the first to launch into an onslaught of questions, wanting to know about blood spillage and body count.

Maybe, Isobel thought, sitting on the couch, wrapped in her pink robe and wearing her fuzzy slippers, no one was saying anything because it was Christmas.

Then again, maybe it was just because her parents were biding their time, waiting for the right moment to confront her about Varen's jacket and formally announce their decision to send her to a shrink.

As for the dream itself, Isobel knew better than to call it that. It had felt real. It had *been* real. Whether Pinfeathers's visit had happened in waking life or within the dreamworld, however, was another question.

But unlike the dream with Varen, the nightmare with Pinfeathers remained fresh and alive in her mind, every horrid detail still sharp and clear. A shudder ratcheted its way up her spine at the memory of the monster's mouth pressed to hers. And that smile. That horrible, jagged smile.

The Noc's visit made her wonder about the shadow she had seen inside her bedroom the day before. And later under the bathroom door.

"Hey," Danny said, calling to her from where he sat on the floor beside the Christmas tree, surrounded by discarded multicolored ribbon curls and box-shaped husks of wrapping paper. "Look alive, space face."

He chucked something at her. Isobel flinched, catching the small brick-shaped package just before it could smash into her nose. Covered in lumpy red paper and too much tape, the thing looked like it had been wrapped one-handed by a toddler.

The box felt light in her hands, as though she would open it only to find wads of old newspaper stuffed inside. Isobel glanced to Danny, but he had since gone back to rifling through his fresh stack of shrink-wrapped video games and console accessories. Behind him, *A Christmas Story* played on the TV, the volume kept low.

Across the room, Isobel's dad sat staring at the television, dark bags under his eyes. A new silver sports watch encircled one of his wrists, and he had on the pair of blue University of Kentucky slippers Danny had given him.

Sitting next to him on the love seat, her mom flipped through a boxed set of mystery novels. Occasionally she would reach up to her collar and brush her fingertips over her new locket.

Isobel looked at the present in her lap. With cautious fingers, she began to peel back the tape and pry open the corners of the wrapping paper. She shucked the glossy red sheath to reveal an old tissue box stuffed with a sheet of crumpled-up copier paper. Isobel yanked the paper free, only to hear something else rattle inside the box. Her attention went to the paper first when she noticed faint blue writing tucked between the crumpled folds. She opened the paper and read the lines of Danny's sloppy handwriting.

> *Consider this another U. O. ME.*
> *Watch and learn.*

Isobel frowned. Confused, she slid her other hand into the tissue box, her fingers reaching through the plastic slot to stumble across something cool and metal. As she pulled the object out, she heard Danny's voice pipe up over the TV.

"Hey, Mom, do we have any hot chocolate?"

In her palm, Isobel held what appeared to be a small silver-and-pink butterfly key chain. It felt heavy in her hand and had a clip-on attachment rather than a split ring. When she tucked

her thumb beneath the butterfly's wings, they fanned upward
and out with a quiet *click*, revealing the round face of a ticking watch. The gift brought to mind her previous glitter-filled
key-chain watch, the one she'd broken back in October.

Isobel turned the watch over in her hand, hardly able to
believe that Danny would have remembered something like
that. Normally, putting the words "Danny" and "thoughtful"
together in the same sentence would have been on a par with
trying to genetically alter jellyfish to fly. Still, she didn't get
what the gift had to do with Danny's cryptic note.

"I think we've got the powder kind in the cupboard,"
Isobel heard her mom say. "Should I make some?"

"Actually, that sounds really good," Isobel's dad said.

The sound of his voice made everyone look in his direction. It was the first time her father had turned away from the
television or said anything since opening his presents.

"Izzy? How about you?" her mom asked.

Isobel studied her brother, still trying to put two and two
together, but he had slipped on the pair of headphones she'd
gotten him and plugged them into his Nintendo DS.

"Sure," she said, "I'll take some."

Her mom gave a tight smile, though Isobel thought she
sensed a hint of relief there too. Then she got up from the love
seat and padded through the archway leading into the dining
room and kitchen.

Folding Danny's note, Isobel tucked it back into the
tissue box.

"Isobel?"

Her dad had stopped watching TV and now, instead, he watched her.

"There's something else," he said.

Isobel set the box aside. What did he mean, "something else"? She looked toward her brother again, but he remained absorbed in his DS, his back hunched and his shoulders curved forward, nose hovering less than an inch from the flickering screen.

"I mean you have one more present left to open."

Brow arched, she looked at the already hefty stack of gifts that sat next to her on the couch. In addition to new gear for cheer practice and a gym bag, her parents had gotten her lavender body lotion, two sweaters, and a pair of jeans. Considering her recent trip to Nationals and her championship ring, Isobel hadn't expected to get nearly as much as she had.

"What is it?" she asked, feeling oddly on guard.

"It's got a few stipulations that go along with it," her dad said. Standing, he walked over to the tree, bent down, and pulled a dark green folder from beneath the tree skirt. Stepping around Danny, he made his way to where Isobel sat on the couch. He had an odd, pinched look on his face as he held the folder out to her, like an FBI agent handing over some sort of top secret document.

"You can thank your brother. He talked me into it early this morning after you . . ." He paused. "Well, after your mother went back to bed. She . . . uh . . . doesn't know yet, by the way. Your mother. So . . . you're going to have to help me with that, too."

Isobel took the folder in both hands. As she flipped it open, her father sank onto the couch beside her. Because of her pile of presents, though, he had to perch on the very edge of the cushion.

Isobel stared at the sheet of crisp white printer paper tucked into one side of the folder.

An image of a blue jet soared across the header. Below, she saw her father's first and last name paired with her own in blocky bold black letters.

It took a full five seconds for it to sink in that what she held was a flight itinerary.

Her jaw slackened as she read the words "Baltimore-Washington International Airport."

Isobel rocketed to her feet. "This . . . ," she said, breathless, "this is . . . is this . . . ?"

Quickly, she scanned for dates. Their departure was listed for five forty-five a.m. on Sunday, January 18. That meant they'd be in Baltimore later the same morning. He'd scheduled the trip for Martin Luther King weekend, just like she'd asked.

Isobel knew that the Poe Toaster visited the graveyard after midnight on the eighteenth, during the early morning hours of the nineteenth. The thought that she would actually be there, that facing Reynolds had now become a near certainty, made her start to quiver all over.

She turned to face her father. "Is this for real?" she asked him. "Are you really taking me?"

Her father rose. Pressing a finger to his lips, he gave a

furtive glance toward the dining room. "Don't get too excited yet," he said, lowering his voice. "I still have to make the appointment with the university. I doubt they'll be open that Monday because of the holiday. That's why we're staying an extra day. So that means you need to—"

Isobel let go of the folder. She catapulted herself at her father, swinging her arms around his neck and pulling him down into a tight embrace. "Thank you," she whispered. "Thank you." Over and over she repeated it. "Thank you, Dad. Thank you. You don't know what this means."

And the truth was that he didn't. He didn't know what it meant at all.

But when it got down to it, Isobel supposed, neither did she. Not really.

Only that she'd somehow managed to establish that first step back into a world of terror, confusion, and chaos.

All the same, it was one that took her closer to finding Varen. And for the moment, that was enough to make her happy.

Tears burned at the edges of her eyes again. She pressed her face against her father's sleeve and breathed in. He smelled so wonderful to her. Like Old Spice aftershave, fireplace cinders, and dark coffee, a smell tied to a million different memories.

Pulling herself free, Isobel turned on Danny, who remained oblivious to the moment. She stepped toward him, her bare feet crunching over wrapping paper, and dropped to kneel on the floor next to him.

"Don't. Even. Think about—"

Isobel wrapped her arms around him, causing his DS

to tumble out of his hands and onto the floor with a thump.

"Watch out!" he shouted. He yanked off his headphones. "Why are you *touching* me?"

He tried shoving her off, but Isobel remained attached long enough to plant a kiss on the side of his head.

"Sick!" he yelled, and pushed her away. *"Get off!"*

Unable to keep herself from laughing, Isobel rolled backward onto the discarded shreds of wrapping paper while Danny scrambled for his DS.

"Augh!" he growled. "That was a freaking boss level! Now I've got to do the whole board over again."

"Isobel?"

All three of them looked up at once.

Their mom stood in the doorway, a bag of mini-marshmallows clasped in her hands. She wore a startled look on her face.

"What's . . . going on in here?" she asked, aiming the question at Isobel's father. "What's so funny?"

"Dad got Isobel and him plane tickets to go see that stupid school in Maryland," Danny blurted.

Their dad shot him a glare, but Danny only spread his arms. "What?" he snapped. "She shouldn't have messed with my game." With that, he gathered his DS and headphones, trudged through the living room archway, and pounded up the stairs.

Her mother's gaze settled on her father. The livid, half-freaked look in her eye caused Isobel's momentary elation to deflate.

"Mom," she said, standing, serious again. "Don't be mad."

Ignoring Isobel, her mother walked to where the green folder lay and plucked it from the floor. She dropped the bag of marshmallows onto the couch, flipped the folder open, and scowled down at the itinerary, her expression growing harder with each passing second.

"It's not like I wasn't going to tell you," Isobel's dad said.

Her mom closed the folder, her chin lifting in that way that said *no excuses permitted beyond this point.* "I thought you and I talked about this just last night."

"Please don't fight," Isobel said. She stepped between them, taking on the full heat of her mother's glare. "Not because of me. Not today."

"We're not fighting," her mom said. "We're talking. Right now, in fact. Sam, can I see you in the kitchen?" She didn't wait for an answer but turned and strode back through the dining room. Isobel watched her slip into the kitchen and stop next to the counter, where she slammed the folder down. She didn't look back at either of them. Instead she glowered at the cabinets, hands on her hips, her jaw set.

Isobel's dad sighed. He rubbed a hand down his face, scratching at the stubble on his chin. Then he stuffed his fists into the pockets of his robe. Giving Isobel a weak smile, he said, "Go on upstairs for a while. Let me see if I can work it out, okay?"

What if she says no? Isobel mouthed the words, too afraid her mom would hear otherwise.

"Why do you think I went ahead and ordered the tickets

this morning?" he whispered, giving her a wink. "Better to beg forgiveness, right?"

He edged toward the dining room but didn't go in yet. He turned toward Isobel halfway, waiting for her to move. She took her cue and pivoted.

She made her way toward the stairs and started up them but stopped midway. Glancing back, she watched her father disappear through the archway.

Wasting no time, Isobel hurried down from the stairs and slipped into the living room once more, doing her best to stay out of sight as she crept up to stand just outside the doorway. Pressing her back to the wall, she turned her head to listen.

"—not comfortable with her leaving home. Not with the way she's been acting," she heard her mom say. "I thought you and I agreed on that."

"We do. I mean, we did. But Jeannine, you saw her this morning. Whatever this is, it's getting worse. Maybe she needs this. Maybe she needs to get away for a day or two. Maybe that's all she's been asking for."

"How can that be it when she just came back from Nationals?"

"That wasn't getting away," he said. "That was *competing*. And I'm starting to think that that was exactly what she *didn't* need."

"Are you saying you don't think she wants to cheer anymore?" her mom asked.

"What I'm saying is that I think she needs a break. A *real* break."

"I don't like it, Sam," she said. "What if this isn't about looking at a school or a squad like she says it is?"

"So what if it's not?"

Isobel's eyes widened with shock. Was this *her* father speaking? Her father the sports guru and drill sergeant? Her father the warden?

"So what?" her mom hissed. "Sam, what if this has something to do with that boy? Did you stop to think about that? You saw her wearing his jacket this morning. I didn't even know she had that thing."

At these words, Isobel paled. Her thoughts freewheeled back to the night before, to the sight of the jacket hanging on her closet door.

If her mother hadn't known it was there, then how had it found its way out of hiding?

The shadow, Isobel thought, her memory latching onto that puddle of darkness that had appeared on the floor outside the bathroom door.

Pinfeathers. The nightmare . . . it had been real. She'd been awake.

It was the only explanation.

A numbing dread prickled in her gut.

If that were true, then that meant Pinfeathers could be somewhere nearby. He might even be watching her right now.

Isobel looked out the living room windows. She searched the snow-laden trees for crows, wondering how it could be possible when she had severed the link.

Nothing from the dream realm was supposed to be able

to enter reality. In burning Varen's journal, she herself had ensured that. The very fact that Varen remained imprisoned there *proved* that.

Yet hadn't Reynolds, with his yearly visit to Poe's grave, already shown that there were other ways to pass between worlds? If he had lied about Varen, what would have stopped him from lying about other things too?

"Did you ever think maybe *that's* what she needs to get away from?" Isobel heard her dad say. "Clearly that kid had issues, Jeannine. And the fact remains that neither of us knows what happened between the two of them, let alone what happened that night. The only thing we *do* know is that our daughter hasn't been the same since."

"What if she's trying to find him?" her mom asked, the anger in her voice giving way to quiet panic.

Isobel drew a quick breath and held it.

"Why would she come to us?" her dad asked. "It's clear she doesn't trust us right now. And why should she, when she's been asking us for help and we've just been pushing that aside, hoping things will eventually smooth over on their own? Maybe if we listen to her, maybe if we let her do something that will take her mind off everything, she'll actually start opening up. You saw her just now, didn't you? When was the last time you heard her laugh? And when was the last time you saw her smile like that? I mean, *really* smile."

For a long moment, Isobel heard only the hum of the refrigerator.

"You could have at least told me before you told her," her mom snapped, her anger renewed. "Why would you leave me out of something like this?"

"Because I knew that if I told you first, then I would've had to wait to tell her. And after whatever that was she went through this morning, I couldn't wait any longer. I had to do *something*."

A quiet knock at the front door caused Isobel's head to jerk up.

"I hate feeling helpless like this," her dad continued. "I don't have a better idea, and honestly, I don't think you do either. It's *Christmas*, Jeannine. All I wanted this year was to see my little girl happy again."

"You don't think I've wanted the same thing?"

Her parents continued to argue, their voices rising over each other's.

They had not heard the knock.

It came again, louder this time.

Isobel pushed away from the wall. Doing her best to move quietly, she crept around the couch and made her way into the foyer, where she moved close to the door.

Peering through the peephole, she found the porch outside empty.

Fear tugged at her gut when she noticed the set of fresh footprints in the snow, which led all the way up the curved sidewalk and concrete steps.

Isobel stepped back from the door. Spotting the brass umbrella stand, she grabbed the handle of her father's large blue-and-white golf umbrella. She pulled it forth slowly, as though drawing a sword from its sheath.

Fastening her free hand to the doorknob, she pressed her ear to the smooth, cool surface to listen.

At first she heard only the faint hiss of the wind. Then the knock came a third time, loud enough to send a painful buzz reverberating through her skull.

Isobel reared back. She flung open the door, then pushed through the storm door and out onto the porch. She held the umbrella in both hands, like a baseball bat, ready to swing.

Outside, the winter air clung to the bare skin of her legs while a few stray flakes drifted from an otherwise tranquil sky.

Layers of white capped the flat tops of evergreen shrubs, which glistened like frosted cupcakes. Across the street, a pair of fluffy-tailed squirrels skittered and chased each other around the trunk of Mrs. Finley's oak.

The sunlight bouncing off the snow seared Isobel's eyes.

She squinted through the glare, scanning the quiet scene of her neighborhood.

Until she heard the storm door creak open behind her.

Isobel froze. Turning her head, she caught sight of a dark blur as it slid away from the brick siding and darted inside her house.

8
Gifted

Heart hammering, Isobel spun. She threw open the storm door and charged back inside, rushing the black-clad figure.

Arms raised, the intruder stumbled backward, sprawling on the stairs with a heavy *clump*.

Isobel lifted the umbrella high over her head, preparing to bring it down like a sledgehammer.

"Don't shoot!"

Isobel stopped short of striking, halted by the familiar voice as well as the wide brown eyes that now peered up at her from behind glinting oval lenses.

Stunned, Isobel lowered the umbrella.

"*Yeesh,*" Gwen said, a nervous tremor in her voice. "You expecting out-of-town relatives or something?"

Isobel took a step back, unsure of what to say or think.

Or how to feel . . .

Gwen sat up, lowering her arms slowly as though she feared Isobel might change her mind and clock her anyway.

Isobel saw that Gwen wore the scarf she had given her last night. She also had on the owl gloves. Slung over one shoulder, the strap of a heavy-looking messenger bag blended in with Gwen's charcoal knee-length woolen coat.

Inside the bag, Isobel glimpsed the green binding of a thick hardback book. Her eyes caught the last word of the gold-embossed title. *Mysticism?*

Quickly Gwen fumbled to cover the book. She looked up, and their gazes met once more.

Despite what had happened between them the previous night, there was an undeniable current of secret joy that surged within Isobel at Gwen's return.

But there was another part of her, a stronger part, that held her back and kept her from betraying any emotion. It brought with it a wave of cold detachment that sent a slow freeze over the initial impulse to start spilling out everything that had transpired since Gwen's all-too-sudden departure the night before.

"What are you doing here?" Isobel snapped.

Gwen sobered. Her eyes shifted to the wall. "I came to talk."

"Yeah?" Isobel said. "I thought you *couldn't* talk to me. Ever again."

This time, Isobel didn't hold out for a response. Instead she deposited the umbrella back into the brass stand with a harsh *clang*. Folding her arms, she faced Gwen again, watching her as she grabbed ahold of the banister and drew herself to a standing position. Her thin frame wobbled under the weight of the messenger bag as she opened her mouth to speak, but Isobel cut her off.

"So remember that time you told me I was a terrible friend?" she asked.

Gwen's jaw clamped shut. A look of wilted misery flittered across her features. At first the reaction gave Isobel the jolt of satisfaction she'd been looking for. A moment later, though, she wished she hadn't said it.

"Look," Gwen mumbled, "I'm gonna say I'm sorry, but I'm not there yet, okay?"

Digging a gloved hand into one coat pocket, she drew out a small mahogany box.

"First things first," she said, and thrust the box toward Isobel. "I'm supposed to give this to you, so take it already. Merry Christmas or whatever. Just open it. After that, if you still want me to go away, then fine, I will."

Isobel frowned at the small, flat, postcard-size box, uncertain whether she should accept it. Did Gwen seriously think she needed to bring Isobel a gift in order for her to accept her apology?

Gwen continued to hold the box steady.

At last Isobel's curiosity outmuscled her indecision. She took it.

Gwen retracted her arm immediately and shoved her hand back into her pocket.

That reaction made Isobel pause.

"What?" Gwen said. "Don't look at me like that. It's not a freaking tarantula. Would you just open it already?"

Isobel clasped the box between both hands and carefully opened the hinged lid. Inside, the thin chain of a silver necklace glimmered. A tiny charm in the shape of an open hand rested in the middle of a black velvet cushion, its fingers decorated with delicate filigree. In the center of the palm, a tiny iridescent opal lay nestled in the dish of a circular setting.

The necklace sparkled like moonlight on water.

Isobel let out a small sound of surprise. The pendant was so beautiful and so intricate that she had no doubt the stone it held was genuine.

It struck her as an extravagant token. At the same time, the well-worn state of the box gave her the impression that the charm was old—an antique, if she had to guess.

Though the pendant had five fingers, it looked different from any representation of a hand she'd seen. It had two thumbs, the tips of which curved outward on either side. It hung from the chain so the fingers would aim downward, toward the wearer's feet.

Gwen sniffed. She rubbed at her nose with her sleeve.

"It's called a hamsa," she said. "Belonged to my grand-mother."

Isobel looked up. She clamped the box shut with a sharp snap and, shaking her head, held it back out to Gwen. "I can't accept this," she said.

Gwen raised a palm. "Too late," she said. "Besides, she was the one who told me to give it to you."

Isobel hesitated, trying to think of a tactful way to say what she was thinking. But there wasn't one, so she just blurted it out. "Gwen, I thought you told me your grand-parents were dead."

Gwen shrugged. "They are. Now put the damn thing on so they'll stop parading into my dreams to tell me how disappointed they are. Do it before your dad finds out I'm here and calls animal control."

"Too late," came a mellow voice from behind them. "Too bad they're not open today."

Both Gwen and Isobel swung around to find her dad standing in the doorway leading from the hall to the kitchen, a steaming white Santa mug in one hand. With the bags under his eyes, his unshaven face, and the scraps of hair poking out around his head, Isobel thought he looked a little like Jack Nicholson in *The Shining*.

"Morning, Mr. Lanley." Gwen gave a stilted full-armed wave, like the swipe of a windshield wiper. "I like your slippers," she said, pointing. "Go Big Blue."

His eyes narrowed to near slits. "Are you supposed to be here?" he asked.

"No," she replied. "But I know you're not gonna kick me out."

At this, her dad actually looked more amused than annoyed. "Oh yeah?" he said. "Why's that?"

As he tilted his mug to his lips, Gwen flashed one of her bright toothpaste-commercial smiles. "It's Christmas!"

"Humph," he said, and gave her another once-over before turning his attention fully to Isobel. "It's safe to come back into the kitchen, Izzy," he said. "Your hot chocolate's ready." He shuffled back around, but paused in the archway. He stood there for a few seconds, as though debating whether or not to say what he was thinking. Finally he gave a long, loud sigh. "Ask Gwen if she wants marshmallows in hers."

Gwen's bag hit the floor with a thud. "Actually, I take mine with whipped cream, but I'll settle for Cool Whip if that's all you've got."

"Super," he said, turning to face them again, a tight-lipped smile in place. "Can I get you anything else while I'm at it? Muffin? Bagel? Taxi?"

"Now that you mention it, I *am* kinda hungry." Leaving Isobel behind, Gwen made her way down the hall toward the kitchen door, shedding her coat.

Isobel's dad stepped to one side, allowing her room to pass. "Jeannine," he called into the kitchen. "Isobel's got company. You remember Gwen, don't you?" he asked, staring down into his mug and swirling its contents as he spoke. "Young lady who called from that illegal warehouse party to inform us that she'd lied about the sleepover and that our daughter was missing?"

"Hey, at least I called," Gwen said. "Is this mug clean?"

Isobel moved to her father's side and laid a hand on his sleeve. "Dad?"

He aimed a thumb over his shoulder toward the kitchen. "She always this polite?"

Isobel gave him a weak smile. It faded quickly, and she squeezed his arm. "What did Mom say?"

He nodded as though he'd been expecting the question. Then he lifted his mug to his lips again, taking another small sip of the steaming liquid before answering.

"She said we'd better dress warm."

*   *   *

"University of Maryland, huh?" Gwen asked after taking a noisy slurp of her cocoa. Leaning forward out of her chair, she reached across the table and grabbed a handful of peanut M&M's from a green-and-red-striped candy dish. "I'd have thought you'd want to go somewhere a little bit closer to home."

Sitting next to Gwen, Isobel opened her mouth to respond, but it was her mom who cut in, glancing up from her stack of newspaper coupons. "Isobel's just going to look," she said. "She hasn't decided yet."

Isobel shut her mouth again and returned to stirring her own cocoa with a long-handled spoon. Every now and then, she glanced at the box that held the necklace Gwen had tried to give her. Isobel had set it on the clear wooden space between their holly-decorated place mats in an effort to communicate to her friend that she had by no means agreed to take it.

"Hey," Gwen said. Perking up, she aimed her half-eaten candy cane at Isobel. "In that case, you should come with me to look at U of K in the spring. And University of Louisville, too. They're close, and they've both got killer athletics departments. Right, Mr. Lanley?"

"Mm," her dad mumbled into his mug.

"I'm pretty sure *I'm* goin' to one of those two," Gwen went on, waving the candy cane back and forth with one hand, fishing for more M&M's with the other.

Isobel's dad gave a low grunt. Pushing away from where he'd been leaning against the kitchen sink, he swiveled and poured the dregs of his cocoa down the drain. "This Maryland joint's starting to sound better and better," he muttered.

Isobel's mom shot him a glare. Then she turned to Gwen, who now held the handful of M&M's close to her pursed lips. She sucked the candy into her mouth one piece at a time, with a high-pitched whistling noise that cut off into a quick, loud spurt of crunching.

"Do you know what you want to major in yet, Gwen?" her mom asked.

"Criminal justice. I'm thinking about becoming a lawyer."

"Ha!" shouted Isobel's dad. Her mom sent him yet another disapproving scowl.

Gwen chuckled. "Just kidding, Mr. Lanley," she said as she chewed through a widening smile. "I knew you'd get a kick out of that." She turned back to Isobel's mom with a shrug. "I'll probably go for a double major in business and costume design."

"Double major. Wow," her mom said. "Why costumes?"

"I like to design clothes and sew, but I'm not much of a fashion guru."

"Could have fooled me," her dad commented.

Gwen went on, pretending like she hadn't heard. "I like more extravagant things. Stuff you wouldn't normally wear."

"Really?" Isobel's mom said. Smiling now, her attention snagged, she crossed her arms over her spread of coupons and leaned forward.

Isobel thought about the frilly pink dress Gwen had altered for her and made her wear to the Grim Facade. She remembered that Gwen's reasoning behind the pink had been to make it easier for Varen to spot her in the sea of black-clad bodies. Currently, the tattered garment lay hidden in the bottom drawer of her dresser, bloodstained and covered in ashen grit. Isobel hadn't had the heart to throw it away. Instead, like Varen's jacket, she'd entombed it beneath layers of less conspicuous garments. It lay sleeping in its compartment, preserved yet unseen, a constant reminder of where she had been, what she had faced, and who she had left behind.

"What kind of shows do you want to design for?" Isobel heard her mom ask.

"Hopefully I'll be doing movies one day," Gwen said. "As far as staged shows go, though, I'd like to do stuff like *A Midsummer Night's Dream* or *Alice in Wonderland*. Plays that leave a lot of room for artistic interpretation."

"Any musicals?"

"Omigosh. *My Fair Lady.* The embassy ball is a costume designer's *dream.*"

"Oh, that *is* a good one."

Until this moment, Isobel had only been half paying attention to the conversation. Now, though, as she looked between Gwen and her mother, Isobel had to marvel at the way Gwen operated, how she could spin any given situation in her favor. How she could play the innocent card right along with that brash attitude and still win every time.

"Actually," Gwen said, "now that I think about it, the horse-race scene would be even better."

"Oh! That's my favorite part!" Isobel's mom said, giggling out of nowhere. "When she starts yelling at the horse?"

"C'mon, Dover!" Gwen crowed suddenly, adopting a gritted expression and a bad accent that sounded part Australian and part British. She slammed a fist down on the table, causing their cocoa mugs to rattle and Isobel to jump in her seat. "C'mon!"

Grinning, Isobel's mom pressed her own hands flat to the tabletop. Their eyes met and together they chorused, *"Move your bloomin' arse!"*

Isobel's eyes popped wide as her mom fell back in her chair with a loud peal of laughter.

Her dad turned a baffled look on her, but she could only shrug.

Isobel had to admit that whatever Gwen was trying to accomplish, it was apparently working. Ten minutes ago, the girl had been a banished delinquent, forbidden from coming within twenty yards of her house, much less inviting herself in for cocoa. And now here she was, sitting pretty at her family's kitchen table, chatting about college and quoting Broadway musicals with her mom.

"Izzy's not sure what she wants to major in yet," her mom said, still grinning. "Right now I get the impression she's more interested in finding the perfect squad."

"Which is fine, too," her dad interjected.

Her mom's smile faltered. "Which is fine, too," she

KELLY CREAGH — 99

allowed. Quiet settled over the kitchen as her mother's focus returned to the stack of coupon pages. Isobel could tell that she wasn't really reading, though.

A tense awkwardness filled the room. Gwen pretended not to notice. She only pulled the candy dish toward her and began to pick through the M&M's, pulling out the reds and leaving the greens.

"You know what they say about the green ones," she muttered to herself.

Isobel looked from her mother to her father, and the picture began to grow clearer.

Even though her dad had said that her mom was okay with the trip, Isobel could tell that she wasn't. Not really. Not only that, but she'd begun to sense an unfamiliar level of contention between the two of them. It was like a loose knot that had gradually started to tighten. She could feel the stiffness in the way they interacted, or rather, in the way that they didn't. It took her only a moment to realize that even though they'd exchanged words, they hadn't really been talking.

Isobel looked down into her mug of cocoa, at the lumps of melted marshmallows floating on the surface like clouds in a murky sky. She told herself that she couldn't think about that. If she allowed herself to worry too much about her parents' involvement or the tension building between them, then she would lose sight of why she was going to Baltimore in the first place. And she couldn't afford that. Not if she wanted to see Varen again. Not if she wanted to keep her promise.

The cheerleader part of her told her the whole thing

would work itself out, even though she knew that kind of thinking was only false comfort. But part of the plan, she had decided, was not to overthink what she was doing. If she took it in steps, if she crossed each bridge as she came to it, then and only then could she keep believing that she would make it, that she would see him again. It was her only tactic for fighting the doubt and the insurmountable darkness that came with it.

"I think I'm going to see who's playing," her dad said suddenly. With that, he turned and marched out of the room.

"Sam," her mom said, her head popping up from her papers. He didn't turn back, though, and Isobel watched her mother sink into herself, her eyes glazing over as she brushed her fingers over the snowflake locket at her throat.

"That's beautiful," Gwen said, her voice slicing through the moment, soft and yet intruding enough to turn her mother's attention away from the empty doorway. "Christmas present?"

Isobel's mom dropped her hand from the necklace with a flutter, as though she hadn't realized she'd been fiddling with it. She smiled at Gwen and nodded, though her eyes remained distant and sad.

"I gave Isobel a necklace too," Gwen said. "You should show your mom."

Placing one hand on the mahogany box, Gwen pushed it toward Isobel.

Isobel glared at Gwen. She was starting to wonder how much she'd underestimated the girl's ability to find a means to any end. When Isobel still didn't take the box, Gwen plucked it from the table herself and pried it open, holding it out toward Isobel's mom the way a waitress might display the label of a particularly fine bottle of wine.

"Oh, that *is* lovely," her mom cooed. "Such a nice gift."

"What can I say?" Gwen shrugged. "She's my bestie."

Bestie? Isobel thought.

"Why don't you put it on, Izzy?" her mom asked.

"Yeah. Put it on," Gwen echoed. "Here," she said as she pulled the necklace free of its velvet bed. The chain unraveled like a silver snake. The hamsa dangled at the end, the opal gleaming, as iridescent as the sparkling snow that coated the world outside.

Isobel's initial irritation turned into an under-the-lid boil, and she trained her eyes on Gwen. Unfazed, Gwen merely unlatched the necklace and stood. Rounding Isobel's chair, she lowered the chain over her head and latched the clasp in place. Next, she scooped Isobel's hair out from underneath the chain and let it fall loose once again.

"Oh, Izzy. It's so becoming. I'm sure you've thanked Gwen already."

"Yeah." Isobel gritted a smile. "I did. It's great. I love it."

Gwen beamed, triumphant.

"Well," she said with a sigh, grabbing her coat, which she'd hung on the back of one of the kitchen chairs, "I guess I'd better let you guys get back to your Yuletide festivities."

"What about you?" Isobel's mom asked. "What are your plans for today?"

"Nothing much," Gwen said. She pulled her coat on and

waved her hat through the air as though batting away a fly. "Hanukkah ended last week. The twenty-fifth tends to be a boring day in the Daniels household. But thanks for the cocoa, Mrs. Lanley. Merry Christmas."

"Oh." Isobel's mom blinked in surprise. "Gosh. Well, in that case, why don't you stay and have lunch with us?"

Gwen paused. She hesitated, clasping her knit hat between her gloved hands. "I dunno. I don't want to *intrude*. I mean, is that gonna be okay with *Mr.* Lanley?"

Isobel's mom seemed to stiffen at this question. "Of course it will be," she said. "Besides, it's refreshing to see Isobel have some company for a change. Here, let me get these dishes, and you girls go upstairs. I'll call you when it's time to eat."

"Gee, thanks, Mrs. Lanley," Gwen said, her voice syrupy sweet as she backed toward the hallway door, looking as sly as a cat with a canary locked in its jaws. Isobel scooted back her chair and stood to follow Gwen through the archway.

When they reached the hall, Gwen stooped to pull up her bag from where she'd let it drop in the foyer, grunting as she hoisted it onto her shoulder.

Isobel glared at her, arms folded. "You planned that whole thing out, didn't you?"

"Right down to the lunch invitation. Now, c'mon. There's something I need to show you."

9
An Eidolon Named Night

"Close the door behind you," Gwen said, dropping the messenger bag onto Isobel's bed.

Isobel shut her door. She pressed her back to it, watching as Gwen threw open the flap on the bag, pulled forth a large green book, and laid it gently on Isobel's comforter.

Gold foil glinted on the cover and spine, revealing floral motifs and elegant lettering. The book's yellowing block of pages looked almost too thick for its own binding.

Curious, Isobel edged closer to the bed. *A Guide to Jewish Magic, Myth, and Mysticism* the embellished title read.

The subject matter sent a worming sensation through Isobel's lower stomach. It made her wonder—and dread— how the information contained in the book connected to what Gwen knew.

Gwen didn't wait for her to start asking questions, though. Opening the behemoth volume, she began flipping through whole sections at a time, as though searching for a name in a phone book. The chunks of pages slapped against one another until finally, Gwen stopped. The page she halted on depicted a single letter, a large and elaborate *L*.

Isobel's gaze followed the path of Gwen's spindly fingers

as they slipped to the top right-hand corner of the book, hooking the thin, almost filmy paper. This time, she turned each separate sheet slowly, the pages whispering against one another as they lifted and settled into place once more.

As Gwen leafed through, Isobel caught glimpses of strange symbols and squiggly characters—probably Hebrew—interspersed between long sections of English text.

Isobel shifted her weight from one foot to the other. She fiddled with the cuffs of her sleeves, then folded her arms, waiting and yet somehow *knowing* what had to be coming.

Gwen continued to turn page after page, past engravings and artist's renderings of scrolls, past detailed diagrams depicting interlaced wheels and six-pointed stars, past human figures cloaked in robes and draped in scarves—until she turned one final page.

An intricate engraving of a beautiful woman unfolded itself, the artwork filling the entire left-hand side of the book.

The image sent a shock wave through Isobel.

Black hair coiled around the woman's head in thick, snakelike tendrils, intertwining with the length of her arms. It twisted upward, too, writhing through the air above her as though caught in a gale. Her white hands clutched and pulled at the swaths of gauzy fabric that encased her, as though she were a moth straining to tear herself free from coils of cobweb.

The lacelike curl of her lashes lay folded down, fringing closed lids, creating spidery shadows against her cheeks.

Innately, Isobel knew the woman couldn't be sleeping.

Her expression seemed too intent and aware, as though she was gazing far into the future.

At the woman's feet, ghouls converged, a mess of sharp, tangled limbs and withered frames, of gaping hollow skull faces and howling mouths filled with serrated teeth. Even though they weren't an accurate rendering of the Nocs, Isobel had no doubt that was who the wasted creatures were meant to depict.

In the background of the etching, the craggy branches of pencil-thin trees poked out from a decorative border that framed the picture. The hunched forms of inkblot birds dotted their knotted boughs.

"Soooo," she heard Gwen say, "I'd ask if this was ringing any bells, but by the look on your face, I can practically hear them myself."

Isobel offered no response.

How was this possible? Here before her was the same woman Isobel had encountered, face-to-face, in the dream-world. The only thing missing was the silver rim of light that had surrounded her, like the ebbing glow that haloed the winter moon.

Staring straight down into the open book, Isobel let her eyes shift to the text that filled the opposite page, right below the title, which read "LILITH" in swirling capital letters.

She shook her head as she sank to her knees, closer still to the book, and stared hard at the writing, waiting for her brain to remember how to read.

She could see the words, identify them as *being* words,

but for some reason, she couldn't seem to concentrate enough to decode their message. She was too distracted, too swept up in a nebulous world of flashing images and floating memories.

Only one word swam into her focus long enough for her to register its meaning.

Demon.

"Now you know why I left," Gwen said softly.

Even through her confusion, Isobel could still detect the residue of guilt in Gwen's words. If their roles had been reversed, if she had known these things that Gwen had, that she was involved with something beyond a vengeful spirit or malevolent ghost, Isobel had to wonder if she would have acted any differently.

Against her will, her eyes insisted on shifting back to the engraving.

"What does it mean?" Isobel asked.

There was a pause, and then a quiet shifting of fabric as Gwen lowered herself into a kneeling position next to Isobel. As she settled, bracelets tinkling, she began to read aloud from the book. Isobel tuned her ears to the sound of Gwen's voice, though her eyes remained fixed on the etching.

"'Lilith, also known as *Li-li*, *Lila*, or *Lilitu*, is one of the oldest recorded demons in existence,'" Gwen read, the tone in her voice suggesting that she wasn't relating anything she didn't already know. "'References to Lilith date as far back as antiquity, and she makes her appearance in a multitude of cultures, eras, and regions, including ancient Egypt, Greece, Babylonia, and Europe during the Middle Ages. In modern times, she is revered by some occult circles as a goddess. Translated literally, her name means "night."'"

Fine threads of ink curled upward and chased one another downward, spreading their way across the page like veins infused with black poison. They connected and layered with one another, intertwining and weaving in and out to depict the curve of a delicate wrist, or to convey the motion of wind through the swells of gossamer veils.

"'She is the harbinger of nightmares as well as death, destruction, and insanity. Said to reign in an alternate dimension, a bleak and desertlike twilight version of reality, Lilith has long been hailed as the queen of mental darkness.'"

With the utterance of these words, Isobel's thoughts flashed to Varen. Sorrow crept over her fear as she remembered the way he had stared at her with eyes devoid of both light and hope. When she had finally found him, he hadn't even believed she was real. In that moment, he had seemed so hollow, so utterly lost. Consumed.

"'In some traditions, Lilith is considered to be a succubus, who enters the dreams of young men, seducing or otherwise influencing them.'"

Drawing in a shaking breath, Isobel forced her eyes shut. But the image from the book remained, drifting forward in lines of glowing white, highlighted against the black backdrop of her eyelids.

Doing her best to ignore the image of Lilith, she attempted to call to her memory the exact words Varen had used to describe "Bess" in his sketchbook.

Despite her efforts, only one sure word surfaced through the jumble. *Need.*

Isobel's expression hardened. She opened her eyes, realizing for the first time just how well this demon had chosen her target.

"'Lilith can take many forms, such as a bright, starlike light or a white owl,'" Gwen continued. "'Most often, however, she assumes the figure of a snow-skinned woman cloaked in white with large onyx eyes. Those who have seen her describe her as possessing a strange and unearthly beauty, characterized in particular by masses of thick ebony hair.'"

As Gwen read on, Isobel soaked up each new bit of information and began to piece them together with all the events that had led to this moment. Varen's writing. His repeated disappearances. What he'd meant when he'd told her that when he didn't want to go home, he went "somewhere else." Like jolts of electric current, her thoughts raced ahead of her to make one connection after another until her mind became a live switchboard of linking sequences.

This creature had *stalked* Varen before entering his dreams. She had watched him and waited for just the right moment. And then she had lured him into her world, making him an offer he could not refuse—an escape hatch into a realm that, to him, must have seemed all too beautiful.

Through deception and seduction, Lilith had found a way to access that hollow part of him that yearned for connection. Like black oil, she had poured herself in, filling his mind, his heart, and eventually his stories. Stories that had not only given her strength, but had opened a gate to *this* world. In short, she had exploited that very characteristic of Varen's that so many chose to judge him by.

His aloneness.

The word drew Isobel's thoughts away from Gwen's voice and back to the poem by Poe that Varen had once told her was his favorite: "Alone."

It made her realize how Lilith must have squeezed her way into a similar chink in Poe's own heart.

Now Isobel thought she finally understood why Varen had gravitated toward Poe in the first place.

In the pages of his stories and the lines of his poems, Varen had discovered a light much like his own. In researching Poe's life, he'd been able to draw parallels between them. He had found a kindred spirit.

He is not like others, is he?

Isobel tilted her head as the words floated through her mind, drowning out her own thoughts as well as Gwen's voice as she continued to read aloud.

It was what Lilith had said to her that night in the attic of Nobit's Nook, when Isobel had asked why she had chosen Varen.

He is special, even in regard to those who have come before him.

Isobel felt her skin prickle as the voice spoke within her head again. The sound of it, crisp and resonant, as merciless as it was melodious, electrified the hairs on the back of her neck. A crawling sensation of being watched stole over her.

She frowned as Gwen's voice began to fade, ebbing away into a distant murmur, replaced by a faint ringing noise.

Her focused snapped to the etching.

The woman's veils—they moved.

Isobel felt the blood drain from her face. She went still as, line by line, the etching began to animate itself. And yet she knew Gwen wasn't seeing any of it because she just kept reading, her voice a dim murmur to Isobel's right, like the sound of a radio playing somewhere in the next room.

Isobel blinked deliberately once, then twice at the etching. But now the branches seemed to be moving too. Like clawed hands, they scraped and scratched soundlessly at the page. All the while, the ringing in her ears grew, loud enough to drown out Gwen's voice entirely before converging into a multitude of unintelligible whispers. Whispers that seemed to be coming from the entanglement of hollow-faced creatures surrounding the swathed figure of Lilith. Like a knot of interlacing serpents, they began to writhe, their skeletal limbs snagging in the tattered scraps of fluttering white veils.

Then the woman's eyes snapped open.

Two black pits bore into Isobel, causing her breath to catch in her throat.

The woman's lips parted. Her mouth opened wide, allowing a rushing sound to issue forth, like a hissing surge of wind through autumn trees. It grew louder as tendrils of ebony hair danced and whipped across the page like black smoke.

In one great *whoosh*, the birds in the background of the image took flight from their perches.

The rasp of their hoarse caws and the flap of wings joined with the hissing whispers until it all rose into a hellish cacophony, converging with the woman's glass-shattering scream.

Isobel fumbled for the book, knocking Gwen aside in her effort to grab it and slam it shut. But it was heavier than she'd expected, and it slid from her hands, tumbling between them. Its spine cracked when it met with the floor, and then it fell flat against the carpet with a thud, still open.

Isobel scrambled backward, away from the book, and crashed into the wall with a *thump*. She clapped her hands over her ears but couldn't block out the monstrous screech emanating from the book.

In the corner of her vision, she could see Gwen shouting at her.

Then they froze, both of them staring at the book as it began to move on its own. One heavy half tipped itself upward, as though pulled by magnetic force. It fell onto the other half with a sharp slam, squelching the piercing shriek at last.

An entire minute passed before either of them made a move.

"What . . . just happened?" Gwen asked in a small voice while Isobel removed quaking hands from her ears.

"It moved," Isobel said. "The picture. Did . . . did you see it?"

"I saw the book . . . move," Gwen said. Then there was silence between them again, enough that she could hear Gwen swallow before she added, "Just now."

"You didn't hear the . . . ?" But Isobel didn't bother finishing her question. It was already clear that Gwen hadn't seen or heard what she had.

Isobel tried to steady herself, willing the thundering of her pulse to slow, willing her nerves to steady themselves and her increasingly tenuous grasp on reality to return.

Reality. The thought of that word caused her to utter a short, sharp laugh because, by now, it had begun to lose its meaning.

Isobel felt Gwen's eyes on her and, turning her head, found herself caught in the beam of Gwen's widest, most fearful stare.

It made Isobel want to laugh again, because it only went to show how much she really was on her own. Even if Gwen wanted to help her, how could she? How could anyone when they couldn't even *see* the things that she could?

Still, the moment with the book made her wonder.

If Lilith already had what she wanted, if she had Varen locked within her world, then why show herself here and now?

Because, Isobel thought, she must know that Varen had found a way to reach her, to communicate. She must know he'd visited her in a dream.

Isobel felt herself beginning to smile, while within her chest, a warm spark of courage ignited like a flare. It brought with it a flash of clarity: Despite everything, she was still a threat.

"Isobel," Gwen said, "I'm really not liking that look on

your face right now. It's a little Chucky meets Buffy, and it's freaking me out. As if I'm not freaked out enough already with you seeing stuff and my dad's book slamming itself shut. How am I supposed to take that thing home with me now?"

Feeling calm for the first time in what felt like a decade, Isobel drew herself slowly to her feet. She went over to the book and, stooping, scooped it from the floor. It didn't feel as heavy as it had before. She tipped it into one hand and passed the fingers of her other along the spine, probing for any cracks or breaks. She felt Gwen watching her as she went to the bed and slid the book back into the black messenger bag.

"Sorry I let it drop," Isobel said. "From what I can tell, I think it's okay."

"What I'm wondering," Gwen said, "is if *you're* okay."

"I'm fine. Especially now that I understand what it is I'm dealing with."

"Whoa, whoa, whoa." Lifting her arms above her head, Gwen knocked her wrists together as though she were a referee calling a foul. "Beep-beep, there, Cassidy, back up the truck. I think this is all getting a little thick up in that blond head of yours. What we're 'dealing with'"—Gwen paused long enough to insert air quotes, her fingers hooking like raptor claws—"is actually more likely the one doing the dealing. With *us*. And don't get me started on your usage of the word 'understand.'" Again with the raptor quotes. "What I need for you to understand is that there *is* no understanding. We're a pair of Tinkertoys to this thing. Do you hear me?

As if that wasn't painfully obvious from whatever weirdness it was that just—"

"It doesn't matter," Isobel said, cutting her off. "It doesn't change anything."

"Uh, on the contrary, *demons* can change a lot of things," Gwen said. She raised one hand, ticking off fingers. "Let's see, their *shapes*, for example. Minds. They can change their minds. Other people's minds, in some cases." She gestured to the book in the messenger bag. "Inanimate objects, apparently. Oh, not to mention they can change *you*. Into somebody dead."

"What I meant is that it doesn't change the fact that I still have to fight this thing."

"Don't you get it?" Gwen said. "What do you think I've been trying to tell you this whole time? You *can't* fight it! Isobel, this creature, this *entity* . . ." Her hands grasped and wrung the air in front of her, the right words evading her at every pass.

Isobel turned away and started pacing the patch of floor at the foot of her bed, thinking.

If only she could *remember* the dream with Varen. If only she could recall more of the details. Why had it seemed so real when it was happening and so amorphous now?

"Are you listening to me?" Gwen said. "I'm telling you that what's happening here is bigger than you or me or Varen or Poe or any of this put together. If you saw something just now, which I know you did, then that means it's trying to get to you. That means it *can* get to you. Isobel, are you not hearing me when I say she can *kill* you? I'm trying to dial through to that pom-pom brain of yours. We're talking about a *demon* here. Believe me, you can't fight it with force and expect to win!"

Isobel stopped pacing. She wheeled on Gwen.

"So is this why you came back?" she asked. "To try to get me to change my mind? To tell me that it's too dangerous? That I shouldn't go?"

"Honestly?" she said. "If I thought it would do any good, I might try."

Isobel gaped at her. "How can you even say that? Especially when you're the one giving speeches about not giving up? Weren't you the one who cornered me and told me I needed to *do* something?"

"I never said we shouldn't do something," Gwen said, anger building in her voice. "I just don't know if going to find this Toaster guy is the *right* something."

"What else is there? How else am I supposed to reach Varen? Did you happen to bring a book with you that answers that question?"

"No!" Throwing up her arms, Gwen plopped down on the edge of Isobel's bed. "Look," she said, bracing one hand at her brow. "I'm sorry. You'll have to excuse me if I'm not too keen on the prospect of attending my best friend's funeral. It's just that I know you don't understand what this all really means. And *that's* why I came here today. So you'd have some idea of what you were walking into. You love Varen. You'll do what it takes. I get that. I do. But there's something you should consider about why this all happened in the first place." She paused before continuing and drew in a slow breath, her hands knotting in her lap. "Demons . . . they don't just waltz into your life and take over for no reason," she said, her voice going soft again. "They might knock on the door, but ultimately, you have to be the one to invite them in."

Isobel sent her a questioning sidelong glare. "What are you saying?" she asked. "That Varen brought this on himself? Gwen, she *lured* him. The book says that. You read it yourself!"

"I don't think it's a secret to either of us that Varen answered the call when the phone rang, Isobel. There's no denying that he went seeking her out in return. You said yourself he was writing about her, giving her power."

Isobel pursed her lips. Unable to counter the accusation, she folded her arms and turned from Gwen, then made her way to her window, where she stared across the street to the line of cars parked in front of Mrs. Finley's yard.

"Listen," Gwen went on, "I know it's not something you want to hear, but somebody has to say it. Varen's missing right now because some part of him at some point wanted that to happen."

Isobel's gaze narrowed, her eyes following a large crow as it swooped down from Mrs. Finley's roof. Rounding the oak in the front yard, it flittered to perch on one of the snow-dusted branches, only a short distance from a second, larger crow she hadn't noticed until now. She hugged herself tighter as they cawed at each other, the feathers around their necks bristling.

"There's one more thing you need to know," Gwen said.

Isobel remained quiet, torn between wanting Gwen to continue and wishing the bombardment would cease.

"I already told you that my grandmother came to me in a dream last night."

Outside, the smaller of the two birds took off, dive-bombing the larger, who swooped out of the way just in time. Then they flew off together, one chasing after the other, their squawking echoing through the neighborhood.

"The hamsa." Isobel lifted a hand to her collar. She brushed the silver metal of the charm, which had grown warm against her skin. "You said she told you to give it to me. Why?"

"Protection," Gwen said. "She said you would need it. So don't take it off."

Isobel's fingers left the charm. Reaching up, she snapped the lock on her window into place. Grabbing the lace curtains, she pulled them closed, then glanced over her shoulder to see Gwen rifling through an outer pocket of her messenger bag.

"It wasn't just my grandmother who I saw in the dream, though," Gwen said. "There was somebody else there too. The whole time, the two of us were just wandering around this mazelike garden, all enclosed and made up of tunnels covered in roses."

Like flint striking in the dark, Gwen's words snatched Isobel's attention.

"What did you just say?"

"A rose garden," she said, and removed a white sheet of paper from her bag. "Sort of like a network of rooms and tunnels covered in roses, all of them red. That's the only way I know how to describe it."

Images of a dome-shaped room surrounded by roses flashed through Isobel's mind, telling her that she had been there too. She could even picture a screen of falling petals, the velvety slips of red tumbling between her and someone else, someone leaning in close.

"At first Bubbe and I were alone. But then I saw someone moving through the garden. When he passed by one of the archways, he stopped to look in our direction, like he was surprised to see us there. And then I woke up. But not before I realized who it was." Gwen stood.

Varen, Isobel thought. Not only had Gwen dreamed about the same place she had, she'd seen Varen there too.

Unfolding the paper, Gwen stepped toward her, holding it out.

Confused, Isobel took the white sheet, an Internet printout of the same black-and-white image of the cloaked and kneeling figure that Mr. Swanson had passed back along with her and Varen's essay.

Reynolds.

Isobel's grip tightened, the paper crunching in her fist.

"Him," Gwen said. "It was him."

10
White Noise

Isobel lay awake that night.

She'd left her door open, giving her a clear view of the darkened hallway.

Occasionally flashes of light sparked from behind Danny's door, though it seemed as if the headphones she'd given him had done the trick of blocking out the sound of sword swipes and repetitious cries of agony.

So far, however, the renewed silence wasn't helping her get to sleep any faster. All things considered, she could have been tucked away in the presidential suite at the Hilton and still be watching the walls wide-eyed.

As midnight came and went, not being able to drift off became its own brand of torture. Especially since, right then, sleep was the one thing she wanted more than anything. Because unconsciousness was the only way she knew to slide back the screen standing between her and Varen.

If she fell asleep, if she began to dream, then maybe he would find her again. Even if she only remembered snippets when the sun rose, even if she woke as soon as she saw him, it would still amount to more than she had now.

At the same time, Isobel could not forget the horror of that morning's encounter with Pinfeathers.

Before climbing into bed, she'd taken care to grab her "Number One Flyer" trophy from her dresser. She kept it buried beneath the covers with her, one hand wrapped around the plastic golden cheerleading figurine, confident that the statue's hard granite base would provide enough of a blunt edge to smash in the Noc's face.

The Nocs were brittle, hollow creatures, their hard outer shells as fragile and breakable as porcelain. But they also held the power to transform themselves to smoke, to slither around in violet, inklike swirls, sliding through the air as intangible wraiths. The trick to shattering one was catching it in solid form, getting it to hold still long enough to land a blow.

Isobel had managed to inflict significant damage to Pinfeathers once before, kicking in one side of his torso and snapping off an entire arm.

She already knew Pinfeathers must have managed to rebuild himself, though. When he had appeared to her that morning, taking on Varen's form, he'd had both arms. The lightning-bolt scar zigzagging down his bare torso now explained itself as well.

Isobel's hand tightened around the trophy.

The Noc might have caught her off guard that morning, but Isobel knew that Pinfeathers's power lay in his ability to surprise her—an advantage she would not allow him to have again. Not now that she knew he'd found a loophole through which to enter her world again.

It made her wonder if a version of that same loophole existed for Varen, if its emergence had any correlation to his repeated appearances in her dreams. Not to mention Lilith's intervention that afternoon through Gwen's book.

Isobel recalled the statue that had stood atop the fountain in the rose garden in her dream. She remembered how the figure had turned its head to look at her, its pair of empty black eyes matching those of the woman in the etching.

Other images of the dream continued to swirl through her mind.

The absence of her reflection in Varen's sunglasses. The interior of his car. The spinning dashboard clock. The nothingness inside those eyes.

Gwen's mention of the rose garden had tipped the first domino of Isobel's recollection, bringing the rest of the dream into stark relief.

It was clear that somehow, some way, they had both visited the same dream space.

If so, why had Reynolds appeared to Gwen and not her? What had he been doing there in the garden?

It made her think about the strange aroma that clung to him. It had been almost overpowering that night Reynolds had carried her home—that musty smell of sweet decay, exactly like roses on a grave.

Isobel rolled onto her back to face the ceiling, the blank white space offering a better canvas on which to connect the emerging series of dots.

The garden, she knew, must be the place from which

Reynolds took the roses he brought to Poe's grave. It made sense.

Still, his presence in the garden didn't explain why Varen had felt the need to take her there.

His face winked into her thoughts, so clear and complete in every detail, close enough that she could almost feel the silken strands of his hair brushing her cheek.

I'm here. Right here. Waiting.

Isobel shut her eyes as Varen's words resurfaced in her mind. In them, she knew she had the answer to her questions.

When she came for him, when she finally discovered a way to step physically back into the dreamworld, she knew she would need to locate the garden. He'd be there, waiting, just as he'd said. *That* had to be what he'd wanted her to know, what he'd needed to convey.

It still didn't explain why Reynolds had been there. But now Isobel realized that Reynolds knew how to get there, wherever "there" happened to be. And after she followed him out of the cemetery in Baltimore, he would be able to lead her to the rose garden.

To the place where Varen was keeping his promise to wait.

The place where she would fulfill hers of finding him.

The smooth softness brushed her arm first, the sensation faint as a sigh.

Isobel rolled onto her side.

The slight silken something returned, though, tracing the curve of her jawline.

She lifted a hand to brush whatever it was away, sending a ripple through the still pool of her slumber.

But the ghostly slip of velvet would not relent.

It passed over Isobel's lips.

She scowled and snatched at the air in front of her face, catching something sleek and stiff within her fist.

Her eyes fluttered open. Shooting upright, she unclenched her hand and frowned down at the object that now rested in her palm.

A black feather.

Isobel jerked convulsively. With a small cry, she released the plume as though it had scalded her.

Scrambling backward, kicking off covers, she collided with the cubbyhole headboard of her bed, causing its contents to rattle.

Isobel scanned the perimeter of her room, searching the silent mesh of shadows for any sign of movement.

Her surroundings lay still, quiet—empty.

Isobel did her best to keep her breathing in check. She swallowed, forcing her panic level down while she waited for each of her senses to check in, to confirm that there really was nothing there.

But her heart refused to match the quietness or slow down.

A flicker of cool blue light drew Isobel's attention to the hallway.

Her focus landed on Danny's door. It stood ajar.

When the flickering came again, the icy flutter filling the

stairwell, Isobel could tell that the source of the light had to be on the first floor.

She wondered if Danny could still be up, if he might have relocated his post-Christmas video-game marathon to the living room.

But then she glanced to where the feather lay amid her tangled covers, and she knew that fooling herself was no longer an option.

Next to the black quill, she caught sight of her flyer trophy half-buried in the crumpled blankets. She snatched it up.

She swung her legs over the side of her bed, and her bare feet hit the carpeted floor.

Nerves prickling, Isobel took a step toward the hall, and then another.

As she moved closer, she had to fight the urge to rush forward and slam her door shut, knowing all too well that locking herself in would block whatever it was out about as well as closing her eyes and pretending she was somewhere else.

Peering out into the hall, she glanced downward, through the banister rungs of the landing. The blue light continued to flash through the foyer; the weird flickering appeared to be emanating from the living room.

Isobel drifted down the hallway with careful steps. She paused at Danny's door long enough to peek inside. The intermittent bursts of light illuminated his bedroom, and she saw that he lay flat on his stomach, nestled beneath a mound of blankets. He breathed heavily, one arm slung over the side of his bed, the tips of his fingers nearly brushing the clothing-strewn floor.

She pulled his door closed, keeping the knob twisted until the wood slid into the frame so that the latch wouldn't click. Then she returned her attention to the light.

Gripping the banister with her free hand, she began to descend the stairs.

She stopped midway down, though, her eye caught by a portrait of herself hanging crooked on the wall amid the array of all the other perfectly aligned family photos. In the image, she wore her cheerleading uniform. Posed in front of a black backdrop, her arms akimbo, she smiled brightly, a blue-and-gold pom-pom resting on each hip.

Isobel reached out to straighten the picture, but her hand froze on the frame when she heard a sharp static sizzle followed by the sound of garbled singing—a woman's airy voice accompanied by warbling piano notes.

"Sleep now a little while
Till within our dreams we wake
Unfolding our Forever
If only for Never's sake."

Isobel tensed.

She knew that song. She'd heard it only the night before. It was the same sad melody that had filtered from the radio when she'd found Varen's jacket hanging on her closet door.

Isobel turned her head toward the music when the scratchy spurts of static broke through and began to drown out the woman's singing.

> *"And . . . to your ever . . .*
> *Let's . . . our eyes*
> *Together . . . through . . . oor*
> *Where autumn . . . ver dies."*

Isobel let go of the picture frame. She tightened her grip on the trophy and, moving steadily, continued down the stairs, her steps keeping time with the ticking of the mantel clock. She made her way to stand in the archway of the darkened living room, the interior of which stood unoccupied aside from its menagerie of familiar furniture and silhouettes.

Through the dimness, the TV glared a flickering blue, throwing the details of the room in and out of view.

Her eyes trailed the row of built-in bookshelves behind the corner lamp stand and moved past the Christmas tree to the front windows, which showed nothing but the slush-covered street.

"Who's there?" she asked the room in a quiet voice.

As though in answer, the TV popped and fizzled, causing Isobel to jump.

On the screen, the image of a young woman seated in profile at a grand piano, her hands trailing back and forth over the keys, began to bleed through the overlay of static corrosion.

The music picked up once more, as if the broken signal had become reestablished, the pattern of trickling notes matching the movements of the figure on the TV.

Oddly, everything within the television's frame, except for the woman's deep violet evening gown, appeared in muted tones of black and white. Her long fair hair, secured partially by a glittering comb, hung in loose strands around her downturned face, concealing her features from view as she played and sang.

The dress that she wore, beautiful and elegant, was floor-length. It hugged close to the curves of her body before opening out just below the knees like the trumpet of a bell-flower.

The woman's hands, nimble and long-fingered, seemed to float over the piano keys.

And yet the way she moved, jerky and quick between smooth slow-motion moments, reminded Isobel of clips she'd seen from old silent films.

Rocking forward and back ever so slightly as she played, the woman sang with a wispy and ethereal voice, one infused with a delicate strength that poured forth in careful pitch and control, less like an angel's and more like that of a ghost, heartrending and full of mystery.

> *"And I'll sift my sands to your side*
> *Before we slip away*
> *Before we're little more than silt*
> *Beneath the rocking waves."*

Isobel lowered the trophy as she entered the room, entranced by the strange scene playing itself out on her family's television, confused and curious as to what it was doing there and where it could be coming from.

Sinking down to kneel in front of the screen, she squinted, trying to see through the crackle and static overlay, which had grown thicker as she'd drawn nearer.

She wished the woman would turn and look her way, if only for a second. There was something so familiar about her. Especially those floating hands.

Had she seen her before?

It made her wonder if she could have been in the dream with Varen.

No, Isobel thought, she didn't think so. But the *song* had.

In an instant, she placed the melody as not only the same one she'd heard in her bedroom, but the same one that had struggled to work its way out of Varen's car stereo. She remembered the way he'd wrenched the portable CD player loose from its cords, pitching the whole thing into the backseat.

What about the music had bothered him so much?

Isobel studied the woman, who continued to play as though locked in a trance, the melody now meandering on without vocal accompaniment, the piano taking over. An interlude of high notes trickled forth in a complicated pattern, accented by a few well-placed chords from the instrument's lowest spectrum. This mixture of dark and light, high and low, hope and despair, worked its hypnotic effect on Isobel, as though she were a small child listening to an intricate story.

And that was when she began to search for more details, to notice the objects that surrounded the movie's central figure. Old-fashioned floral-print wallpaper. Fancy antique furniture. A shelf-lined wall bearing indiscernible pictures in frames and nondescript knickknacks. A mirror, too.

Isobel's sense of déjà vu grew twofold, the sensation threatening to spill directly into her conscious recognition until, like murky waters, gray and black rolls and squiggles rose up the television screen to scribble the woman away, and fizzing white noise eclipsed the music.

"*No,*" Isobel whispered, snapping to as though released from a spell. "Wait." She placed a hand against the screen, but it blinked to blue again, resuming its silent fluttering, flashing in her face like cold firelight.

"Don't worry," an acidic voice rasped from behind her. "They don't work anyway."

Isobel shot to her feet. She spun to find him sitting in an armchair next to the darkened Christmas tree.

Leaning forward, elbows resting on his knees, he sat staring down at the floor in front of him. His hands hung in between, one overlapping the other, the curved tips of his razor claws aimed toward the floor.

"Lullabies, I mean," he whispered in the corrosive hiss that never failed to set her on edge. "Never have."

He didn't look up at her when he spoke but remained motionless.

Every so often, the light from the TV burst strong enough to flare across his scarecrowlike frame, illuminating the crimson curve of long claws and the pointed, slicked-back black-to-red spikes of his coarse feather-and-quill hair.

Pinfeathers.

11
Of Ill Omen

"Why are you here?" Isobel asked him, her tone guarded. In her hand, her "Number One Flyer" trophy began to feel slick, greased by her own sweat. She clutched it tighter.

Part of her had suspected that the black feather had been the Noc's way of announcing himself, of dropping off a quiet calling card before retreating and waiting to be received.

It was a far cry from his usual jack-in-the-box style of popping up out of nowhere, all demented smiles and gleaming malice.

But what was he seeking to gain by entering her world like this?

More important, how was he doing it?

Pinfeathers blinked, his black eyes remaining downcast. Tilting his head to the side and knitting his brow, he seemed to contemplate the question. He didn't answer, though. He only looked the other way, toward the Christmas tree, so that with the next flicker from the television, Isobel caught a glimpse of the jagged hole in his cheek.

It made her wonder—if he could reconstruct his arm and side, what kept him from doing as much for his face?

But there was something in his demeanor, in the heavy

way he sat, that warned her against asking and launching the opening bid for a match of verbal tag-you're-it with the Noc.

Instead she shifted her weight from foot to foot and kept her eyes trained on him, waiting for him to speak or move again. When neither of those things happened, Isobel's anxiety began to build, its intensity magnified by the ticking of the clock on the mantel.

The clock.

Isobel shot a glance in its direction long enough to see that the second hand moved at its normal pace.

That time remained steady helped to solidify the notion that she had to be awake. And why was he just *sitting* there anyway? Was he waiting for her to offer him leftover Christmas cookies and a glass of milk?

Finally his sullen silence became too much.

Raising the trophy, she took a quick step toward him, feigning the intent to strike, as though he were a snake she could scare off.

His eyes alone flicked up. He shot her a withering glare.

"Mature," he said.

Isobel felt her face burn. His response, so infuriatingly snide, left her wishing she'd gone ahead and taken a crack at his jaw instead of pretending. Now she'd given him the upper hand, the knowledge that she wouldn't attack unless she had to. Something even *she* hadn't known until that very moment.

"You're—You're not supposed to be here," she said, stammering in her effort to remain calm.

"We could also argue that I'm not supposed to *be*," he replied. "But one thing you and I seem to have in common, cheerleader, is our knack for existence. Though it would appear I'm not quite as adept at evading destruction as you. For there you are." He pointed at her with one curved claw. "Yet . . . here am I. And if you look carefully in between, you can see everything we *knew* would happen. Or wouldn't," he added with a flippant wave.

His gaze returned to the floor.

Isobel shifted uncomfortably where she stood.

While she was used to his speaking in riddles, she didn't know what to make of his uncharacteristically dour mood. Was it just a show? Another game?

"Look," she said, raising the trophy again and aiming it at him as though it were a gun she could blast him into bits with. "I already know this isn't a dream. So tell me how you're doing it. How are you entering the real world again?"

He laughed, a low, deep sound that sent a cold shiver running through her.

"Still so convinced that everything revolves around *you*," he said, at last drawing himself to a standing position, his spindly frame towering over a foot above her own.

Despite the sudden rush of adrenaline that gushed through her veins, Isobel refused to allow her body the backward step it so desperately wanted to take. Instead she remained rooted, determined not to do or say anything else that would betray her escalating fear. Even though she knew Pinfeathers held no power to harm her physically, everything about him, from his caustic voice to the twitchy birdlike way he sometimes moved, terrified her.

"Dreaming aside," he went on, "how can you be so sure *your* world is the real one?"

Without waiting for an answer, he began to take slow and cautious steps toward her, as though *she* were the cornered animal poised to either strike or bolt.

It was certainly how she felt.

Widening her stance, Isobel clutched the trophy close to her, wishing it were an ax instead of a flimsy piece of plastic affixed to a tiny block of granite.

"I swear, if you so much as try to touch me . . . ," she warned him, the threat trailing off as she began to consider her options.

Now that she was face-to-face again with the nightmare creature in all his gruesome glory, he appeared less vulnerable than she remembered. Not only that, but Isobel couldn't seem to recall why she had thought the trophy would have done her any good as a weapon. Why did she seem to have a knack for trying to defend herself with stupid objects anyway? Why hadn't she done herself a favor, feigned an interest in baseball, and asked her parents for a Louisville Slugger for Christmas?

Unable to hide her fear any longer, she began quivering all over, her stomach clutching at the memory of the monster's thin, pale lips fastened to hers. She couldn't take that kind of torment anymore. Worse, she didn't know what she would do if he dared assume Varen's form in front of her even one more time.

As her courage began to collapse in on itself, Isobel started to realize how wrong she'd been to think the Noc couldn't harm her. Obviously, he could. In more ways than she knew.

As though sensing her heightening alarm, Pinfeathers halted his advance.

"I can't *help* it that I'm susceptible to you," he whispered. "You know that. It's just that you're so . . . *unreal* . . . and so I *have* to touch you. If only to be certain that *I'm* not the one who's dreaming. You see, I hear that sort of thing is going around."

"This isn't a dream," she snapped. "I know I'm awake. I know what's real and what's not. I know you can't hurt me, and now what I *want* to know is how you're getting here. I'm not asking again, and if you won't tell me, I *will* smash in your foul, ugly—"

"We are here," he growled, edging closer again, crimson teeth bared in a grimace, "because of what *we* know. And that is how. *She* taught us. And what one can do, so can the other."

Isobel watched him closely, too distracted by his continued approach to absorb his meaning. "What—what are you saying?" she stammered. "That the other Nocs can—?"

In an instant, he dispersed into smoke, rushing her like a gust of wind.

She had no time to scream before the tendrils of vapor wrapped around her throat.

Isobel dropped the trophy. She heard it thud against the carpet in the second before she lifted her hands to claw at the looping threads of swirling mist.

Her nails scraped her own skin, but the tightness remained.

"*We* didn't *want to be right about you,*" his voice seethed in her ear.

Isobel twisted. Stumbling backward to escape, her heel caught on the brick ledge of the fireplace. She fell, almost landing in the hearth.

The inky swirls whisked around her and Isobel held her breath, afraid of what would happen if she dared breathe in any part of it.

"*But we were,*" he whispered as he re-formed and crouched over her, hands braced on his knees.

Turning his head to the side, he glared at her through one black eye the same greedy way a bird inspects a shining beetle.

She watched his teeth, serrated and gleaming, part and come together through the cavity in his cheek as he spoke. "All along. We were right."

Isobel fought the urge to shut her eyes, to shut him out. "You *know* you can't hurt me," she said, more in an effort to affirm that to herself than to him. "You can't *do* anything. So why do you keep coming back? What do you *want?*"

"*There,*" he said, leering at her, cupping her chin with one cool clay hand. "Good for you, cheerleader. You're finally asking the *right* questions."

He drew his hand slowly back, his claws grazing her cheek. Isobel winced as the razor tips raked her skin. There was no pain. Only the surge of dread as his face drew nearer to hers. "I want what I thought we both did," he said.

Isobel kept her eyes squarely on his, wide and unblinking.

Meanwhile, she trained the fringe of her vision on the wrought-iron stand that sat only inches to her right, her attention zoning in on the handle of the fireplace poker sticking out of the very middle.

"You don't scare me anymore," she said, even though she could tell by the wistful smile he wore that he knew it was a lie. She didn't care. She only needed him to stay distracted long enough for her to make her move. "So why do you keep trying?"

He brushed his thumb across her lips. "I guess you're not as easy to forget as we'd hoped."

Growling, Isobel jerked her head away from him. She lifted a knee and kicked hard.

His body loosened, and her leg went through smoke.

Seizing her chance, she rolled onto her side, groping for the iron poker. It rang out with a low clang as she snatched it from its stand. Scrambling to her feet, she began taking swipes at the darkness around her.

The poker sliced through the tendrils again and again with no effect. The haze slid back from her, and Pinfeathers's face, translucent and vaporous, re-formed within the tangle of violet wisps.

"Your necklace," he snarled. "It's a clever trick, but it won't help you."

Isobel charged him, the poker whistling as it arced through the air. Again the monster slithered back, his face dissolving, lost once more amid the thickening murk.

"It's true she won't be able to touch you," hissed his

disembodied voice, the violet mist now drifting toward the ceiling and out of Isobel's batting range. "But at this rate, she won't have to."

Isobel eyed him as he took solid shape again, his back pressed into one high corner, his arms outspread to brace himself, heels planted against the wall behind him, making him look like an enormous spider.

With that thought, Isobel stooped and grabbed her trophy where it lay on its side next to the couch. She launched it at him.

Pinfeathers caught the trophy with one clawed hand. His face screwing up with rage, he flung it back at her. Isobel yelped, clutching tighter to the fireplace poker as the trophy smashed the fat-bellied lamp that sat on the end table just beside her.

"*Listen to me!*" he railed. "Why won't you ever *listen* to me?"

"Give me one good reason why I should!" Isobel screamed back at him.

Fury overcame him. With a deafening howl, he dove for her, claws outstretched.

Isobel swung the poker again, but he dispersed at the last second, splitting into multiple wisps, each separate strand whisking off in its own direction until she wasn't sure which way to turn.

"*Because,*" his voice seethed, seeming to come from every-where at once.

Isobel went suddenly still as she felt the tendrils return,

wrapping their way around her waist from behind before transforming into arms.

She felt him pull her to him. His voice, acidic and sharp, buzzed in her ear. *"Soon . . . I'll be all that's left."*

"I told you"—Isobel raised the poker and jabbed it backward—"not to touch me!"

The iron rod sailed through nothing, the momentum of the action serving only to knock her off balance.

She teetered, catching herself on the armrest of the love seat before wheeling around, swiping blindly and wildly in all directions until a sharp click brought a burst of bright light into the room.

Isobel spun to find her father standing in the living room archway, one hand still fixed on the light switch, bleary eyes aimed directly at her.

He watched her with a hard, confused look, his expression a mix of shock and disbelief.

There was fear there too, she thought.

Fear for her. Fear *of* her.

He raised one palm toward her, as though she were a careening car that needed to slow down.

"Isobel?" he said, his voice husky with sleep. "What . . . what are you doing?"

She heaved in sharp, quick breaths, and her gaze darted all around the room.

But Pinfeathers was gone.

The TV was off too, its screen black.

At her feet, the end table lamp lay in shards, and her

Number One Flyer trophy was facedown amid the mixture of broken slivers.

"Isobel?"

She heard her father draw nearer, saw his shadow stretch wider as he made his way toward her. Yet she still flinched when he wrapped a hand around the fireplace poker clutched between her own hands.

Finally glancing up at him, Isobel watched his red-rimmed eyes scour her face as though in search of some evidence that she was still, in fact, his daughter.

"Isobel, honey," he began again, using one hand to brush back a lock of her hair while at the same time attempting to extract the poker from her grasp with the other. "Are you even awake right now?"

All at once, she felt her focus return. Her eyes met directly with her father's.

She let go of the poker, releasing it into his tugging grip.

Parting parched lips, she spoke at last.

"I—I don't know."

12
Grim Returns

Contrary to Gwen's Christmas Eve prediction, it took an entire week for most of the snow to melt. Still, icicles hung from the roofs and sides of homes and businesses, dripping from gutters like strips of torn lace. Like crusted barnacles, hard clumps of charcoal-colored sludge clung to the underbellies of cars and trucks.

The world had a drowned and washed-out look by the time Isobel returned to school, and though the thick coating of white had receded, no color had returned to take its place.

Even the grass looked gray, poking up through the lingering swiss cheese patterns of snow on Trenton High's front lawn.

But despite the lack of scenery, Isobel was glad to finally get out of her house, even if it felt like she was simply leaving one prison for another.

A light rain began to fall as she stepped through the line of rumbling buses and the lingering haze of exhaust fumes.

She stopped to stand on the sidewalk that led up to the school's side entrance.

Hooking her thumbs in the straps of her backpack, she scanned the building's regal structure. Far above, beyond its ridged outline, tattered clouds crawled across a slate sky. Flashing silver in the overcast light, the windows did their best to coordinate themselves with winter's drab gray palette, to blend in just like everything else. Just like her.

It was January now. A new year. Exactly two weeks until Poe's birthday.

After her second strange encounter with Pinfeathers, though, Isobel had stopped having dreams about Varen. Or anything, for that matter.

Like the falling snow, her connection to the other side, to *him,* had abruptly ceased to be, leaving her small collection of recent experiences to thaw in the stark glare of reality.

To her left and right, students passed her, hurrying to silence and stuff cell phones into pockets and bags. At first Isobel didn't think anyone noticed her. Then she made the mistake of removing the hood of her sky-blue parka as she entered the school.

She knew she wasn't imagining the looks, the blatant stares, the whispers.

By this time, she'd grown used to them. They'd become a staple of her daily life at Trenton. Everyone knew who she was. Of course they did. She was the last person seen with Varen Nethers. "You know," she'd heard one of the junior boys say to a group of buddies before the break, "that weird goth kid who went missing on Halloween night. That girl, the cheerleader, she's his girlfriend. Or was, anyway."

Isobel did her best to ignore the gawkers and murmuring as she made her way through the hall.

It wasn't that she hadn't expected them to be here when she got back. She'd just hoped that there would have been enough winter-break drama and gossip to provide even a minuscule amount of distraction.

But there would be no respite.

Whispers and turning heads, glares and fleeting looks of sympathy alike followed her all the way to her locker.

She put up her mental blinders, steering her thoughts in the direction of the day's schedule. Classes. Lunch. Classes. Practice. Dinner. Homework. Sleep.

Sleep. It was the one thing she still looked forward to. Strangely enough, it was the one thing that made her feel as though she was *doing* something.

But each night, the dreams refused to return.

Why, when she had finally learned how to become lucid while dreaming, when she'd discovered how to communicate with him, had he vanished from the radar?

She was sure it all had something to do with the night she'd found Pinfeathers in her living room. It was obvious now that he'd been trying to tell her something. But in the end, nothing he'd said had made any sense to her. Nothing except his mention of her necklace, the hamsa, which Isobel wore night and day, holding fast to her promise not to remove it.

Pinfeathers's sneering face swam to the forefront of her mind when she stopped in front of her locker. She heard his words echo through her head as she dialed her combination.

It's true she won't be able to touch you. But at this rate, she won't have to.

At what rate? What did that even *mean*?

"Hey."

Isobel jumped. She turned to find Nikki standing behind her.

"Whoa, easy there," Nikki said as she pressed one shoulder against the door to Gwen's locker.

"Sorry," Isobel said. "I just . . ." She shook her head without finishing, pulled the lock free, and kicked the dented bottom corner of her locker. The door popped open.

"Too many espresso shots in the latte?" Nikki asked. Rolling to lean her back against Gwen's locker, she swept aside the dark swoopy bangs of her new haircut, a layered look that framed her face in sleek wisps, accentuating the crystalline blue of her eyes.

"Just . . . still waking up." Isobel made an attempt to smile. "I like your hair," she said.

"Thanks."

Nikki pursed her lips. When she spoke again, she kept her focus on the bronze polish coating her fingernails. "Hey, how come you didn't return any of my calls last week? Or, you know, text me back?" she asked. "And why didn't you come to Stevie's New Year's Eve party? You were kind of the only one from the squad not there."

Isobel thought she heard a genuine note of disappointment in Nikki's voice. Sharp as a nail file, a stab of guilt whittled its way between her ribs. She shrugged in response, deciding to try and play it down. "Sorry," she said. "I asked, but Dad wouldn't go for it. Apparently, the solitary confinement sentence went through to the end of the year."

There was a pause before Nikki spoke again, her brow scrunching with affected confusion.

"Yeah . . . but you didn't really ask, did you?" she said, still absorbed in the lacquered paint covering her fingernails. "'Cause you and I both know your dad always lets you do squad stuff. I mean, he let you go to Nationals, didn't he?"

Again Isobel shrugged, then stripped off her parka. She didn't know what answer she could give now. She'd already been caught in a lie.

"Yeah. No biggie," Nikki said. "It's okay. I totally get it. I mean, you've been going through some stuff."

Once more Isobel threw up her mental blinders, keenly aware of the hint of sarcasm that had begun to slow-drip into Nikki's tone. She started to shove things into her locker, stuffing her coat in without bothering to hang it on the inside hook. It tumbled out again, landing in a heap on the floor in front of her feet.

"Halloween and everything," Nikki went on, sighing in mock sympathy.

Isobel stooped to gather her parka, hands working fast. But not fast enough.

"Going to covert parties. Lying to your dad. Lying to your friends. Then your loner boyfriend pulls a shocker

and goes AWOL. You *were* officially together, weren't you?
Vernon. Was that his name?"

Isobel shot to her feet, anger flaring inside her.

She shoved her locker door shut with a bang loud enough
to grab the attention of half the hall.

Immediately Nikki stopped the scrupulous inspection of
her nails. Her eyes, like two gleaming marbles, slid in Isobel's
direction.

"You *know* his name," Isobel seethed in a heated whisper,
all too aware of the multitude of gazes now aimed in their
direction. "At least you should," she snapped. "It was right
there on his shirt tag that night you, Brad, and Alyssa decided
it would be fun to trash the place where he worked. Or did
you happen to forget that, too?"

Nikki scowled and looked away. Instead of stomping off
like Isobel expected her to, she only stared at the floor, her
hair falling to shield her face.

Disgusted, Isobel twisted in her locker combination
again. She kicked open the door, wadded up the parka, and
thrust it inside.

"I'm sorry," she heard Nikki murmur. "I didn't mean
to . . . it's just that . . . lately it's been hard getting your attention."

"Like you said, I've had a lot on my mind."

"I know that," Nikki went on. "I know you well enough to
tell when something's . . . not right. The only difference now is
that you won't talk about it. Actually, you don't say much of
anything. It's almost like you're suddenly . . . somebody else."

Isobel sighed, her shoulders dropping as she held open the door to her locker, staring in at the contents, a mixture of mundane items that could have belonged to any given high school girl. "Maybe I am," she muttered.

"Yeah," Nikki said, "well, that wouldn't make you the only one." Pushing off from the row of lockers, she paused to add, "Speaking of, I should probably let you know that Brad's back today."

Isobel turned to regard Nikki with stern surprise.

She had not seen her ex-boyfriend since that night at the rival football game when the Nocs had attacked him on the field in the middle of a play, causing him to sustain a compound fracture to the leg. Isobel could still picture the glinting white bone poking through the flap of skin. The injury, combined with blood loss, had been severe enough to put Brad out of school for two full months.

"Is he . . . okay?" Isobel asked.

It was Nikki's turn to shrug. "Except that he won't play anymore."

"He quit the team?"

"*No,*" Nikki said, and uttered her trademark *tch* of impatience. "I mean he won't because he can't. Like, ever again. The doctors told him last week that he's done. And you would have known that before now if you'd pick up your damn phone once in a while."

With that, Nikki spun on her heel and stormed away, leaving Isobel to gape after her.

Brad? Not being able to play football? Ever again?

That would be like someone telling her she was done cheering, that she'd never throw another stunt, that she was fastened to the ground for good.

He had to be devastated.

"Hope you don't mind that I opted not to interrupt."

For the second time that morning, Isobel started. Swinging around, she found Gwen standing at the locker next to hers, twisting in her own combination.

"I figure at this point, the less full of cheer I am the better. But she's got a point about your phone. And here I'd made up my mind this morning not to say anything about it because of my special place in the cockles of the warden's heart. But you haven't been talking to anyone, have you?"

"I've just . . . been doing a lot of thinking."

Gwen's face went grim. "What happened?"

"Nothing. That's just it," Isobel said, having already made up her mind not to go into either of her most recent encounters with Pinfeathers. Aside from the fact that Gwen didn't know much about the Nocs, Isobel didn't really think she wanted to try to put either experience into words. If anything, she wished she could forget they'd ever happened.

"No more dreams?" Gwen asked.

Isobel shook her head. "No. You?"

"Nothing of relevance."

Their eyes met and a pregnant pause elapsed, a beat in which both of them seemed to understand that there was something the other wasn't saying.

Gwen broke the connection first, returning her attention to her locker.

"So," she said, crouching down and grunting as she worked to unearth a pastel-green binder from beneath a stack of loose papers and ragged spiral-bound notebooks. "I'm guessing Scarlett O'Hara already mentioned your ex's less-than-graceful reemergence into high school society this morning."

"How did *you* know Brad was back?"

Gwen ceased struggling long enough to shoot Isobel a skeptical "C'mon, it's me" kind of look. Then, finally wrenching the binder free, she stood and tucked it under her arm. She reached into the top compartment of her locker to scrounge for something, then used one booted foot to smash stray handouts back inside her locker. Along with the sound of crunching paper, Isobel heard a light plastic rustling. When Gwen's hand reappeared, it held a powdered doughnut hole, which she popped into her mouth.

Isobel watched in appalled fascination while Gwen chewed, wondering if the open package had been in her locker over the entire two-week break.

"*Please*," Gwen said, the word sending out a puff of powdered sugar. "I know it all." She licked stray bits of the white dust from her lips and fingers. "And this time, it's not pretty, I'll tell you that."

"You mean you saw him?"

"Hard not to notice someone on crutches."

Isobel frowned. The more she heard about Brad's return, the more she dreaded the prospect of running into him.

"I think you'd better talk to him," Gwen added. "Find out what happened. Today if you can swing it."

Isobel drew in a sharp breath. She hadn't prepared herself for this. And why would Gwen suggest that she *talk* to him? What would she say? She wasn't even sure how much Brad remembered about the whole ordeal, if anything. Then again, there was always the prospect that he remembered everything.

Isobel wasn't certain which scenario would be worse.

"Oh," Gwen added. "And before I forget, do you mind if we skip our usual lunchroom date today? Mikey and I are sneaking out to the new pizza place across the street." She grabbed one last doughnut hole before slamming the door to her locker closed, then she began to drift away, walking backward. "I'll make it up to you by picking you up from practice."

"Wait a second. *Mikey?*" Isobel asked, trying not to blanch outwardly. "Are you still seeing that guy?"

"Eh. It's an on-off thing." She shrugged. "What can I say? He's got nice hands."

Flashing a coy smile, Gwen winked and turned, skirts swishing as she vanished around the corner.

When the bell ending third period rang, Isobel gathered her things slowly. She took the long route through the halls, using the added time to prepare herself for the most torturous hour of the day.

Mr. Swanson's English class.

In that room, Varen's empty desk might as well have been a ghost. One whose hollow, vacant stare never relented.

She knew better than to try and skip the class; instead she trained herself not to look at that part of the room, or if she could help it, even think about the desk being there.

No one ever tried to sit at it. And no one ever commented on it either. It seemed the general consensus was to pretend Varen was out sick. Or maybe she was fooling herself with that thought. Maybe it was more like the room you left untouched out of respect after the death of its occupant.

Isobel tried not to let these thoughts repeat themselves in her head, circling around on a never-ending carousel. Instead she did the only thing she could think of that could occupy her mind.

She paid attention.

It wasn't always easy, but over the two-month period that Varen had been missing now, she'd gotten better at it.

But it wasn't so much the threat of distractions or wandering thoughts that made it difficult. Rather, it was Mr. Swanson and the way he looked at her whenever they happened to catch each other's eye.

The expression "if looks could kill" came to her mind whenever it happened. But Swanson never dealt the accusing dagger-and-knife kind of look that usually went with that saying. It was more of a slow and painful hemlock poisoning kind of kill that came in the form of questioning glances and looks of general concern. There was a sadness reflected in those eyes too, a weighty sorrow glimpsed behind the oval lenses of his spectacles.

If there was one adult she wanted to tell everything to, it

was Mr. Swanson. And maybe that was why Isobel found his looks so unbearable. Because she knew they were an invitation. One that he extended time and again, over and over, every day if he could manage to sneak it in.

What happened? those looks seemed to be asking her.

Under that pleading gaze, Isobel felt the plaster-patched cracks in her projected veneer of innocence and ignorance start to open until she began to actually entertain the idea of talking to him.

She often caught herself daydreaming about it, thinking of what she would say and how she would tell him and where she would begin. Whenever she got to that point, though, she forced herself to look down at her paper full of notes. Then, once she'd severed the connection, she told herself to *think*, drilling herself with the questions she knew he, or anyone, would respond with.

What do you mean he's in a dreamworld?

Poe? What does he *have to do with any of this?*

And, worst of all: *Don't you think this is something we need to mention to the police?*

Always, that last one became the deciding factor in her decision to remain silent and appear as clueless as everybody else.

Up until today, it had been a good plan.

Near the end of class, however, Mr. Swanson gave them a reading assignment to finish while he went around the room, handing back the pop quiz on *The Crucible* he'd sprung on them the Friday before break.

Even though Isobel had missed only one of the questions, she found a neon-green Post-it affixed to hers.

Please see me after the bell, it read, the words scrawled in her teacher's loopy cursive writing.

Wonderful, Isobel thought.

Whether she was up for one or not, it seemed she was in for a Swanson chat after all.

13
Grave Danger

When the bell did ring, Isobel's first impulse was to pretend she hadn't seen the note and book it straight out the door. One fatal glimpse in Mr. Swanson's direction, though, and she knew there would be no slipping past his radar, especially since it seemed to be aimed straight at her.

Like a chess club's version of a bouncer (complete with sweater-vest and tucked-in necktie), Mr. Swanson stood poised beside the door as everyone filed out. Hands stuffed into the pockets of his pleated khaki pants, he shot several pointed glances her way between quick exchanges with the students now headed for the lunchroom.

Already halfway out of her desk, Isobel gritted her teeth and sank back down again.

She felt a surge of sudden resentment toward him for making her stay like this, for breaking his unspoken promise that he wouldn't bring up Varen unless she came to him first.

But maybe he'd begun to sense that that was never going to happen.

Trapped, she waited for the classroom to empty.

To avoid fueling the gossip mill, she did her best to appear as though she was only taking her time in pulling her things together. Tugging her backpack into her lap, she rifled through the front pockets like there was something inside that she just *had* to find before heading out.

She looked up only when she heard the door click shut.

Staring straight at her, Mr. Swanson wore a blank expression, which Isobel thought must be his stab at a poker face. The fixed, deadpan look gave her the distinct impression that he was pulling a Clint Eastwood, waiting for her to draw first. It was like he hoped that any second now she would freak and launch into a word-vomit session of the whole truth and nothing but the truth.

Isobel tried to keep her face as blank as possible as she held up the quiz paper, Post-it side out. "I didn't cheat," she said.

Mr. Swanson frowned, his wiry white-and-gray eyebrows drawing in close enough to touch. He pressed his thin lips together, rocking on his heels with his hands still tucked inside his pockets.

"I know you didn't," he said. "Actually, this isn't about the quiz."

Shocker, Isobel nearly muttered. Instead she did her best to look perplexed.

"It's about your project paper on Poe," he said.

This time, his words did manage to catch her off guard.

Isobel watched him as he went to stand behind his desk. He slid open the top drawer, extracted a small stack of stapled papers, and dropped them onto the desktop. "I'd like you to tell me how much of it you actually wrote."

Uh-oh, Isobel thought, realizing that Swanson must have made copies of all the papers before handing back the originals. Of course he had. Knowing him, he probably kept a backlog of every single assignment he'd ever given. He probably had an FBI-style database of every student he'd ever taught too.

Isobel picked up her pen, twisting it around and around, trying to think of an honest yet nonincriminating way to answer his question.

There wasn't one.

The truth about the gargantuan ten-page essay was that Isobel hadn't written a single word of it, something Varen had assured her wouldn't be a problem.

Obviously, among other things, he'd been wrong about that.

But it wasn't the possible change in her grade that made Isobel nervous so much as the prospect of a call home from a teacher. After the night her father had found her swinging the fireplace poker in the living room, he'd of course drawn the false yet inevitable conclusion that *she* had smashed the lamp. Even though Isobel had been able to convince her dad that she'd been sleepwalking, she didn't need another reason for either of her parents to reconsider the Maryland trip. And she certainly didn't need another instance of her involvement with Varen being brought up, least of all by Mr. Swanson.

Isobel tucked a strand of hair behind her ear. "Um," she began.

"It's okay," he said. "You don't have to worry. Last grading period's grades are locked in. Report cards already went home, remember? Besides, I wouldn't change the grade even if I could. I'm not doubting that you earned it. That's not why I'm asking. It's just that I happened to read over the essay again during the break and . . . well, it made me curious, is all."

Over the break? Seriously? Was that what he did in his spare time? Reread old papers when he ran out of pop quizzes to grade? Or had he reread the essay because it had been hers and Varen's?

Maybe he had thought the same thing about the paper that he seemed to presume about her—that it held some kind of special information.

Isobel sat up in her chair. She cleared her throat. "Everything kind of got down to the wire," she said.

Mr. Swanson nodded as though she wasn't telling him anything he hadn't already concluded for himself. "Mr. Nethers has a very distinct writing style," he said, "even when he tries to hide it." Rounding his desk, he folded his arms and perched on the edge of one corner. "And so now I guess it's only fair," he went on to say, "that I ask how much of the presentation Varen contributed to."

"We worked on it together," Isobel said. "Whenever we could, that is," she added. "Sometimes stuff . . . got in the way."

A stern look of concern clouded Mr. Swanson's features. "You know," he said, "despite what I'm sure the two of you must have thought, I didn't pair you together on purpose.

I really did draw names at random. Though I have to admit, I did get a kick out of seeing the two of you side by side on the day you presented. . . ." A wistful smile breezed across his face, vanishing as quickly as it appeared. "I take it then that you two got to know each other fairly well."

"Fairly," Isobel allowed. Her grip on her pen tightened.

"That day," Mr. Swanson said. "He . . . he seemed a bit strange, don't you think? Stranger than usual, that is. Kind of out of it. Did you notice?"

Isobel glanced down at her notebook. She shifted uncomfortably in her seat, aware that this was Swanson's not-so-subtle way of looking for an in. And aside from the fact that she couldn't think of a single response that wouldn't give him just that, she found herself once again struggling to come up with a comprehensible answer concerning that particular hour of Halloween day.

It was the one big paradox of the entire twenty-four-hour period, a giant piece missing from a fragmented puzzle already riddled with so many holes.

That day Varen had been here, in this very room, present for all to see and yet, supposedly, also fast asleep in the attic of Nobit's Nook.

"I remember," Mr. Swanson said, his voice cutting through her thoughts, "that he wouldn't take off his sunglasses when I asked him. He's never done that before. Looking back, I should have known right then that there was something the matter."

Isobel maintained her silence. She told herself not to

say anything, to just nod, unable to trust herself not to give something away.

So many times she had played and replayed the events of Halloween in her head, always starting with the enigma of Varen's strange dual existence during Mr. Swanson's class. She could also recall how, after everything was over, even Reynolds hadn't been able to explain the why or how of what had happened. He'd even seemed shocked when Isobel had brought it up. Or if not shocked, at the very least dismayed.

"I hope you don't mind my asking," said Mr. Swanson. "But did Varen happen to . . . mention anything to you about what might have been going on?"

"I . . . ," Isobel began. She started to nod again but caught herself. "No." She shook her head. "He didn't."

At this point, she knew that it was time to go. From here, the questions could only get more specific and her resolve not to answer them would only get weaker.

Sliding from her chair, fumbling for her things, she gathered her backpack, pen, and notebook while out in the hall, the bell indicating the beginning of lunch sounded with a shrill cry.

"About the project paper," she said, avoiding eye contact with him as she slipped her quiz into an open pocket of her bag. "Was that all you wanted?"

After a beat, he clasped his knees and said, "Yes. I . . . suppose it was."

Isobel made a beeline for the door. She could feel Swanson's eyes following her.

That she wanted to leave his classroom so badly must have been a dead giveaway that she knew more than she was letting on. But she needed to get out of there as soon as possible. To regroup. She was going to have to try and figure out some way to get through the next two weeks of his class—of life—without blowing her own cover.

The entire Baltimore trip depended on it.

Gripping the doorknob, Isobel froze, her hand tightening around the cool metal fixture as a new thought struck her.

Letting go of the knob, she pivoted to face him.

"Mr. Swanson?"

"Yes, Miss Lanley?"

"Speaking of the project paper," she said, "do you . . . do you remember that article you handed back with our grade? The one about the—"

"Poe Toaster?"

"Yeah," she said. "Him. How . . . how did you know about all that?"

Mr. Swanson stood from where he'd been leaning against his desk. Arms remaining folded, he glanced down at his loafers. "Oh well, you know us scholarly types," he said. "When someone goes to such extremes to pay tribute to one of the famous dead litterateurs, we can't help but take an interest. Now that I think about it, he's due fairly soon, isn't he?"

"The nineteenth," Isobel blurted.

"That's right," Mr. Swanson said. Looking up, he squinted at her in surprise. "The morning of Poe's birthday. I should give you extra credit for remembering that. I'm sure there'll be quite a crowd there this year. It's becoming more and more popular, you know. I daresay I'd like to go myself one day. Wouldn't that make for a heck of a field trip?"

She watched him round his desk. Picking up Varen's paper on Poe, he sighed and stuffed it back into the top drawer. "Doubt I could get the board to sign off on *that* one, though, much less the county."

"Sorry," Isobel said, "did you say crowd?"

"I did. It's kind of a big to-do up there. Or didn't the article say?"

Isobel shook her head. "N-no."

"Oh, people come from all over to stand outside the gates and watch," he said. Turning his back to her, he picked up one of the chalkboard erasers and began to sweep away that night's homework assignment. "It's even gotten to the point where they've had to have special security lined up for the event."

"Security?" Swallowing, Isobel felt her heart drop into her stomach. "But . . . doesn't the Poe Toaster come super late or something? Like, after midnight?"

"Well, so does the Great Pumpkin," Mr. Swanson said with a chuckle. "But that doesn't stop Linus from staying up every year, now, does it?"

Isobel frowned.

"If I'm correct," Swanson went on, "the Poe Toaster appears at the grave sometime between midnight and six a.m. And still, droves of people go every year just to stand outside in the freezing cold for a mere *chance* at sighting him.

Maniacs, I'm telling you. There's even a committee of people who watch from inside the church just to make sure no one attempts to get in the Toaster's way or, heaven forbid, unmask the poor fellow."

"Hold on," Isobel said, blinking hard. "You mean people have tried?"

"Of course they have," he said. "With anything like this, you're always going to have the occasional nutcase who wants to ruin the mystery for everyone. Don't worry, though. So far, no one's ever been successful. Somehow the Poe Toaster always manages to give everyone the slip. From what I understand, the whole thing is over very quickly."

"But . . . ," Isobel said. Hugging her notebook close, she took a step toward his desk. "If everyone goes to watch for him every year, why aren't there more pictures of him circulating on the web? How come there's only the one?"

"Ah." Dropping the eraser into the chalk tray, he turned to face her again, dusting his hands off. By the coy smile on his face, Isobel could tell that he was enjoying the barrage of questions. "That's because no one ever actually sees him. Unless of course you're inside the graveyard itself, like the group that watches from the church. You see, what many people fail to realize is that there are *two* gravestones in that cemetery bearing Poe's name."

"*Two?*" Isobel said. "How can anyone be buried in two places at once?"

"Oh, while I'm sure that's quite possible if you use your imagination," he said with a wry laugh, "the reason Poe has two gravestones is because one stands as the marker of his original burial place. That's the stone that you see in that grainy photo where the Poe Toaster is kneeling. Sometime in the late 1800s, Poe was exhumed and moved to a more prominent location at the front of the cemetery. This was so those wanting to pay their respects to the famous author of 'The Raven' wouldn't have to go traipsing through the back end, searching for a grave that happened to be unmarked anyway. The monument that stands at the front gate of the cemetery is where Poe now rests. A very visible spot, but sadly, not the one the Toaster chooses to pay tribute to. I'm surprised you two didn't come across any of this in your research."

"You said Poe was buried in an unmarked grave?"

Mr. Swanson nodded. "For a long time, that's where he remained. He never really had a proper funeral. The original ceremony was very quick and cheap. There were only a few people in attendance, somewhere around eight or nine. Quite sad if you think about it."

"Yeah," Isobel said. "Sad."

"Perhaps when Mr. Nethers, our resident Poe expert, returns we can ask him what *he* knows about it."

At his mention of Varen, Isobel glanced up at him and their eyes met.

Yet another well-devised trap she realized too late, because now she couldn't seem to break away, caught yet again in the unflinching beam of that pleading look she found so impossible to evade.

"You *do* think we'll see him again in the near future, don't you?" he asked.

Isobel started to respond, but no words would come. How could she offer him an answer to that question when she didn't even have one for herself?

It was going to be like this every day from here on out, she thought. Even if he didn't hold her behind to question her outright like he had today, as long as Mr. Swanson thought she knew something, as long as he thought she *cared*, then Isobel knew he would stop at nothing to extract the truth from her.

Suddenly, with that thought, it dawned on her exactly what it would take in order to deflect him. Before she could give it even one more moment of consideration, Isobel began to speak.

"Look, Mr. Swanson," she began. "I know there are a lot of rumors floating around about what went on between me and Varen but . . . none of it's true. For starters, we never went out," she continued, taking care to keep her gaze squarely on his. "Believe me, that would *so* never happen."

Again, his brows drew in close together. Clearly, her words confused him.

In her chest, her heart began to pound wildly, hard enough and loud enough that she actually feared he might hear. "In fact, we never saw each other outside of class except those times we *had* to meet for the project."

As Mr. Swanson listened, his face grew more and more grim. He didn't say anything, but Isobel could see a dimness settling in around his sharp gray eyes as well, as though someone had turned down the wattage of his hope.

"To be honest," she said, plowing on, unable to stop herself, "we didn't even get along. But I had to put up with it because I needed a passing grade. Otherwise, I wouldn't have been able to go to Nationals." Isobel raised her hand, flashing the championship ring. "When he and I started working on the project together, it turned into this big thing." She shrugged. "Something new for everybody to talk about, like we were part of some cheesy reality TV series or something."

Isobel paused long enough to draw in a shaky breath. Never in her life had she looked an adult in the face and delivered such a bold-faced string of lies. And yet, never in her life had the act of lying come so effortlessly. Still, she knew that if she wanted to convince him entirely, she couldn't leave it at that. She had to be sure to eliminate all doubts.

"And ever since he ran off or whatever, everybody seems to think I know where he went," she said, "but I don't. Not any more than you do. At this point, I'm just kind of ready to forget about it and move on, you know?"

His gaze dropped from hers, and Isobel felt the tightness in her chest ease a little. A new and more ruthless wrenching came to replace it a moment later, however, as soon as she heard him utter the words, "I'm sorry." Crestfallen, he stared down at the floor, his brow knotted. "I didn't mean to seem presumptuous. I just thought that maybe . . . he might have confided something in you. The two of you seemed to . . . connect on some level. From what I'd witnessed during those weeks, I . . . I was under the impression the two of you had become friends."

"It's no big deal," Isobel said. "I mean, I know you liked him a lot."

Feeling the stinging threat of tears, she began to back away, retracing her steps to the exit. "And I do hope they find him soon. But . . . as far as knowing anything about what happened that night? I'm honestly the last person who would."

Isobel turned.

Without another word, she opened the door and slipped out into the empty hall.

Grabbing her parka from her locker, Isobel took the sandwich and soda she'd packed that morning outside and into the vacant courtyard.

It had stopped raining sometime after third period, so it wasn't difficult to locate a relatively dry patch on one of the stone benches.

She sat with her back to the long spread of large cafeteria windows and hoped that the slender oak, which stood in the center of the yard, would help to obscure her form from view.

With everybody already through the lunch line and seated at tables corresponding to their various social spheres, Isobel wasn't about to go strolling in there this late, especially since Gwen wouldn't be waiting for her at their usual table.

The only thing less pleasant than waltzing through the cafeteria right at that moment might have been walking up the steps of a gallows, hands secured at her back, cloth sack draped over her head.

So she'd opted to spend the last ten minutes left of lunch outside in the cold.

The thirty-degree dampness, laced with the occasional sweep of icy wind, didn't bother her, though. And for once in her life, neither did eating alone.

Aside from wanting to avoid the prying eyes and the unceasing stream of whispers, Isobel needed time to think. Though there was so much swirling around in her head, she wasn't even sure where to begin.

At least she'd managed to solve one problem for herself among her growing list.

During the next several days leading up to the Baltimore trip, Isobel knew she would be free of Mr. Swanson's prying glances and prodding questions. From what she could tell, he'd bought the self-absorbed cheerleader bit. Though she'd hated acting that way—like she didn't have a soul. Like it hadn't been ripped in two from the day she'd learned Varen hadn't returned.

Isobel closed her eyes. She pressed her thumb to the band of her championship ring, which suddenly felt too heavy for her hand. Even though the ring had helped her to seem convincing, Isobel wished she could take it off. She wanted so much to throw it away someplace where she'd never have to look at it again. Because that was the only reason she'd ever put it on to begin with. Not to honor something she'd accomplished, but so she could persuade the world—her parents and teachers, fellow squad members, and classmates— that she hadn't changed. That a single kiss from a boy who knew how to walk through dreams, who himself now seemed to be a dream, hadn't irrevocably altered her.

Dropping her hand, Isobel opened her eyes.

Mechanically, she reached for her sandwich, but unable to force herself to take even one bite, she abandoned it for her soda.

Needless to say, the meeting with her English teacher hadn't left her with much of an appetite. She even felt nauseated, as though all the lies she'd told him had followed her out here and were now trying to claw their way back inside her.

With trembling hands, Isobel popped the tab on her soda.

The sound cracked through the vacant courtyard, startling a nearby group of pigeons. They took off in a flurry, their frenzied flapping causing her to shrink into herself with a shudder.

She took a hurried sip of the soda.

In a way, she was glad Mr. Swanson had asked her to stay after class. If he hadn't, she might never have found out about the special security setup at the graveyard on the eve of Poe's birthday, or the hordes of people who gathered to watch. *Or* that there happened to be *two* gravestones.

That Reynolds actually had a legion of *fans* (she wasn't sure what else to call them) only served to intensify the sickened feeling that continued to roil in the pit of her empty stomach. It grew more intense when she thought of the committee Mr. Swanson had also mentioned, the group apparently dedicated to *protecting* him.

All of it was certainly going to make her venture into the graveyard that much more difficult. Maybe even impossible.

Despite the combined mixture of anger and panic that the existence of both groups aroused within her, Isobel knew she had no right to blame either for their actions.

Unlike her, they didn't know what they were dealing with.

Deep down, Isobel knew that every one of them must assume that after the night was over, this dark figure, like them, just went back to being a regular person from somewhere normal like New York City or Pittsburgh or even just down the street. The mystery and the drama, the chance to be a part of the moment itself, was what they sought.

And like the good performer that he was, Reynolds was giving them everything they wanted.

That's why they protected him.

Up until now, Isobel hadn't even begun to realize how difficult it was going to be just getting *to* the graveyard, let alone inside. She'd been so caught up in trying to find a way to Baltimore itself that she hadn't stopped to consider that the ritual might actually be a *tourist* attraction.

It made her wonder what time people started gathering. Since Reynolds wouldn't arrive until after midnight, spectators would probably only begin to accumulate at the gates after dark. And then there was the group inside the church to worry about too.

How was she supposed to slip past them? And how would she even get in to begin with?

Suddenly Isobel found herself wishing Gwen hadn't cut

lunch to meet up with Mikey. She needed to talk right then. She needed Gwen.

Lowering the faux-fur-lined hood of her parka, Isobel risked a quick glance behind her toward the congested and brightly lit cafeteria.

As far as she could tell, no one seemed to notice she was out here.

She saw Mr. Nott, the cafeteria monitor, drifting between the tables, his hands clasped behind his back like a drill sergeant patrolling a mess hall.

Bending to reach into the front pocket of her backpack, Isobel groped for her phone. She had turned it off earlier that morning, but she knew that Gwen, unable to bear being out of the loop for even a moment regarding anything, usually kept hers on silent.

Isobel decided to send her a quick Mayday text to let her know something was up. Then maybe she could get a hall pass and they could meet in the library sometime next period.

Isobel drew her cell into her lap, using her body to shield the action.

She flipped open the phone, her thumb drifting toward the power button, but she stopped cold, arrested by the face reflected in the cell's darkened LCD screen.

He stood just behind her, peering down over her left shoulder.

His eyes, black, met hers through the screen, their gaze piercing, cold.

Varen.

14
Twisted

She had seen him. She knew she had.

One moment he'd been there, his gray-toned image mirrored in the screen of her cell phone as though he'd been standing mere inches behind her. Close enough to wrap his arms around her. Close enough for her to have felt his breath on her neck or the heat of his body against her back.

But she hadn't felt anything.

Then, when she'd turned around, there'd been nothing there. No one. Just the wind, the cold, and the ashen oak.

Isobel had checked her phone again, but Varen's reflection had vanished.

Too shocked to think, she forgot about texting Gwen.

The bell rang and, dazed, she returned to class.

That afternoon during cheer practice, Varen's face, so close, so clear, continued to haunt her.

"IS-O-BEL!" Coach's voice, amplified through the squad's blue-and-gold megaphone, slammed through Isobel's concentration.

"C'mon!" Coach yelled. "Up and at 'em, Lanley! You're not going to start that space-case business again, are you?" Coach waved her toward where the rest of the squad stood waiting, already lined up in their stunting formations. "Break's over. Just because the competition season ended doesn't mean it's time to slack off."

Isobel jumped to her feet from where she'd perched to rest on the corner of the bottom bleacher. When she stood, though, her water bottle tumbled out of her lap and hit the floor with a *thwack*, inciting titters from Alyssa Wilkes and her posse of sidekicks.

Setting down the gigantic cartoon-size megaphone, Coach made a show of sighing, her round hip jutting to one side.

"Thirty minutes left before I've got parents in cars breathing down my neck to release you all, Lanley," she said. "Let's go already! We gotta get through these drills or basketball season's going to be chock-full of claps and boring ground-level jumps. Hustle!"

Isobel left the water bottle behind on the floor as she jogged to the place where Stevie and Nikki waited for her along with her two spotters, Stephanie and Deja.

At the far end of the line, Isobel could hear Alyssa yawning loudly.

"That's enough, Miss Wilkes," Coach snapped. "Focus should be on the stunt at hand, not your next nap. Now let's hit it, team. Remember, we're going for a wave effect here, but our sidelines aren't gonna give us a lot of room, so keep it tight. Don't worry about the letter boards yet, Ashley. Leave them there for now, we'll add those in when we get our timing down on the lifts. Starting with your group, Stevie, and on down the line. Clean and prep by the count of eight, then I'll begin the count again. Group two, don't forget that your flyer needs to be up two counts after Isobel. Group three, two counts after Carly, and so on. We all stay up for eight, then it's the same count in reverse, with the pop cradle for our dismount." Coach raised the megaphone again. *"Ready?"*

Isobel didn't bother offering so much as a glance in Alyssa's direction, channeling her attention instead on the prep and load as Stevie and Nikki, her two stunt bases, squatted on either side of her. They held their hands out for her feet while her spotters sank down in front and back of her, ready to brace her during the lift.

After Nationals, Coach had been quick to rearrange the squad's regular grouping. And it had come as no surprise to Isobel that Coach had chosen to separate her and Alyssa, taking care to place them as far apart as possible during any given formation. Considering how complex Coach Anne's choreography tended to be, though, Isobel wasn't sure how long the reprieve would last.

While Coach counted, her voice lilting up and down with every other number, Isobel placed one hand on each of her bases' shoulders and pushed off from the floor, popping into the load.

"Five, six, seven, eight!"

On the last count, Isobel shot tall, rising high above the gymnasium floor. Keeping her knees locked, she mimed the action of flipping up her assigned *H*-for-"HAWKS" letter board.

Since they were taking the stunt in a wave pattern, Isobel and her group would have to hold their position the longest. While she waited for the count to restart and the wave to make its way back down the line, she tried to keep her mind on maintaining her balance without allowing her thoughts to circle back, yet again, to what she'd seen in the courtyard.

But that was almost more impossible than trying to convince herself that the moment hadn't been real.

She'd *seen* him.

It *had* to have been real. At least as real as anything else that had been happening to her. As real as drawings that came to life in old books. As real as masked figures who could walk in and out of reality. Real as the monster that had appeared in her living room.

Or, Isobel thought, her gaze drifting toward the clock that hung above the gymnasium's open set of double doors, then again, maybe not.

On a normal day, practice ended between four thirty and four forty-five. By this time, they'd been working for well over an hour. And hadn't Coach just reamed her out about how they had only thirty minutes left?

Why, then, did the time on the gym's clock read five past three?

"—six, seven, eight!"

Isobel felt her bases dip her. She wobbled just before they popped her into the air. Her body, kicking into autopilot, prepared for the drop, but it was too late to gain full control.

Isobel floundered as she fell, landing slantways in the arms of her squad mates, who stumbled under her lopsided weight.

"Whoa, whoa, whoa!" Coach yelled, abruptly stopping the count as Stevie and Nikki brought Isobel to her feet. "What happened?" she asked. Eyes bugging, she shook her shaggy head. Behind the barrier of her thick blue sweatband, Coach's frizzy hair shook in spongy clumps.

"I sure hope it wasn't my flyer that time," she said when no one in the group spoke up to rat her out. But it would seem no one had to.

Walking over to Isobel, her tennis shoes squeaking, Coach leaned in. "I thought taking topples was so last year, Izzy," she said.

Muffled snickers erupted from Alyssa and her entourage.

Isobel felt her face redden. She knew Coach hadn't meant it as a jab, that she was just trying a tougher approach in order to get her focused. Still, her words stung.

"Okay!" Coach shouted. "Let's try that again!"

"Izzy," she heard Nikki hiss at her. "C'mon."

But Isobel had to turn back to glance at the clock one more time.

True, the hands weren't spinning like they had been on the dashboard clock of Varen's dreamworld car, but they weren't moving the way they should either. They weren't moving at all.

She had to wonder if it could be a sign that she was asleep right now, that all this was a dream. If she *was* in a dream, then that would explain why she had seen Varen in the court-yard. Maybe he had been trying to connect. Maybe he had to work his way into her awareness.

But the world around her, the people, the gym and the lighting, it all seemed so normal, so real.

The American flag, suspended against the far wall, hung where it always had. Two basketball goals extended down on metal armatures from the walls at opposite ends of the wide room. Glancing up, Isobel could even see a small blue balloon from the last pep rally still lodged between the steel rafters.

Then again, she reminded herself, this was exactly what made dreams so tricky. Because no matter what, if you were in one, a dream always seemed real.

"Hey," Stevie called to her. "Let's go. Coach is heading back this way."

"Coming," Isobel mumbled, but she stayed put.

This *was* how all the other dreams began, always with her at cheer practice.

Could she really have dreamed the events of an entire day, though? Or was that how it always went, and she just forgot about all that later, after she woke up?

Isobel watched the double doors, waiting a moment longer for Varen to appear and settle the internal tug-of-war between her reasoning and instinct. But the doorway remained empty. Above it, the clock's face stayed frozen.

Maybe she *wasn't* dreaming. Maybe the clock was just stalled because the battery had run down over winter break. But if she couldn't be certain by looking at a clock, then how else *could* she tell?

Coach drew closer, and Isobel swiveled to face her stunt crew.

As Coach passed them, Isobel recalled something else Reynolds had once told her.

That if she could wake up in her dream, if she could realize she was in one, then, to some extent, she could control the things that happened.

How else had she been able to make the door appear in the floor at the Grim Facade just when she'd needed it most?

One thing was certain. If she was asleep right now and dreaming, then that had to mean she would be able to do things she couldn't in waking life. Or at least, something she'd never tried before.

Isobel pivoted away from her stunt group to face the gym's wide-open floor. It shone as though greased by a thin layer of oil. In the center of the floor, the embossed head of Henry the Hawk scowled at her with one angry yellow eye, as though warning her not to even *think* about it.

That was just it, though. If this was a dream, then she shouldn't have to think about it.

She just had to do it.

"Izzy," Coach said. "Hello. We're starting!"

Ignoring her, Isobel broke forward in a sprint.

"Lanley!"

Isobel lifted her arms. Bending forward, using her gained momentum, she launched into a round-off.

The world blurred, becoming a mesh of light and streaking colors.

Catapulting into a midair Arabian, knees tucked in, she became weightless. Then *bam*, her feet met the bare floor, ankles jarring from the impact on the hard, mat-free surface.

But like a windup toy set into motion, there would be no stopping.

A millisecond later and she'd completed the second round-off, pulled through the hands-free whip, and finished the back handspring, air whistling in her ears.

Her feet slammed the ground and she pushed off for the last time, hard as she could. Clutching her arms in tight, she launched upward, recognizing somewhere in the back of her mind that this was the longest pass she'd ever attempted.

The air greeted her, holding her like a stray leaf in its nonexistent grasp as she twisted once, *twi*—

The ground rushed toward her, as fast as the grille of a speeding semi. She completed the rotation and her heels connected with the floor, but like a spinning plate, the gym floor whizzed out from beneath her.

She heard a collection of gasps and gave her own strangled cry, which the floor pounded out of her as it slammed her back hard, like the palm of a giant's hand.

Isobel lay motionless, her muscles going slack.

There was a moment of silence as she stared up at the rows of piercing lights high, high above. She focused again on the lone blue balloon, and it helped to steady her swirling vision. Then her ears began to ring, the blood rushing through her skull loud enough that she didn't hear the sound of stampeding sneakers until a moment before several members of the squad converged on her.

Through the circle of stunned faces, Coach's appeared at

her right, chili-pepper red and blotchy with anger. Lacking only the smoking nostrils, she looked like a dragon, puffed up and prepared to heave fire.

Isobel struggled to sit up, her entire body humming with a mixture of adrenaline and humiliation.

Even though she felt no immediate pain, she knew better than to think it wasn't coming. It would. Later. Tonight. Worse in the morning.

"Lanley," Coach grunted. The low, rattling way her voice shook reminded Isobel of the sound a pot top makes when the water inside begins to boil. "You hurt?"

"N-no?" she managed to croak. Her voice sounded small and far away in her still-ringing ears. She felt suddenly tiny herself, too, as though she were a gnat in a room full of elephants.

"Then get your ass up off the floor and out of my gym. The rest of you, back to your positions."

With that, Coach whirled away.

Isobel's squad mates turned to follow, not a one of them wanting to draw attention to themselves and risk unleashing Coach's scarcely contained wrath by speaking to Isobel or offering to help her up. Even Stevie and Nikki jogged back to their places, though Isobel liked to think that Stevie might have lingered for half a second.

Slowly, achingly, Isobel brought herself back to her feet. As she hurried to gather her bag, somewhere from her retreating squad mates she heard Alyssa's stifled laughter and the whispered word "loser."

No, Isobel thought as her head began to pound.

This was definitely *not* a dream.

She got dressed in the girls' locker room, thankful for the solitude.

Out in the gym, she could hear Stephanie calling the names of various stretches as she led the rest of the squad through cooldown, and Isobel was glad no one had been sent in to retrieve her.

No matter how she spun it, there was no way she'd be able to explain her actions.

She knew how it must have looked: like she was trying to give Coach the showdown after being corrected in front of everyone; like she was a huge brat who had something to prove.

Isobel slammed her locker shut, her face flaring hot with renewed mortification.

How could she have done something so *stupid*?

And to top it all off, Alyssa had witnessed everything firsthand. She must be throwing herself a little squee session inside that pigtailed, baby's-rattle head of hers, loading her verbal gun with clever little jabs to send Isobel's way when they passed each other in the hall tomorrow.

Worst of all, Isobel couldn't be sure if she could still count herself as a member of the squad at all. Coach hadn't formally kicked her off, but still, Isobel had broken her number one rule to never (*ever*) throw a pass without mats or someone spotting. Not to mention that the pass itself had been an illegal one, since twists greater than one rotation were always forbidden. Not that Isobel had been able to accomplish the full double ending anyway.

But since she had tried, she could now officially consider herself resigned to cheerleader limbo, where she would have to wait until Coach either summoned her for judgment or clipped her wings for good.

Whatever the case, Isobel sincerely doubted a cheer-format apology would do any good at resurrecting her standing *this* time.

In one fell swoop, she'd managed to jeopardize *every-thing*. Now the one thing she'd been so desperate to avoid, a phone call home, seemed inevitable.

How was she going to explain this to her dad? It would be the last straw; she knew it. If Coach called him, which she might be doing right that very second, he'd cancel the Baltimore trip for sure.

What had she been *thinking*?

Isobel grabbed her coat, shouldered her gym bag, and pushed her way out of the locker room, eager to evacuate before Coach dismissed everyone else.

Then, glancing up, she was suddenly reminded of *exactly* what she'd been thinking, since once again, she found herself questioning if she really could be awake.

Because the thin, pale person hobbling into the boys' locker room on a pair of crutches could not possibly be who she thought it was.

15
Haunted

As the door to the boys' locker room began to shut behind Brad, Isobel broke into a fast walk. She hurried down the corridor and stopped to catch the metal handle. Pulling it open again, she slipped silently inside, keeping her back pressed to the door as it eased into the jamb.

At first, she didn't see anyone. But the metal click and squeak of a locker being opened told her he was close by.

Setting her coat and gym bag to one side, she stole forward, past a U-shaped section of blue lockers. Straight ahead, she noticed her reflection in a narrow full-length mirror affixed to the wall at the end of the aisle. It hung right next to a door that she knew must lead into the showers.

Isobel crept farther down the aisle, toward the sound of clanking and rustling, then stopped when she caught sight of him within the next alcove.

He stood with his back to her, scrounging in one of the blue metal cabinets.

BORGAN it read on the front of the door, which was open toward her, obscuring his head. Below his last name, the number twenty-one, his jersey number, stood out in bold yellow.

When he began pulling things out, padding and gear, Isobel thought that maybe she shouldn't have been so quick to follow him in. It now felt as though she was intruding on some private rite, his time to detach.

She wondered if she should say something or make some kind of a noise to let him know she was there. Or should she just retrace her steps and duck out again?

Seeing him like this, so different, so changed, made it difficult for her to do anything but stare.

His once thick arms, corded with strong muscles that used to strain against the sleeves of his shirts, now looked more like thin tree branches poking out of the cuffs of his retro tee. He had on a baggy pair of crisp and new-looking dark-wash jeans, the left pant leg of which had been rolled up over a Trenton blue midthigh-to-ankle cast.

He worked at a slow pace, as if he were a robot teaching itself how to move.

A blue-and-gold jersey hit the floor while he tossed a plain white T-shirt onto the duffel bag that sat on the bench behind him.

Isobel's gaze traveled down the length of his shrunken form, stopping to take in the thick cast coating his leg. There were no squiggly lines of black Sharpie where friends or teammates might have signed their names. Only clean, hardened bandages molded to the shape of his thigh, knee, and calf.

He stood with his weight on his right leg, his crutches propped against a pair of lockers at his side.

Whenever he began to teeter one way or the other, he would stop and place a hand against the wall of metal doors to catch himself.

Isobel fidgeted. She opened her mouth, then let it shut again. It felt wrong to stand and gawk without saying something, but what *could* she say?

She hesitated, then cleared her throat.

The sound made him pause, though he didn't startle. Not until he turned his head.

When their eyes met, his body jarred as though shocked by a jolt of electricity. He stumbled backward, the lockers banging and clattering as he tumbled into them.

Isobel took a step toward him. "Sorry! I—"

"No!" He threw up a hand, palm out, fingers splayed.

His fear made her pull back.

"I—I didn't mean to," she stuttered, aiming a thumb over her shoulder. "I mean, I saw you—but I wasn't—I just thought I'd—"

She realized she was babbling, so she stopped and took in a deep breath.

With no more meaningless words pouring out of her, Isobel found herself with nothing left to do but gape.

His face, drawn, worn, and full of fright, seemed so altered from the face she remembered. His features, now gaunt and haunted-looking, no longer held their sharp and chiseled all-American boyishness. His eyes, too, had lost that piercing blue-diamond luster that could cut as much as convince. Along with the former beach-tan hue of his skin, their color had since faded, dulled to a slate-metal tone that reminded Isobel of steel bars.

Isobel watched as he struggled to right himself. He fumbled for his crutches, using them to maneuver his way out of the corner she seemed to have driven him into.

"Wait," Isobel said.

To her surprise, he stopped when he reached the open walkway between the locker-room entrance and the door that led to the showers. He stood stock-still with his back to her, his head down.

For the first time, Isobel noticed the streak of white at his temple, showing up like a patch of frost against his otherwise coppery curls.

He trembled where he stood and kept his face turned away from the mirror, his eyes rolling in her direction, pupils expanding. Tiny beads of sweat began to form on his upper lip.

"Aren't you supposed to be in practice right now?" he asked her in a shaky whisper.

Isobel swallowed. "I got out . . . early."

"What do you want?"

"To talk," she said. "Just to talk." She reached a hand toward him but pulled back when he cringed and angled away from her.

"You're going to ask me what happened," he said. "Just like everybody else. Aren't you?"

Isobel didn't answer.

"Except," he continued, "unlike everybody else, Izo, you

know what happened. In fact, you're the *only* one who knows what happened. You were there. I saw you."

She watched as he hobbled back to the bench. Bracing his crutches against the lockers again, he lowered himself next to his duffel, extracting from it a black trash bag. Bad leg extended, he leaned forward at the waist and began to stuff the things lying on the floor into the bag.

"You . . . remember that?" she asked.

"Every single time I shut my eyes," he said.

Isobel shifted uncomfortably where she stood. She knew they were talking about Halloween night, but she couldn't be certain yet if he recalled any of the time he'd spent in the dreamworld, or if he was simply referring to what happened on the field when the Nocs cornered him during a play, snapping his leg.

Immediately after the attack, he'd fallen unconscious on the turf. Isobel had been there with him, calling out to him. But she didn't find out until later that his spirit, his "astral form" as Reynolds had called it, had been dragged from his body by the Nocs and taken by force into the dreamworld. It was there that Isobel later discovered him, alerted to his presence by desperate screams only moments after she'd found Varen locked inside another room.

Promising Varen she'd come back for him, Isobel had gone to try and save Brad from being tortured by the Nocs. But she'd arrived too late.

She'd watched Brad, against his will, become the blood-drenched figure of the Red Death, his soul sucked into a cemetery statue that burst into life, its gray stone robes transforming into sodden sheets of tattered crimson.

She could still picture the way the phantasm had moved, floating over the ground with its cloak billowing behind. Helpless, Isobel had watched from within the pit of an open grave as the hooded figure descended from its plinth. With one wave of its skeletal hand, the creature had sent the dirt walls of her prison caving in, burying her alive.

Reality and the realm of dreams had already begun to merge by that time, and under the Red Death's control, Brad entered the real world again, ready to carry out the final events of Poe's gruesome story.

Only Reynolds had prevented him from killing everyone at the Grim Facade.

After rescuing her, he had fought to keep the Red Death at bay while she returned to the woodlands to destroy Varen's journal, severing the link between worlds. Though doing so had been enough to free Brad and allow him to return to his body and to reality, it had not been enough to ensure Varen's return. In fact, it had done just the opposite.

"Brad," Isobel began, "listen. I'm sorry about . . . what happened on the field. And . . . I'm sorry that you can't—"

He laughed, a bitter, cold sound. "You know I'm not talking about what happened on the field," he said. "And keep your pity for yourself. I hated football." She watched him shove the blue-and-gold jersey into the trash bag.

Isobel gaped at him, stunned. "What?"

"You heard me," he said. "I hated the games. I hated the

practices. I hated the tailgating and the stupid pep rallies. The only reason I did it was because everyone told me I should. Because it made my old man happy. Because I thought it made *you* happy."

He shook his head, yanking the yellow ties so the neck of the bag drew tight. He tied them off in a knot. "Now," he said, and stuffed the nearby stack of T-shirts and locker photos into the duffel. Isobel thought she even recognized Nikki's smiling face in one of them before he zipped the bag shut. "Now I can just forget about it. Right? Start over. Be something else. So thanks for that, Izo. But please . . ."

He looped the strap of the duffel over his head and positioned the bag on his back. Anchoring himself with one of the crutches, he pulled himself onto his feet again. "Don't do me any more favors."

He picked up the black garbage bag with his free hand and limped toward her. Isobel stepped aside to allow him access to the enormous trash can behind her. He hoisted the bag over its edge and let it fall in with a *whoosh*.

Then he turned to her and pointed to the remaining crutch. Wordlessly, she handed it to him.

He slid it under his arm.

Isobel expected him to walk right past her after that, to leave without saying anything else. But he lingered, edging in closer, his crutches creaking.

"You know . . . ," he began, his voice dropping to a whisper, "I still hear the screaming. If my head ever gets too quiet, that's when it starts up. It's like when you hit the snooze button and then, just as soon as you begin to doze, the alarm goes off again. Sometimes I wake up in the middle of the night and there's blood all over my hands. And all down my arms." Adjusting his weight, Brad extended one of his arms out in front of him, staring at it as he flipped it from front to back. "And I have to blink several times before it'll go away." His gaze shifted back to her. "What about you, Izo? What do you see?"

Isobel didn't move. Her eyes remained trapped by his. She told herself not to speak, not wanting to let on how much he was scaring her.

"Can I tell you something?" He tilted his head, moving in closer still, so close that she could feel his breath against her cheek. "Do you want to know what my grandma used to say about kisses on the forehead?"

He pressed his lips to her brow, holding the silk soft kiss for a long moment while Isobel stood in place, unable to bring herself to shove him away.

"She told me it's the kind of kiss we save for the dead."

Isobel's eyes snapped open wide. She took an immediate step back from him, her hands forming into fists.

But he wasn't looking at her anymore. Instead he seemed transfixed by something behind her. "A word to the wise," he added in a murmur. "Cover your mirrors. That's how they find you."

With that, he turned away from her, his crutches clanking as he moved toward the door. He pushed through without looking back, leaving her there alone.

She stared after him, suddenly hyperaware of the mirror at her back.

A nagging feeling settled over her. It was that same sensation she'd felt that night in the park behind her house before being chased by the Nocs. Like there were a thousand invisible eyes aimed at her back, waiting for her to notice them so they could descend and devour.

Her body told her to start moving, to walk away as fast as she could, to leave right that second and not look back. But her mind, her *instinct*, told her there was something she needed to see.

She pivoted slowly in place, like a music-box ballerina winding down on its pedestal.

There, in the mirror, standing only a few short feet behind her, Isobel saw him.

It was the pure blackness of his eyes that stopped her breathing. They peered right through her. White ash caked his boots like flour, turning them from black to gray.

"Varen?"

He watched her with an expression as unreadable as it was unchanging. It was that cold and stark blank-canvas look of his she'd always found so unsettling, that mask of nothingness that refused to give anything away.

He blinked, and the lights flickered.

Isobel stood paralyzed, helpless to move or utter a single syllable as he slipped between the lockers and vanished.

She spun to look behind her. The aisle stood empty. As she ran the length of it, checking between each of the alcoves, panic swelled in her chest. Still, she found no trace, no scrap of evidence that he'd ever been there.

She whipped her head to look back at the mirror, confronted only with the mad confusion of her own reflection.

16
Dark Reflections

Isobel left the boy's locker room and ran toward the doors leading out into the central hallway, her gym bag jouncing at her side.

She needed to catch up to Brad, to ask him what he knew. What else he'd seen. She needed him to tell her what he'd been talking about, what he'd meant when he'd said—

"Isobel!"

She whirled.

Looking harried, with her glasses askew, Gwen came hurrying after her, bracelets jangling. Behind her scurrying form, through the open doorway of the gym, Isobel could see a small cluster of squad members as they glanced up in their direction.

Isobel shrank back farther into the hall and out of their line of sight.

"Wait!" Gwen called, jogging in Isobel's direction, the strap of her messenger bag looped across one shoulder. "I've been looking all over for you," she huffed. The bright flush in her cheeks told Isobel that she must have gone searching outside as well. "Did you forget I was picking you up? Why weren't you in there with the rest of the gladiators?"

Isobel didn't answer. Turning away, she started down the

hall at a faster pace, following the line of lockers, stopping only when she rounded the corner. But Brad wasn't there. He wasn't anywhere.

"Where are you go—*oof.*" Gwen collided with Isobel's back, her bracelets clanking like cutlery.

Isobel spun to face her.

"Gwen, I saw him."

"Who?" Gwen asked. She straightened her glasses, then tugged at her hair, trying to loosen several strands from where they'd become caught between the sets of silver bangles. "Your old flame? Yeah, I saw him too. Just now. Watched him get into the car and ride off with *Mizz* Scarlett." Gwen batted her eyes, flipping her hair in imitation of Nikki. "Did you talk to him?"

"No. Gwen." Isobel gripped her by the shoulders. "I saw *Varen.*"

Gwen went rigid in Isobel's grasp, her expression faltering. In an instant, her cheeks lost their rosy hue, giving way to a pasty white. She clutched at Isobel's wrists, which made her realize that she'd been digging her nails into Gwen's shoulders.

Isobel let go.

"Where?" Gwen asked. "How?"

"In—in the—" Isobel looked over her shoulder, back in the direction of the gym. Then another memory surfaced through the jumbled murk of her confusion.

The first time Reynolds had appeared to her, hadn't it been through a mirror?

Isobel grew still, her heart speed doubling as her thoughts returned yet again to the moment in the courtyard after Mr. Swanson's class. Suddenly there was no longer any doubt in her mind about what she'd seen in the darkened screen of her cell phone.

Reflections . . .

That's how they find you, Brad had said.

But what had he meant by "they"? And if mirrors really were a link between the dreamworld and reality, then why hadn't Varen tried to reach her through one before now? And why hadn't he spoken to her or, at the very least, attempted to convey some kind of message? Why had he only stared at her like that?

"The way he looked at me . . ." Isobel glanced slowly back to Gwen. "It . . . it was as if . . ." She trailed off, suddenly realizing where it was they were standing.

She remembered turning this corner after practice once before. That day she'd found Brad hovering over Varen, threatening him in low tones. And then the way Varen had glared at her, thinking it had been all *her* doing, that she'd sent Brad after him on purpose.

It seemed like such a faraway moment, but she could never forget the hatred in Varen's eyes that day. Like two pyres burning in the dark, they had branded themselves into her memory forever. In them, he had shown no fear. Not even anger. Only empty contempt.

Just now, in the locker room . . . why did it feel as though she had relived that moment?

She felt Gwen grab her by the arm, jostling her. "Isobel," she said, "talk to me. Tell me what happened."

"The kiss," Isobel said, the words tumbling out of her mouth in the precise moment they occurred to her.

"*Kiss?*" Gwen asked. "Whoa, whoa, what kiss? What are you talking about?"

Isobel's eyes met with Gwen's, her jaw squaring. "He saw Brad kiss me."

"So," Isobel's dad said as he reached for the saltshaker. "First day back. How was it?"

Isobel stopped pushing her green beans around on her plate long enough to give her father a cautious glance.

"Okay," she lied.

Resuming construction on the tepee-shaped pile of beans, she looked at Danny, who sat next to her, preoccupied with his DS, and then at the empty chair across from him, glad that Monday was her mother's Pilates night.

After dropping Isobel off at home, Gwen had initially invited herself to stay for dinner but then opted out as soon as she discovered that Isobel's mom wouldn't be there to act as a buffer between her and Isobel's dad.

For once, though, Isobel was grateful to be free of Gwen's company. Aside from wanting to escape the endless barrage of questions she didn't have answers for, she would need solitude in order to conduct that night's after-dinner plan of action.

"Glad to hear it," she heard her dad say as he shook salt

onto his mashed potatoes, not bothering to look up. Isobel's gaze remained downcast as well while she stabbed at the slice of roast beef on her plate.

So far, her father hadn't brought up hearing from Coach. If she *had* called, Isobel couldn't fathom why it wouldn't have been the first thing out of his mouth as soon as he walked through the door. Since he had yet to mention anything about it, Isobel had to believe that he didn't know what she'd done in practice and that she was still in the clear regarding Baltimore, at least for the time being. She had to trust that, because right now, there were more immediate things that needed her attention, like her dresser mirror.

Isobel swept the sliver of beef around and around in its pool of thin gravy. If she could just bring herself to take another bite, if she could just down enough food to clear half her plate, then there was a slim chance that she *might* be able to excuse herself. Then she could go to her room, close the door, and face the mirror without having to worry about being interrupted.

She'd once conducted a similar experiment, in the bathroom at school. There, in desperation, she'd confronted one of the mirrors in an attempt to summon Reynolds, calling out to him by name.

It hadn't worked.

Yet later that day, when she'd again encountered the mysterious masked figure, she recalled very clearly how he'd chastised her. *I am not a dog to be called,* he'd said.

In other words, he'd *heard* her.

"Isobel, did you hear me?"

"Huh?" She looked up. Bringing her fork to her lips, she forced herself to take another bite. Roast beef squished against her tongue like a tough sponge.

"I said, how was practice?"

Isobel coughed. She lifted her glass of lemonade to her lips and, taking a sip, managed to force the food down. She nodded in response while taking another gulp of her drink. "Good," she said, her voice raspy.

"Really," he muttered. "That's not what Coach said."

Isobel froze. Slowly she lowered her glass.

"Did you know she called me on my cell?" he asked.

Isobel didn't answer. Vines of panic began to wrap their way around her insides.

Turning her fork on its side, she used the edge like a mini snowplow, shoving the goopy, too-smooth glob of instant mashed potatoes from one edge of her plate to the other. The action made a long, high-pitched scraping noise, which caused her little brother, even though he had on his headphones, to glance up from his game. He glowered at her before returning his attention to the tiny flashing screen.

Normally, neither of them were allowed to have anything electronic at the dinner table. Isobel knew that if their mother were there, she'd have confiscated the DS for sure by now.

"Said you pulled an outright kamikaze on her," he went on, elbows working as he sawed at his food with fork and knife, the movement causing the table to wobble slightly.

"Her words exactly." He stabbed at the meat, stuck the fork in his mouth and, chewing, continued to stare at her.

Isobel wished she held the power to shrink to a pinpoint and float off. More than that, she wished that she could blink and make the rest of the two weeks before the Baltimore trip pass by in an instant. That way, she could avoid doing all the stupid things that would prevent her from going at all.

She sank into her seat.

"I threw a pass when she wasn't looking," Isobel confessed. "There wasn't a mat and no one was spotting. I missed the last rotation, and I fell."

She assumed that he had his reasons for remaining silent until now. It could only mean he'd made up his mind regarding what he was going to do about it. Taking that into consideration, Isobel knew it was better to just go ahead and match stories with Coach's instead of playing verbal dodgeball in hopes of finding out exactly how much had been said. When it came down to it, she needed to know what fate he or Coach or Mom or school would sentence her to. After what had happened that day, after what Varen had seen, or thought he'd seen, the only thing that mattered was getting to Baltimore, finding a way to find him. She would need to know if getting there, to the city and to the cemetery, was something she was going to have to do on her own after all.

"An *illegal* pass," he corrected her.

"The double just sort of happened," she said. "Or actually, it didn't."

"Coach said you almost landed it."

"I . . ." Isobel frowned. Glancing up, she watched her father's face carefully, trying to gauge not only where this calm, almost detached reaction was coming from, but where it was going. Shouldn't the yelling have started by now?

"How many rotations?" he asked, and took a sip of his ginger ale.

Isobel's eyes darted to Danny, who remained absorbed in his game. Then she glanced back to her dad. "I . . . don't . . . know." She shrugged. "I just— "

"Coach said it was more than three at least," he cut in, sounding strangely excited. "Whatever you did, she seemed pretty impressed by it. But don't tell her I told you that. Anyway, do . . . uh . . . do you think you could do it again?"

"Do it . . . again? Dad. I think it's fairly safe to say I'm off the squad."

He scrunched up his face and waved her off. "I talked to Coach," he said. "Told her about us going up to Maryland. She said you hadn't mentioned it to her. I told her that's probably why you did what you did. She seemed to calm down after that."

Isobel watched her father push his half-full plate away and fold his arms across the table. Chin down, he angled his gaze up at her, several creases running across his broad forehead.

"You're really serious about cheering, aren't you?" he asked.

Isobel remained silent, opting to just nod.

"Good," he said. "Because I called the university today

and made arrangements for you to meet with the head coach. I told her about Nationals, and she mentioned that you might show her a few things. Sort of like an unofficial tryout."

"You *what*?"

Isobel's fork slipped. It clattered against the table, causing Danny to flinch. Her brother scowled, and this time left the room, taking his plate with him to the kitchen.

Her dad paused, his ginger ale poised just in front of his lips. He lowered the can, setting it down before he spoke again. "Thought you'd want to meet her while we were there," he said, studying her closely.

Isobel stared at him in abject horror. He had gotten her a one-on-one with the head coach? *And* an unofficial tryout? It seemed unthinkable. How?

Her heart constricted in her chest, clenching tighter with each beat.

In that moment, she knew she should never have involved her father in the plans to reach Baltimore. She should have figured something else out, found some way to make it there on her own.

"You know . . . ," he prompted. "At this super-special university we're flying up to see week after next?"

Mouth open, Isobel's lips trembled in an attempt to form words.

He'd meant this to be a surprise—a *good* surprise.

She did her best to force a smile. Meanwhile, her mind shot into overdrive, trying to calculate how much this would complicate things.

"Are—are we going to have time for that?" she asked.

"I mean . . . that's the whole reason we're going, isn't it?"

She sat back. Gripping the table, she nodded. "Yeah," she said. "Wow. I—it— Thanks . . . Dad."

He gave her a funny, squinty-eyed look. "Gosh, Iz, I thought you'd be a little more excited than this."

"I *am* excited," she insisted. Leaning forward in her chair, she touched his arm. She smiled again but didn't push it, not wanting to lay it on too thick too late. "I just . . . got nervous there for a second is all. I don't really have anything prepared, you know?"

"Well, like I said, kiddo, it's not official or anything. Right now, I think they just want to see a little of what you've got. You're still only a junior. And you've got some time to practice, though you ought to be in pretty good shape from the competition. You don't have to do the pass if you don't want to." He nudged her elbow. "I mean . . . you're not having second thoughts about the whole thing, are you?"

"No!" she shouted.

Her dad cocked an eyebrow at her.

Isobel sank back in her chair. She ducked her head and stared at the soupy contents on her plate. The smell of the food began to make her already knotted stomach churn in loop-de-loops. She felt suddenly light-headed and queasy, like she'd spent the entire day on a carnival ride that had only just begun to slow down.

"I mean no," she said more quietly. "I *do* want to go."

"Okay," he said. "Well then, we're still on, don't worry. I

booked our hotel, too. We're flying up that Sunday, and we'll be staying in the city two nights, right in the Inner Harbor. Then we'll check out Tuesday morning, load up the rental, and drive to the school. That'll be a long day, because we'll have to turn around and come back later that night to catch our flight home. I've got to be back in the office the next morning, too, so we gotta— Isobel, are you listening?"

Isobel nodded. In truth, she'd tuned him out right after he'd mentioned the day of the flight. Sunday was the eighteenth, the same night she needed to be in the graveyard. That meant she'd have to ditch him almost as soon as they arrived.

"Yeah," she said. "Sure. That works. Um, hey, Dad?"

"Yeah?"

"Can I . . . be excused?"

He pointed to her plate. "You didn't eat much."

"I know," she said. "I'm not that hungry."

She needed to get away from the table, away from her father and all his well-meaning plans. She didn't want to think about hurting him, because that's what she was going to do. She wouldn't make it to the special meet-and-greet tryout he'd arranged. Neither of them would, because she would be long gone. And he would be there, alone in that huge city, doing whatever he could to find her.

She could practically hear her parents arguing over the phone, her mother's frantic I-told-you-sos, her father beside himself with guilt and self-blame.

She could *feel* the fissure forming in her family now,

before any of them were even aware the crack existed. Or that she had been the one to put it there.

Isobel's breath hitched. She balled her napkin in her fist, trying to play it off as a hiccup. Cringing inwardly, she decided to pull the fail-safe girl card. "Cramps," she said.

Her dad leaned back in his chair. "Mm," he said.

Isobel stood. She slid a hand under her plate, but her dad held up a palm. "I'll get that," he said.

She backed away. Turning, she hurried up the steps.

Ducking into her room, she shut the door behind her.

17
Inversion

Isobel sat on the corner of her bed closest to her dresser mirror. She watched the glass from an angle that did not show her own reflection, only that of the room itself.

From here, she could see the dark square of her window and the white-lace curtains that flanked it. The mirror also showed her nightstand and fringed bedside lamp, which she'd switched on.

The darkness seemed to press in around her, as though waiting for her to make a move or dare to step beyond the cone-shaped pool of yellowish lamplight.

But Isobel wasn't afraid.

Her eyes remained steady on the surface of the mirror as she spoke.

"I don't know if you can hear me," she said. "I can't tell if you're listening. I'm not even sure how this works . . . if it works . . . but I know that you've seen me. And . . . and I know what you saw today. What it must have looked like." Glancing down, she took in a breath, then let it out in a long sigh before continuing. "But it wasn't what you think it was. You *know* that's not who I am anymore. Don't you?"

She lifted her head, her eyes returning to the mirror.

"Varen . . . if you can see me, if you can hear me, why won't you appear like before? Speak to me. Tell me how to reach you. Show me how to find you. Because right now, I don't even know if what I'm doing is right anymore."

The mirror remained clear.

Pushing off from her bed, Isobel went to stand in front of it.

Not liking the way the dim light exaggerated the shadows on her face, Isobel glanced at the reflection of her digital clock and the inverted neon numbers that blazed through the gloom.

"Varen," she whispered, "I miss you."

She saw the last digit twitch, a minute having passed by. She waited, and when another sixty seconds elapsed, the number changed again.

Time continued to crawl by, yet Isobel stayed in front of her mirror, hoping that any moment she would see his face appear at her window, that he might step up behind her, or that she would hear him say something. *Anything.*

But the only thing that changed was the time.

After several more long minutes, Isobel heard the front door open, and her ears perked at the sound of her mother's voice calling through the house, "I'm home!"

Only then did Isobel break her gaze with the mirror.

She crept to her door and, opening it a fraction of an inch, peeked out into the hall. Through the banister rungs of the landing, she saw her mother standing in the foyer below. Stepping out from the living room, her father took her coat while they exchanged words too low for Isobel to make out.

"Upstairs," her dad said.

Before her mother could look in her direction, Isobel took a quick step back. Hearing shuffling on the stairs, she hurried to her bed. She threw back the covers and slipped under them, then rolled to face her window and shut her eyes.

The hinges of her bedroom door squeaked as it opened.

Even though no other sound came for some time after, Isobel could still sense her mother watching her.

Isobel kept her breathing even and heavy.

She heard the rustle of clothing and then the quiet click of her bedside lamp.

The darkness behind her lids became absolute.

A moment later and she felt her mother's lips, still chilled from the night air, brush her temple. The remnants of that morning's spritz of perfume invaded Isobel's nostrils, an airy blend of apricots and field flowers in full bloom—a breath of midsummer in the bleakest part of winter.

Even after Isobel's mother left her room, the calmness she had brought with her remained, soothing Isobel's nerves and robbing the pressing darkness of its power.

In its place, sleep closed in to claim her.

Standing on the sidewalk, right at the edge of the curb, Isobel tilted her head back to peer up at the front of the bookstore.

Above the pointed rooftop, just beyond the crumbling chimney, a thin layer of low-lying clouds rushed by. The fast-moving backdrop created the optical illusion that the narrow building housing the shop was tipping forward, on its way to crush her.

A high-pitched squeaking noise drew her attention directly overhead, to the once straight-hanging sign for Nobit's Nook. Now, though, the wooden board dangled lopsided from its iron bracket. Suspended by only a single link, the sign whined as it rocked and swiveled.

But why was the lettering . . . backward?

The wind swished past her in a low hush, dragging cool fingers through her hair.

Isobel looked toward the front window of the shop when she heard someone inside begin to cough.

She listened as the hacking grew distant and knew it had to be the elderly bookshop owner, Bruce.

Stepping forward, she peered through the glass. Though the lights were on in the main room, she saw no one standing near the book-swamped checkout counter or amid the tall rows of packed shelves. The shop appeared deserted, identical in every aspect to how she remembered it—save for one difference.

It was all reversed, everything completely flipped.

Just like the image in a mirror.

Isobel backed away from the window. She spun to look around, suddenly realizing where she was, that she was not only currently asleep in her bed and dreaming, but that somehow she was also standing within the dreamworld.

As far as she could see, the woodlands stretched long in every direction, their darkened borders occupying the space that in the real world would have held a string of storefronts.

The trees themselves stood in thick union, close as grass

blades, almost as though they had conspired to merge nearer to one another in order to block anyone who might dare cross their boundaries. Or, she thought, try to escape them.

Layers of ash spilled out from between the blackened tree trunks. The dust reached far enough to swallow the legs of a bus stop bench as well as the bases of signposts and all the streetlamps, which gave off an eerie glow through the mist-filled air.

Like a slumbering black dragon, a certain vintage car sat parked close to the curb, only a few feet away from where she stood. White ash caked the treads of its tires.

Varen. He was here.

Isobel hurried up the short stoop to the door. Though the flip sign read CLOSED in reverse, she tried the handle anyway.

The belt of bells jangled as the door swung open. Isobel entered the shop, the floorboards moaning underfoot.

"Hello?"

At first there came no answer. But then a small, soft voice, that of a woman's, sliced through the silence.

"Hello there."

Isobel halted.

Raising a hand to her throat, she groped for the pendant Gwen had given her. The hamsa felt warm and solid in her fist, and again, she had to remind herself that this wasn't real. Or at the very least, that it wasn't reality.

Willing herself to stand her ground, Isobel waited for something else to happen, steeling herself to move in the event that it did.

"It's okay." The woman's voice, overlapped by a faint crackle of static, broke through the quietness of the shop, her tone reassuring. "You can come in."

Isobel turned her head in the direction of the voice, which seemed to be coming from somewhere near the checkout counter.

"I shouldn't play so late," the voice said. "Did I wake you? Since you're up, if you like, I could let you hear the rest. It's our song, after all, and it *is* almost finished. Here, let me sing you the last verse."

As the tinkle of piano notes trickled through the shop, Isobel's initial fear began to subside, and she pressed on toward the counter. There, sitting amid the stacks of books, stationed atop an enormous pair of thick volumes, she saw what looked to be an old-fashioned gramophone.

The device had a hand crank, which turned itself around and around as familiar music poured forth from its enormous funnel-shaped horn. Then the voice began to sing.

"And side by side we'll fight the tide
That sweeps in to take us down
And hand in hand we'll both withstand
Even as we drown."

Isobel sidled up to the counter, drawing closer only to discover that the gramophone held no record. Its needle hung suspended off to the side, too, away from the empty turntable, which spun at a lazy speed.

She listened, hypnotized, as the piano notes carried on anyway. Then the music faded off, ending in a sharp clang of keys as though something about the song's execution had frustrated its composer.

"I don't know." The voice on the gramophone sighed. "Do you think that last part's too sad? Well, don't just stand at the door, silly," she said through a laugh. "Come, sit with me on the bench awhile. Let me play you the whole thing from start to finish, and then you tell me what you think."

The gramophone's crank continued to rotate. It circled around and around as though propelled by the hand of a ghost, the hushed overlay of crackling continuing through the brief moment of silence. Then the melody picked up again, that same sad song Isobel had heard three times before now— the lullaby.

> *"Sleep now a little while*
> *Till within our dreams we wake*
> *Unfolding our Forever*
> *If only for Never's sake."*

A low creak from overhead drew Isobel's gaze to the ceiling.

Beside her, the gramophone began to skip.

> *"Till within our dreams we wake—*
> *Till within our dreams we wake—*
> *Till within our dreams we wake—"*

"I *am* awake," Isobel whispered.

The moment she spoke out loud, the gramophone stopped playing, its crank halting mid-rotation.

As she continued to listen, she heard footsteps—*booted* footsteps, their gait even and slow—begin to make their way across the upper floor.

There was somebody upstairs, in the attic.

Isobel headed toward the rear of the shop, but a distant sound, hissing from behind, stopped her before she reached the open archway.

Glancing over her shoulder, back toward the gramophone, Isobel watched as the crank began to revolve again, this time in the opposite direction as before. The hissing transformed into whispers. Then the whispers became words, which began to drift from the horn's black hole, growing louder and more discernible with each revolution of the crank.

"Believe me," a girl's voice cut through the static, "that would *so* never happen."

Isobel's mouth fell open as she recognized the voice as her own.

"In fact, we never saw each other outside of class except those times we *had* to meet for the project. To be honest," the voice—*her* voice—continued, "we didn't even get along. But I had to put up with it because I needed a passing grade."

Isobel shook her head. "No," she said.

"At this point, I'm just kind of ready to forget about it and move on, you know? But . . . as far as knowing anything about what happened that night? I'm honestly the last person who would—I'm honestly the last person who—I'm honestly the last person—the last person—honestly—hoooonnestly—hooooneeessstly."

The crank ground to a halt, the repeated word dropping several octaves, slurring into one incomprehensible drone before dying out.

"I didn't mean it," Isobel murmured. After a moment, she shouted, "I didn't mean any of that!"

Startled by the sound of a low click followed by a long creak, Isobel whirled to face the open archway leading to the rear of the shop. Through it, she could see that the door leading to the attic, the DO NOT ENTER door, the BEWARE OF BESS door, had opened itself.

Approaching the door, she could see the narrow set of stairs just within.

She crossed the threshold and, looking up, saw that where the ceiling should have been lay only open skies. The low-flying clouds skimmed past at a frightening speed, the cavernous spaces in between their folds illuminating with brilliant flashes of violet lightning.

Fighting vertigo, Isobel groped for the stairs. She mounted them, watching her feet climb until she reached the top landing.

When she raised her head again, she saw that just as there had been no ceiling, no walls existed either. Only their blackened and charred remains fringed the parameters of the open room.

Black trees crowded the freestanding platform, their arms outstretched to the passing clouds.

In the middle of the room, wearing a long black coat she had never seen before, stood Varen, his back to her.

Between his shoulder blades, the image of the same upside-down crow from his green mechanics' jacket blazed in pure white against the ebony fabric. Only, just like everything else, the bird was reversed, now upright with its wings outspread as though in the midst of taking flight.

Clenched in one fist, she saw that he held her pink ribbon, the sash belonging to the dress she had worn to the Grim Facade. When she'd been there with him, on the other side of the purple chamber, unable to free him, Isobel had untied the ribbon from around her waist and given it to him as a token. A symbol of her promise to return for him.

He turned to face her slowly, the wind teasing at his hair, tugging at the hem of his long coat.

Isobel took a step toward him but stopped the moment their eyes met.

His stare, black and soulless, so far from the penetrating emerald gaze she remembered, rendered her immobile.

Lifting his arm out to the side, he let the slip of pink satin dangle from his hand. Then he unclenched his fist, letting go of the ribbon.

It fell, pooling right in the center of a blackened scorch mark that marred the floor.

"Wait!" she called as he began to turn away again.

But it was too late. Her eyes were open and she was back in her bed, awake and alone in her darkened room.

18
Burned

"You want me to go in with you?" Gwen asked.

It was the one and only question she had posed to Isobel between picking her up from practice and arriving at Nobit's Nook.

Isobel had not told Gwen about the previous night's dream, but she hadn't had to invent a reason to go to the bookshop, either. Gwen's response to Isobel's request for a ride had been uncharacteristically though blessedly simple. "Okay," she'd said, "let's go."

Now, staring out the passengers'-side window of the Cadillac, Isobel blinked at what she saw and then blinked again, as though doing so would make it disappear.

But the Cougar remained, parked exactly the same way it had been in the dream.

Its ebony finish gleamed in the late-afternoon sunlight, which had begun to break through the thinning screen of clouds. From where they sat parked on the opposite side of the street, Isobel could clearly read the hateful words YOU'RE DEAD FREAK, which Brad had once carved across the driver's-side door.

She forced herself to look away.

"Isobel?"

"Stay here, please," she murmured, and grabbed the door handle.

"What about that old guy?" Gwen asked as Isobel climbed out. "What if he tries to yell at you or tells you to get out? At least let me play decoy."

"He'll remember you from last time," Isobel said, glancing back. "Besides, he won't see me."

"Yeah, nobody does incognito like a cheerleader," Gwen scoffed.

Isobel tried for a smile, but it didn't want to come. "It'll only take a second," she said, and shut the door. Rounding the Cadillac, she checked for traffic and was about to cross the street when Gwen rolled down her window and leaned out.

"You have your phone on you, right?"

Isobel nodded. She waited for a car to pass, its tires swishing over the rain-slicked pavement as it rushed by. Then she zipped her parka all the way to her chin, tugged the hood over her head, and hurried across the street.

She paused in front of the store and glanced up.

The sign for Nobit's Nook hung crooked, dangling from its rusted bracket by a single metal loop. This time, though, the letters were not in reverse.

The tightness in her chest squeezed harder and she struggled to draw her next breath.

For the entire day, she had carried a knot of dread within her. Through each agonizing hour at school, her pulse had beat with an uneven rhythm, her gut churning with sick anticipation of this moment.

Could Varen really have heard her say those things to Mr. Swanson? Was *that* why she had seen his reflection in her phone during lunch? Could he have been there with her somehow, following and listening in?

Even if he *had* heard her, he wouldn't really believe she'd meant any of it, would he?

But then . . . there had been the kiss in the locker room, too.

Isobel gripped the cuffs of her sleeves as a swift breeze stung her cheeks and caused the sign above her to rock and creak.

She channeled her focus to the front door of Nobit's Nook and the flip sign inside that read OPEN.

Though she knew she would not have the answers to all her questions until she came face-to-face with Varen, she also knew that the answer to at least one of them could be found inside this store.

Isobel's thoughts returned to the first time she'd ever dreamed of Reynolds.

That night he'd entered her room like a phantom, warning her about the danger behind Varen's actions while also returning the volume of Poe's complete works she'd discarded earlier that afternoon. And though Reynolds had assured her from the start that she was dreaming, Isobel still found the book the next morning, a solid testament to the realness of the encounter.

But did that mean she would find what she feared she would here, upstairs, in the attic?

The only way she had avoided falling into the sinkhole of doubt until this moment had been to hold on to the possibility that when she finally arrived at the bookstore, she would discover no evidence to prove that what she had witnessed in her dream had truly taken place.

After all, how could she trust what she'd seen when she had been tricked by false images before?

Gwen had said that demons could twist minds.

But it was hard to tell whose mind Lilith was trying to turn with lies. Isobel's or Varen's?

Though both the car and the hanging sign matched up with her dream, it all brought to mind something Mr. Swanson had once said back at the beginning of the year when they'd been studying *Othello*. He'd explained to the class that what made the villain, Iago, such a convincing liar was his ability to make things *appear* a certain way to his enemy.

Perception had been his weapon.

With that thought, Isobel gained the courage to move. She hurried up the short flight of stairs, twisted the knob, and pulled open the door. As she slipped inside, the stiff scent of aged paper, dust, and stale air greeted her. She turned to face the door as it closed, careful not to allow its hanging belt of Christmas bells to jangle too harshly.

She kept her back to the shop interior, listening and waiting to see if anyone had noticed her come in. With her head down, her face partially hidden by the hood of her parka, she risked a glance over one shoulder. Seeing no one, she took a quick inventory of her surroundings.

Tall wooden bookcases stood in close proximity to one another. Their shelves, once stuffed to the point of bowing, now seemed to hold a much lighter burden. There were even a few barren spots in between clusters of worn-looking volumes and stacked tomes.

The high-reaching shelves stretched long across the floor, halfway blocking the copper-colored light that struggled to illuminate the tight aisles in between.

Isobel heard rustling and, glancing the other way, spotted a round middle-aged woman in a navy-blue raincoat. She stood over a bin of old magazines with a handwritten sign on the side indicating that they'd been marked down to twenty-five cents an issue. The woman looked up, offering Isobel a distracted smile before going back to leafing through the magazines.

Other than the woman, the store appeared to be empty of customers.

Careful to keep her steps as quiet as possible, Isobel slunk between two of the tallest shelves. She placed one foot directly in front of the other as though walking a tightrope and trailed close to the shelf at her right.

Her ears strained for the sound of Bruce's haggard cough, though she heard nothing.

A few more steps took her to the end of the bookcase, and peeking around its edge, she found him.

The bookstore owner sat behind the glass display case

that served as the front counter, half his face obscured by the ancient push-button register.

His single visible eye, its center dark as black coffee, stared directly at her.

Isobel gasped. She darted behind the bookcase again. Whipping her head around to peer back toward the front of the shop, she had to fight the urge to make a run for the door. Instead she held her breath, squeezed her eyes shut, and waited, but the yelling she had anticipated never came. When she didn't hear coughing, either, she suddenly remembered what had happened the first time she'd ever walked into the store. The old man had stared at her then, too, but she'd discovered a moment later that apparently that was the way he slept—with one of his eyes (the one that just so happened to be glass) wide open.

Isobel leaned out to peek around the bookcase again.

The shop owner sat in the exact same position.

He looked frailer than she remembered, his once round body having shrunken enough so the sleeves of his thick brown sweater hung from his arms in loose folds, like the skin of a bloodhound. His hair had thinned as well since the last time she'd seen him, the shock of Einstein-white gone, leaving mere wisps on his otherwise bald head.

His breathing, slow and rhythmic, came with a wet, rattling sound. He didn't blink. But when he didn't cough, either, Isobel took that as the most telling sign of all.

She released the breath she'd been holding and took a cautious step out from behind the shelf. Watching him closely as she crept past the counter, Isobel paused again when his other eye came into view. As she'd suspected, it was pinched shut.

At the far end of the counter, opposite where Bruce sat, a gramophone, identical to the one in her dream, caught her eye.

The seed of dread within her dropped out of her heart and into her gut. There it grew, transforming into quiet panic.

She hurried to the rear of the shop, taking the short step up and through the archway, into the section that housed the nonfiction books and encyclopedias. She ignored the stacks of boxes and the emptied shelves, heading straight for the door that would take her to the attic.

Below the DO NOT ENTER sign, she saw the yellowing and far more ominous handwritten note that bore the familiar words BEWARE OF BESS.

Before she knew what she was doing, Isobel ripped the handwritten sign free, crumpled it, then let it drop to the floor. She pulled the door open.

The enclosed stairway stretched up before her. Above, the attic room appeared to be intact, no longer exposed to the sky as it had been in the dream. Solid walls met with the wood-and-rafter ceiling, and cold light poured in from the window above the staircase, dust particles drifting through the sharply slanted shafts like flotsam.

Isobel moved beyond the threshold, pulling the door shut behind her. She mounted the stairs, and as she moved through the patchwork of light and dimness, she thought she could smell the bitter scent of seared wood.

She opened her arms and placed her hands to the wood

paneling on either side of her. Her fingers trailed the coarse surface, bumping over the grooves as she used the walls to guide herself up, every step taking its turn to groan beneath her.

When Isobel reached the top landing, she found the attic room just how she remembered it, right down to the little café-style table and matching chairs that sat beneath the small oval window overlooking the street below.

For a second, Isobel felt as though she was reliving a moment she'd experienced before, that time she'd rushed up the steps after forgetting the Poe book Varen had lent her.

She'd heard voices coming from the tiny attic room. His, and a woman's . . .

But when she'd reached the top of the stairs, she'd found the room empty, just like it was now.

Her attention fell on the odd black scorch mark that marred the very center of the floorboards, taking the place of the ragged orange-brown throw rug, which lay rolled up against the far wall.

Her ribbon did not lie within the perimeters of the black mark. Or anywhere else.

The fear that had gripped her throughout the day loosened in an instant, but only by a fraction. Because, despite her ribbon's absence, the attic's emptiness answered nothing. Her uncertainty remained, growing twofold as she stared at the burn mark.

Isobel drifted toward the spot, keeping her footsteps light as she made her way to stand in the center of the starburst-shaped blot.

Only when her shoes matched up with two similarly shaped smudges branded into the wood did she realize where it was she stood.

This was the spot in which she had ignited Varen's journal in the dreamworld.

In that moment, the two worlds had been so close, practically superimposed over each other. She had belonged to both realms, and like the floor, she should have burned.

Yet she hadn't.

Her thoughts went back to what Pinfeathers had said in her living room about how she had evaded destruction.

Even Reynolds hadn't had much of an explanation for why she had survived. His response to that particular question had been murky at best, filled with flimsy guesswork—another reminder that, despite what he wanted her to believe, he didn't know everything.

The low pulsing buzz of her cell phone cut the strand of her thoughts.

She drew her phone out and flipped it open. Scowling at the screen, she watched the time display jump, the numbers changing at random. The service bars faded down, flickering.

Isobel moved toward the window, hoping for better reception. But as soon as her feet left the black marking, her normal display returned. The bars reappeared and the time showed five forty-five.

She glanced from the phone to the black mark and then back again, this time reading Gwen's text.

WHAT'S GOING ON?

I'M IN THE ATTIC, Isobel thumbed in. She hit the send button.

Her phone hummed loudly in her hand.

AND?

AND NOTHING, she typed. I'M COMING BACK DOWN.

She felt her phone buzz a third time, but she ignored the incoming text and shut the device. Then she made her way to the stairs and sped down them.

Placing a hand on the knob, she stopped short of twisting it when she heard a slam, and a harsh clang of bells.

Her first thought was that the woman browsing through the discount bins had left in a hurry.

But the deep, angry voice she heard next told her she'd guessed wrong.

"Where is he?" a man growled. "Wake up, Nobit! We're going to do this every day. Every day until you tell me where he's gone. Do you hear me?"

Isobel shrank back from the door.

That voice . . . she knew it. She had heard it yell and threaten like this before.

It belonged to Varen's father.

19
Things Buried

Isobel took a timid step forward. She pressed herself close to the door, listening.

"I'm old, but I'm not deaf, Mr. Nethers," she heard Bruce say. "If you're going to shout, you can turn around and take yourself back outside. My ears can't take it."

"You know what else will be hard to take?" Varen's dad said. "A lawsuit. For obstruction of justice. That's *lying*, Nobit."

"I haven't lied to anyone," Bruce said. "I'm not keeping anything from you. I don't know where your son is, Mr. Nethers. I've already told the police everything I know. In detail. So stop coming into my shop day after day, scaring off my customers and bellowing like a *fool*. If you weren't the boy's father and I didn't see this for the deferred if not profoundly mangled attempt at parenthood that it is, I'd slam you with a lawsuit of my own. For harassment!"

"You *are* a liar!" Varen's dad said, shouting again. The sound of a sharp, rattling bang made Isobel jump. She could picture Varen's father slamming an enormous palm on the glass countertop. "How am I supposed to believe a damn word you say? You've lied to me before when I've come in here looking for him!"

"I didn't lie when I told you I hadn't seen him. If I haven't seen him, that doesn't mean he's not here. You've taught him, however indirectly, to be very cautious with his whereabouts, Mr. Nethers. And I can't say I blame him for that. Besides, I'm too old to be trekking up and down stairs after teenage boys. He wanted a place to study, undisturbed, and so I gave it to him."

"Along with too many other excuses not to come home," Varen's dad snapped. "That stupid job, for one. That junk-pile car sitting outside."

Suddenly it dawned on Isobel why Varen's car had been parked outside the bookshop. When his father threatened to take the car away, Isobel remembered how Varen had argued that Bruce had been the one to cosign the loan, not him. And since the Cougar was here now, that had to mean Bruce must have paid the loan. He must be keeping it on purpose, she thought, believing that Varen would return.

"Your son earned that car, Mr. Nethers," Bruce said.

Isobel lowered herself to kneel in front of the door. Closing one eye, she peered through the old-fashioned keyhole.

Beyond the open archway, she could see Bruce standing behind the counter, his shoulders stooped and bent at a slight angle. He scowled at the man on the other side of the register, a tall, straight figure dressed in a spotless black business suit. He stood with his broad back to Isobel, his glossy hair shining like coal.

"Earned it how? Working for *you*?" Varen's father pointed a finger in the old man's face. "You are not his family," he seethed.

Isobel felt her blood surge hot in her veins. Rage flared within her, and she had to clench her hands into fists to keep from tearing the door open and starting her own yelling. The fear of being caught, however, kept her rooted to her hiding place.

"I'm not so certain he has a family," Bruce said. "He never talks of one. His mother left, that much I do know." He kept his own voice steady and low, wielding inflection in place of volume. And it seemed his aim had landed true. Varen's dad turned his head in her direction, almost as though he'd been dealt a slap, and she saw his face for the first time.

His sharp and angular features collapsed before hardening again.

"Our family's business is none of your concern," said Mr. Nethers. The anger and bravado in his tone had drained away and was replaced by a cold matter-of-factness.

Bruce spoke again, wheezing between his words, his throat clogged with suppressed coughs. "I'm . . . afraid that the reality here . . . is that *he* is no longer any of *your* business. Not anymore. He turned eighteen week before last. But you knew that, of course."

Varen's birthday had passed? Isobel had never even asked him when it was. And now he'd turned —

"Eighteen, Mr. Nethers. Do you know what that means? It means that even if he *does* choose to return, he no longer has to go back to you, sir."

Isobel could see the tremble begin in those big, meaty

hands, the quake traveling up his solid frame as they formed into boulder-shaped fists.

The outburst came like a roar of thunder. "He is *my* son!" Varen's dad shouted, loud enough to cause the bowl-shaped light fixtures to ring. "You are *not* his father. *I* am!" He pounded the counter again, causing a row of stacked paperbacks to slide.

"Then why don't you try acting like it," Bruce said, at last starting to shout himself, "instead of waiting around until it's too late? Until he's run into trouble at school or vanished altogether? Where have you been, Mr. Nethers? Where have you been all this time besides at the bottom of a bottle?"

A hush fell over the shop.

The sound of her breathing became unbearably loud in Isobel's ears.

Her phone vibrated in her hand. She fumbled to open it and found two texts from Gwen. The first, she realized, was the one she'd received upstairs but had neglected to check.

WHOA. SOME DUDE JUST PULLED UP IN A LEXUS. LOOKS LIKE PACINO FROM THE GODFATHER.

WHAT'S GOING ON IN THERE? WHO IS THAT GUY? WHY IS HE YELLING??? I CAN HEAR HIM FROM OUT HERE.

Isobel hurried to type a response. V'S DAD. STAY THERE. Her thumb slid to the send button, but before she could press it, the phone slipped out of her grasp. She gasped as it hit the floor with a loud *crack*, snapping itself shut like a clamshell.

She clapped both hands over her mouth, staring at her phone in wide-eyed horror.

"What was that?" Varen's father demanded.

Isobel's eyes shot back to the door. Her heart began to pound like a fist against her sternum.

"Wh-what was what?" Bruce stammered. "What are you talking about?"

"That sound."

"I didn't hear anything."

"Of course you didn't."

"Really, Mr. Nethers, I'm surprised you can hear anything at all above your own— Wait! Where are you going?"

Footsteps. Hard, heavy footsteps. She heard them thumping against the worn wooden floorboards, getting closer.

Isobel began to quiver all over, bolted to the spot like an animal about to be eaten alive, knowing the predator had already caught her scent.

"You can't go back there!" she heard Bruce call. "Stop! Do you hear me, I said stop!"

"*Varen!*" called Mr. Nethers in a gruff voice.

She stumbled back from the door, knowing that there was nowhere she could hide. There was nothing upstairs. No closets, no furniture. Nothing. She was stuck. Trapped.

Snatching her phone from the floor, Isobel clutched it tightly and whirled.

"Varen!" the voice boomed from just outside. "*Varen!* I swear to *God* if you're here . . ."

She clambered up the stairs, hands over feet, but the toe of her tennis shoe caught on the lip of one of the steps. The stair pulled loose with a clatter.

Isobel fell forward, the edges of the stairs jutting into her ribs and banging her shins. Wincing, she bit back a cry and twisted to look behind her, at the plank she had inadvertently yanked free. Beneath it lay a long black hole, a hollow space like a small, narrow grave, large and deep enough for a person to fit through sideways.

The doorknob jiggled, then began to turn.

Isobel sprang for the hole and dropped inside, landing on her feet. The top of her head still poked above the open stair. She reached an arm out to grab the loose plank and pulled it over her. Hearing the squeak of hinges, she sank down quickly, the board settling back into place with a muffled *thump*.

Isobel squatted in the tight space. Balancing on the balls of her feet, she tried not to think about the cobwebs she couldn't see or the pill bugs or brown recluse spiders that might be crawling over her shoes at that very moment. Not when there were worse monsters stalking the world directly above.

Isobel's phone, still in one hand, vibrated continuously. Isobel knew that Gwen must be trying to call her, but she silenced the hum and sent the call to voice mail.

Overhead, footsteps hit the stairs like grenades on a battlefield. Dust and grit shook down around her, pieces of grime landing in her hair.

A heavy shadow tromped up the spine of the staircase, momentarily blotting out the horizontal strips of light that peeked through the thread-thin cracks between the rise and tread of each step.

"I know I heard something," Varen's dad muttered when he reached the top landing.

"What you heard," Bruce grunted, "is an old house full of noisy ghosts. You won't find anything up there, Mr. Nethers. At least nothing tangible enough for you to lay your hands on and bully around."

"Ghosts . . . ? I don't believe in ghosts."

He began to descend, the step she had dropped through complaining the loudest beneath his weight.

"If you see my son," Varen's dad said, his tone calmer now, more controlled—businesslike, "tell him he needs to come home. So his stepmother can get some rest. So that god-damned cat of his will stop its whining. "

After that, the footsteps began to fade away. Like a storm that had blown itself out, the thundering tapered off into hollow thudding, growing farther and farther away until she heard the jingle of the bells, followed by the slamming of the front door.

Bruce's whistling breath dissolved into a stream of fresh coughing. Listening, Isobel heard him shuffle off, panting and winded.

She looked down at her phone as it buzzed yet again.

She flipped it open, ignoring the scroll of texts waiting for her.

IS HE LEAVING? she typed.

NO. NOT YET, Gwen texted back. HE'S SITTING IN HIS CAR. I THINK HE'S CRYING. ARE YOU OKAY?

Crying? Isobel reread the text. She found the image difficult to conjure.

YEAH. I'M OKAY. TEXT ME WHEN HE
LEAVES AND I'LL COME OUT.

K. HE'S JUST SITTING THERE WITH HIS
FACE IN HIS HANDS. WHAT HAPPENED???

I'LL TELL YOU IN A SEC. WATCH HIM.

Isobel shut her phone and tucked it into her coat pocket. She straightened and, lifting her arms above her head, pushed against the loose board. She had to hit it twice with the side of her fist to dislodge it from where it had become pressed into place. The action sent not only a cloud of dust particles surging around, but also new shoots of fresh white light. Isobel poked her head through and, shifting one foot forward, angled herself so as to set the board aside.

Her toe brushed against something solid. It fell over with a quiet clank.

Isobel ducked back into the hole again. She looked down at her feet to see a half-melted candle in a tiny glass holder. She tilted her head at it, then glanced over her shoulder.

Beyond the crisscrossing frame of two-by-fours that

supported the staircase, Isobel saw a small box-shaped area—a tiny room. A gray sleeping bag lay unrolled and pushed against the left side of the cramped crawlspace, its pillow positioned in the crook of one corner.

Her hands fell from the board. She swiveled away from the underbelly of the stairs toward the pocket of space, which was no bigger than the inside of a small walk-in closet.

Stepping forward, Isobel ducked and threaded her way through the support beams.

Drawings lined the plaster wall right next to the sleeping bag, the pictures etched in a soft and looping hand that Isobel recognized right away. Some of the etchings had even been colored with paint.

An image of a horse seemingly made of smoke reared its head, eyes bugging, hooves pawing at the air. A patch of clouds lit by purple lightning rolled beside a tuft of white lilies, their heads drooping under crowns of raindrops. Black trees marked the center of the wall. Tall and pencil thin, their limbs tangled with one another to create a twisted net dotted with the limp bodies of shriveled leaves. Or were those birds?

Isobel's eyes followed the sprawl of the mural to the images closest to the sleeping bag's pillow. There, the likeness of a certain Siamese cat seemed to hover just over the place where the sleeper might lay his head. The painted cat had a bright and curious look on her face, her eyes beaming through the gloom, the perfect piercing hue of ice.

Isobel sank to kneel on a thin burgundy throw rug sprawled across the concrete floor. Nearby, a pack of matches lay on top of a pile of books, next to a brass dish filled with the ashen bodies of burned incense cones, their stale scent barely detectable.

A small wooden box sat beside the books, its sides and lid carved in bas-relief with delicate rose patterns. A short stack of spiral-bound notebooks occupied the opposite corner, several sheets of loose-leaf paper sticking out around the edges. A coffee mug full of pens, pencils, charcoal sticks, and paintbrushes sat sandwiched between the notebooks and a bin full of multicolored paint tubes.

Locating another candle, Isobel took the box of matches, struck one, and lit the wick.

Warm flickering light filled the space, sending shadows leaping up the walls and across the slanted ceiling.

It didn't surprise Isobel that Varen would have a secret like this—a hiding place within a hiding place.

That thought made her smile, though her grin faltered as she passed the candle across the carved wooden box. The sputtering light revealed the fancy lettering of a name engraved into the lid.

Isobel set the candle aside and reached to draw the wooden box toward her.

Her fingertips traveled across the deep grooves and notches that formed the name MADELINE.

20
Lady Madeline

Isobel opened the box. The hinged lid tilted back, held at ninety degrees by two violet strips of ribbon in either corner.

A stack of photographs littered the top layer of the box's contents. Beneath, Isobel saw an assortment of odd trinkets and pieces of old jewelry.

Her fingers went first to the photographs, and she pulled free the topmost picture, recognizing it as one that had come from her own cheerleading scrapbook.

Dressed in her blue, gold-trimmed uniform, the one with the smooth A-line miniskirt and the THS shell top, her own image beamed up at her from the glossy paper, pom-poms held up to either side of her head like giant puff-ball ears. She had one shimmer shadow–caked eye pinched shut in a squinty pirate–style wink while she puckered her lips at the camera for a kiss. Her hair sat on top of her head in a ponytail of corkscrew ringlets, and a painted star glittered on her left cheek.

All in all, she looked ridiculous.

She remembered that Nikki had snapped the photo at a regional competition last year, right before their performance.

But how did it get here?

She thought back to that night Varen had snuck onto her roof. After leaving her bedroom for several minutes, she'd returned to find him no longer waiting on the roof but perched on the edge of her bed. He'd had her cheer album in his lap, his nimble fingers flipping through it. Her face burned when she realized he must have slid the photo free from its plastic sheath and tucked it away somewhere during the time she'd been gone.

For a moment, she couldn't decide whether she should be infuriated or flattered—or if it was better to default to the ever-appropriate choice of mortified.

Why, out of all the other pictures in the album, did he have to pick *this* one? Why not one of the ones with her actually *posing*, like, without a goofy face, bad hair, or stupid pom-pom antlers?

She flipped the photo over so she wouldn't have to look at it anymore, when she noticed something written across the back.

Short lines scrawled in deep violet blazed against the white watermarked Kodak paper. Bringing the photo closer, Isobel began to read. She felt her heart stammer a beat when she realized that it was a poem. About her.

I keep telling myself
That you're
just a girl.

Another leaf blown across my path

Destined to pass on
And shrivel into yourself
Like all the others.

Yet despite my venom

You refuse to wither

Or fade.

You remain golden throughout,

And in your gaze I am left to wonder if it is
        me alone

Who feels the fall.

Isobel's hand sank, as though the photo had become too heavy for her to hold.

Like tiny knives, his words lacerated her heart.

Isobel pushed the photo back inside the box, prepared to shut the lid and leave, but through her bleary, stinging vision, she caught sight of another photo in the stack.

At first she could glimpse only the edge, and it was the wisps of soft, honey-colored hair that made her draw it free.

The woman in the picture watched the photographer with a steady pair of large eyes, her chin tilted slightly upward. Her beauty, natural and free of cosmetics, was undeniable.

Her lips, shapely and petal pink, seemed as though they wanted to smile, even though they didn't. Her wavy blond hair lay in a gentle swoop across her smooth forehead, the soft flyaway ends disappearing behind her in what Isobel thought must be either a low ponytail or a loose braid.

The woman, slender and pale, wore a plum-colored peacoat buttoned to her chin, while a black knitted scarf laced her throat.

Even though the physical resemblance was subtle, Isobel knew that this was a photograph of Varen's mother.

It was the woman's eyes, the same hue of polished jade, that gave her away.

Taking a closer look, Isobel began to notice faint lines showing through from the other side. Curls and slanted loops appeared in raised bumps around the edges, like Braille, as if Varen had pushed too hard with his pen while writing.

Isobel hesitated before flipping the photo over, afraid of what she might find. She turned it slowly, allowing the candlelight to reveal another poem.

Previously, Varen had only mentioned his mother in passing, saying that she'd left when he was eight. He hadn't elaborated, and Isobel had refrained from asking questions, knowing all too well how quickly his walls could snap into place.

Now, ten years later, he was still thinking of her, still holding on to the last remnants of her existence in his life.

Isobel found herself reluctant to read even a single line.

It was true that she had never hesitated to pry into Varen's writing before. That was part of how this had all started, that day when she'd gone snooping in his journal. But there was something about *this* poem that made her dread its message. Perhaps it was the title, presented like a simple salutation in a letter. "To Madeline," it said at the top, the letters scriptlike and looping, written in his best hand.

Isobel could not recall a single instance in which she had ever called her own mother anything other than "Mom." Of course, she couldn't recall a single instance in which her mother hadn't been there, either.

Swallowing, she began to read.

> *To Madeline,*
>
> *This subtle second self*
> *Sheaf of me*
> *Can do more than you ever could.*
>
> *Like you, it can leave*
> *And go*
> *Somewhere else.*
>
> *The night splits me in two.*
>
> *I disconnect—*
>
> *To sink, to fall, to fly*

And rage

Forever

And always

Without you.

Isobel read the lines again and then again. From the crater-like feeling of emptiness the words themselves left within her, there bubbled up a familiar echo, a repetition of things heard and learned of in the past.

Second self?

Lucid dreaming. Astral projection.

Isobel glanced back to Varen's sleeping bag as, all at once, its presence there held new meaning. Her eyes returned to the mural on the wall, suddenly knowing that his canvas — his hideaway — stretched much farther than this room.

Isobel pressed the picture of Varen's mother facedown on the floor next to her, then picked up the remainder of the stack. She flipped through the rest of the photos slowly, one at a time. There were no more people, though, only images of stone figures, and artsy shots of the same autumn tree, its red-and-gold-sleeved limbs in various states of undress, like he'd been in the process of creating a flip book.

There were more pictures of turrets and iron gates, passageways glimpsed through keyhole doorways and windows. There were also a few shots that showed snarling gargoyles who leered from rooftops, and still more depicting stone angels mourning from their high perches atop cemetery monuments.

Much like books, Isobel could tell how voiceless things had provided a brand of companionship more compatible to Varen's nature than human friendship had ever been. These things, locked in their inanimate ways, fed him ideas, she thought. They whispered their tales to him through unmoving lips and he listened, opening himself to their world so much more than any normal passerby. That much was evident in the *way* he'd taken the photos, as if he'd caught each soulless thing in a candid moment of secret animation. Like they'd sensed him coming and so turned themselves his way because they knew that he held the power to translate their silence into words.

By putting their stories on the page, he could give them life.

A beautiful gift that had turned dangerous.

Maybe none of this would ever have happened, she thought, if Varen's mother had stayed.

Isobel had often wondered why his mother had left. Always, her presumed answer pointed at one individual: Varen's father. But even if she—Madeline—had needed to escape, even if she'd *had* to get away, how could she have left her son behind? She must have *known* about him, that he was different. Special.

Hadn't she cared?

Lost in her thoughts, Isobel hadn't realized that she'd

flipped to the last photo in the stack, one that showed a solitary stone face that peered out from an alabaster wall.

Isobel looked closer, realizing that she knew that face. She recognized it from one of the houses on Varen's street. It was one of the "green men" he had told her about, the group of gargoyle busts said to act as protectors against evil.

"Sleeping on the job," Isobel muttered at the photo.

The face of the gargoyle glowered up at her. He looked almost human, except for the oversize, orblike eyes that stared sightlessly forward.

Isobel sighed and gathered the photos. Before tucking them back into the box, she took a moment to sift through the remaining contents, a collection of bits and pieces strewn along the violet crushed-velvet lining. Broken typewriter keys lay intermixed with antique jewelry, buttons, and brooches, and folded slips of . . . sheet music?

Isobel snatched up one of the papers. She was about to unfold it when she noticed the glimmering object that had lain beneath, concealed.

A lady's elaborate hair comb, encrusted with amethyst gemstones, winked at her in the candlelight. Isobel dipped her hand back into the box and lifted the comb free. She held it up for inspection and it sparkled in her grasp, as if each jewel held its own glowing ember within.

She had seen this comb before, but where?

Isobel's phone began to buzz in long pulses from within her pocket. She pulled it free and answered.

"Yeah?" she said, keeping her voice at a whisper.

"He's gone," Gwen said. "Just left. But he did something weird before he drove off."

"What?"

"He put something in Varen's car."

Isobel paused. Varen's dad had put something *in* his car?

"What was it?" she asked. "Did you see?"

Isobel returned the comb to the box. She laid the stack of photos on top and then closed the lid. Carefully she slid the box back into its original place against the wall.

"No," Gwen answered. "I was trying to make it look like I was busy reading. Which is hard to do when all you've got laying around are road maps and gas receipts. But I thought I saw him open the glove compartment."

Dusting herself off, Isobel stood.

"I'm coming out." With that, she closed her phone, blew out the candle, and went to the narrow hole in the stairs.

She pulled herself out, replacing the plank before hurrying to the door.

It was still open. She poked her head out first, though she didn't see Bruce behind the counter. Maybe, she thought, she could slip out while he was occupied somewhere amid the stacks. She listened another moment for coughing or heavy breathing. When she didn't hear either, she took a cautious step out.

"I don't know how you did that," a voice behind her said.

Isobel stopped midstride. She glanced over her shoulder to find Bruce sitting on a stool and facing one of the wall shelves. A cardboard box half-filled with books sat near his feet.

He turned his head to look at her with mismatched eyes, one brown, one ghostly gray.

"Nor do I want to know," he added. "I'd prefer you keep it to yourself. I get in trouble when I know too much. And just for future reference, it's *this* one that's glass," he hissed, and aimed a finger at the gray eye.

Isobel gulped. She shrank to press her back against the wall behind her and waited awkwardly for whatever would come next. She wanted to make a break for the front door, but she couldn't decide whether it would be better to stay and try to conjure up some excuse for herself.

She started to speak, but he cut her off.

"No," he grunted, holding up a hand to silence her. "Don't say anything. I'm glad you're here. Even if I feel like he could do better."

Isobel's mouth snapped shut, her teeth clicking together. For real? Did he just *say* that to her?

"But if he was dead, I doubt you'd be sniffing around here. And that's something I'm grateful to know. Besides that, you're probably the one who's got the best chance of reaching him. So when you do, if you haven't already, I need you to pass on a message for me, do you hear?" He shook a finger at her. "You tell him I'm going to sell that car. I've already got an interested buyer. So you tell him I'm not a holding garage, do you hear me? He's got till March. *March*, you got that? Don't forget."

Miffed by his words, Isobel didn't respond. She couldn't trust herself not to say something scathing or to tell him that, as far as best friends went, he didn't quite get her Varen-worthy stamp of approval either.

He grunted when she didn't speak and went back to pulling books from the shelf, letting them fall into the open box one at a time.

Isobel turned and stalked toward the front door.

"Wait!" she heard Bruce call as soon as she placed a hand on the knob.

She halted. Back rigid, she complied, even though she wanted to walk out on him.

He started coughing again, and though he tried to talk through the fit, he only succeeded in getting out one or two unintelligible words.

She looked back to see that he held one knotted hand over his mouth and the other extended toward her.

"Don't . . ." He shook his head. "I'm sorry," he said, at last regaining his composure. "Don't tell him that. Don't tell him I'm going to sell it. Just tell him March. He needs to come get it by March if he still wants it. Tell him that's . . . tell him that's what the doctors said."

"Doctors?" Isobel asked. What was *that* supposed to mean?

He rose, using one of the shelves to help him pull himself to his feet. "Go on now," he said. "We're closed."

"But—"

"I said we're closed!" he growled, waving his arms at her as though she were an alley cat he could frighten away. "Now get out!"

"I—"

"I said go!"

She bit back her questions and pushed through the door just before he could reach her. She stumbled out onto the sidewalk as he flipped the OPEN sign to the CLOSED side. The lights inside the shop went out with a snap, and his dark brown eye lingered on her a second longer before he slipped backward into the shadows.

"What the heck happened in there?"

Isobel turned to find Gwen standing on the curb right next to the Cougar, a folded slip of paper held ceremoniously between both hands. Without asking, Isobel already knew that Gwen had pulled the paper from the glove compartment of Varen's car.

"He thinks Bruce knows something," Isobel said.

She kept her eyes steady on that white slip as she wrapped her arms around her middle. Dusk had already begun to settle over the street, causing the lamps to glow brighter and the bite in the air to grow stronger. Isobel hugged herself tightly, shuddering as she wondered what the paper held. At the same time, she wished she wouldn't have to find out.

"About Varen?"

Isobel nodded once.

She'd already decided not to tell Gwen about the secret room beneath the stairs, or the foreboding message Bruce had asked her to relay. Both of those things felt off-limits, knowledge meant for Varen only. More things to be added to her growing list of isolating secrets.

"His dad is convinced that he's still around somewhere,"

Isobel said. "Hiding. But . . ." She shook her head. "I can't understand why. He has to know someone would have reported seeing him by now."

"Um," Gwen said. Her eyes flitted to the ground and then to the side. She pressed her lips together and stepped forward, holding the paper out to Isobel. "Hope you don't mind. I sort of read it already."

Isobel took the slip. She unfolded it, revealing a hand-written message to Varen from his father, the brief sentences formed with sharp and slanted lettering.

> *You think it's funny to walk out in front of my car? You almost drove me straight into the fountain last night. You could have been killed.*
> *It's time to stop playing morbid games.*
> *No more vanishing acts.*
> *Come home. Now.*

A brisk wind rattled the paper in her hand.

Isobel glanced up in time to see Gwen quiver, her teeth chattering. "You—you said you saw him too . . . didn't you? As in, not dreaming?" Gwen asked.

"Yeah," Isobel murmured, turning to stare at her reflection in the car window. "Twice."

21
Dissemble No More

At the first red light they came to, Gwen took the opportunity to raise her hand to her lips and bite her fingernails. Even though the noise it made was loud, like popcorn popping, it could do nothing to distract Isobel from the whirlwind jumble of her thoughts, from the inconceivable notion that since his disappearance, someone else, someone besides her, had seen Varen in waking life.

According to his note, Varen's father had almost run him over just last night. Yet Isobel already knew that reflections could not stroll out in front of moving cars.

Was it possible that Mr. Nethers had only *thought* he'd seen his son?

Maybe, Isobel speculated, he'd been drinking right before.

But Varen's father had been so adamant in the bookshop. His words with Bruce had been as fierce and sure as his clenched fists. And the way he'd stomped up into the attic, so furious and so certain he would find what and who he'd come looking for.

I don't believe in ghosts, he'd said.

The declaration made her wonder if Varen's father had

uttered that statement more for his own benefit than for Bruce's. Had it been self-reassurance? Or denial . . . ?

The traffic light flicked to green.

Gwen stopped biting her nails. She stalled for a moment. Then, putting on her turn signal, she shifted the car into gear, hit the gas pedal, and swerved to the left.

"Hey!" Isobel gripped the dashboard. "Where are we going?"

Gwen didn't answer. Instead she steered the Cadillac into the right-hand lane and, swerving a second time, left the road for a parking lot.

"Why are we turning here?" Isobel asked. Leaning forward, she craned her neck to peer up at the enormous burger-shaped sign stationed on its post high overhead. It glowed like a beacon.

"Because," Gwen said, "I need something greasy to soak up all the norepinephrine."

"The what?"

"My nerves are shot. Time to eat."

"It's . . . getting late," Isobel protested. "My parents are probably wondering where I am. Dad especially."

"Send him a text. Ask him if he wants something." Gwen swiveled the Cadillac behind a minivan already idling next to the freestanding back-lit menu. "Tell him I see they've got something called a Classic Melt and it made me think of him."

"Gwen, please. I have to play by his rules until Baltimore. You *know* that."

"I'm thinking onion rings and an iced tea," she said. "What about you?"

Isobel sank into her seat again. She shook her head. "I'm not hungry."

"What's that?" Gwen hooked a hand around one ear in a "didn't quite hear you" gesture. "Fries and a milkshake?" she asked. "Very Sandra Dee of you."

Isobel started to argue, but the car in front of them pulled ahead and Gwen pressed down on the gas pedal. They jerked forward to the intercom. Switching off the heat, Gwen cranked down the window, hung an elbow out the door, and leaned into the cold.

"Welcome to Mighty Burger," a jaded male voice broke through the speaker. "Would you like to try one of our Mighty combo meals, or perhaps our two-for-two Mighty drink special?"

Gwen's breath puffed out in small bursts of white as she spoke. "You know," she said, "I can almost *hear* the little TM implied after every time you say the word 'Mighty.' You've got great inflection."

"Ma'am?"

"Uh, yeah, can I get a large onion rings, large fries, large chocolate milkshake, and a large *unsweet*—that's *no* sugar— as in I come back and challenge you to a plastic fork duel if I even *think* I taste a *hint* of sugar—iced tea?"

There was a pause before the monotone voice returned through a crackle of static. "So I've got a large Mighty onion rings, one large Mighty fries, a large Mighty chocolate shake, and a large Mighty *extra* unsweet iced tea. Will that be all?"

"Now he's *trying* to get on my nerves," Gwen muttered

under her breath. "Yeah," she barked at the speaker, "that's all."

"That'll be nine sixty. Please pull through to the second window."

Gwen eased off the brake, allowing the Cadillac to glide past the first window to the next.

"Tea was never meant to be sweetened," she said, more to herself, it seemed, than to Isobel. Reaching into her patchwork purse, she scrounged before pulling out a ten. "Soon as you cross the Mason-Dixon it's like everything turns into molasses and corn syrup." She smacked her lips. "I can feel myself getting a cavity just thinking about it."

Beside them, the drive-through window squealed as it swung open. A greasy-haired guy in a blue apron and white envelope hat handed Gwen their drinks in exchange for the ten. Ducking inside for change, he pulled the window shut again.

Isobel took the foam cup and straw that Gwen thrust her way, while Gwen slid her own into the holder next to her. With hurried and nervous fingers, Gwen ripped the paper free from the straw, jabbed it through the plastic lid, and leaned down to suck in a gulp.

As though tasting for poison, she swished the liquid back and forth in her mouth. Then, with a satisfied nod, she swallowed.

"Good man," she said. "Mighty man."

A moment later the drive-through window opened again. Grabbing the grease-stained bag, Gwen tossed it into Isobel's lap. Then she stuffed her change into her purse, rolled her window up, and pulled out of line.

"And you had better drink that shake," Gwen said. "You're starting to look a little waifish."

She steered the Cadillac toward one of the parking lot's tall lampposts and slid into a slot just underneath the wide circle of light.

"Wait," Isobel said, "why are we parking?"

"Because, talented as I am, I can't shift and stuff my face at the same time." She pointed at the milkshake. "That's not going to drink itself."

"I told you, I'm not—"

"Straw in cup. Now."

Taking in the strained, almost panicked expression on Gwen's face, Isobel bit back her objections. She slid the straw from its paper sheath and, after shoving it through the plastic lid of her shake, forced herself to take a sip. After a few attempts to suck the cement-thick substance through the straw, the creamy liquid finally made contact with her tongue. Though the coldness of the drink made her shudder, Isobel had to admit it *did* taste good.

Mollified, Gwen snagged the bag and fished inside with one hand, the paper crinkling loudly. The smell of fried food permeated the cab as she removed an onion ring. She bit into it, chewing fast as she stared sightlessly forward through the windshield.

Isobel looked down into her lap at the milkshake, which she'd nestled between her knees. One at a time, she pressed down each of the plastic lid's bubble tabs indicating diet, tea, and other.

She could tell from Gwen's sudden edginess and fidgeting that she had again reached her freak-out limit. She hadn't started asking questions yet, though.

Maybe, Isobel thought, she'd learned her lesson in that regard.

"Not enough salt," Gwen said. Then she added, "By the way, I hope you know that I'm well aware there's an exorbitant amount of stuff you're not telling me these days."

Isobel stiffened. Her eyes slid in Gwen's direction.

"Like why we went back to that bookshop today," she continued. "And what you were looking for, and whether or not you even found it. You've had more dreams, too, haven't you?" She finished off the onion ring and immediately scrounged for another.

Isobel took a moment to deliberate before speaking, searching for the right words.

"It's just things . . . have kind of gotten . . . intense . . . lately," she said. "I don't know what's happening anymore, let alone how to explain it. There's just so much. I'm . . . I'm starting to think it's . . . better this way."

"Sure." Gwen nodded. "Maybe it is," she conceded. "Maybe the less I know, the more I'll be able to . . . I don't know, to go along with this quietly like you want me to. With you going to find him. After all, I'm sure it makes it easier on you not to have someone calling foul on whatever you think you're gonna do when you get there." She gave a short snort of a laugh. "'Cause if I don't really know what's going on, then how am I supposed to keep reminding you you're on a suicide mission?"

"Gwen," Isobel began. She shut her eyes, hoping that if she didn't allow herself to look at her friend or read the fear on her face, she could keep her own at bay. "We've been through this. You know I've made up my mind."

"I know," Gwen said. "That's why I'm coming with you."

Isobel opened her eyes and whipped her head to face Gwen. "What did you just say?"

Gwen tossed the bag back into Isobel's lap. "Friendly reminder," she said. "The fries go in your mouth, not your ears. I said I'm coming with you."

Gwen ate the onion ring she held in one bite.

Isobel gripped the bag of fries. She shook her head, uncomprehending. "Um, Gwen." She waved a hand at her. "Reality here. Yeah, my dad's *never* going to let you go with us. Not to mention how bringing that up would make both my parents even more suspicious than they already are."

Gwen chewed and chewed, her gaze distant yet determined as she continued to stare forward. At last, swallowing, she turned her head to look Isobel square in the face. The lenses of her glasses glinted in the dark, making her eyes disappear, so that for a moment she looked like some kind of mad genius.

"Not everyone in high school still lives in the Stone Age,

Pebbles," she said. "I have one of those motorized things with wheels? I believe you're sitting in it right now. In your language, I think they call it a *car*."

"You're going to *drive*?"

"No, I'm gonna hopscotch. Yes, I'm gonna drive."

"But what about your parents? Won't they—"

"Unlike you, I live in a land of democracy. Convinced them to let me take a road trip up to Brooklyn to visit my cousins and see a concert. Shelly and Greta owe me one. They already know to cover for me when my mom makes her inevitable check-in calls."

Again Isobel shook her head, dumbfounded at how much of the scheme Gwen already seemed to have figured out. "Gwen, there's no way I'm going to let you—"

"*Let* me?" Gwen barked a laugh. "Since when have you ever *let* me do anything?" Snatching the bag back, she pulled out a french fry and aimed it at Isobel's nose. "I do and you deal. Besides," she went on, "how are you going to get to the cemetery? You gonna *walk* there? At night? Alone? Do you even know what part of the city you're staying in? Have you even looked at a map?"

The truth was that Isobel hadn't thought that far ahead. At least not about the specifics. At least not yet. All her energy had been poured into getting to the city and keeping up the alternating "I'm okay" and "I know nothing" charade in the meantime. She'd had to work overtime just to keep all her masks in place. And then with the dreams and the visions . . . she'd been so distracted.

"They have taxis there," Isobel said, even though she wasn't sure.

"Yeah," Gwen said, "right along with a crime rate that makes the Big Apple blush. And in case you forgot, taxis cost money. A lot of money. And forgive me for mentioning it, but last time I checked, your brother's troll bridge tax rate hadn't gotten any lower. Like I told you before, you're going to need a plan. And you're going to need help." This time, Gwen aimed the fry at herself. "*My* help," she said, then popped the fry into her mouth.

Isobel struggled to come up with some valid reason why she didn't.

"You know there's gonna be a ton of people there that night, don't you?" Gwen asked. "And security, too. Turns out the Lone Ranger's got quite a following," she added before chomping down on a handful of fries bundled together between her fingertips.

"I might have heard something about that," Isobel mumbled. "How—how did you know?"

"Google *is* a verb now," Gwen said.

Isobel lifted the shake's straw to her lips. She took a long tug, swallowed, and then took another. Brain freeze radiated through her skull like a crawling frost, but the pain felt good in a strange way, an active reminder that she was, as yet, still among the living.

"And you're right," Gwen said. "It probably is better if I don't know any more than that. Otherwise, I might actually come to my senses and try to stop you. So I'm figuring why not just cut the crap and go along so I can keep you alive myself?"

Isobel smiled sadly as the slow freeze inside her head gradually subsided.

"You're really coming?" she asked.

"Couldn't stop me if you tried. It's one of those pesky things we have in common."

"You do and I deal, right?"

"Finally," Gwen said. She lifted her tea from its holder and raised the foam cup toward Isobel as though in a toast. "You're starting to catch on."

That night, no matter how hard she tried, Isobel could not fall asleep.

She rolled back and forth on her mattress, flipping from one side to the other, unable to make up her mind whether it was better to face her window or to have her back to it.

Neither felt comfortable. Or safe.

Nothing did anymore.

Finally she settled on lying flat on her back and staring up at her ceiling. But then her doorway, which stood open and empty across from the foot of her bed, took on a menacing presence, as though it might fill at any moment with some horrible new nightmare, or the scenery beyond would transform from white walls into woodlands back-lit by violet light.

She already knew it would do no good to shut the door. So she shut her eyes instead.

As she lay there, exhausted and yet firmly wired into wakefulness, Isobel thought she was beginning to understand something Pinfeathers had once told her in the moments before she'd first come face-to-face with Lilith.

Open this door, and no matter what, you'll never close it.

By degrees, Isobel had grown to fear the night, to fear what the veil of sleep would allow to worm through her slumbering mind, what holes its images could burrow through her heart. And the seeds of doubts it could plant in her soul.

She rolled onto her side again, facing her closet. Huddling into herself, she clutched her blankets tightly. What she'd seen in the dreamworld, with Varen in the attic of the reversed bookshop, couldn't have been real. It had been a fabrication meant to confuse and detour her. Something Lilith had concocted to distract her and cause her to lose hope so she would give up.

Because if it *had* been real, Isobel would have found the ribbon that afternoon. It would have been in the bookstore, just like the gramophone and the crooked sign and the black burn mark on the floor and everything else that had been the same. But the ribbon, the only thing that had mattered, hadn't been there at all. And that alone should have proved to her that what she'd seen had been an illusion. That Varen still had to have the ribbon in his possession. He would never let it go. He would never let *her* go. She had to believe that. They'd been through so much.

Sitting up, Isobel wrapped her arms around her knees,

hugging herself into a tight ball, and lifted her eyes to the smooth surface of her mirror.

If Varen existed within the world beyond the mirror, trapped there without the ability to return, then what or who had his father seen last night?

Had Varen truly stepped out of nowhere, causing his dad to swerve and almost careen into the fountain that sat in the center of their old Victorian neighborhood?

The fountain.

Isobel's thoughts bounced back to the dream in the rose garden, when Varen had taken her to the very same fountain. She thought about the bookstore, too, realizing that she had now dreamed him in two places that paralleled reality. And like Varen's father, she'd even seen him once in reality itself.

On Halloween. The day their project on Poe had been due.

Varen had shown up in class, yet supposedly he'd been at Nobit's Nook at the exact same time.

Isobel frowned, recalling how Varen had refused to shake Isobel's father's hand during their presentation. In fact, he hadn't touched anyone. And when he'd picked up her boom box, the speakers had spiked with static, even though it had no batteries in it. Then, right after class, he'd vanished into thin air.

Just like a ghost.

I don't believe in ghosts, Varen's father had said.

And yet, he'd seen one.

Just as she had that day in Mr. Swanson's class.

With that thought, Isobel tossed back her covers and climbed out of bed.

Her digital clock read 4:40 A.M.

That left her with just under two hours before she was supposed to be up for school.

Isobel scrambled to get dressed in the dark, thinking that it might be just enough time to get there—to the fountain— and back before anyone noticed she was missing.

Pedaling fast on Danny's mountain bike, it took Isobel just over twenty minutes before she arrived at the entrance to the stately and quiet neighborhood.

She had dressed in layers, but the stinging predawn air still managed to singe her lungs each time she drew a breath. The ski cap that she wore, pulled low over her ears, protected her head from the cold, though her cheeks burned from the sharp wind that had pressed against her the whole way, almost like an invisible force trying to hold her back.

Isobel's heart thrummed as she steered the bike around the last corner and onto St. Francis Court, the street where Varen lived.

Used to live . . .

Brown leaves plastered the pavement beneath her wheels, their slick bodies smoothed sticker-flat by the rain and the tires of passing cars. The gas lamps lining the grass median between the two one-way lanes glowed with live flames that fluttered tall and thin within their glass holders.

She stopped pedaling and let the bike roll on its own,

gliding between the two rows of darkened Victorian homes while she took a moment to catch her breath.

Their wide windows, like so many eyes, seemed to follow her as she went.

Isobel clutched the handle brakes as she drew nearer to the solemn redbrick house Varen had once invited her into. Even though she had not planned to, as soon as the darkened stained-glass front door came into view, Isobel extended one foot and pressed her toe to the pavement, stopping the bike. From the middle of the street, she watched the house.

Looking up at Varen's bedroom window on the third floor, she felt as though something within was watching her back. But she could see nothing beyond the darkened panes.

Isobel turned away and pushed off on the bike once more, telling herself she couldn't afford to linger. Not when she needed to be back in her room before her mother woke to make her dad's coffee and pack Danny's lunch.

As she approached the fountain, she again squeezed the handlebar brakes. The tires squealed very slightly, and she did not wait for the bike to reach a complete stop before standing up on the pedals, swinging one leg over, and dismounting.

She walked the bike to the circular curb that surrounded the fountain and, gently lowering it to the pavement, strode across the brief strip of grass all the way up to the ornate grillwork railing that separated the dry concrete reservoir from the frozen turf.

Wrapping her already numb hands around the painted metal, Isobel peered up at the fountain. Floodlights, nestled just below the drained concrete base, lit the tarnished bronze basin from every angle, illuminating the leaf-and-scroll-flourished underside of the shallow and empty, goblet-shaped basin.

Isobel glanced to her left and then to her right.

Even though a row of parked cars lined both of the lanes and a few sconce lights glowed beneath porticos and wrap-around porches, the neighborhood felt eerily deserted.

Her grip on the railing tightened, and with a sinking sensation, as though she were standing in quicksand and not on solid ground, she began to wonder why she'd come. What had she been hoping for? That he would appear before her the way his father's note said he had last night?

Maybe, she thought, she'd been holding on to the distant hope that, like the bookstore, the place he had told her she would find him in the dreamworld had some connection to its real-world counterpart. Some traversable link.

But if not Varen himself, then there at least had to be *something* for her here. Some kind of token or sign that would reassure her that he was still waiting for her, still holding on.

Even something as minute and simple as a single red rose petal.

There was nothing, though.

Instead the entire street felt hollow, drained of the timeless beauty it had possessed that autumn afternoon when he'd first brought her here.

Isobel looked back at the fountain.

Curly-haired cherubs frolicked beneath the basin in

a captured moment of abandon. Though the figures might have seemed playful in the daylight, something about the mix of shadows and stark light cast on their small faces by the floodlights made them appear more mischievous than free-spirited, more impish than gleeful.

The large swans that reveled with them, rearing back with wings outspread, looked somehow frantic.

Isobel took a step back and then another.

Blocked by the wide bowl of the basin, the lights could not reach the sultry figure of the nude woman who stood at the very top of the fountain, her veil billowing out behind her. She remained swathed in shadow, a silhouette that belonged to the night.

"You won't win," Isobel whispered under her breath.

Her gaze locked on the woman's face, featureless in the dark.

"Whether what I've seen is true or not," she went on, her voice growing louder with conviction, "no matter what you've made him believe, you won't stop me. As soon as I find him, as soon as he sees me, he'll know you've lied. Demon or not, you can't scare me anymore. I *will* bring him back. And then I'll find a way to stop you for good. To keep you from doing this to anyone ever again. I swear it."

Isobel turned her back on the fountain. She strode to the curb and bent to pick up Danny's bike.

"Is that some kind of bad habit of yours? Making promises you can't keep?"

Isobel halted. That voice . . .

Slowly she turned, glancing toward the fountain again. Then, lowering the bike, she let it drop at the last second before hurrying to make her way around its circumference in quick strides, stopping when she found him.

He sat with his back pressed to the fountain's base, just below one of the unfurling swans. To his right, one of the bronze cherubs seemed to lean toward him with cautious interest.

The buckles of the Noc's tight straitjacket-style coat were open, exposing a portion of his alabaster chest. Right where his heart should have been, Isobel saw an open crater the size of a softball.

Next to him sat a pile of what at first glance looked like a collection of small rocks. That was when she realized they weren't rocks at all but shards, broken bits of Noc.

Isobel did her best to keep her face free of expression as he lifted one of the shards between the crimson claws of his finger and thumb. He held the shard up to the floodlights and studied it like a jeweler would a diamond. Then he brought the shard to his chest, carefully fitting the sliver into the gaping black cavity. She heard the piece attach with a quiet *tink*.

"Our jacket," Pinfeathers said, selecting yet another shard without glancing up from his task. "The one you found on your closet door. Have you guessed yet that wasn't me?"

22
Secret Deeds

Though it was a gruesome thing to witness Pinfeathers piecing together the gaping black hole in his chest, Isobel couldn't seem to bring herself to look away. She also couldn't help but wonder how he'd acquired the damage, but she knew better than to ask.

"Why are you following me?" she demanded, doubting the Noc would give her a straight answer. "Is she sending you to spy on me?"

"On the contrary, cheerleader," he said. "I've been here all along. Waiting for *you*." He smiled his jagged grin. "Of course."

"How—"

"—did I know you would come?" he asked, finishing the question for her. "Because." He glanced up for the first time, his soot-black eyes locking with hers. "You said you would."

She shook her head, a slight motion. "I never—"

"You did," he corrected, interrupting her a second time. "Even if *you* haven't been listening, cheerleader, we have. Speaking of . . ." He cocked his head to one side and blinked. "Didn't you hear what I just said?"

Isobel's jaw tightened. She pinched her lips together, not allowing herself to speak until she could trust herself not to say something that might provoke him. She liked him right where he was: at a distance, sitting and with hands occupied.

She *had* heard what he'd said about Varen's jacket, though.

"If it wasn't you," she asked, deciding to humor him, "then who?"

"Us," Pinfeathers replied, his gaze dropping as he fixed another chalk-white piece into the shrinking crater in his chest, his work nearly complete. "But not me."

Isobel's mouth twisted with unease and frustration. When it came to dealing with Pinfeathers, she'd learned that whenever possible, no reaction was the best reaction.

"You're saying it was Varen then. How?" she demanded. "If he can come into this world like you, then why isn't he here right now?"

Pinfeathers remained silent, rooting through the remaining shards with one claw.

Isobel stomped up to the fence. "Answer me!" she cried, and gripped the railing.

"The masked man," Pinfeathers said, ignoring her questions. "The hidden one you'll soon leave in search of. He took that jacket from us, you know. He has the power to take what he wants. And go where he pleases. Power he should not possess."

Isobel felt her scalp prickle and the hairs on her arms and the back of her neck stand at attention. But it wasn't the chill in the air that was making her skin crawl.

Her thoughts jumbled in her head like a scrambled signal as she tried to comprehend how Pinfeathers knew about her plan to go to Baltimore and find Reynolds. Then, all at once, it dawned on her.

"That night with Gwen," she said. "The shadow I saw moving around in my room, that *was* you, wasn't it? You were there, listening the whole time. You *have* been spying!"

"The other was wise to run," was all he said.

"And then later outside the bathroom door. You were—"

"I told you, cheerleader," he said, his tone infuriatingly calm as he fit one final fragment into position, wincing as it snapped into place. "The jacket wasn't me."

Grabbing one of the loose straps on his coat, he threaded it through the corresponding buckle with practiced ease and pulled, cinching the thin black material back over his chest. He did so again with the topmost buckle, once more concealing the spiderweb patch of hairline cracks. Then he stood, unfurling himself limb by spindly limb from the base of the fountain.

Isobel stumbled backward, away from the railing, nearly tripping over her feet.

She hated feeling this defenseless against him. It was true she could wound him if she got lucky. But what could she possibly do to him, when clearly they both knew he was the one with all the answers?

For the first time since she'd met Pinfeathers, Isobel found herself fearing that any second he would evaporate and be gone, taking with him her one solid connection to Varen.

"Tell me he's okay," she said, pleading. "Please. Tell me the dream in the bookstore was a lie and that he still knows I'm coming. Tell me he has the ribbon."

She watched Pinfeathers as he stepped toward her slowly, even gracefully, and it occurred to her that he was moving that way on purpose, as though making a conscious effort not to alarm her.

The hilarity of that thought might have made Isobel laugh if she hadn't been so close to tears.

The Noc stopped at the railing. He extended his arm out to her, his hand opening like a bear trap.

"Come," he said, "there's something you need to see."

Isobel shook her head. "I'm not touching you," she said. "And I'm not going anywhere. There's no way." She took another step backward, her heel meeting with the concrete curb. She could run if she wanted to. She knew that. She also knew that if he wanted to catch up to her, she wouldn't get very far.

Pinfeathers did not lower his hand. He didn't come any closer, either, but stayed behind the railing as if to say, *This is as far as I go.*

"No tricks this time," he said, "no false realities. Just a memory caught in passing. Something that might interest you. You said yourself that I can't hurt you."

Isobel's eyes darted from the serrated edges of his shark's teeth, clamped together through the open pit in his cheek, to the needle-point tips of those crimson claws.

Despite his macabre exterior, everything about him in that

moment, from the planted way he stood to his grave, ascetic expression, resonated through her like an echo.

"You're . . . different," Isobel said, the urge to turn and run dissipating like the white fog of her own breath. "Why? What happened to you?"

"Change of heart?" he said through a thin smile that was as bitter as it was brittle.

Though her body screamed against doing so, Isobel took a tentative step toward him. She told herself it was a test step, just to see how he would react.

His smile faded, his expression becoming suddenly sober and serious—more human than she had ever seen it. Almost . . . recognizable.

Pinfeathers's claws clicked together as he beckoned.

Isobel took another cautious step toward him, then another.

She had come here tonight in search of Varen's ghost.

Maybe, Isobel thought as she cleared the distance between them, finally fitting her hand into the Noc's porcelain grip— just maybe—she'd found it.

His hand closed tightly around hers, the claws of his fingers and thumb crisscrossing one another like some kind of wicked locking mechanism.

He squeezed hard, and Isobel opened her mouth in a silent gasp of pain.

Just when she thought she'd made a terrible mistake, her hand yielded and his fingers passed through hers, as if she'd suddenly become as intangible as a mirage.

KELLY CREAGH — 269

Almost as if preparing to waltz, Pinfeathers stepped backward, drawing Isobel forward. But her body remained paralyzed, rooted in place while some separate part of her began to slide forward, drawn by his pull.

It felt as if she were being peeled away from herself.

And that, it seemed, was exactly what was happening.

Her vision went double while the open-air sounds of night, wind, and rustling leaves became muted in her ears. Then, in a flash, everything disappeared, winking to crystal white.

She floated in a world of nothing, weightless, alone, and strangely unconcerned about what had just happened or where she was or if she would come back. It was like teetering between waking and falling asleep, and it made her wonder if this was what dying felt like.

Something pulled at her, and her senses returned.

Looking down at her side, she saw her hand still clutched in Pinfeathers's grip.

Disoriented, Isobel glanced up to find herself no longer standing in front of the fountain. Gone were the houses and the trees, the cars and the flickering lamps. In their place stretched a long and dark corridor, lined on either side by plain utilitarian doors. All of them were closed.

She looked up at Pinfeathers, who pressed a single bloodred claw to his lips, calling for silence. Then he loosened into smoke and, with a rustle and flit of feathers, re-formed as an ebony bird, perching on Isobel's left shoulder.

The weight of the bird's body felt almost nonexistent, as if even in this form, the Noc was still only hollow within.

Aiming his beak forward, he gave a hoarse and urging croak.

She faced the dimly lit hall, which seemed to stretch on forever into a far-reaching pit of blackness. She wondered where Pinfeathers had brought her and why, but the bird only bobbed his head and snapped his beak with several impatient clicks. Clearly he wanted her to proceed.

Isobel did so with cautious steps, her footfall making no sound on the worn floorboards.

Between each of the doors, antique oil lamps burned with steady yellow flames, their glass holders warping the light into hourglass shapes along the barren walls.

The scent of kerosene and the antiseptic smell of iodine mixed with alcohol permeated the air. Beneath that, though, Isobel could detect another odor, a hint of putridity like the stale reek of a sickroom.

A quiet squeaking drew Isobel's attention to the right, and she soon saw someone gliding toward them—a woman dressed in white.

She stopped cold. Fear pierced her gut like a spear, holding her in place.

A trap, she thought. She'd been stupid enough to trust Pinfeathers, and now it had landed her right where she should have known it would, straight into Lilith's waiting grip.

As the woman drew closer, however, her figure became more discernible, and Isobel saw that instead of white veils, she wore what appeared to be an old-fashioned nurse's uniform. With a starched white cap sitting atop her pouf of dark brown hair, she looked like a costumed actress straight out of a period movie. A matching apron cinched her narrow, corseted waist while long, heavy skirts swished around her feet.

The woman, her gaze intent on the path before her, took no notice of Isobel as she bustled by, even as her skirts nearly brushed Isobel's legs.

Behind the woman, a teenage girl, dressed in the same uniform, wheeled a gurney, the source of the high-pitched squeaking. On it, an old man with skin like raw dough lay prone and listless.

Isobel turned her head to watch their grim procession as they passed.

A hospital, Isobel thought. She was in some sort of old hospital. But why would Pinfeathers have brought her to such a place?

He'd called this a memory, and clearly she was viewing something from the past, but when? With the gas lamps and the way the nurses had been dressed, Isobel's first guess was the 1800s. But if they'd gone back *this* far, then whose memory could this possibly be? Certainly not Varen's.

A low wailing drew Isobel's attention forward once again.

There, at the very end of the passageway, a door that she knew had not been there a moment before swung open by itself.

Pinfeathers cawed softly in her ear and, with a loud flutter and flick of feathers, took flight from her shoulder. She watched the bird soar ahead of her, flapping his wings, then shooting straight through the open door and out of sight.

Isobel hurried down the corridor after him, preferring to have the company of a monster than to be left alone in this place.

As she drew closer to the door, the wailing emanating from within grew louder and more distinct. The sound began to build toward shouting, and soon—screaming.

"REYNOLDS!"

The cry, ragged and frayed, caused her to stop in her tracks. Standing frozen in place within the frame of the door, she took in the scene before her.

In the center of the room sat a narrow bed. A dark-haired man lay on the white sheets, his face gaunt and sickly pale. He writhed amid the tangled linens, howling and moaning while, above him, a thick smear of rippling black clouds spread wider against the ceiling.

"REYNOLDS!" the man on the bed shrieked.

Beside him, a young doctor dressed in a black coat, the white collar of his shirt rumpled and sweat-stained, stooped over his patient.

"Edgar!" the doctor said as he wrung the struggling man's pallid hand, oblivious to the otherworldly storm that churned above them. "Edgar, you are safe!"

Poe, Isobel thought with dull shock. This man twisting in agony before her . . . it was Poe.

Her eyes grew wider as they swept upward, toward the fog roiling directly over his bed. Sharp faces and snatching claws swam through the haze, surfacing to snap at their tormented victim like frenzied sharks.

Terrified, Poe whipped his head from side to side on his pillow as though the rest of him were bound by invisible fetters. His chest rose and fell with quick breaths. He moaned and ground his teeth, the veins on his broad forehead bulging, standing out like blue cords.

That was when Isobel saw it—the thin silver string that stretched between the vapors whirling above the bed and the center of Poe's heaving chest.

The quivering strand seemed to be made of a luminous and ethereal light, as wispy as gossamer.

Poe arched against the bed, shouting, while streams of shadows began to pour out of the tempest. Swirling tendrils of black smoke invaded the room, shooting out in every direction. The streams floated through the air like coils of ink in water and glided across the floor, skimming the walls before forming into the wraithlike figures of the Nocs.

But these were not the Nocs *she* knew.

Though they had hollow, shell-like bodies, they did not possess the red tint to their quill-coarse hair and claws like Pinfeathers and the others. Instead their claws were a deep blue, their hair and teeth indigo.

Then Isobel realized that she *did* recognize one of them. It was the Noc from the marble crypt she had stumbled into while in the dreamworld, that same creature who had asked her help in piecing himself back together. Here he appeared complete. Intricate carvings lined the salt-white skin of his naked chest. Etchings of ships tossing amid tumultuous waters sailed across his porcelain torso, while the detailed image of a diamond-scaled sea serpent wound its way down the length of one arm.

Scrimshaw, Isobel thought, remembering his name in a flash.

The Noc moved to hover over Poe. Leaning down, he grabbed for Poe's other hand, his claws digging into his wrist, threatening to puncture the skin. The creature grinned. Mocking the doctor, he began to whisper in Poe's ear.

"You made the mistake of trying to outsmart yourself again, didn't you?" he hissed. "Now look where it's got us." He pointed a claw toward the ceiling. "Trapped. Right in the eye of the storm."

"*Edgar,*" spoke a voice from within the fog.

The first sign of white came in the form of veils, the gauzy, silken material fluttering amid the eddying maelstrom.

Dropping Poe's hand and shrinking back, Scrimshaw dissolved into wisps with the clipped cry of *"Teka-lili!"*

The other Nocs followed suit with the same strange outburst. They shot away in different directions, slithering into the walls and between the floorboards like snakes.

Poe's screaming intensified when Lilith's face surfaced through the murk.

The clouds of darkness rolled back from her flawless features. Her white arms, encircled in twining veils, stretched out from the abyss.

Her hands fastened around the silver cord as though grabbing hold of a rope, and she began to use the swaying ethereal strand to pull herself from the vapors.

"Edgar," she whispered again, her dark hair flying back into the tumult that raged behind her. *"You are bound to me. You must return."*

"REYNOLDS!" Poe screamed again.

The utter despair in his voice shook Isobel from her shock-induced trance. She looked around, searching for something—anything she could do to stop the torment.

She spotted Pinfeathers, still in bird form, perched in the sill of the rain-spattered window. With a flap of his wings, he took flight, soaring across the room, circling to light on her shoulder. His movement from one corner of the room to the other, unnoticed by Poe, Lilith, or the doctor, reminded her that there was nothing she *could* do. Nothing at all. Because the events unfolding before her had already transpired.

Isobel felt her knees grow weaker with every inch Lilith managed to draw herself from the chasm. She could feel Pinfeathers switching restlessly from foot to foot, rankled as well by Lilith's presence, even if her visage was only a shadow from the past. Isobel knew he wanted to leave and hide just as the other Nocs had done. But he remained with her. And in spite of everything he had ever done to her, she was grateful.

Poe, his teeth gritted, turned his head away from the demon clawing her way toward him. He clamped his eyes shut to block it out, his face transforming into a tight knot of resigned anguish.

Reynolds, she thought. Poe had been calling for Reynolds. Where was he? Why wouldn't he come? Why hadn't he stopped this?

"There is nothing here that can harm you," Isobel heard the doctor insist. "Edgar, listen to me! It's over. Do you hear me? Whatever has happened, it is over!"

For one instant, the world turned black. Isobel blinked, trying to regain her vision. She felt Pinfeathers's talons clamp her shoulder more tightly. Then the blackness lifted and that was when she realized someone else had entered the room, walking *through* her.

A tall, cloaked figure now stood before her.

Her eyes traveled up his broad back, stopping at the wide-brimmed fedora hat that sat atop his head. She saw the edge of a white scarf.

Reynolds.

Lilith's attention broke from Poe, and she blinked in surprise as Reynolds drew forth one of his twin cutlasses. Her lips peeled back from sharpened teeth in a snarl. "Stop, you fool!" she hissed. "You'll kill him!"

Poe grew suddenly still on the bed. Isobel watched as he rolled his head to face the doctor, uttering something indiscernible while Reynolds coiled his arm, preparing to strike.

"No!" Isobel shouted, her cry rising in exact unison with Lilith's.

In the next instant, Reynolds slashed his sword forward in one clean swipe, severing the silver cord that stretched between Poe's body and Lilith's clutching hands.

The demoness howled as the cord snapped in two. Her face contorted with fury as the silver light vanished from her grip. She flew up, sucked into the ceiling, while the fog transformed into a whirlpool. Then, in a rush, the miasma dissipated, swept into the smooth plaster until no trace of its presence remained.

Isobel gaped, watching as Reynolds stepped aside and sheathed his sword.

Her gaze fell to Poe, who now lay lifeless, his eyes glazed and unseeing.

"Edgar," the doctor called.

The figure on the bed made no response.

Reynolds turned, and as he began to stride toward her, a wave of hatred washed over her. With a scream of rage, she threw herself at him, fists swinging.

Pinfeathers fluttered up and away from her, feathers flying, his rasping squawks filling the silent room.

Isobel's fists passed through Reynolds's ever-calm visage. He walked through her without so much as a ripple, and Isobel's efforts sent her stumbling forward.

She stopped and, looking up, froze to find herself standing at the foot of Poe's bed. She watched as the doctor reached out a trembling hand to close the two sightless eyes, which seemed to have been fixed directly on her.

As he did so, the surrounding walls, floor, and ceiling fell away like playing cards, throwing Isobel into a bottomless vat of darkness.

She fell backward through the dark, and as she did, a glimmer stole her attention. A silver cord glowed in the expansive nothingness, terminating in the center of her body.

It wavered like a ribbon caught in the wind as she flew back and back, falling faster and faster.

Then, suddenly, the cord snapped taut. It began to pull her forward, like a kite being reeled from the night sky. Light broke through her consciousness, and from a place high above, she saw herself—her body—standing in front of the fountain on Varen's street, her arm still extended as though to take Pinfeathers's hand, even though the Noc was gone.

She could see there was someone else there now. A stranger, who approached her from behind.

A jab of fear sent Isobel rushing toward herself. The world whirred into a blur as her two selves snapped into one.

Isobel blinked dry and stinging eyes. She dropped her arm, her bicep screaming as if she'd been standing that way for hours, and swung around to face the person who had nearly touched her shoulder.

23
Conscience Grim

"Oh!" The woman jumped, pulling back her hand the moment Isobel whirled to face her.

Young and blond with pretty gray eyes and a complexion too tan for this late in winter, the woman, who had to be somewhere in her early thirties, wore a fashionable heather-gray coat along with matching gloves. Her hair, straw colored and straight, lay neatly arranged on either of her shoulders, making her look like a model from a Macy's clothing ad.

The woman regarded Isobel with caution, as though she couldn't be certain if she'd stumbled on an insane asylum escapee.

"Did you not hear me?" she asked. "I said, is this your bike sitting here in the middle of the street?"

The woman pointed behind her to Danny's blue bike, which still lay on its side next to the curb. Isobel's gaze darted from the bike back to the woman and then beyond her willowy form to the chrome-colored Lexus idling in the road. The driver's-side door hung wide open, as if the woman had jumped out quickly, hoping to jump back in just as quickly.

"I—" Isobel stammered, and then looked toward the fountain again, her momentary confusion lifting at the sight of it.

She'd been gone, she realized. Not physically. Her body had remained here while her astral self, her spirit, had been transported elsewhere—to a memory from the past.

She was back now, though, and she knew in her bones that what Pinfeathers had shown her had been the truth.

Reynolds had killed Poe. He'd told Isobel that Lilith was responsible for his death, but that had been another lie. But why had he done it? Why, when Poe had been crying out to him, pleading with him for help? Why, when Reynolds had told her they'd been friends? Had that, too, been just another falsehood?

"Are—are you lost?" the woman asked.

Yes, Isobel wanted to say. *More than ever before.*

Glancing skyward, she could see that it had begun to get lighter, though just scarcely so. Enough for her to wonder how much time had elapsed since she'd first arrived at the fountain.

"What—what time is it?" Isobel asked the woman.

"Early," she replied. "High school doesn't start for at least another hour. Is that where you were headed before you stopped here? Where do you go?"

Isobel didn't answer. She was too busy making time calculations. If she had an hour before school, then that left her with thirty minutes to get home before her alarm went off. Less if her mom decided to pop her head in and check on her. If she hadn't already.

God, what would her mother think if she looked in and found her bed empty?

She'd freak for sure. She'd call Isobel's dad and then . . .

"Are you . . . is everything all right?" the woman asked.

"You look a little . . ." She stopped, her glossed lips still parted as if her next words had simply flown out before she'd had a chance to utter them. Squinting at Isobel, the woman tilted her head to one side. "I'm sorry. Do—do I know you?" she asked abruptly.

Immediately, Isobel realized who she was talking to.

This was Varen's stepmother.

They'd seen each other only once before, on that night Varen had argued with his father. After his parents had left his room, Isobel had come out from hiding in his closet and, together, she and Varen took the fire escape outside his window. Just as they'd climbed into his car, this woman had run out onto the porch and down the sidewalk, calling out to them. She and Isobel had locked eyes for only a split second before Varen pressed his foot to the gas pedal and took off, but apparently, that had been long enough.

Isobel shook her head, even though she could already tell it was too late for denial.

"No," the woman said, and pointed at Isobel with one gloved finger. "I *do* know you. You were with Varen that night he— What are you doing here? Who are you? Tell me your name."

"I—" Isobel broke off.

Turning, she lunged for Danny's bike. Plucking it from the road, she began to run alongside it.

"Wait!" the woman cried. "Stop!"

Isobel swung herself onto the bike seat and began to pedal hard.

She could hear the scamper of footsteps coming after her, and then moving away again. Isobel stood up on the bike and drove the pedals harder as the clap of a car door echoed through the neighborhood.

Reaching the end of St. Francis Court, Isobel swung the bike onto the connecting street. The thin, cold wind whistled high in her ears as she headed pell-mell for the main road. Behind her, she could hear the approach of the Lexus and stole one quick glance back. Varen's stepmom leaned out of the driver's-side window. She honked the horn as she drove and shouted for Isobel to "please stop."

The note of desperate pleading in the woman's voice grabbed Isobel's heart hard, and for an instant, her feet stopped pedaling. She coasted, her hands poised to clamp down on the handle brakes. The Lexus was right behind her now. She could hear its quiet purr growing louder.

"I'm just trying to find him!" the woman called. "If you know something, then please—"

Her words caused Isobel's fear to spike again. Her arms acted for her and she cut the handlebars sharply to her right, swerving down an alleyway lined with city trash cans and carriage house garages.

Behind her, the tires of the Lexus squealed as it missed the turn. Isobel swerved again—this time up a short incline and into the parking lot of an old stone church.

She zoomed past and, making a quick scan for traffic, raced across the connecting street, her tires bumping on the curb as she maneuvered the bike onto the sidewalk.

She rounded the corner. Then, just before she shot beyond a row of tall brick buildings, the Lexus appeared, turning onto the street she'd just left, and Isobel knew she'd been spotted. She also knew she was out of room to run.

Isobel jerked the bike to the left and rattled into a dead-end gravel lot behind a coffee shop. Squeezing the brakes, she slid to a halt, her tires kicking up a cloud of white dust. She hopped off the bike and, giving it a push, let it roll behind an enormous Dumpster, where it crashed against the wall and clattered to the ground.

Isobel hesitated only a heartbeat before lifting up the Dumpster's flimsy lid, hoisting herself over the lip of the metal bin, and dropping inside.

She landed with a whoosh, her fall broken by a cushion of foul-smelling trash bags.

The flap banged closed behind her, plunging her into darkness.

The stench of spoiled milk and rotten food filled her nostrils, making her gag. She coughed and clamped a hand over her nose and mouth. She grew still and waited, listening even though her ears could pick up only the sound of her own ragged breathing and the shift of plastic bags and compacting trash. She hoped those noises were a result of her own body weight and not the scampering of rats.

Closing her eyes, she held her breath and waited.

When she finally popped her head out of the Dumpster, she sucked in gasps of oxygen, hoping Varen's stepmother had moved on from the area.

After climbing out of the Dumpster, she retrieved the bike and began to pedal homeward, as fast as her legs could carry her, praying the whole way that her mother had not yet opened the door to her bedroom.

Hiding Danny's bike in the backyard bushes, Isobel hurried up the lattice on the side of her house. She made her way across the slanted roof ledge, her legs weak from having pedaled so hard and so far. She slid her window open and climbed back in the way she'd left.

The alarm clock sitting on top of her cubbyhole headboard had already gone off, blasting a continuous and shrill tone, the numbers blinking 6:33.

"—sobel!" her mother's voice boomed from somewhere downstairs.

Isobel slammed her window shut and turned her head to look toward the door when she heard footsteps on the stairs.

Shedding her coat, she scrambled into her bed, tossing the covers over her head. She heard her doorknob wiggle and yanked off the black ski cap, stuffing it under her pillow the instant before her door swung open.

"Izzy!" her mother called into the room. "Glad to finally see you getting some sleep, but can we *please* shut this thing off?"

Isobel peeked over her comforter. She did her best to slow her breathing, careful to keep her body concealed so her mother wouldn't see that she was fully dressed.

Stopping at her bedside, her mother reached over Isobel's

head to hit the alarm's snooze button.

"There," she said with a sigh, and ran a hand through her hair, which had been combed and curled. In place of her usual nightgown and slippers, her mother wore a wool skirt and her moss-green cashmere sweater. "C'mon," she said, giving Isobel's leg a double tap. "Let's go. Danny's got a teacher conference this morning, so I'm giving you both a ride to school. Up and at 'em. We need to leave early."

Isobel nodded. "I'm awake," she said.

Her mother walked away but stopped at the door and turned to look back, her nose crinkled. "What's that smell?" she asked. "Have you been leaving food up here?"

Isobel rolled over onto her side, feigning grogginess. "Yeah," she said. "I'll get it in a sec."

"You do that," her mom said. "I don't know how you can stand it. And no more snacks in the bedroom, please. You know better."

With that, her mom bustled out. Isobel waited half a beat and then sat up, kicking back the covers. She was about to make a beeline for the bathroom when her brother's voice broke from the hall.

"Shower dibs!" he shouted, his words punctuated by the slamming of the bathroom door.

Gwen set her tray on the table in front of Isobel's. Hiking her skirts, she threaded legs, clad in black spandex and gray legwarmers, through the picnic-table-style bench and sat with a sigh that seemed to say *at last*. Her hands fluttered over her tray, fingers twiddling as she searched for her fork and knife, as though she were a magician about to perform her first trick.

Locating her fork, Gwen prepared to stab her salad. She paused, though, and glanced up slowly.

"You know," she said, "if you wanted to sit by yourself today, all you had to do was ask."

Isobel leaned an elbow against the table. She put a hand to her forehead, her shoulders sagging. Her eyelids fell closed as though weighted by sandbags, and it felt good to block out the stinging glare of the fluorescents, even if only for a moment.

"Is it that bad?" she asked, already knowing the answer.

"It's bad," Gwen said. "What happened? Been spending quality time with your brother?"

Isobel kneaded the bridge of her nose between her finger and thumb. "Long story."

"Mm," Gwen said. "Would have been better, I think, if you hadn't spritzed the body spray over it. You know when somebody tries to cover up a fart by lighting a candle?"

"Gwen?"

"Eh?" she said, popping a cherry tomato into her mouth.

"Not today, please."

"You don't look so good. Didn't sleep much, I'm guessing," Gwen said. "Can I ask why, or is that another thing stuffed in the ever-thickening 'no share' file?"

Isobel frowned. Opening one eye, she uttered the question her brain had been drawing circles around all morning long.

"Why do you think he does it, Gwen?" Isobel asked. "Every year he comes back, and every year he leaves the roses. It's been going on for decades now, and why? What's the point?"

"You know," Gwen said as she unfolded her paper napkin and laid it in her lap, "corpses *are* notorious for playing hard to get."

Isobel dropped her hand, letting her arm flop against the table. She shot Gwen a scathing glare. "I'm being serious," she said.

"Well," Gwen started, thinking. "Obviously, he gets the flowers from the rose garden. The one I saw in my dream."

"But why?" Isobel pressed, her frustration growing even though she knew full well that Gwen would be unable to answer her questions, especially since she did not know half of what Isobel did. Ever since Pinfeathers had shown her the scene from the hospital, Isobel couldn't stop turning the events over and over in her mind. It had become like a sore she couldn't stop worrying and picking at. Or more like a nightmare she couldn't forget.

Gwen shrugged and bit into her roll. She chewed thoughtfully, her foot tapping against the checkered linoleum floor beneath their table, a clear sign that Isobel had once again said something to ramp up her nerves. "I dunno," she said. "Paying respects? That's a given. I don't think anyone really knows just why he does it. From what I understand, that's part of the mystery. Call me clueless—which, remember, I pretty much am—but I would have thought that if anyone knew why, you might."

"I . . . I thought I did," Isobel said. "But . . . I don't. Not anymore."

Isobel looked down at her chicken patty. A moment of silence passed between them while the surrounding sounds of talking and laughing swelled louder. Then Gwen reached her fork across the table and stabbed one of Isobel's Tater Tots. "FYI," she said. "Dunno about you, but I'm all set for the trip. Even got a gas card the other day so my parents can't track my debit when I refill."

"Gwen. I'm . . . I'm really scared."

"Finally," Gwen said without missing a beat, even though her fingers trembled while she tried to tear open the plastic packet of salad dressing. "Your first healthy reaction."

"Things are different," Isobel said. "They're changing. I mean . . . they've changed," she corrected.

"How about your mind?" Gwen glanced up, feigning hopefulness. "Tell me that's changed."

"No," Isobel said. "I . . . I know what I have to do. I just . . . Gwen? I . . . I need you to do me a favor."

"Should I just put that on your tab?"

Isobel ignored the joke. "If . . . if I don't come back from this—"

Gwen dropped her fork onto her tray, her hands snapping into a referee's time-out gesture. "This conversation is not going to happen."

"Please," Isobel said. "It's important."

"*Listen.*" Gwen propped her elbow on the table and aimed a finger in Isobel's face. "Say what you gotta say, get it out of your system, and then keep it zipped about the not-coming-back crap," she said. "This is the first *and* the last 'if I should die before I wake' spiel you get. Got it?"

"It's not a spiel," Isobel said, "it's just, I need to know if you'll do something for me."

"What?"

Isobel took in a breath and let it out. "Varen's stepmom," she said. "I . . . sort of ran into her this morning. She . . . doesn't know who I am, but she saw me with Varen on the night before he disappeared. I think she knows I was involved. So, if . . . if I don't come back, will you give her this?" Isobel pushed a hand into her pocket. Taking out a folded slip of well-worn paper, she pressed it to the table and slid it toward Gwen.

"What is it?" Gwen asked. She plucked the paper from the table and began to unfold it.

"Don't," Isobel said. "Please. It—it's a note from Varen. The last one he gave me. I found it in the pocket of his jacket after . . . I just thought that—if—if I can't—I mean, if neither of us ever—it might help her . . . not understand, but . . ." Giving up on trying to find the right words to explain her reasoning, she said, "I just thought that maybe the one thing that gave me hope . . . can be the one thing that will give her closure. If it comes to that." She shrugged. "That's all."

Gwen refolded the note. Without asking any more questions, she tucked it away in her purse.

"I'll keep it," she said. "Then, when you get back, after you and the dark one are done making out and planning a future filled with little blond-haired, green-eyed, pigment-challenged rug rats, I'll bring it over and you can add it to your scrapbook, right before you start cooking me dinner. I like vegetarian lasagna with cottage cheese instead of ricotta."

"Gwen?"

"And don't forget the mushrooms. Garlic bread, too, please. That is, as long as your vampire lover doesn't object."

"I want to say thank you," Isobel said. "For . . . everything."

"No," Gwen said, "thank *you* for the delicious dinner. I can almost taste the baklava you and Darth Vader will be making for dessert. Something tells me you're gonna have to look that one up, though." Snatching her napkin out of her lap, Gwen pulled a pen from her purse. Scribbling the dessert name onto the flimsy paper, she slid it across the table to Isobel. After a slight pause, she twiddled the pen and then snatched the napkin back. "Oh, hell," she said. "I'll just write the whole damn recipe down. In the meantime, you can stop looking at me like I've just pulled you out of quicksand or something."

"But it feels like you have," Isobel said.

Gwen's eyes flicked up to meet with Isobel's.

"Well, I haven't," she said.

24
Charmed

Isobel did not dream during the next week and a half. At least not as far as she knew. She did not see Varen in passing reflective surfaces. Pinfeathers did not return to explain the vision he had shared with her or how he'd known she would go to the fountain. The pictures in her books remained motionless, and her radio played only pop songs and commercials.

In the place of upheaval, normalcy, or something that felt close to it, settled in. It laid over life like a fresh coat of paint, and for once Isobel fell habitually, if not easily, into the routine of playing all her various parts: student, daughter, sister, cheerleader.

On the night before she and her father would depart for Baltimore, Isobel stared into her empty suitcase.

She had put off pretending to pack for nearly the entire day. Now that the sun had sunk into the horizon, it remained the last task left to perform.

But there was something daunting about the futile act of collecting and tucking away things she knew she wouldn't need, especially when she had already done the real packing the afternoon before.

The previous day, as soon as Gwen had dropped her off

from school, Isobel had gone straight to her room and emptied out her backpack. She'd refilled it with the essentials: a pack of granola bars swiped from the pantry, two water bottles, a black hoodie, and a pair of hiking boots.

Her backpack sat underneath her bed now, hiding in the shadows, waiting.

Inside it, sitting on top of everything else and folded with care, lay Varen's green mechanic's jacket. He would need it when they came back, she thought. After all, Baltimore would be cold.

Isobel turned from the bag and made her way to her dresser, opening the top drawer. Without looking, she pulled free a stack of T-shirts. Returning to the suitcase, she tossed them onto her bed instead.

She couldn't do this. She couldn't pretend anymore. Grabbing one of the big pillows from her bed, she stuffed it inside the bag, then closed the flap and zipped the sides.

Done.

At least this way, it would shorten the guesswork on her parents' part. It would leave them with no doubts that she'd tricked them and used them, that she'd planned her escape right from the start.

Maybe knowing would somehow lessen their pain.

"Packing a little light, aren't we?"

Isobel glanced over her shoulder to find Danny standing in her doorway. Arms folded, he leaned against the frame. His usual smirk seemed to be in hiding, plastered over by an uncharacteristic look of solemnity.

He nodded toward her suitcase. "Generally speaking, I think hotels stock those."

Scowling, Isobel grabbed the handle of her suitcase and picked it up, shrugging in the same motion. As she made her way to the door, she had to wonder how long he'd been standing there, watching.

"I like my own," she said, setting the bag upright and flush with the wall.

"Yeah," he said. "I bet you also like your own underwear, but I didn't see anything like that go in there either."

She sighed, hands going to her hips. "Don't you have anything better to do than spy on me? What do you want?"

His eyes drifted to the carpeted floor. "I dunno." He kicked the doorjamb with the toe of one sneaker, then lifted his shoulders all the way to his ears in a shrug before letting them drop.

"I mean, I *was* going to go nuclear on you about the scuff marks I found on my bike, but I know it won't do any good. You won't tell me why you took it. Or *where* you took it. Or what made you decide to drag it behind you instead of, y'know, riding it."

Turning, Isobel went to her closet to fish out her parka. "I don't know what you're talking about," she said.

"Are you running away for good?"

She stopped. Looking over her shoulder at him again, she scanned her brain for a prepared answer, realizing too late that she didn't have one.

Her brother stared at her in blatant accusation, like a

lawyer who'd just asked his obviously guilty client, "Did you do it?" There was something else there too, hidden beneath. It was something she hadn't seen in her brother's face since he was very small. Vulnerability.

She had to wonder how long he'd seen this coming. Apparently long enough at least for him to have had the opportunity to tell someone. Their mom or dad or even a school counselor. But for some reason, Danny, Snitch King of America, had kept his observations to himself. Then she remembered that if not for him and his special powers of persuasion, their father might never have gotten her the plane tickets to begin with.

Could it be that Danny had guessed her plans from the very beginning?

Regardless, Isobel knew it would be useless, not to mention cruel, to evade his candid question. If he'd wanted to blow the whistle on her, he'd have done so already.

"No," she said. "It's just . . . there's something I've got to do is all."

Taking the shift in her attitude as an invitation to come in, Danny strolled across the threshold and into Isobel's room. Wandering over to her dresser, he said, "Like, Luke Skywalker leaves Dagobah to save Han and Leia gotta do, or Dick Grayson stops being Robin to go to Blüdhaven and become Nightwing gotta do?"

Isobel's eyebrows shot toward the ceiling, and she regarded her brother with an expression somewhere between bewilderment and hilarity.

She fought against the urge to grin but found herself

powerless to resist, knowing that her brother had asked the question in all seriousness. "The first one? I think?"

"Oh," he said, picking up some small item from her dresser and turning it over and over between his fingers. "In that case, I guess your room's not up for grabs." He shrugged. "Just, y'know, beware the Dark Side. And don't forget this." He held out the trinket he'd been tinkering with, the small butterfly key-chain watch he'd given her for Christmas.

"Right." Isobel plucked it up from the center of his palm. "I won't."

He started for the door and then, catching himself before walking out, turned back. "By the way," he said. "I heard Mom and Dad talking the other night. Dad said something that made Mom freak, something about you and the fireplace poker. I heard her say that if you didn't start acting like yourself again when you and Dad got back, like, for-real you and not plastic you, then she was going to take you to see a shrink."

"*What?*" Isobel said. "You mean like . . . a doctor?"

Again he shrugged. "Psychologist or psychopediatrist. One of those 'psycho' people," he said. "Just thought you should know. I mean, you'd tell me if Mom and Dad were thinking of giving *me* up for medical experimentation, right?"

Isobel's brow furrowed.

"See," Danny said. "Normally, this is the part where you're supposed to say something like 'Oh, you don't have to worry about that, they've already got plenty of chimps' or 'They're only interested in acquiring *intelligent* life-forms.' C'mon, Iz. I'm dying here. I mean, if there was such a thing as a little brother union, I'd have filed a grievance back in November."

She didn't respond. She only looked down at the butterfly watch in her hand.

"Okay," he said. "Or I could just leave you alone to conduct your sad emo transformation in peace."

He sighed, then turned and shuffled down the hall to his own room.

Isobel's cell phone, sitting on her bedside table, gave a soft *ting*, indicating she'd received a text. But she didn't have to check the screen to know who had sent it or what it said.

Shutting her door, Isobel pulled her backpack out from underneath her bed, taking a moment to fasten the butterfly key chain to one of the front zippers. Then she took her backpack to the window and opened the sash, sliding it all the way up the frame.

Her curtains billowed on either side of her as she leaned out into the night air.

Over the roof's ledge, she saw Gwen standing in her backyard.

Gwen raised a hand to her throat, which was wrapped in the scarf Isobel had given her.

Isobel, understanding the gesture, touched her own collar, lifting up the tiny hamsa charm as proof that she had not taken it off, that she still had it.

Gwen gave her a thumbs-up, her glasses glinting like signal lights through the gloom. She held her arms out in

front of her, and without hesitating, Isobel pitched the backpack over the roof's ledge.

It soared straight into Gwen's waiting grasp.

After that, they gave each other only one last parting
glance before Isobel ducked back into her room and Gwen
hurried to wherever she'd parked her Cadillac.

Isobel shut her window, turning the locks.

As she got ready for bed that night, somewhere in the
very back of her mind, she wondered if she was doing so for
the last time.

They arrived at the airport well before dawn the next morning.

Isobel's mom dropped them off near the front sliding
doors of the terminal, while Danny stayed in the backseat,
comatose, a bit of drool glistening in one corner of his open
mouth.

After hugging her mom good-bye, Isobel leaned down to
peer at her little brother through the darkened window. She
found it hard not to envy the peaceful look on his face, even
with the drool.

During the flight, Isobel put in a pair of earbuds that
would keep the threat of conversation with her father at bay.
She didn't think she could afford any more heart-to-hearts.

As it turned out, she didn't have to worry about chitchat.
Shortly after the plane leveled out at maximum altitude, her
dad reclined his chair and closed his eyes. It wasn't long until
his breathing became deep and steady. It made her wonder if
he had slept at all the night before either.

They landed just after daybreak and left the airport in the rental car, a gold coupe. As they reached the highway, the sun began to open its lazy eye. Weak light filtered through the crisscrossing branches of the barren trees lining the highway. Beyond, the horizon flushed a reddish pink.

Soon the highway grew wider, and the outline of tall buildings loomed into view. The coupe shot like a pinball down the final ramp, coming to a stop at the end of a four-lane row of easy-flowing traffic.

Isobel leaned forward in her seat in order to peer up at the skyscrapers, while every so often, her dad would point out a landmark or statue.

Tiny doughnut shops and fast-food restaurants sat squished in narrow strips at the bottom of taller buildings, while pigeons bobbed along on the sidewalks outside their neon-lit windows, attacking bits of bread and wadded-up wrappers.

Her dad made a right turn onto another wide street embedded with metal tram tracks.

A homeless man in a long coat lay huddled within the recesses of a darkened doorway. He clutched a tattered blanket close to him, the soles of his worn shoes poking out from underneath.

Sirens erupted somewhere behind them. Their whine seemed to blare on forever, growing to ear-piercing volume as an ambulance crept past on their right, screaming with urgency even though it didn't rush like the ones back home.

It didn't take Isobel long to realize that was because it

couldn't rush. Instead the ambulance conducted an odd "excuse me, pardon me" scoot and slide through the rows of cars doing their best to angle this way and that in order to make room.

Leaning closer to the window, Isobel looked skyward, noticing how every tall streetlamp bore its own purple banner, each depicting a cartoon bird's head in profile, a big yellow *B* stamped on its neck.

When they passed a covered bus stop, its plastic siding lined with posters and advertisements, Isobel noticed the bird again, along with a slogan for the Baltimore Ravens football team.

"Oh yeah," her dad said, following the path of Isobel's gaze. "Home of the Ravens. Named for Poe's poem."

Isobel stiffened at the mention of Poe.

"You know," he said, an odd look crossing his features, "now that I think about it, isn't Poe supposed to be buried somewhere in the city? Maybe we should go out after breakfast tomorrow and try to track him down. Ask him if I got it right. What do you say?"

Isobel turned to face her window, afraid of what he'd be able to read in her expression. To her relief, the harbor drew into focus, patches of silver dancing amid gray waters.

"Hey, Dad," she said, pointing. "Look."

A wide and open redbrick pedestrian walkway stretched from the road down to the water. Flanking the walkway, two long identical glass-paneled malls faced the harbor shore.

"Oh yeah," he said with a sigh. "Right. Shopping. Or we could do that."

As they turned into a jammed intersection, her dad went quiet, his expression turning stern while he concentrated on navigating out of the mess. Isobel was relieved that he made no further mention of Poe, and by the time they arrived in the lobby of their hotel, she was sure he'd forgotten about his suggestion of visiting the writer's grave.

At least until they entered the check-in line.

"Huh," he said, squinting. "That's an odd coincidence, isn't it?"

"What?" Isobel said, glancing around.

Her dad stepped out of line, going to the nearby wooden stand filled with paper pamphlets advertising local attractions. He returned with a glossy postcard paper that bore Poe's picture front and center. It was the same image Isobel had found in the *Complete Works of Edgar Allan Poe* book that Varen had once lent her, the one that depicted him with hollow and haunted-looking eyes, their centers like two black marbles.

"Join us for the annual Edgar Allan Poe birthday celebration," her dad said, reading the header on the brochure. "Six o'clock January nineteenth. That's tomorrow."

His brows came together while he flipped the postcard from front to back.

"Humph," he said. "That's kind of funny, don't you think, Izzy?"

"Yeah," Isobel replied, nodding, though she didn't dare meet his gaze. "Weird."

25
Sweet Sorrow

That evening Isobel's dad took her to the Inner Harbor for dinner, deciding on a seafood restaurant one of the hotel clerks had suggested.

As soon as the hostess seated them in a booth, Isobel took out her phone.

It had been at least two hours since Gwen's last text update, in which she'd said something about being in Chinatown, New York. Isobel knew that since Gwen was using the Brooklyn trip for her own cover, the text was most likely a coded message indicating her arrival in Baltimore. That would clock Gwen's entire drive at right around the projected eleven hours.

Isobel had responded immediately, texting back that she and her dad were spending the afternoon at the aquarium. After that, she'd waited, and waited, her phone never leaving her fist. She'd expected to receive some response that would let her know that Gwen had received the info and that she was now headed in Isobel's direction. But that never came.

Isobel was starting to think that maybe she and Gwen should have planned better. Maybe she should have snuck out last night when Gwen had come to pick up her backpack. That way, they could have left together and made the drive overnight. Of course, that would have caused more commotion. Neither of them would have their current cover and both would be as good as fugitives on the run, especially if Isobel's parents guessed they were together. At least this way, no one was looking for either of them. Yet.

"Away at last and you're still hot-wired to home," her dad sighed from behind the thick, plastic-coated menu. "Who are you texting with?"

Uh-oh, she thought. Sensing an impending end to her phone usage and, consequently, her only link to Gwen, Isobel typed in a quick message, knowing she would need to make it count.

JUST GOT TO THE M & S GRILL AT THE
INNER HARBOR. BUT I THINK DAD'S
READY FOR ME TO DITCH MY PHONE.

She hit the send button just as their drinks arrived.

Isobel clamped her phone shut. She kept it tight in one hand, waiting for the buzz that she hoped would follow any moment.

Her father folded his menu as their waitress, a thin young woman with a straight-up-and-down figure, hovered close to the table. She wore red lipstick and a matching headband lined with silk flowers. Her dull expression reminded Isobel of the blank look the seniors got during the last few weeks before graduation.

"Do you know what you'd like?" she asked Isobel, pen poised against her notepad.

"Uh." Isobel glanced down at the menu in front of her for the first time and flipped it open, still never letting go of her phone. "Um, what are you getting, Dad?"

He watched her from across the booth. Chin in hand, elbow on the table, he seemed to affect the exact same expression as their waitress. "Crab cake platter."

Isobel refolded the menu and held it out to their waitress. "Same," she said.

Their waitress tucked both menus under one arm and, without writing anything down, slid the pen and notepad into an apron pocket and zipped out of sight.

Alone with her father again, Isobel became keenly aware of his unwavering gaze. She tried to ignore it, but with her phone now disqualified as a suitable distraction, she began to feel like an ant caught in the incinerating beam of a magnifying glass.

She pulled her lemonade toward her. Taking a sip, she swirled the pink liquid with her straw. The ice clinked against her glass, the sound seeming to drown out the thrum of the low chatter around them.

She looked up and her eyes met with her father's.

"What?" she asked.

"It's a phone," he said, "not a game show buzzer." He gestured to the hand that clutched her cell. "I honestly doubt you'll miss anything crucial if you put it away for a while."

Reluctantly Isobel pressed the phone to the table. She had to peel her fingers back one at a time in order to force herself to relinquish it to the starched white tablecloth. It sat there, three inches from the edge, like a pink hand grenade waiting to go off.

"Okay," her dad said, "that's a start. But how about you put it in your coat pocket instead?"

Isobel reached for the phone again, but just as her fingers came in contact with the plastic, the cell gave a short buzz, Rattling against the table.

"Mind if I do the honors this time?" her dad asked.

She stiffened when she saw her father's hand float toward the phone, his fingers stopping to hover just above. She had to tuck her hands between her knees to keep herself from snatching the phone out from underneath him.

"Sure." She shrugged. "Go for it."

Picking up the phone, he flipped it open.

His face glowed in the white light of the LCD screen.

Isobel felt her breath catch. Beneath the table, her foot began to waggle. She squeezed her knees together, keeping her hands captive as she watched his eyes narrow and his brows creep toward each other, forming an angry knot in between as he thumbed through the texts.

Oh no, she thought. This was it. Gwen *had* run into trouble. And now she'd made some desperate response, blowing their cover without meaning to.

Whatever the situation, Isobel knew she couldn't stay here with her father any longer. She would have to make a run for it. She'd need to find Gwen on her own and still hope they could make it to the graveyard before midnight. Gradually, inch by inch, Isobel edged her way down the seat, preparing to bolt. She stopped, however, the moment her father's head snapped up.

Isobel felt the blood rush from her face as he thrust her phone out to her, screen first.

Her eyes widened at Gwen's response.

DON'T HOLD IT AGAINST HIM. YOU CAN TELL THE POOR GUY'S NEVER KNOWN WHAT IT'S LIKE TO BE POPULAR. BY THE WAY, HOW'S THE HARBOR? I'M PARKED RIGHT BY THE HUDSON MYSELF. I CAN SEE ALL THE WAY TO NEW JERSEY. IF ONLY THERE WAS SOMETHING TO SEE.

Despite the insult, Isobel felt her shoulders ease in relief. She knew the message, again coded, must mean that Gwen was nearby, waiting somewhere outside and in sight of the harbor.

Regardless of what would happen now, it was time to move.

"Uh . . . sorry about that, Dad. You know Gwen. She's kind of . . ."

"Rude? Yeah, I know."

Isobel reached out to wrap her hand around the phone still clutched in her father's outstretched grip. She had to tug it to get it free from his hand. "Listen, Dad. I think you're right. I think I'll just turn it off for a while, okay?"

Isobel held the power button until the screen on her phone

went dark. Next, she snapped the phone shut and pushed it to his side of the table. "Here," she said, "you keep it."

"Humph," he said. He picked up his tea, the redness in his face ebbing away. She almost had to wonder if what she'd perceived as anger had really been embarrassment. "I'd be happy if you could just find a way to turn *her* off," he muttered before taking a sip.

"Hey, Dad?"

"Yeah, okay. I'll can it," he said, "but I'm taking you up on the phone blackout." Picking up her cell, he leaned to one side, the booth seat groaning underneath him as he tucked the phone into his back pocket. "If this isn't going to be a Gwen-free *trip*, it should at least be a Gwen-free meal, don't you think?"

Isobel had to force herself to move. She slid down the booth, leaving her coat and scarf tucked against the wall.

"Hey, where you going?"

She aimed a thumb over her shoulder. "I just . . . bathroom. I'll be . . . back." She nodded toward her things, hoping to draw his attention away from her face. "Watch my stuff?"

"Like it's going to sprout legs and walk off while you're gone."

Isobel turned to go, but she couldn't seem to take another step away from the booth. It was as if something magnetic was holding her in place, a pull that told her she wasn't quite done there yet. She glanced back to her father and saw that he had since picked up the dessert menu and seemed to be eyeing the caramel apple pie.

She took a moment to study his features one last time and

really absorb the details of his face, like taking a mental snapshot. She loved how he looked whenever he went a day without shaving. It was his Sunday afternoon look, she thought. The pepper-colored stubble on his chin always made her think of old rough-and-ready yet sophisticated movie-screen rogues like Harrison Ford and Sean Connery. Guys who you knew would always save the day, no matter what.

"Dad?"

"Yeah?"

"Um . . . I just . . . Thank you," she said. "For bringing me here. I needed to go. I mean . . . to come. I don't think you'll ever know just how important this is."

He lowered the menu to the table and folded his hands in front of him. "I know it's important." He ducked his head in a low nod. "That's why we're here, right?"

"I love you, Dad."

He arched a brow at her. She knew she probably shouldn't have said it, that it would only raise a red flag. But she also knew she didn't care anymore. If she was going to do this, if she was going to walk away right this moment, then at the very least, she needed him to understand that it wasn't because of him.

"I love you, too, kiddo," he said. He watched her with one eye keenly squinted. "Is everything okay?"

She nodded. "Yeah. I'll be back," she said, and she hoped that the statement wasn't a lie.

"Okay," he said, and smiled.

Turning again, Isobel strode down the line of booths, this time without looking back.

Her legs felt stiff beneath her as she left her father behind, knowing that, fifteen minutes from now he'd be panic-stricken, left to wonder what had happened and where he'd gone wrong. She pushed the thought aside, reminding herself that she'd already made her decision. That the decision had long since been made *for* her.

She walked on.

At the last booth before the pathway opened toward the exit, Isobel noticed a family of four, their table jam-packed with glasses and plates of food. A little girl in a red jumper sat next to a man who shared the same corn-silk hair. The little girl watched her father, swinging her legs while he leaned over her to cut her chicken strips for her.

Isobel did her best not to stare at the two as she made her way past. Before her guilt could swallow her whole, before she could change her mind and turn back, she pushed through the front doors of the restaurant and out into the cold.

Without her coat on, it was like taking a plunge into a vat of ice water.

Outside, darkness had stolen over the harbor while minuscule flakes of white filtered down, lighting on the brick walkway. Mottled moonlight glistened on still waters, mingling with the slightly warmer glow emanating from the tall lamps and storefront windows. Shoppers, huddled in thick coats and scarves, hurried toward doors that would lead them into warmth.

Above, troops of puffy-cheeked clouds waited in the sky, frozen in place.

Isobel squinted through the darkness toward the road, where she saw a familiar navy-blue car pulled close to the curb. It waited just beyond the line of flagpoles, its yellow flashers blinking.

Glancing back at the restaurant one last time, Isobel noticed a trio of servers standing in the light of the propped-open kitchen door, smoking. Then she saw the flowered headband, the smear of red on black visible in the bright white light fixed above the door.

She kept her head ducked and her back to the restaurant while she strode quickly toward the Cadillac, hoping her getaway would go unnoticed by their waitress. At the same time, she knew it would be hard not to spot someone walking around without a coat in twenty-degree weather.

Just as the thought occurred to her, a cold sting of wind whizzed past, gusting in from the direction of the harbor. Sharp and knifelike, it carried the scent of the salty sea air. It made her hair whip at her face while, above, she heard one of the flag lines clank against its metal pole.

Isobel grabbed the cuffs of her long-sleeved T-shirt and pulled them down over her fists. She hunched her shoulders as she hurried to the curb where the Cadillac waited.

Opening the rear passenger door, she all but fell into the backseat, where she found her backpack waiting for her.

With the winds picking up, she only had to pull lightly on the handle and the door swung shut on its own. Behind them, someone laid on their horn.

Without so much as a "long time no see" to Isobel, Gwen

cranked down her window, just enough to stick her head out and shout "Bite me!" at top volume. The offending car blasted its horn again in a string of Morse-code bursts. Collapsing back into her seat, Gwen shifted the car into gear. She put her foot to the pedal, and Isobel was slammed backward as they lurched away from the curb.

Other horns joined in now, honking like a flock of feather-ruffled geese.

"Try telling *him*!" Gwen railed at the surrounding cars. "Think anybody here's ever heard of the phrase go *around*? Look at the blinkers, you schmendricks. When the blinkers are blinking, that doesn't mean you sit there and blink with them. You go *around*!"

As they gained speed, Isobel twisted to peer through the rear window. She saw the young waitress staring after them. Dropping her cigarette, she stamped it out with one foot, crossed her arms against the cold, and disappeared back into the kitchen.

"What is it?" Gwen asked. "Somebody see you?"

"Gwen, to quote you directly, I think *everybody* saw."

Gwen switched lanes, putting on her signal before veering left as the light changed. "Did you expect me to just put up with that back there?" Isobel heard a click from the dashboard area, followed by a burst of heat. "By the way, I hope you packed a coat in your bag of tricks back there, 'cause it's supposed to start snowing, and there's no way we're playing pass-the-parka with mine."

Isobel grabbed her backpack and, placing her thumb

under the silver wings of the butterfly watch, popped them open to reveal the time as just after eight.

"Gwen, they locked the cemetery gates an hour ago," Isobel said. "How are we supposed to get in?"

"Actually, they locked them an hour and seven minutes ago, if you want to get technical about it," Gwen said. "On the website, Westminster lists their hours as eight until "dusk," and I have to say, they were pretty accurate."

"Wait a second, you were *there*?" Isobel grabbed the seat in front of her and leaned forward as Gwen made yet another turn.

"Of course I was there," Gwen said. "What do you think I've been doing all this time? Crocheting mittens? It's called doing reconnaissance. Why aren't you wearing your seat belt?"

"Jeez, Gwen! You could have texted me. I mean, I've been going crazy thinking you might be stranded on the side of the road somewhere or lost or, I don't know, kidnapped!"

Gwen rounded the next curve, then slowed to a stop as the traffic light switched from yellow to red. Around them, the glowing window fronts of bars and businesses grew fewer and farther between. The number of pedestrians plodding along began to dwindle as well.

"While you seem to underestimate my abilities concerning self-preservation," Gwen said, making a point to press down on her door's locking mechanism, "I think you also *over-estimate* my creativity. So sorry if I couldn't think of a good New York–related activity that might accurately compare to scouting a creepy fan-freak-filled cemetery. Did you know there was a guy in there actually dressed as a raven? At least I think it was a guy. Not to mention that I was a little busy trying to explain how I'd found my way into the catacombs when they did the five-man sweep to clear the grounds before locking the place up!"

"Wait," Isobel said. "Did you say *catacombs*?"

"Yeah," Gwen said, "I did. But it's not underground like you'd think. Not really. Turns out the whole church was built on *top* of a huge portion of the graveyard. I found them by slipping in through one of the gated doors on the side of the church."

Isobel yanked off her shoes as she listened. She dug to the bottom of her backpack, took out the hiking boots, and pulled them on. Next, she rifled through the pile of clothes and took out the black hoodie she'd borrowed from Danny's closet. She drew it on over her head and tugged it down, grateful for the fleece lining. Finally she went to unroll Varen's jacket.

"I thought the door led to a cellar where we could hide," Gwen went on, "but guess again. Now, I can't say it's the lobby of the Ritz-Carlton, but at least it cuts down on the wind. I figured it's as good a place as any to lie low. At least until midnight."

Isobel brought Varen's jacket carefully into her lap and smoothed her hands across the silhouette of the upside-down bird. She let her fingers trail the rolled edge of the patch of white cloth safety-pinned to the thicker green material.

An image of the long black coat she'd seen Varen wearing

in her dream of the bookstore flashed in her mind. It was not lost on her that in addition to being reversed, the bird on *that* coat had been white.

Slowly Isobel lifted the green mechanic's jacket from her lap. She threaded her arms through the stiff material and allowed it to settle onto her shoulders, heavier somehow than she remembered.

"We're here," she heard Gwen say.

Isobel glanced toward her window, noticing immediately how it was quieter in this area, the road narrower, the atmosphere darker, with fewer lampposts to offer relief amid the accumulating shadows.

The Cadillac slowed to a crawl as they rolled past a set of tall iron-gate doors. Isobel slid into the opposite passenger's seat for a better view. Through the window, she saw that the metal bars of the gate were knotted together in the center by a snakelike coil of silver chains. Through the iron rungs, Isobel glimpsed a smattering of what looked like squat stone houses. Tombs, she thought. There were traditional gravestones, too. Slanted and flat-faced, they stood crooked amid patches of grass.

The stones slid out of sight behind a wall as the car continued to move forward.

Gwen steered the Cadillac around the next corner, making a right onto Fayette Street. Here the brick wall gave way to pure iron, each tall bar tipped in a wicked spike. Isobel squinted through the window as Gwen rolled to a complete stop beside the front gates of the cemetery. There she idled, and the car hummed a soft and steady note while the exhaust fumes gathered behind them. The wind blew the steaming billows toward the gate, creating the illusion of fog.

"I'd tell you it's more pleasant in the daytime but I don't like to lie," Gwen said.

Through the row of black iron bars, the large stone monument that marked Poe's grave stood like a sentinel, a guardian of the gate, each of its four sides illuminated by small display lights embedded in the brick walkway.

Above them, the enormous church, Westminster Hall, loomed like a disapproving sentry. Its bell tower, topped with four hornlike spires, stretched to meet with the black cloud-filled sky.

The car began to roll forward again, and Isobel had to stoop low in order to crane her neck and take in the full extent of the church's Gothic facade through the front windshield.

Gwen angled the Cadillac toward the curb, sliding it behind a row of cars parked next to the church's front entrance—a pair of windowless double doors. She switched off the engine and yanked the keys from the ignition. Immediately the heat snapped off. The coldness that waited for them outside crept closer, pressing in on the thin barrier of their windows.

Isobel turned to peer through the rear windshield toward the front gate, focusing on the simple brass lock that held the metal doors in place. "How are we going to get in?" she asked in a whisper.

Isobel heard Gwen's seat squeak, and she glanced back at her just in time to see Gwen lean over and pop the latch on her glove compartment. The little pocket door swung out, sending a rush of maps onto the floor mat, along with a little black case.

"Same way everybody else does," Gwen answered, plucking the case from the scattered stack of maps.

26
Cemetery Sighs

"Are you *kidding* me?" Isobel whispered. "Gwen, someone's going to see us!"

"Would you just hold the flashlight still?" Switching angles, Gwen lowered herself onto her knees in front of the gate. She peered up at the padlock and, taking one of the two metal tools she'd pulled from the black case, slipped its flat, spatula-looking end sideways into the keyhole. Holding the lock steady with one hand, she pressed her thumb against the long, sticklike handle of the spatula tool, adding tension. Next she took the second tool, its tip a thin, sharp point, and shoved it into the toothy slot, wiggling it back and forth. The faint sound of metal scraping against metal echoed through the cemetery.

Isobel stood directly over Gwen, hoping to shield her actions from the sight line of any passing cars. Or security patrol vehicles. Or officers on foot.

In one hand, Isobel held the black leather zip-up case inside which lay a full assortment of long metal tools. In her other hand, she squeezed the tiny flashlight attached to Gwen's mad tangle of keys so that a dim ray shot out from the miniature bulb, casting just enough of a glow to illuminate the lock.

Turning her head from side to side, she glanced either way down the sidewalk and then behind them, across the street.

"Would you quit moving?" Gwen snapped.

"I'm trying to keep a lookout."

"Well, stop it!" she hissed. "I told you. The entire gang who watches from inside the church left for dinner thirty minutes ago. Why do you think I waited so long to come get you? The way I see it, we've got an hour and a half easy. Maybe longer if they spring for martinis. And the Poe Toaster fan club shouldn't start showing up until after nine at the earliest."

"Yeah, but there are people crossing the street over there. And how do we know the church doesn't have cameras?"

"It doesn't," Gwen said. "I checked."

Isobel dropped into a crouch next to Gwen, laying the leather case open against the patch of sidewalk in front of the gates. "How long does this take?"

Gwen turned to glare at her. "Maybe you'd like to find a place where we can dig ourselves *under*? Say hello to Edgar on our way up. Or how about this?" She pulled the picking tool free from the padlock and pointed its spindly end at Isobel. "*You* can try shimmying up and over while I go in the normal way, because I'm not hiking my tuchus over any walls."

"Okay, okay!" Isobel said. "Just . . . can we hurry up?"

"Can I get my light back?"

Keys clanking, Isobel aimed the tiny flashlight at the lock.

"Hmm," Gwen said. She tapped the metal tool against her lips before holding it out to Isobel the way a surgeon might

offer a used scalpel to her nurse. "Hand me the ligature direc-
tor, would you? It's the one that looks like a claw."

Isobel snatched the spiked tool from Gwen. She tucked it
into a random spot in the open case and turned the flashlight
toward the others. She scanned the row of neatly aligned
sharp metal objects, each secured with its own elastic band. It
seemed as if at least half of them had ends hooked like claws.
"Which one is it?" she whispered. "I can't tell. And what are
you even doing with a lock-picking tool kit anyway?"

Gwen grabbed the hand that held the flashlight and, aiming the low glow in her own face, eyed Isobel with a baleful
glare. "They're not lock-picking tools," she said. "They're
orthodontic *instruments*. My dad keeps a set in both cars in
case he ever has to make hospital calls for face trauma patients."

"And you use them to pick locks?"

"I always sterilize them when I'm done."

Isobel twisted her hand in Gwen's, aiming the flashlight
at her own face. "Okay, Gwen, what I mean is—how the hell
do you know how to pick a lock in the first place?"

Dropping Isobel's hand, Gwen reached down to the
black leather case and extracted the instrument she needed
before returning to her work. "When I was a kid, I wanted
to be a magician when I grew up," she murmured. "Harry,
the all-time master, was my idol. I still have a poster of him
hanging in my room."

Isobel's face scrunched with incredulity. *"Potter?"* she
asked.

Gwen's head snapped toward Isobel. *"Houdini*, Isobel,"

she all but shouted. "Harry Houdini. The friggin' Handcuff King!"

"Okay!" Isobel threw up both hands, nearly dropping the keys. "Sorry!"

Gwen snatched for Isobel's wrist, aiming the light toward the lock again.

"I've since learned that picking a lock is a lot like talking to a guy," she said. "Sometimes all you need is just the right amount of . . . *force*."

Click.

Isobel's mouth fell open in the same moment the shackle popped free. Quickly Gwen stood.

"Here," she said. "Take these."

Isobel rose, still gaping as Gwen shoved the instruments into her hand.

Checking over her shoulder once, Gwen yanked the lock from the gate and gave the metal doors a light shove. They eased open with a low and rusty groan.

Gwen hurried in.

"C'mon," she said, turning back. "I think I hear a car coming."

Isobel stooped to grab the case full of tools, then darted through the gates. She had heard it too, the hushed monotone hum of a vehicle's slow approach. Together, she and Gwen turned to push the gates shut, and while Isobel held the iron doors steady, Gwen threaded one thin arm through to snap the padlock back in place, effectively locking them inside the cemetery.

"Quick," Gwen whispered. "Get down. Doesn't have its lights on, so it's gotta be a cop."

Isobel backpedaled away from the gate, searching for somewhere to hide. She froze, though, when she realized that she was standing right in front of Poe's grave.

Shaped like an enormous white chess piece, the monument stood taller and wider than a person, raised off the brick walkway by a square-cut stone base. Embedded in the center of the memorial was a portrait of Poe embossed on a giant bronze medallion. His eyes, two chiseled holes, seemed to watch her with an expression that in the mix of shadow and light looked nothing short of stricken.

It took her back to the vision Pinfeathers had shown her. Poe's final moments played out again in her mind's eye, like a horror movie she couldn't turn away from.

"What are you doing?" Gwen rasped, rushing to her side. "I said get down!"

Grabbing hold of Isobel's wrist, Gwen pulled her behind the side of the monument that faced away from the front gates. Together, they pressed their backs against frozen stone, the contents of Isobel's backpack digging into her spine.

Isobel squeezed Gwen's arm. She pointed at the elongated Siamese-twin shape their shadows cast against the side of the tomb directly across from them. They sank down in unison, their shadows melding into one, blending in with humpbacked silhouettes of the surrounding stone markers. Staying low, they balanced on their haunches, listening to the sound of squeaky brakes as the car eased to a halt.

A flashlight beam shot past them, slicing through the darkness. Like a searchlight, it trailed down the walkway and over the slabs of stone. Isobel huddled closer to Gwen, pulling her own shoulder in from where it had been poking out on one side of the grave. Isobel held her breath, and she could tell that Gwen was doing the same.

A sudden scratchy burst of static erupted from what sounded like a two-way radio. A man's voice broke through the fuzz. "Unit ten, we've got a call for backup at the harbor."

Isobel strained to hear, unable to help but wonder if the call had anything to do with her disappearance. She had no doubt that her father would have contacted the police by now. Had he already called Mom, too?

"Copy that," a voice answered. "Just checking on old Westminster. It's still quiet over here, so we're on our way."

The flashlight beam made one more arc over the cemetery before bouncing away. Beside her, Isobel could feel Gwen releasing her breath in a slow exhale.

Isobel began to relax too—until one last burst of static zipped through the air, carrying with it a snatch of melody, a woman humming. Three notes, haunting and beautiful, drifted through the cemetery before a motorized drone, like the sound of a power window rolling up, cut it short.

Isobel knew that melody. The lullaby.

Quickly she craned her head around the side of the grave. She glanced toward the front entrance of the cemetery just in time to catch the red glow of the patrol car's taillights as it slid out of sight.

Isobel gripped Gwen's leather case of tools to her chest. "Did you hear that?"

"Yeah," Gwen answered in a whisper. "But whatever it is, I doubt it'll keep them busy for long. Let's go before someone else circles by."

With that, Gwen pushed away from the monument and stepped down onto the pathway. Isobel turned to follow, but something on the side of Poe's grave marker caught her eye.

"Gwen, wait," Isobel called, forgetting for a moment to keep her voice low.

"Shh!" Gwen hissed. Isobel could hear her hurrying back up the walkway. "Come on, Isobel. You can pay your respects during normal business hours. Right now we need to hide!"

"No, look," Isobel said. She placed a hand on the stone, her fingertips tracing the carved letters that arced in a rainbow shape.

VIRGINIA CLEMM POE

BORN

AUGUST 15, 1822

DIED

JANUARY 30, 1847

"Poe's wife," Isobel whispered. "I didn't know she was buried here too."

"Well, say hello if you have to," Gwen said, "but make it quick. One, it's freezing out here, two, we're officially breaking the law, and three, I think you're standing on her anyway."

"She died so young," Isobel said. "No wonder he was always so sad."

"Yes, it's breaking my brittle little freeze-dried heart. Isobel, please. Can we at least get out of the spotlights?"

Isobel felt Gwen latch hold of her arm again and pull her forward. Yet her eyes lingered on the stone, unable to break away from Virginia's name, highlighted by the warm yellow light.

How had Varen said she'd died? Tuberculosis? She thought that sounded right.

She could recall Varen telling her to write it down on one of the index cards the night before the project. Back in Poe's era, though, the disease had been called "consumption" because of the way the sickness seemed to slowly devour its victim from the inside out, causing its sufferer to cough up blood.

Varen had told her that Virginia had been playing the piano for Poe and her mother the day the illness had revealed itself. She'd been singing when, out of nowhere, a single drop of blood landed on her bottom lip.

Red Death, Isobel thought.

"Psst!" Gwen hissed. "This way!"

Isobel stepped back from the grave. Adjusting the straps of her backpack, she turned to follow after Gwen as she moved farther down the redbrick path that skirted one side of the huge church.

Ahead, Isobel saw that the path tapered as it made its way between two rows of stone sepulchers. The low-lying tombs sat facing one another, like neighboring houses on a narrow street.

Isobel strode toward them, and the shadows around her grew thicker. Glancing down, she noticed a long white slab set into the center of the brick walkway, someone's name chiseled into the alabaster stone. Stepping around the slab, she hurried to catch up with Gwen, who waited for her between the two rows of aboveground crypts.

Tiny flecks of snow began to light on the pointed roof-tops of the squat stone chambers. Isobel glanced at the hinged doors that adorned the face of each, the iron panels large enough to allow for a single coffin to slide through. They reminded her of the kind of doors found on old-fashioned furnaces. Or morgue refrigerators. She had to wonder, though, why these doors needed hinges at all if they were never meant to be reopened.

"Watch out for the drain," Gwen said, pointing toward Isobel's feet.

"Drain?"

Still clutching Gwen's keys, the case of orthodontic instruments now tucked under one arm, Isobel pressed the on button for the flashlight. As the bulb sprang to life, she aimed the slim beam downward, illuminating a cement drain entrenched in the walkway. It ran between a pair of parallel tombs that, unlike the other face-to-face crypts, flanked the walkway lengthwise. No doubt the drain was meant to keep the tunnel-like section from flooding with rainwater.

Moving to one side of the drain, Isobel placed her hand

against the tomb to her right, allowing the rough stone to guide her.

Gwen pressed onward, navigating a path Isobel could tell she had taken before. She turned left and disappeared behind one of the tombs. Isobel spurred herself forward, entering an open courtyard. To her right, next to an ancient and gnarled tree, stood the set of gates that looked out on Greene Street.

"Over here," Gwen whispered.

A squeaking sound drew Isobel's attention away from the street to where Gwen tugged at another gate recessed beneath a brick archway, one that seemed to lead into the lower portion of the church. Smoky glass backed the iron bars, hiding from view whatever lay within. Isobel knew right away that it must lead to the catacombs Gwen had mentioned before.

Isobel took a step in the direction of the door but paused, glancing toward the rear portion of the cemetery, where the ground arched into hilly terrain dotted with slabs and still more large and closely quartered aboveground tombs.

As she looked out over the crowded landscape, it struck Isobel as odd that there didn't appear to be any angels or other decorative figures guarding any of the stone burial chambers. There were no seraphs or weeping women bearing laurels. There were no lyres or even crosses. Only stone and mortar, marble and granite. Even though they *were* in a graveyard, the scene struck her as very lonely.

"*Isobel,*" Gwen hissed.

She turned to see Gwen hanging out the catacomb door. "Would you get in here? You can take the tour later!"

Isobel glanced behind her to the gates that faced Greene Street. A car whooshed by, and somewhere in the distance, she thought she could hear a faint chattering growing nearer. She turned and jogged to meet Gwen, who stood back from the door, allowing Isobel to slide into the musty chamber.

Underneath the church, it smelled like chalk and earth.

Taking the miniature flashlight from Isobel, Gwen shone it through the darkened space. More vaults lay scattered around a cavernous room. Gravestones, too, poked up through a floor of dust and dirt.

"That door," Gwen said, pointing across the room to yet another iron gate backed by the same opaque glass as the one they'd entered through. It seemed to glow, lit from behind by nearby city lamps and building lights. "It lets out to the rear of the cemetery. Right behind another row of mausoleums. From there, you've got a straight-shot view of Poe's old grave. But I thought we'd hang out in here till midnight," she said, and aimed the beam of her flashlight upward, illuminating the underbelly of the church. Stone archways filled with pockets of spiderwebs stretched across the ceiling. "If we're lucky, we'll be able to hear the Poe Patrol whenever they get back from dinner."

Isobel stared at the door that led to the back of the graveyard as she strode forward through the gloom, moving toward its dim glow. She stopped at the place where the light from the small flashlight reached its limit.

While she could discern the tops of tombstones and the general perimeters of the room, she could barely make out the dirt floor itself. The darkness created a thick blanket that hid the outline of steps and short brick barriers and squat grave markers.

"What time is it now?" Isobel asked, her voice echoing.

"Almost nine, I'm guessing," Gwen said. "I'm not sure. I turned off my phone so it wouldn't give a signal. You did too, right?"

"Left it with Dad," Isobel murmured.

"Even better," Gwen said.

Isobel turned to face Gwen again, watching as she swept her skirts up from the dusty ground to tie them in a knot over the pair of thermal stretch pants she wore. Gwen lowered herself with a grunt to sit on the ground, her back pressed to the front of one of the long tombs. After that, she twisted to aim her flashlight up at the name engraved above the rusted iron door.

"Well, hello . . . J . . . Meredith," she said. "Hope you don't mind the intrusion. No, no. No need to get up. We're not the fancy type. I'm Gwen and this is Isobel. Isobel, J. Meredith; J. Meredith, Isobel."

Isobel took the black case out from beneath her arm and offered the tomb a pinched smile and a slight wave with her free hand. She drew up to the mausoleum and let her backpack slip to the ground, then lowered herself to sit next to Gwen on the other side of the metal door.

Gwen let out a long sigh as she tilted her head back to rest against the tomb, while Isobel reached for her backpack.

"I'm going to put your dad's tools in my bag," she said.

Gwen rolled her head in Isobel's direction. "Not tools," she muttered. "Hammer and wrench are tools. Orthodontists use *instruments*."

"You hungry?" Isobel asked. Digging deeper into the bag, she pulled out two of the granola bars she'd packed.

"*Always,*" Gwen replied, and snatched one up. She tore open the package. "Dunno if it's really kosher to dine in catacombs, though," she said, taking half the bar in one bite.

Isobel fumbled to open her own bar. Even though she didn't feel hungry, she knew she needed to eat. She chewed her first bite without tasting.

The sound of their munching seemed to fill the otherwise silent space. After a moment, Gwen released her hold on the tiny flashlight button, allowing the darkness to turn both of them into shadows too.

"Where do you suppose your dad is right now?" Gwen asked.

"No telling," Isobel said, and even though she had half the granola bar left, she nudged Gwen, offering her the rest. "Police station, maybe."

"Thanks," Gwen said. She took the bar, and Isobel could hear her chew and swallow loudly.

"I have water, too," Isobel said.

"I'm good."

They were quiet for a long time after that. Then, when the soundlessness began to grow loud in Isobel's ears, she spoke again.

"I bet Dad's called Mom by now," she said softly. "She's

probably scrambling right this second to get a plane ticket. And someone to watch Danny."

"Mmm," Gwen said.

"I can't help thinking about it," Isobel whispered. "About what I'm doing to them right now. About how crazy they must be feeling. The things they're saying to each other. The things they're thinking."

Isobel pulled her knees close, hugging them to her chest.

"Sometimes," she went on, "I wonder if any of this would have ever happened the way it did if I could have just *talked* to them about what was going on. I mean, what was *really* going on. Maybe it wouldn't have made a difference if I'd told Dad about the things I was seeing, about Varen's journal and the Poe book and the dreamworld. I don't think he would have ever believed me. But not just because of the weird stuff." She paused. "Until I met Varen, it was never like that, where I couldn't just go to my dad and tell him . . . whatever. Because no matter what it was, I never had to doubt whether he'd be on my side. I mean with something that *really* mattered."

Isobel stopped again, dropping her forehead to her knees.

Gwen said nothing, but Isobel kept talking anyway, the words spilling out from some inner wound she hadn't realized had begun to bleed.

"Why?" she asked. "What about Varen changed all that?"

Taking in a shuddering breath, she tasted dust. "I guess," she continued, deciding to take a stab at answering her own question, since Gwen had yet to offer one, "I guess that by wanting to keep us apart, Dad thought he was protecting me.

I'm trying to understand that, to get that, but it's hard when he never even gave Varen a chance, you know? When he decided in a split second, after just one look, that he couldn't accept Varen even being in my *proximity.* No one could. His friends, *my* friends, my parents, the entire school—everyone wanted to pretend like, together, Varen and I formed some kind of . . . I don't know . . . combustive chemical mixture that could blow everything up. I think you were the only one, the only one in the whole world, who it didn't make any difference to, Gwen. Did you know that?"

Isobel waited. When Gwen still made no response, she glanced over to hear that her friend's breathing had turned slow and measured.

Asleep . . .

Taking into account the drive Gwen had made that day, coupled with her earlier survey of the cemetery and the stress of picking her up from the harbor, Isobel didn't doubt that she'd probably dozed off after Isobel's third sentence.

But that was okay, she told herself. Because it hadn't been Gwen who she'd been speaking to anyway. Not really.

Leaning back again, Isobel shut her eyes and, releasing a sigh, rested the back of her head against the tomb.

More than anything, it felt as if she'd been delivering a final speech. Her last words to herself. *For* herself. For the girl she'd once been but could never again resurrect, the girl her father had been so afraid of losing and had lost anyway.

But, Isobel thought with a bleak and sad smile, what better place to bury what was dead than in a cemetery?

27

The Most Lovely Dead

A soft scraping noise made Isobel open her eyes.

She scanned the outline of tombs but saw no movement within their ranks. Listening, she heard only the high, keening whistle of the wind as it whipped along the sides of the church.

Isobel rubbed one eye with the back of her hand. She turned her head to see if Gwen was still asleep, only to find her gone.

"Gwen?" she called into the darkness, which seemed to eat the syllable right out of her mouth.

There was no answer.

Hands fumbling, Isobel groped in the dirt for the knot of Gwen's keys. She found the flashlight amid the tangle of metal and plastic and, squeezing it, aimed the glowing bulb toward her backpack. The key-chain watch, still clipped to the front zipper, gave off a sharp glint. Isobel pulled the bag into her lap and flipped open the butterfly's silver wings.

The tiny clock's three thin black hands did not show the time, but spun chaotically, chasing one another in fast loops.

A dream? Impossible. She couldn't have fallen asleep. She'd only shut her eyes for a moment.

The sudden sound of soft humming caused Isobel to drop both the watch and the flashlight. She scrambled to her feet and squinted through the gloom toward where the door leading to the rear of the cemetery now stood ajar.

A dim blue glow emanated from the slight gap, lighting a path through the obstacle course of broken stones, low-lying crypts, and uneven ground.

"G-Gwen?" Isobel called, louder than before. Again, she received no response.

The melody, as though drifting up from the depths of some fathomless well, continued to echo through the catacombs.

It was the same song that had filtered through the stereo in Varen's car in the dream where he'd taken her to the rose garden. The same collection of notes that had squeezed past the static of her bedroom radio the evening she'd found his jacket. It was the lullaby she'd heard playing through the living room TV that night with Pinfeathers, and over the crackling hush of the gramophone in the dreamworld bookshop. The very same one she'd heard only minutes before in this very cemetery.

Isobel began to move in the direction of the humming. She stopped as soon as the toes of her boots met with the edge of the slanted porcelain-blue shaft of light that spilled from the door. Hesitating, held in place by her own indecision, she wondered if she dared look inside.

Did she even have a choice?

Maybe, she thought, she should do something to try and

wake herself. If she cried out, would Gwen hear her and be able to rouse her?

While Isobel deliberated, the humming beyond the door grew stronger, the melody rising and falling in its familiarly haunting and melancholy pattern.

Curiosity overriding her trepidation, Isobel took her first step into the blue light, where the coldness of the catacombs seemed to intensify. A draft rose up around her, sending a chill through to her bones, as though every spirit trapped within had decided to come out and watch her approach.

But toward what? Or whom?

One tenuous step after another brought Isobel closer and closer to the door until she stood just beside it.

The door swung inward at her slightest touch, making no sound as it moved.

Where she knew she should have found the cold night and the back of the cemetery, Isobel instead discovered another chamber in the catacombs.

Immediately her focus settled on the source of the humming, a shrouded figure who lay faceup on the lid of a horizontal tomb.

Positioned in the center of the room, the coffin-shaped crypt sat atop a set of stairs stationed directly below a blue stained-glass skylight embedded in the stone ceiling.

Moonlight, sheer and diaphanous, poured through the sapphire panes. It bathed the slender body that lay concealed beneath a snow-white sheet in dappled patterns.

The melody drew Isobel farther, beckoning her like a siren's song into the room.

Something crunched under her foot, but she ignored it, too distracted by the array of broken and empty-eyed Noc faces that seemed to watch her from their perches on the rows of shelves lining the narrow chamber's four walls.

Suddenly realizing where she stood, Isobel froze.

She was back. Back in the dreamworld. Back in the blue marble crypt that held the sarcophagus with the stone woman lying on top.

But unlike before, the lid of the tomb was no longer ominously shifted open.

While the shrouded figure kept on humming, Isobel glanced to the far corner of the room, to the place where she had first encountered the blue-haired Noc who had called himself Scrimshaw—the same Noc she had seen in the vision of Poe's death.

The space he had once occupied was empty, cleared away to reveal the stone floor. Like Pinfeathers, Scrimshaw must have managed to piece himself back together. And now he was out somewhere, roaming the woodlands.

Lifting a hand to her collar, grasping the hamsa, Isobel drew nearer to the tomb. She mounted the steps, and as she edged closer to the shrouded form, the woman's humming began to slow.

She reached out a quivering hand and grabbed a portion of the stiff fabric close to the woman's face. Keeping her other hand firmly clamped around the hamsa, she began to draw the sheet slowly away.

The figure beneath stopped humming.

Inch by inch, the sheet slipped free to reveal a girl dressed in a pink party dress, the same one Isobel had worn to the Grim Facade.

She uttered a clipped cry.

Blond hair lay in a halo of loose ringlets around the girl's head. Soft curls framed an all-too-familiar face—*her* face.

Isobel let go of the sheet. The covering continued to slide off the sarcophagus, the cloth pooling onto the stairs and tumbling over Isobel's shoes.

Inky splotches began to seep through the material of the pink dress, the layers of skirts and bodice transforming to pure ebony.

Isobel watched with mounting horror, unable to look away.

The girl lay prone on the slab, her still lips painted a false pink, her eyes closed. A slanted needle-thin scratch marred her right cheek, the cut a deep purple against her ashen skin.

Bound to her stiff and pale hands by a pink ribbon, the same pink ribbon Isobel had given Varen, the corpse held a bouquet of pristine white lilies. Their stifling perfume, now unleashed, filled the tomb, lacing the stagnant air with their choking fragrance.

A twin version of Isobel's hamsa circled her double's sallow neck. It gleamed in the frosted moonlight until a blanket of cloud cover passed over the skylight, turning the opal in the center of the charm dim and milky.

Isobel took a step backward and stumbled down the stairs, nearly falling.

She whirled for the door but it was gone now, replaced by flat stone.

"No!" she shouted, the word reverberating around her.

Rushing to the wall, she beat her palms against the place where the door had stood wide open only moments before.

Trapped, she spun to face the interior of the tomb again, but the sudden motion caused the room to reel and tilt. Tossed off her feet, Isobel slammed onto cold stone that pressed into her back and shoulder blades like a slab of ice.

Reaching out, kicking her legs and thrashing, she found herself boxed in by close narrow walls of smooth marble.

Isobel screamed. Contained within the narrow coffin-shape space, the sound of her cries, she knew, would pierce only her own ears.

The sarcophagus— Somehow, she'd become sealed within.

28
Unraveled

Isobel woke with a sharp gasp.

The outline of long tombs and graves swam into her focus. Hunched in the gloom of the catacombs, they looked like shadow creatures waiting to attack.

Beside her, Gwen sat propped against the tomb of J. Meredith, her head lolled onto one shoulder, her mouth slightly agape, emitting soft snores.

Isobel twisted where she sat, whipping her head to look in the direction of the door that had taken her into the separate chamber of the marble crypt. It was closed, and the light filtering in through the opaque grime-stained sheet of glass no longer shone ethereal blue, but a dull bone yellow.

She'd been dreaming after all. Or was she still?

Isobel grabbed the flashlight once more and felt a funny sense of déjà vu as she reached for the butterfly watch next. She unclipped it from her backpack and clicked it open to see if the hands were still spinning, but they remained still, except for the second hand, which twitched along at its normal rate.

The moment her brain registered the time, a strange prickling sensation spread through her, causing the metal casing of the tiny watch to turn ice-cold in her palm.

The hour hand and the minute hand were almost aligned; both aimed a full notch past twelve.

It was five after one. More than an entire hour past midnight.

Isobel shot to her feet and dropped the keys. They landed on her backpack with a muffled *clank*. Shoving the watch into one pocket of Varen's jacket, she launched into a run, leaving Gwen behind as she scuttled around tombs and hopped over broken stones. Blindly, not caring if she fell, she made her way to the door that she hoped would, this time, take her out of the catacombs and into the graveyard, to the site of Poe's original burial.

But what if she found that the roses had already been placed? What would she do if she'd missed him? If Reynolds had already come and gone?

Pushing all thought aside, Isobel pulled the iron handle of the door, yanking it open. The rusted hinges shrieked, their cries echoing through the catacombs. A gust of frozen air laden with a cascade of powdery snow whirled in over the threshold, sweeping between her feet to mingle with the dust, creating ghostly swirls.

Isobel paused to give one last backward glance toward Gwen, who still lay sound asleep, bundled to her chin in her coat, and the scarf Isobel had given her, looking like someone's lost doll.

Before she could change her mind, call out to Gwen and wake her, she ducked through the door and out into the darkened cemetery.

Snow sifted from the sky in downy flakes, giving the tops of the tombs thin, fleecy blankets. It collected on the walls and gathered in the crooked elbows and outstretched fingers of the withered trees. Flecks of white caught in Isobel's lashes, blurring her vision. She blinked them away. Then, from somewhere close by, she heard the echo of voices.

The sound of people chatting and laughing arose from beyond the far wall. A woman's high-pitched laugh ricocheted through the cemetery, bouncing off silent headstones and tombs, their slate faces impervious to her glee.

Isobel set her footsteps down carefully as she ascended a small set of brick stairs that led from the catacombs. She glanced from side to side, only to find her view blocked by several tall crypts, and entered into a narrow space between two garage-size tombs. She put her hands against the walls on either side of her to help guide her as she pressed forward through the tight passageway.

She stopped when she reached the end. From where she now stood, Isobel could just make out the silhouette of Poe's old grave, recognizing its shape from the grainy photo of the Poe Toaster. Thick and heavy-looking, like a milestone marker, the solemn stone stood between two squat, snow-capped shrubs.

Even though she could not make out the writing on the face of the stone, the tiny figure of a raven engraved into the top curved portion left her with no doubt that it was the one she sought.

Unable to see the base of the grave due to the shrubs,

Isobel could not tell if the roses had been left. But she could still hear the nearby jumble of voices as the talking and laughing continued to grow in volume.

Crouching low, she poked her head out slightly and peered around the side of the tomb, leaning forward just enough to catch sight of the crowd that watched from beyond the Greene Street gates.

They stood huddled together in a tight cluster, gloved hands wrapped around the iron bars.

Most of the onlookers wore heavy coats, hoods, and ski caps, but there were several decked out in long Victorian-style cloaks as well. At least one of the men sported an old-fashioned top hat. Thick scarves wrapped their throats, while plumes of white breath accompanied their loud talking.

Isobel saw that some of the watchers held cameras; the lenses glinted silver in the glow of the streetlamps, and the red dots of power lights pierced the darkness like demon eyes.

She sank slowly back into her hiding place, aware that one wrong move on her part would no doubt unleash a flurry of flashes. She knew the observers had to be combing the spaces between tombs and scanning the landscape for even the slightest hint of movement among the gravestones. And that fact alone was enough to allow her a small measure of relief.

Reynold's fan club wouldn't still be here if he'd already come and gone, right? If he'd already paid tribute, the crowd would have dispersed by now for sure.

Then again, Isobel thought, *maybe not.*

Taking a brief glance back to the place where Poe's marker stood, Isobel saw that the view from the Greene Street gates to Poe's old grave was completely blocked by another aboveground tomb. No one watching from the street could ever get a clear shot, just like Mr. Swanson had said. And that had to be why so few pictures of the Poe Toaster existed.

Still, something told her the group wouldn't be waiting, watching with an almost palpable, nervous excitement, if they weren't expecting something to happen at any moment.

Isobel's ears perked up when one of the voices emanating from Greene Street, a man's sturdy baritone, lifted above all the others and began to recite lines from "The Raven."

> *"Nothing farther then he uttered — not a*
> *feather then he fluttered —*
> *Till I scarcely more than muttered, 'Other*
> *friends have flown before —*
> *On the morrow he will leave me, as my*
> *Hopes have flown before.'*
> *Then the bird said, 'Nevermore.'"*

She wrapped her arms around herself, tucking them in close in an effort to fight off the cold. Willing Reynolds to appear, she kept her eyes on Poe's grave, and as she listened to the poem, it occurred to her that some of the watchers might have come to the graveyard in previous years. It was possible they knew something she didn't since they congregated at the side gates of the cemetery rather than the front where she and Gwen had first entered. Maybe they were hoping to catch a glimpse of Reynolds as he wove his way through the cemetery grounds.

It made her wonder if she should try to get closer now. Or was it better to wait here, at a distance?

In the end, she knew making a move sooner rather than later wasn't worth the risk of being spotted. Besides that, there was no telling from which direction Reynolds would enter the cemetery, if he hadn't already. How could she know when she had witnessed Reynolds creating an entry between his realm and hers only once before.

He had done so from the midst of the woodlands on that first occasion Isobel had found herself within the dreamworld. He'd fixed one gloved hand around an imaginary knob, and the door had appeared at his silent behest. And then he'd opened it to reveal the interior of Isobel's very own bedroom.

Though she knew that he *could* pass from one reality into the other, how he did it still baffled her. If what he had said about the worlds becoming separate when she'd broken the link was true—if the dimensions once again became parted, untraversable from either side, then what allowed *him* the ability to pass back and forth at will? Furthermore, what prevented her? Or Varen?

Isobel frowned at that question.

Apparently, there was not much that *could* prevent Varen. Hadn't he *and* Pinfeathers already proven on more than one occasion that there were other ways of reemerging into this world?

A harsh wind blew through the graveyard, whistling over the tops of the tombs. It moaned above her as it coursed through the passageway of her hiding place, bringing with it a surge of snow flurries.

Isobel shuddered against the rush of frozen wind. She took in a deep breath, drawing the cold into her lungs. Exhaling again, she reminded herself that her questions would have to wait. Right now, she needed to keep her mind clear.

Whenever and however Reynolds chose to appear, she would have to be ready.

There was no sign of him yet, however, just the audience of the dead, and that of the living, too. The Greene Street crowd continued to chirp and chortle from their barrier point, a few of them inserting comments as the reader within their ranks bore onward with Poe's poem, his resonant voice rising above the rest.

> *"'Prophet!' said I, 'thing of evil!—prophet still,*
> *if bird or devil!—*
> *Whether Tempter sent, or whether tempest*
> *tossed thee here ashore,*
> *Desolate, yet all undaunted, on this desert*
> *land enchanted—*
> *On this home by Horror haunted—tell me*
> *truly, I implore—*
> *Is there—is there balm in Gilead?—tell*
> *me—tell me, I implore!'*
> *Quoth the raven, 'Nevermore.'"*

Leaning out again, Isobel saw a set of metal steps a few feet away to her right. They extended down from the back door of Westminster Hall and led out into the yard. At the top of the stairs, a tall and slender set of double doors made entirely of glass revealed another small gathering of people she hadn't noticed before. Unlike those huddling in the cold outside the gates, this group stood within the warmth of the hall, sharing an unobstructed view of Poe's original burial site.

These, Isobel thought, must be the Poe scholars Mr. Swanson had told her about—the ones who gathered every year to oversee the ritual and to protect the Poe Toaster.

Seeing them there made her doubly glad she'd decided to stay put.

At the front of this cluster stood a man with a beard and glasses; stern-faced, but not unkind-looking. While the others behind him continued to chat among themselves, this man seemed restless. He kept taking his hands in and out of his pockets, checking his wristwatch, and occasionally glancing toward the Greene Street gates.

What was he so worried about? Did he think the Poe Toaster wasn't coming? If nothing else, his anxiety assured her that, as of yet, Reynolds had not shown. Then she remembered what Mr. Swanson had said about people climbing the gates in years past, attempting to intercept the rite.

How fast could security get there if they were called into action? Probably within seconds.

A low scraping sound called Isobel's attention away from

her thoughts and back to Poe's marker. Silence spread over the cemetery as the crowd of onlookers watching from the gates settled into hushed tones, shushing the man who had been reading aloud.

When the scraping noise came again, Isobel's gaze narrowed on the crypt that stood catty-corner to Poe's old grave.

She stared in disbelief as the slab door, which faced Poe's marker, began to wobble in its frame. Then, gradually, an inch at a time, it started to shift inward, with the heavy, thunder-like rumble of stone sliding against stone.

A gust of wind rushed out of the open tomb, sending forth a burst of white substance, something heavier than the snow, denser. The ash flowed out to mingle with the frozen flakes in a flurry just before one black boot appeared at the threshold, imprinting itself into the virgin snow.

Isobel's heart jarred in her chest. She rose to her feet, the rush of blood in her ears blocking out all other sounds. She kept her eyes on the figure that emerged from the black mouth of the tomb. Like caressing hands, the inky darkness within clung to his form, as though reluctant to let him go.

Isobel stood in shock within the recess of her hiding place, her body tingling from head to foot, a vibration starting inside of her and growing so intense, so electrifying that she wasn't certain she would be able to bring herself to move at all when the time came.

She watched as the masked man strode forward toward the grave marker. As he came out into the open, she forced herself to take a step back, allowing the shadows to envelop her fully.

Flurries began to light on his black hat, filling the wide brim, their whiteness matching the scarf that concealed the lower half of his face. Tall and straight, his shrouded form cut a sinister figure amid the scattering of tombstones. His cloak swirled around his feet as he walked, the fabric nearly brushing the ground.

He moved slowly, his chin down, the brim of his hat pulled low over his eyes so that no part of his face showed.

Midway to the grave, he paused, causing Isobel to stiffen. He stood motionless for a moment, his head remaining bowed. In one gloved hand, she saw the three long-stemmed roses she had read about in the article. In the other, Reynolds carried a bottle, and a brandy glass was tucked between his fingers.

Isobel slid farther backward into her hiding place, afraid that he had somehow become alerted to her presence. Her eyes remained on him, the adrenaline within her building, telling her to move, to *do* something.

He turned his head in her direction, and she stilled her breathing.

Could he see her? Even through the veil of darkness cast between the tombs, had he been able to perceive someone watching?

She saw him give a slow nod, a deep and purposeful inclination of his head. Heart pounding, she tried to think of how to react as he raised one gloved hand—the same hand that held the roses—to meet the brim of his hat. That was when Isobel realized that he hadn't been looking at her at all, that the gesture must have been meant for the group watching from inside the church. This was a signal, she thought. Reynolds's own salute to the Poe scholars, a sign that told them he was the one. And one of them.

Isobel glanced back at the glass doors at the top of the iron grate stairs, just in time to see the man in the glasses return the gesture of acknowledgment with one of his own— an open palm.

She wondered if they'd seen Reynolds come through the tomb door. She didn't think so. The crypt stood only a few feet in front of and below the door from where they watched. To them, it must have looked like Reynolds had simply stepped out from between the tomb and the side of the church.

She saw the other scholars smiling as they scrunched closer together in the doorway, their faces nearly pressed to the glass.

They looked excited, even giddy, their expressions lit with the glow of eager anticipation, like they were watching the dramatic opening act of a play.

But what would they do, Isobel wondered, if they had seen what she had? If they knew the things she did about what this man, this . . . *being*, whatever he was, had done? That it was his hand, the same hand that now clutched the roses of supposed remembrance, that had severed the line of Poe's short life?

They didn't know the truth behind what they were seeing. Like Varen, they were interacting with something they didn't understand. And like him, they did not comprehend the danger.

Isobel forced herself to look away from the scholars, back to Reynolds. But her eyes skirted past him to the open tomb door. And somehow, it clicked with her that that doorway was the opportunity she'd come for, her one hope of reaching the dreamworld. Of finding Varen.

Suddenly she knew she couldn't wait for Reynolds to finish his one-man show so she could follow after him. There would be no time for that and no way she would be able to cover the distance without being seen by everyone, including him. If she hesitated, if she didn't go right now, right this very second while Reynolds's back was turned, then it would be too late.

She crept forward on trembling legs, coming to stand just at the edge of the two tombs that concealed her.

She hunkered down, preparing to bolt.

But then she made the fatal mistake of taking one last look at Reynolds just as he lowered himself reverently onto one knee before the stone, about to play out his moment of mock tribute. One look at him there, bowing his head before Poe's grave, paying homage to the very man he had slain, doing so in full sight of people who believed he was something he wasn't, Poe's own patron saint—it caused something within her, all the weight she had been carrying up to this moment, to shift. And implode.

The memory of his lie reignited within her.

Her muscles acted without her consent, her legs carrying her out of her hiding place and into the open. The wind bit at her skin. She could hear it whistling in her ears along with the surprised cries of those who watched from the street.

Possessed by everything she had tried to repress, by the rage and frustration she hadn't been allowed to feel, Isobel surrendered control.

The snowy world around her melted away until all she saw was the dark figure who called himself Reynolds.

So absorbed in the part he'd been playing, he looked only at the last moment. By that time, it was too late for him to move away or draw one of the twin swords she knew he carried.

Isobel plowed straight into him with a shriek of fury.

The bottle and glass he held flew out of his grasp and smashed to bits against Poe's gravestone.

She heard him grunt as they fell back together, landing in the middle of one of the evergreen shrubs.

Isobel gripped his collar, the scent of fermented roses filling her nostrils. Her grip tightened around his cloak, and rolling one over the other, they tumbled from the bush and out onto the hard and frozen turf.

Using all her strength to throw the last whip-snap revolution, Isobel pulled herself on top of him, straightening her arms to slam his shoulders to the ground. His head hit with a dull thud, causing his hat to tumble away.

She bared her teeth at him as his eyes focused on her in utter shock.

"*Isobel!*" he hissed.

That's right, she thought as she reared back one fist, ready to smash her knuckles straight through his face, *it's me.*

The blood in her veins seemed to reach its boiling point as she brought her fist down hard toward his scarf-swathed nose.

In that moment, she wanted nothing more than to hear the crunch of bones. But the sound did not come. He stopped her, his large hand wrapping almost entirely around her own. Growling, Isobel yanked back on her arm, but his clutch tightened, causing her shoulder to jam in its socket.

Isobel bit back the urge to cry out. Still, tears stung at the corners of her eyes, less from the pain than from frustration. She wanted him to know what he'd done. She wanted him to feel everything he had caused her to feel. She wanted revenge.

Before he could stop her, she grabbed his white scarf with her other hand and yanked the fabric free.

It unraveled, revealing the face of the man who had taken so much from her.

29
Entombed

Almost as though she *had* struck him, Reynolds released her at once.

Startled by her own gall, Isobel fumbled back. She scrambled in a crab crawl over the frozen ground, doing her best to put distance between them before pulling herself to her feet. She dragged his long white scarf with her, tightening her grip on the fabric when the wind attempted to tug it free.

He, too, rose, his cloak snapping in the breeze.

Before her stood a man with hollow cheeks, his lips thin and pale, his nose sharp and hawkish.

No monster. No demon or angel. Only a man.

Reynolds glared at her, his dark hair, disheveled from their tussle, hanging in loosed strands around his unmasked face.

Younger than Isobel had imagined him, he had a haunted and weathered gauntness to his features. Aside from the blackened centers of his eyes, it was the one thing that suggested his true age. And yet his youth surprised her less than the fact that as far as secrets went, his face seemed to reveal none.

Could *this* really be the face of Reynolds?

If so, then why the mask? What had he been trying to hide?

"Who are you really?" she heard herself ask.

He did not answer, his jaw set in stiff defiance as they stood opposite each other.

Even with the sounds of people shouting from the gates, Isobel dared not look away.

His gaze penetrating and accusing, he held one gloved hand out to her, palm up. It was a gesture that seemed to ask for the return of his scarf.

But Isobel knew better than to come any closer.

She stepped back instead, her boots sinking into the snow.

"*Give it to me,*" he rasped, his voice urgent. His out-stretched hand balled into a fist. She saw it quiver and knew she had been right in guessing that anger simmered just beneath the surface of that austere veneer.

It was so strange to hear his familiar voice, so full of age and grim authority, coming out of someone who looked so young. *Deceptively young,* she thought. But deceptiveness was Reynolds's game. It was the hand he had always played, right from the beginning, and Isobel knew better than to gamble with him again. The stakes were too high.

"You there!" someone shouted from the church.

It was the man with the beard and glasses. He now stood outside the church on the top landing of the stairs leading out from the glass doors, a flashlight in his hand. Its beam winked toward them.

When Reynolds threw up his arm to shield his face, Isobel took another step away from him. Behind her, she felt a slight rush of air wash over her. But it wasn't like the crisp winter wind that whipped the snow about them.

This breeze felt different, cool but not frigid, the air tinged with the acrid scent of earthy decay, of ash and dust and moldering trees. Of roses. And ink.

She risked a quick glance behind her.

The tomb door stood at a distance of mere yards, still open—waiting, it seemed, for her to make the decision to enter. And Isobel knew that this doorway was really what she had come for. Not for retribution. Not to punish Reynolds or even to try to understand who he was or all that he had done. The only thing that mattered, the only thing that had *ever* mattered, she knew, was getting to Varen.

"Out of the way," she heard someone shout from the gates. "Security! Everybody, move!"

Isobel released her hold on Reynolds's scarf. It puddled at her feet, blending into the white snow. If she ran now, she thought, she could make it. She was close enough that he wouldn't be able to stop her.

"You cannot reach him," he said as though he'd somehow been able to read her thoughts. "Not that way."

In the distance, the gates rattled, followed by the sound of chains being pulled free.

"Do you seriously expect me to believe anything you say?" Isobel asked him.

"I told you what I had to," he said. "To protect this world. *Your* world."

"Did you?" Isobel took a step back and then another. The

speed of her heart, already racing, tripled when she saw him match her movements. "Is that what happened with Edgar, too?" she continued, her eyes darting to the hilt of one of his swords as it flashed silver within the shadowy folds of his cloak. "Did you do what you had to when he was calling out for you, begging for your help?"

He stopped midstep, though his expression remained unchanged.

"You said he was your friend," she went on. "And I guess now you're going to try to tell me that wasn't a lie either? I saw what happened in the hospital. I know what you did." She continued to move as she spoke, putting more and more distance between them. She kept her eyes level on him. "Whatever you are . . . whatever *monster* it is you've become . . . you should know that it is everything you deserve to be."

With that, Isobel turned, rushing headlong for the open tomb.

Somewhere far off, getting closer, she heard the wail of sirens. People yelling. Iron hinges groaning.

"Stop!" Reynolds shouted.

She ran toward the tomb, the ground racing beneath her feet. She felt as if she was rushing straight into her own grave, about to catapult herself into the yawning jaws of death itself.

"Isobel!"

She could sense him just behind her—inches away.

On the ground, she saw his shadow gaining on hers, then falling away the moment before something fast and strong—a hand—caught her around the ankle. She tripped forward and fell flat onto her stomach, the air bursting out of her lungs as the frozen snow soaked through her clothes.

Isobel groped for the archway, for anything to grab hold of. Her fingernails scraped over the stone threshold as she felt herself being drawn backward.

"No!" she shouted.

Twisting onto her side, Isobel saw him behind her, on his knees in the snow, one hand fixed like a manacle around her ankle. She pulled up the knee of her free leg, preparing to kick him, but missed when he yanked her toward him. Cringing, she cried out, gritting her teeth as the hardened, gravel-coated earth grated against her side. Then, as though she were nothing more than a rag doll, Reynolds drew her to her knees before him, bringing her to face him.

He held her by her shoulders and, shaking her once, forced her eyes to meet with his.

"Listen to me," he said. "If you cross that barrier, you *will* die! And if you die while bodily within that realm, you will become like the rest of us. The same soulless class of monster you have so ardently accused me of being!"

She only half heard these words, her attention drawn to the sudden movement that came from behind Poe's old grave marker. A familiar figure, visible over one of Reynolds's black-clad shoulders, rose up from behind the monument, her face luminous as a ghost's.

Gwen.

"Heed my words, Isobel—"

Isobel looked quickly back to Reynolds as Gwen made

her approach, hurrying toward them. Stooping, she gathered the hem of his cloak and then, just as he turned to look, Gwen pulled the fabric taut, tossing it over his head as though bagging a live rabbit.

"Heed this!" she growled as she locked her twiggy arms around Reynolds's neck in a choke hold, clamping the cloak into place over his head.

Reynolds released Isobel at once and his hands rushed to grip Gwen's arms. Gwen did her best to hold fast, clutching him tighter. Her eyes met with Isobel's, glasses knocked askew.

"Go!" she yelled.

Isobel scrambled to her feet. She hurried toward the tomb door even as Reynolds's cries for her to stop continued. At first they came muffled, distorted by the fabric of the cloak. Then, after a high-pitched shriek from Gwen, his shouting became suddenly clear again.

Isobel reached the darkness of the doorway, not bothering to slow down as she shot through to the other side. She gasped as her body passed beyond what felt like an invisible screen of static electricity. Her limbs became numbed as the sound of her footsteps echoed on the stone floor.

Whirling, she grabbed hold of the slab that lay partially shifted aside from the open archway. She shoved at it, and to her amazement, the door began to move, the thick stone grinding its way shut, following the command of her slightest push.

Through the shrinking wedge of dim light, she could see

the cemetery filling with people. The man who had watched from the church. Police officers, hands poised on their holstered guns. And Gwen sitting nearby, huddled against one of the gravestones, cradling an arm against her chest. Tears streaked her face, but her figure soon became eclipsed by another.

Reynolds ran toward her. Throwing his cloak back, he pulled free one of his swords with a harsh scrape of metal.

Isobel shoved harder against the stone door, willing it to close faster.

The gap shrunk to a mere slit.

She let go, and the stone continued to slide on its own.

Isobel stood back as Reynolds slammed to a halt before the thinning crevice.

She saw his eyes just before the door slid all the way shut, black coin-size holes fixed on her with murderous intent.

Then, with a low *boom*, the door snapped into its frame, blocking him out completely, sending a puff of ash and grime into Isobel's face.

She coughed and fumbled through the dank and enclosed space.

Throwing her arms out, she found a narrow set of walls on which to brace herself. She turned, but her toe caught on something hard and she faltered, collapsing onto an ascending stretch of stone steps. Pushing herself up on trembling arms, she peered toward the top of the stairs.

Light peeked through the clearing haze of dust. Several feet above, she saw an open doorway.

Squinting, Isobel could detect a curtain of green vines hanging over the archway in a spilling cascade. Flowers dotted the vines, their heavy heads lolling sleepily amid waxy green foliage.

With a gasp, she pulled herself onto her feet. She mounted the ash-coated stairs and rushed to the doorway. Parting the vines with one hand, she passed through the archway and into a circular room. Countless crimson buds climbed the iron-gate perimeters, their interlacing boughs and vines thick enough to form a living wall between the interior of the room and whatever lay without.

The vines and flowers commandeered the domed ceiling as well, though Isobel thought she could detect the mesh of black tree limbs and the hint of violet light through one of the thinner sections.

Gazing upward, Isobel thought there must be thousands of the flowers, maybe even hundreds of thousands—every single bud the same deep bloodred hue. In addition to the climbing roses, long-stemmed roses grew along the base of the trellised wall, their blooms blending in with all the others.

Their overpowering fragrance, like the smell from a shattered bottle of perfume, filled her nostrils with every breath, making her light-headed.

A carpet of ruby petals covered the circular marble floor, while several open archways lined the curved wall, all of them leading out into what appeared to be rose-lined tunnels.

Though Isobel saw no sign of the fountain, she knew she was in the garden from her dream—the place where Varen had told her he would be waiting.

At last, she'd made it.

She took a step toward the center of the room, her sight set on one of the open archways. But then she stopped, distracted by a staticky voice that came from behind.

"Now, there's a surprise," the voice said.

Isobel's momentary elation withered in an instant, replaced by a crawling fear that caused her heart to leap into her throat.

"I didn't expect to see *you* here. Gone and locked out my old friend, did you?" the acidic voice asked. "And here I've been waiting *so* long to find him. Ever since he broke my . . . well, everything."

Isobel turned slowly.

He sat on the ground next to the doorway through which she'd entered, looking just like he had the night she'd discovered him in the blue marble crypt. The only difference now, though, was that he was no longer in pieces.

Grinning at her, showing a mouth full of spiked teeth the color of blue quartz, the Noc shifted to stand, his gangly frame rising to tower over her.

She watched in horror as he laid one indigo-clawed hand across his bare chest, right over a sprawling patch of porcelain skin that, unlike the rest of his body, appeared void of intricate carvings. Instead, it displayed a crackled jigsaw pattern of broken bits reconstructed.

"But, as you can see," Scrimshaw hissed through his saw-toothed smile, "it's true what they say. Time heals all wounds."

30
Double Time

"So tell me what I am to do now," he said, tilting his head at her with a quick twitchlike movement. The Noc blinked, his enormous black eyes closing tightly, then reopening even wider than before.

Isobel staggered back from him. Her mouth fell open, and though she tried to speak, no words came. Her throat was too tight, constricted with sudden terror.

He took a step toward her and then another, his black boots crushing velvet petals.

"*Maybe,*" he said, "since our masked companion won't be joining me after all . . . *you* would like to play instead."

"St-stay away," Isobel stammered. She risked a glance to her left, searching for the nearest archway, her closest escape. When she looked back, though, she jumped to find him standing right in front of her.

Before she could utter so much as a yelp of surprise, a single indigo claw shot out like the knife of a switchblade, the tip catching her beneath her chin.

"The name of the game *was* going to be vengeance," Scrimshaw said, lifting her face to his. From this close, Isobel could detect the mesh of thin, interconnected hairline fractures that covered his features, like the crackled glaze of a china teacup. "And maybe it still could be," he went on in a contemplative whisper. "After all, you were there. As a matter of fact, as I recall, *you* were the entire reason it happened to begin with, weren't you?"

Isobel jerked her head away from him. "I—don't know what you're talking about."

He retracted the claw, frowning at her. "Oh, come now. It's no *fun* if you don't know *why* I'm gutting you when I'm gutting you. Think!" he said, and used the same claw to tap her temple.

Isobel smacked his hand away and took another retreating step.

Annoyance flittered over the Noc's face, but then his expression changed, morphing into a look of coy amusement.

"No need to be so short-tempered," he said, flexing spidery fingers. "I *could* offer you a hint if you like."

Isobel didn't answer. Instead she focused on the closest archway, one to her right. But just as she mustered the courage to make a break for it, Scrimshaw sidestepped to block her path.

"The park," he said, grinning again. "You'll remember our little jaunt through the park, I'm sure."

Isobel spun and dashed for the archway directly behind her.

It was no good, though. A black fog swept ahead of her, and Scrimshaw reemerged from the murk, his angular form filling the door frame, the sudden rush of movement sending down a flurry of petals between them.

Opening his arms wide, Scrimshaw pressed his hands to either side of the frame, his palms smashing the heads of several flowers. He crooked one leg and crossed it over the other, smiling down at her expectantly, clearly enjoying the one-sided game he'd enlisted her in.

"That's where it happened," he said. "Right when I almost had you. Right behind the place where you live." He pressed the tips of his claws to his lips in a gesture that seemed to say *oops.* "Pardon me," he corrected. "*Lived.* Don't you remember?"

Suddenly it dawned on Isobel that, just like the previous time they'd spoken in the blue crypt, he was referring to the night the Nocs had entered into the real world and chased her through the park behind her house. Reynolds had been there as well, and apparently, at least according to Scrimshaw, he had been the one responsible for the damage the Noc had sustained.

Isobel *did* remember. She remembered hearing a crash just as soon as she'd reached her front yard.

But for all she knew, the story Scrimshaw was telling her could be fabricated. What was to say he hadn't been waiting outside the tomb door for Reynolds to return because they had been in league with each other? Was this just one more trick meant to confuse her? She didn't know. But something she *did* know, she reminded herself, was that even if the Nocs could touch her, they held no power to harm her.

Steeling herself, Isobel ducked under one of the Noc's outstretched arms. As she made her way down the curving tunnel, she forced herself to walk, refusing to let her fear show by running.

She heard him laugh. The sound, like the raspy chuckle of an animatronic fun-house clown, sent spikes of cold dread through her midsection. She knew it meant he wasn't going to let her pass him by this easily.

"You know," she heard him call after her, though she didn't dare stop or look back, "I hear they also say that you can't be in more than one place at a time. But as one who speaks from experience, I find that particular saying to be less true."

As soon as she reached a fork in the tunnels, Isobel again felt a rush of air skim by her, this time tousling her hair. She brushed the loosened strands from her face as the darkness accumulated in the tunnel archway to her immediate left. Scrimshaw re-formed once more, tapping his chin in thought with one tapered claw.

"I myself ended up in at least seventy-eight that night," he said. "But I'm not quite so broken up over you anymore. In fact, I've just now come to the conclusion that we would all do *so* much better without you. Tell me, how many pieces would *you* like to be? While I can't promise I'll be exact, I'll try to keep your request in mind."

"You can't hurt me," Isobel said, meeting his black gaze.

"Hurt you?" He recoiled in mock horror and folded his hands together, his claws clicking loudly as they interlaced. "No, no," he whispered. "You've got it all wrong, dear child. I don't want to hurt you. I want to *kill* you. And that I *can* do."

Again, fighting against the nearly overpowering instinct to run, Isobel instead gave him her back, if only to prove that she knew he was bluffing, and veered into the tunnel on her right.

Black wisps shot past her a third time. He solidified again, closer than before, his grin growing wide enough to deepen the zigzag crack that ran up one side of his skull.

No longer able to ignore the urge to retreat, Isobel back-pedaled toward the tunnel passageway he'd occupied the moment before. At the same time, she couldn't bring herself to turn around and start running, either, hypnotized by the dark resolve burning within his eyes.

"I'm not afraid to fight you," she snapped.

He gave her an appraising once-over, raising a clawed hand to hover above her head as though making a note of her height. "While the attempt to do so would certainly be an appropriate if uninformed response given your circum-stances"—he lowered his hand, lifting a single claw—"you seem to be missing one vital element in the whole situation. It's something you need to understand, I think, before we can get started. And that is that I"—he pointed at himself— "as you might have guessed, am not like the others. I'm what you'd call *special*. A one-of-a-kind specimen, a Ming vase amid pale imposters." He laughed at that, throwing his head back before refocusing on her. "The very last of my ilk, in fact," he went on. "Unique in that I bear no connection whatsoever to the outsider who has found himself trapped here, that boy who I know you came all this way to reclaim.

The one whose adoration shields you from all the others. Blah, blah, *blah*."

Isobel's eyes widened as he spoke, her mind returning to the vision in the hospital room and the moment when Scrimshaw had appeared at Poe's bedside, whispering to him in hissing tones. Instantly she felt her blood congeal in her veins as the truth invaded her consciousness. Her legs stiffened beneath her while her lungs ceased to take in air.

Scrimshaw wasn't one of Varen's Nocs. He couldn't be and he never had been.

He was Poe's.

Eyeing her closely, taking one step toward her for every two she took to get away, he seemed to have been monitoring her expression, waiting for the moment of realization to wash over her. And Isobel knew right away that her face must have betrayed her sudden understanding, that her mounting terror must have become apparent, because all at once, he stopped his advance.

His smile deepened into the voracious grin of a piranha.

Bringing his hands to his face, he crisscrossed claws in front of his open eyes as though to cover them. He watched her, unblinking, through the cagelike barrier.

"One," he said. "Two."

Isobel bolted, taking the path directly behind her, the walls of roses whizzing past.

"Threeeeee."

Met with a dead end, Isobel skittered to a halt. "No!" she shrieked.

"Fouuuur," she heard Scrimshaw drawl. "Some more numbers. Aaaand—nine-ten!" he shouted, cackling.

Isobel whipped around, only to find the passageway now empty, two foot-shaped depressions imprinted in the snowlike ash in the place where the Noc had stood a moment before.

Panic rose within her as she hurried back down the long vine-covered corridor, over the footprints, choosing her next direction at random, no longer certain from which way she'd come.

The roses seemed to watch her like thousands of spectators as she passed, their delicate heads bobbing in her wake. There was no sign of him around the next corner, or even the next. As Isobel took one passageway after another, she couldn't help but feel that she was winding her way deeper and deeper into the garden's maze and into Scrimshaw's snare.

The soles of her boots slapped the marble floor, the sound muffled only slightly by the thin coating of petals and ash that carpeted each passageway.

Isobel whirled to stare at her tracks, wondering if she should try to cover them or just keep running. She knew the Nocs were too fast for her to outrun. If Scrimshaw had wanted her dead right away, he'd have killed her already. He was looking for a chase, for the hunt before the kill. And as long as she panicked, she would be giving him just that. She had to get a grip. She had to think her way around him— invent her own rules.

Know when you are dreaming, she thought.

Isobel dug one hand into the pocket of her jacket. She brought out the butterfly watch and flicked open the wings. The black hands spun around one another, wheeling faster and faster. She willed them to slow, and to her astonishment, they did. Just like she'd been able to close the stone door of the tomb, the hands of the watch responded to her thoughts.

"Show me the way to the fountain," she whispered aloud.

In response, all three hands, joining in one line, aimed themselves at the twelve and, like the needle of a compass, pointed her forward.

She began to run again. As she did, she pictured in her mind that in the next tunnel and the next one after that, there would be no ash to record her steps.

Turning the corner, Isobel suddenly found herself in another circular room identical to the first. But now, the rose-covered corridors leading out of this clearing appeared to have been swept clean of ash. Isobel checked her watch again. She saw the hands split apart. They rotated in opposite directions and joined together again, aligning at the number nine. *Left!*

Isobel made the turn. She hastened toward the end of the covered hall, through the opening, and into the largest clearing yet. And here, in the center of the room, stood the very thing she sought—the fountain.

High above the brass statue's head and arcing veil, a blanket of roses twined with the decorative domed ceiling, their vines braided with the scrolling wrought-iron bars. A breeze entered through the gaps between flowers and metal, sending a cascade of petals raining down.

Everything was just as it had been in her dream. Everything except for one detail.

"Varen?" she shouted.

There was no response. He wasn't here. There was no one here. Nothing.

Isobel bit her lip, cursing herself in her mind, knowing that by yelling, she'd given herself away.

Checking the watch, she found that the hands had gone back to spinning.

"Take me to Varen!" She shook the silver charm and checked it again. This time, when the hands stopped, they pointed her in three separate directions. What did that mean? Was the watch telling her that *any* way would take her to him, or that *no* way would?

Why wasn't he *here* like he said he'd be?

"I told you you'd come," said a nearby voice, one Isobel knew well. "You said you would."

She lowered the watch.

With careful steps, she moved closer to the silent fountain. Rounding the ornate grillwork gate, she discovered Pinfeathers sitting against its base, occupying the exact same space he had the morning she'd gone to Varen's neighborhood, his head hung, held between his clawed hands.

"*Pin—?*"

"You shouldn't have, though," he said, and looked up, his face twisted with anger. "Even if we knew you would, you shouldn't have." He got up and began moving toward her. "*Why,*" he growled, "when we will only show you we are not worth it? Why, when we have no other choice but to prove to you we're not worth it?"

Isobel swallowed and began to back away from him.

She didn't know what he was saying, what any of it meant, or where it was coming from, but the rage contorting his broken face made it clear that, like Scrimshaw, she was dealing with something that wanted to rip her to shreds. And even if Pinfeathers couldn't do it himself, she knew by the look in his eye that he would settle for watching.

She sprinted toward one of the doorways, trying to think of some way to control this, some way to change what was happening to her, knowing Pinfeathers would be on her in a second's time.

Ahead of her, Scrimshaw turned the corner, filling the frame of the archway she'd almost taken. Isobel stuttered to a halt, dropping the watch, which hit the floor and became lost in the ash with a muffled *clank*. She looked behind her and saw that Pinfeathers had already started toward her at a fast walk, his crimson claws bared, his furious gaze trained on her.

She looked to Scrimshaw, whose smile broadened at the turn of events.

Isobel tossed her head from side to side, glancing between the two of them, out of options for escape.

Then Scrimshaw launched himself at her, claws raised, jaw unhinging as he unleashed a shrill screech.

She broke away in a dash, already knowing it could only

end in her death. Any moment now, someone's hands would catch her by the throat. Pinfeathers would seize her and Scrimshaw would rake through her with his claws, spattering the roses with her blood.

Reynolds had been right. She *would* die here.

As she reached one of the archways that would lead her back into the maze, she heard a fierce yell, followed by a crashing sound. Loud and unexpected, it made her stop even though her body urged her to keep running. The noise, like a porcelain bowl smashing, sounded just like the splintering of a Noc.

Isobel whipped around to find Pinfeathers standing erect in the center of the domed room while Scrimshaw, half-shattered, missing one arm and half of his torso, knelt several yards off, surrounded by the scattered pieces of his broken body.

Isobel gaped at Scrimshaw as he peered around at the fragment-strewn floor, his eyes flitting from his severed arm, the one portraying the etching of the long-haired and diamond-tailed mermaid, to the smashed shards, and finally, to the unlikely figure who had wrought the destruction.

As he stared up at Pinfeathers, the look of shock on Scrimshaw's face began to fade, transforming into demonic rage. He opened his mouth, let loose a howl, and dispersed into swirls of black ink. Re-forming on his feet, Scrimshaw ran full tilt toward Pinfeathers, who stood ready.

Scrimshaw closed the distance between them. He pulled back his remaining arm and prepared to swing at Pinfeathers, who at the last moment dissipated into wisps of violet ink. Then Scrimshaw loosened once more into black swirls, slithering through the air to entwine with the purple vapor.

The two of them merged into one cloud, a virulent mixture of opposing currents, each struggling to overpower the other. Together they flew across the room, past Isobel, who pressed herself to the floor as they collided with a patch of wall just behind her. A torrent of rose petals burst forth.

Their faces, sharp and snapping, swam up through the murk of the smoke as they shot along the concave ceiling, cutting a sawlike path and sending down a spray of more bloodred petals.

Isobel pushed herself to her feet. She ran out into the center of the room, to the fountain. Grasping the railing, she peered up into the domed ceiling, her eyes seeking out Pinfeathers. Was he . . . could he possibly be . . . *protecting* her?

One of them, she wasn't sure which at first, transformed into a bird. Flapping giant wings, the enormous creature suddenly switched its path of attack, aiming itself straight for her, talons bared.

Isobel screamed and, falling to her knees, lifted her arms to cover her head just in time to shield her face from the claws that slashed the flesh of her wrists and hands. They raked at her mercilessly, and the sound of her own cries joined with the creature's piercing screeches, until a second bird swooped in to divert the first.

In a flurry of tearing feathers and stabbing beaks, the

two birds freewheeled far up and away from her. They fluttered madly against each other, almost seeming to become one beast for a brief moment, until with talons locked, they began to plummet toward the ground. They tore apart at the last second, the larger of the two birds ripping free one wing of the smaller.

The smaller bird—a crow—squawked as it burst into murky violet wisps, re-forming with a hollow cry into the figure of Pinfeathers, his arm now missing from the shoulder socket down. The second bird, a raven, hurtled itself fast as a bullet toward Pinfeathers, who had lost sight of the other Noc.

"Behind you!" Isobel cried as she saw Scrimshaw solidify at his back.

Pinfeathers swung around, just in time for Scrimshaw to plow into him.

Isobel heard a sickening crunch, the sound of a delicate glass object wrapped in cloth being smashed to bits. A second crash followed as Pinfeathers tipped onto the floor, half of his side caving in on impact, the back of his head collapsing inward like the shell of an egg.

"Pin!" she cried, and ran toward him.

She saw his eyes flicker out and become empty pits, as hollow as the hole in his cheek.

She stopped as Scrimshaw looked up from the body of his slain opponent. His eyes narrowed on her, no longer full of morbid playfulness or cryptic mirth but genuine malice and hate.

"*You,*" he seethed. "This is all because of *you*. I am *tired* of you. It ends . . . now!"

He rushed her and Isobel fell back, sprawling against the floor as his shadow grew long over her. He raised his arm, claws gleaming.

All she could do was cover her face with her hands and wait for the deathblow to rain down.

31
Crushed

The blow never came.

For what felt like an eternity, Isobel stayed crouched where she was, curled into herself.

Was he waiting for her to look up? Was it that he wanted her to see it coming?

Isobel refused. She would not lift her gaze. She couldn't give him the satisfaction of seeing the terror on her face.

Her thoughts, those that would surely be her last, went to Pinfeathers and his efforts to try to save her.

Whatever he'd been, whatever tortures and horrors he had brought with him before, here, in this moment, he had tried to protect her. He had tried and he had failed. Why?

Isobel shifted her eyes in the direction where Pinfeathers had lain, scattered and broken. But she did not see him there.

Except for a few splintered bits, he was gone.

She risked a glance up and saw Scrimshaw's single hand now groping at his throat, attempting to pry away the red-clawed fingers that gripped him there, squeezing.

Trembling, she watched as the hairline crack along Scrimshaw's skull began to widen. Others soon appeared as the pressure increased. The web-thin fissures spread quickly across his startled face like black veins.

Pinfeathers continued to tighten his hold on Scrimshaw's neck until, at last, the blue Noc succumbed, sinking to his knees.

For a moment, it seemed as though Scrimshaw might try to speak, to say something to her, but his words were cut off, crushed into silence along with his neck, which caved at last under Pinfeathers's unrelenting grip.

Isobel shrieked, cringing as Scrimshaw's head toppled from his shoulders. It fell to the floor, where it shattered amid the layer of dust and petals. His body followed soon after, slumping slowly to one side, then toppling to the floor.

Isobel stared at the empty torso, transfixed by its hollow interior. Her eyes skimmed the surface of the remains, focusing on the few beautifully carved images that, despite the extent of the destruction, had managed to remain intact. A swirling whirlpool, a rolling cascade of waves and foam, the curling tentacles of a giant octopus. There was the sailing ship too, only half of which now existed, the other half seeming to have dropped off into the jagged and open cavity of his side.

Looking closer still, Isobel noticed what seemed to be a miniature portrait among the carvings. Engraved just above the heart, the image showed the quarter profile of a young woman, her head turned as though she was peering back at something over one shoulder. Her eyelids, heavy and drooping, veiled her downcast eyes, which seemed as though they wanted to close. The girl's dark hair, etched with care in minute curving lines, was bundled around her head in an old-fashioned style. Isobel thought she recognized the image, but before she could place her finger on it, her attention was drawn to Pinfeathers's wavering shadow.

Isobel tilted her head up to find the Noc still hovering over her.

He swayed, seeming disoriented, even lost as he peered down and around himself. It made her wonder if he even knew what had just happened, what he had just done, or exactly how much damage he had sustained.

She watched as he lifted his hand to his collar. Grabbing hold of the top strap of his jacket, he wrenched it loose, baring his chest. He touched the fragmented area just above his heart, the place he had repaired the morning Isobel had found him sitting by the fountain. He cringed as several shards tumbled forth, falling to clink against the marble floor.

"I . . . told you," he wheezed, his words almost entirely voiceless. It was as if, like a shattered violin, he had lost the ability to resonate sound. "Didn't . . . didn't I tell you?"

Holding his hand over the open crater in his chest, he tottered away from her, away from the mess that was Scrimshaw. As he moved, his whole frame creaked, groaning like a rickety structure preparing to collapse in on itself.

Isobel placed her palms on the ash-powdered floor, about to push herself to her feet, when a quiet *pop* made her stop. It was the sound of one of his knees fracturing. He began to list to one side, then slip straight down toward the floor.

He landed on his knees with a *crack*. The weight of his torso caused his upper body to tip forward, like the trunk of a tree whose base had been sliced cleanly through.

Fumbling forward, Isobel caught him as he toppled into her open arms. His hand fell away from his chest, allowing a slip of fabric to pour halfway out of him as he slumped against her.

Keeping a firm hold on him, his broken form as light and lifeless as a marionette's, she guided him gently to the floor. Then her eyes went to the thin length of smooth cloth that had tumbled from his chest and partially into her lap.

Isobel frowned at the sight of the pink satin ribbon. *Her* ribbon.

She seized it and peered down at Pinfeathers, who stared upward and past her at something above them.

She glanced briefly at the statue of the woman who stood atop the fountain.

"You *let* her win," the Noc rasped. "You make it *so* easy."

Isobel returned her gaze to him. "Pinfeathers," she said, hoping to bring his attention back to her.

"Present," he said, his eyes shifting to meet hers, "if unaccounted for."

She held up the pink ribbon. "Where . . . where did you get this?"

He squeezed his eyes shut as though the question pained him. When he opened them again, his lips began to move, attempting to form words. "You gave it to us," he whispered, making a feeble gesture with his hand before turning his head from her, refusing, it seemed, to meet her gaze. "Asked us to keep it. Said you needed it. Or don't you remember?"

"I . . ." She shook her head. "I gave it to *Varen.*"

"*Yes,*" he hissed.

Scowling, confused, she looked down at the ribbon, one end held in her quivering hand, the other still tucked inside his empty shell of a body.

It made her realize that when Pinfeathers had been piecing himself back together that morning at the fountain, he'd also been sealing the ribbon inside himself. But how had he gotten it?

"The bookstore," she said, murmuring the words aloud as soon as it occurred to her. "You took it from the attic in the bookstore, didn't you? It *was* there. The dream *was* real."

His eyes narrowed into slits. "We . . . *took* it," he said, the words clipped and sharp.

"*Why?*" she demanded.

"Because!" He snapped his head toward her, his frame crackling. Isobel flinched as a new fracture erupted across his face. "We wanted it," he said.

"I—I don't understand—"

"You *can't* understand us. We don't even understand ourselves."

"Please," she said, "please help me. Promise to help me find him and—and I can try to put you back together."

He laughed, the sound low and continuous, deep and corrosive. And as he laughed, he began to crack apart, his body crumbling while the fault line in his face threatened to split wider. Then, as suddenly as it had come, his laughter ceased and his smile fell away. He seemed to relax as he rolled his head carefully in her direction, as though he knew that his next movement could prove to be his last.

"Is that why you came back?" he asked. "To fix us?"

The way he was looking at her now, his half-splintered face shorn clean of its malevolence—it reminded her of another face. A calm and quiet face.

"*Varen?*" she whispered.

His eyes, which had begun to fade out, the black murk within thinning into a filmy and translucent glaze, suddenly grew solid again.

She scooted herself still closer to him, cupping his cold, hard face in her hands.

"Tell me where he is," she said, her voice shaking. "I know you're connected to him somehow. I know you know where to find him."

He lifted his hand toward her, and even when she felt his claws graze her cheek, she did not pull back.

"We're still so very far from you, cheerleader," he said. "Never as close as we appear."

"*Tell me where.*"

"Home," he said, smiling his jagged smile. "We are ever and always home now."

With that, he allowed his arm to fall. As it met with the floor, it sent a vibration ricocheting through his body. The fissure in his face could bear no more. It split wide, and his head cracked in two. Instantly his eyes became empty sockets.

Staring down at him in numb shock and disbelief, Isobel scanned the rubble of the nightmare creature who had once taken so much delight in tormenting her. But no measure of relief came with his demise. Instead, as she pulled the ribbon free from his crumpled chest, a wave of sorrow swept over her as she thought she finally understood what he was.

In some way, he had belonged to the deepest essence of Varen's being. All the broken pieces of himself that Varen had buried, all those bits that terrified his own mind, all accumulated into one beast, a deranged creature born out of everything he knew he wasn't supposed to do or feel. An entity made of desires and emotions and all the longings Varen could never admit to anyone—not even himself.

And if the Nocs were demons, she thought, then they were the most personal kind. Shrapnel of the soul, Reynolds had called them. But then, did that make them soulless?

Isobel turned her head to look back at the shattered form of Scrimshaw, knowing at once whose portrait she had seen carved into his chest. It had been Virginia, Poe's young bride. His Lenore.

Like Scrimshaw with the tiny etching just over his heart, Pinfeathers had carried *her* close too. Hidden within.

And just as Pinfeathers had changed, so had Varen.

It was the only thing that made sense. It was the only explanation for why Varen wasn't here now. Why Pinfeathers had been waiting in his stead.

The shift she had feared had happened. Her dream of Varen in the bookstore attic had been no dream.

She felt something warm slide down her cheek.

Frowning, Isobel lifted one dust-caked hand and pressed her fingers to the place where Pinfeathers had touched her a moment before.

She lowered her hand and saw a smear of crimson.

Blood.

32
Melancholy House

With a careful hand, Isobel wound the satin ribbon slowly around one trembling wrist.

Its softness helped to calm her, if only for a moment.

She avoided looking down as she moved forward through the wreckage, the bits and pieces, the empty limbs strewn across the floor. Making her way to the wall of flowers, she did her best to block out the sound of shards popping and crunching beneath the soles of her boots.

She stopped at a section of interlacing iron and vines uninterrupted by any archway. Reaching out, she clasped the empty air next to one of the iron bars, and as she did so, a matching ornate door handle materialized in her fist.

Isobel twisted the handle and the door swung outward.

As she'd suspected, the world outside the rose garden held the muted and gray landscape of the woodlands.

Trees, black and dead, stood innumerable before a glowing violet horizon. Leaden and tattered, the clouds hung low in the slate-colored sky, while the interlocking boughs of the trees created a webwork of shadow patterns over the ash-coated ground.

Within the dense forest, Isobel could discern two rows

of old-fashioned lampposts, their glass holders lit with violet flames.

She stepped out of the garden, drawn by the flickering of their otherworldly light, her boots sinking into the spongy ash.

On either side of her, through the network of trees, she could also see a line of familiar houses, though their structures were far less recognizable now.

The foundations beneath supported mere frames, the facades themselves in crumbling ruin. Doors and windows lacked panes and wood, giving the homes the appearance of blackened skulls, their vacant entrances like slack-jawed mouths gaping in shock.

With the fountain at her back, Isobel did not have to guess to know where she was.

It made sense.

Like the bookshop, Varen's neighborhood had a mirror-image dreamworld counterpart.

A twilight version of reality, she thought, remembering the words Gwen had read aloud from the book describing Lilith's domain.

That was why she had found Pinfeathers at the fountain on the morning she'd ridden Danny's bike here—to the *real* here. Like the Noc had said, he'd been waiting for her all along.

And Pinfeathers . . . in the moment before he'd shattered apart, hadn't he told her that Varen was "home"?

Isobel glanced in the direction of Varen's house. Through

the thick cluster of trees, she could determine only the vague outlines of the homes farther down the street.

She moved onward, trying to ignore the sharp sting of the scratch that marred her cheek.

But the pain, like the thought of what the wound meant, would not relent.

Pinfeathers . . .

The way he had touched her had seemed so gentle. Like a caress. But she now knew that he'd inflicted the cut on purpose.

It had been his last act of protection. His final warning.

His way of telling her that Varen . . .

No.

Isobel stopped, refusing to let her thoughts stray in that direction. She knew better than to let the things that occurred in this world take root in her mind and grow. If she allowed that, she risked forgetting what was real, forgetting that what she'd had with Varen was real. That it still was.

It had to be.

A burst of wind slipped past as she continued to make her way down the desolate street. It was the first breeze she had felt since leaving the garden. Cool and brisk, it carried with it that familiar scent. Incense, spice, crushed leaves.

Ahead, the solemn structure of Varen's house loomed into view, a darker twin of its real-world equivalent, its facade in complete reverse.

Unlike the other houses, which all looked as if they'd been blown through from the inside out by well-thrown grenades, Varen's, though distorted, seemed to be intact.

The now-blackened windows gave the mansion a wounded look. And the stained-glass front door, no longer golden hued, hung slanted in its frame. A deep violet glow emanated from its colored panes, reminding Isobel of the purple chamber from the Masquerade, the room where she had left Varen on Halloween night.

The most obvious disfigurement of all, however, was the crack that zigzagged from the crown of the structure down to its very base, effectively splitting the house into two. One side, the right side, stood straight, bricks and windows in solid order. But the left side tilted downward, the second-story window askew, like a sorrowful eye.

Isobel stopped between a pair of trees that occupied the very place where the front sidewalk should have been. She looked up, seeking Varen's bedroom window through the tangle of limbs, and saw a tall shadow slide by. It passed quickly, but she would know its shape anywhere.

"Varen," she whispered, and hurried onto the sloping porch. But as soon as she touched the doorknob, an unexpected sound caused her to pull back.

Music. Piano music. It came muffled through the door, the lullaby drifting out in lingering tones.

Isobel set her hand on the doorknob again. As she did so, she felt the metal twitch beneath her fingertips. She heard a sliding back, followed by the *clunk* of the heavy metal dead-bolt. Then the door drifted slowly and silently open, moving inward on its own.

A screen of pure darkness greeted her.

Like the house itself, the blackness that pulsated within seemed somehow alive, made of the same substance she had seen churning on the ceiling of Poe's hospital room. It was the same murk that had stolen out of thin air to wrap its way around Varen during the Grim Facade, pulling him into its depths.

Isobel listened as the piano music continued to flow forth from beyond the sheet of darkness.

She hesitated, wondering if following the music through the black miasma was exactly what Lilith wanted her to do. Lifting a hand to the hamsa at her throat, Isobel wrapped her fist around the amulet.

Even if this *was* a trap, she thought, what other choice did she have?

She stepped into the house.

As she moved through the doorway, she felt the blanket of shadows engulf her. Black smoke tendrils slithered over her. Like tentacles, they wrapped their way around her arms and waist. She felt them pull her inward.

The darkness smudged her surroundings into nothing as the piano music became garbled in her ears. Though it grew louder for an instant, closer, the notes themselves began to tremble and shudder. They warbled and echoed, almost as though she'd been plunged far underwater.

Then, as suddenly as they had taken hold, the shadows released her.

Like a thick fog, they receded from her, leaving her standing in the foyer of Varen's house, a few clinging wisps slithering over her now-bare shoulders and arms.

Glancing down, she found herself wearing a dress of pure ebony, her gritted and ash-caked clothes, along with Varen's jacket, having vanished. A pair of black slippers took the place of her boots.

Wham! The earsplitting crack of the door slamming shut behind her made Isobel swing around. She watched the lock's brass thumb latch twist itself to one side, the deadbolt sliding into place once more.

Isobel backed away from the door, layers of stiff fabric rustling around her legs.

Like the pale pink dress she had worn to the Grim Facade, this dress had a strapless bodice and a set of full skirts that ended at her knees. But without the frills and lace fringe of the former, this one seemed to be its dark opposite.

She did not have to strain to remember where she had seen it before. It had been worn by the corpse lying on the lid of the sarcophagus in her vision of the blue crypt.

Her corpse.

Isobel's hand sprang to her cheek, the silken satin ends of her ribbon, still tied to her wrist, brushing against her arm. She touched the scratch Pinfeathers had left, realizing that it, too, had appeared on the body.

A sudden clang of piano keys made her jump.

"No, no," came a woman's soft voice from somewhere behind her. "Not a C there. How about a D instead?"

The music began again, and Isobel turned to face the reversed interior of Varen's house.

White sheets covered all the furniture. Black draperies hung from the windows.

Above, weak violet light flickered from a flame-lit chandelier with no chain. It hovered over her head, suspended by an invisible force, the crystal prisms and pendalogues jagged and broken.

To her right, the stairs that led up through the rest of the house looked loose and dilapidated. Glancing to her left, she saw that the sliding doors to the parlor were closed. Through the long slit that separated the wooden panels, however, she could just make out the edge of the piano as well as someone sitting at its bench.

The floor creaked beneath her as she drew nearer to the doors.

She heard the melody stutter, stop, and start again.

This time, a woman's soft humming accompanied the haunting tune.

Isobel crept closer and closer, pausing only when she saw a flash of light from the corner of her eye. Her attention snapped to the painting on the wall. It hung above the sheeted hallway table that held the model of a schooner, now bedecked with black sails.

For a moment, the painting within the gilded frame appeared to be nothing more than a canvas of pure black. Another flash, however, revealed otherwise. A bolt of lightning contained within the square frame flickered to illuminate an old-fashioned ship as it tossed about on choppy nighttime waters. The fierce waves in the painting rolled and swelled, the whole tumultuous scene fluttering in and out of sight as the lightning continued to flare in the background. It lit the tar-colored underbellies of the clouds as well as the ship itself, which seemed as small as a toy amid the storm-tossed seas.

Isobel caught the name GRAMPUS across the ship's stern during one long barrage of lightning strikes.

Then the humming from within the parlor changed to singing, and her attention returned once more to the pair of sliding pocket doors.

Quickly she slipped to stand just in front of the drawn panels, peeking through the slim space in between.

She saw a pair of elegant hands wandering over the white keys as the music rose and fell, every note melding with the woman's wispy voice to create a liquid sound.

> *"Sleep now a little while*
> *Till within our dreams we wake*
> *Unfolding our Forever*
> *If only for Never's sake."*

Inside the ornate and orderly room, an eerily familiar scene unfolded before her. The old-fashioned decorations and the stately piano, the woman's elegant violet evening gown, the glittering comb in her hair—it all matched what had played on the TV that night she'd found Pinfeathers in her living room. And the comb. It was identical to the one she'd found in the box beneath the stairs at Nobit's Nook.

"And take me to your ever after
Let's hide behind our eyes
Together pour through that door
Where autumn never dies."

Isobel pressed her palms to the wooden doors. She leaned in, bringing her eye even closer to the slit.

"And I'll sift my sands to your side
Before we slip away
Before we're little more than silt
Beneath the rocking waves— "

All at once, the music stopped. The woman at the piano snapped her head toward Isobel, her emerald eyes lit from within by fear and surprise.

Isobel's breath caught in her throat.

The woman scooted to the edge of the piano seat. She placed a hand on the keyboard cover and tensed, as though preparing to throw it down.

When their eyes met through the crack, however, the woman's trepidation fell away in an instant, replaced with a soft smile of relief and even gladness. Her face was one Isobel had seen before in a faded and bent photograph.

"Hello there," Varen's mother said, speaking to Isobel through the gap. "It's okay. You can come in. I shouldn't play so late. Did I wake you? Do you want to hear the rest of our song? It's almost finished. Here. Let me sing you the last verse."

Isobel frowned, realizing she'd heard this voice speak these same words once before. Along with the song, they'd played in this exact order over the gramophone in the dream-world version of the bookshop.

When the woman swiveled toward the piano again, Isobel began to understand that whatever she was witnessing, it wasn't happening in real time. Like the vision of Poe in the hospital, she was seeing a moment from the past being replayed.

Just like . . . just like a memory.

Madeline's lips parted as she lifted her hands to the keys. Once more, music swelled, filling the room.

"And side by side we'll fight the tide
That sweeps in to take us down,
And hand in hand we'll both withstand
Even as we drown."

The final notes, deep and resonant, reverberated through the door, sending a barely perceptible vibration through Isobel's hands. For several long seconds, Madeline remained still, staring at the keys as though they had done something she hadn't expected them to.

"I don't know," she said, half mumbling to herself. "Do you think that last part's too sad? Here, let me play you the whole thing, and you tell me what you think."

The song began again.

Hooking her fingers in the brass grooves set into the doors, Isobel tried to pull them apart. They refused to budge, however, so she spread her feet, angling for a better grip, and then tugged again.

All at once, the wooden panels flew open with a bang. The piano music halted.

Madeline was gone.

The room now stood empty and wrecked, the furniture toppled and strewn about. The tattered curtains, pulled free from their decorative tassel ropes, hung limp over the tall black-paned windows. The overturned piano bench lay on its side, reams of loose sheet music spilling from under its hinged lid.

Black notes, all hand drawn, dotted the thin lines of musical staves, their corresponding lyrics written beneath in a looping and elegant hand.

Behind the piano, scattered and broken picture frames lined the built-in shelves, though none of the frames, save for one, actually held any images or photos. Like the windows, the frames had all been blacked out, except for the picture that sat in the very middle of the center shelf in an oval frame. It was a portrait of Madeline, a larger copy of the photo Isobel had found at Nobit's Nook.

Except the more she looked at *this* picture, the more it seemed to change.

Going to the shelves, Isobel took the frame between both hands. She held the life-size oval portrait out in front of her, studying the contours of the woman's face as they shifted and morphed, as though the portrait's subject couldn't seem to decide how she wanted to look.

Then the image began to dissolve, eaten through by another. In its place, Isobel's own face appeared, complete with the angry red slit that now marked her right cheek.

Isobel took in a sharp breath as details of the room's dilapidated interior—the doorway, the hall, and the chandelier—began to fill in around her reflection until it became evident that in place of a picture frame, she now held a mirror.

"Memories," came a melodious voice from behind her. "They are the cobwebs of the mind."

Isobel whirled, dropping the mirror, which shattered with a deafening crash as it hit the floor, shards flying out to scatter across the wood.

The owner of the voice stood just outside the parlor entry, her lithe and luminous veil-swathed figure framed by the wide doorway. Isobel had not seen her there in the mirror.

"You can try and sweep them away," Lilith went on, her dark lips moving behind the translucent screen of gauzy fabric. "But it seems as if some trace always remains."

Isobel watched her without budging, a numbness spreading its way through her, causing her skin to prickle and her entire body to hum with a terror that had not quite clicked within her brain yet.

"You—you don't have a reflection," she murmured.

"Though it would appear as if you have two," Lilith replied, smiling a small, close-lipped smile. "At least in his mind."

Isobel swallowed. Knowing Lilith meant Varen, she forced out her next words. "Where is he?"

"Occupied."

"If you won't tell me," Isobel said, taking a step toward the doorway, a step toward the demon, "then I'll find him myself."

"I would welcome you to look all you like," Lilith said, and strode forward as well, passing through the doorway and into the parlor.

Distracted by the odd clicking noise Lilith's feet made when they came in contact with the hardwood floor, Isobel glanced down. *Bird's* feet, she realized with horror as she laid eyes on the enormous scaly black talons that peeked out from beneath the hem of the demon's gossamer robes.

"But the fact is," Lilith went on, "you would never find what you seek. I'm afraid it no longer exists. Just as will soon be the case with you."

Isobel looked up again to see that the closer Lilith came, the more gaunt and inhuman she began to appear through the transparent barrier of her veil. With every step toward her, the white flesh of Lilith's cheeks sank farther inward to reveal the contours of her skull, her lips shriveling back to expose rows of tiny needle-thin teeth. Her nose dissolved into a hole while her eyes, hollowing, became sunken pits lit by two distant pinpricks of light.

Isobel staggered back, her leg catching on the overturned piano bench. She fell, sprawling onto her side, and landed among the broken shards of mirror, which winked at her, reflecting light from the foyer's floating chandelier. But the glow trapped within those shards was not violet, but a warm amber.

And in the closest shard, one that lay nearest to her hand, there was something else, too. A face.

Isobel met the familiar woman's startled gaze and the lady paused for an instant, her straight blond hair draped forward around her features as if, somewhere on the reality side of the mirror, she was bending or stooping to pick something up. Just when Isobel recognized the woman as Varen's stepmother, a large black talon slammed over the shard, crushing it.

Isobel looked up to see the hideous thing that was Lilith looming over her.

Lifting a hand to the veils that covered her face, her skin no longer milky smooth but chalk white and tightly stretched, the creature pulled free the gauze with clawed fingers. Her ebony hair tumbled around her now racklike shoulders. Scraggly and thin, it began to fall out in stringy clumps.

Isobel pushed herself backward, scrambling over the glass-sprinkled floorboards. When her spine met with the base of the bookshelves, she grasped at her throat for the hamsa.

Lilith laughed, a sound that was altogether girlish.

"You think your silly talisman will save you?" the demon asked, her eyes flicking to Isobel's necklace. She raised her hand again, this time reaching for Isobel's clenched fist, her fingers moving to hover just over the hand that held the amulet.

Isobel made no move, even though her heart thundered in her chest. For a moment, she feared that the thing standing before her, this gruesome creature, more ghoul now than woman, would snatch the necklace free with her skeletal finger, toss it aside, and rip into her with her awful teeth.

Instead Lilith's hand began to quiver, her outstretched fingers stopping just short of Isobel. Then, like paper caught by a wayward flame, they began to wither and flake. A flicker of pain crossed her now-monstrous features as her hand began to crumple, her fingers curling back on themselves before dissolving into ash.

Those twin points of light widened as they continued to bore into Isobel. Vines of blackness climbed up Lilith's neck and jawbone, her cheeks and forehead, appearing like black reeds on her pasty complexion.

"It won't," the demon said, her voice no longer sensuous or girlish, but deep-throated and low, like that of a beast that had somehow learned to speak. "I don't have to touch you to destroy you. I have . . . other means for that."

As she dragged back her clawed bird's feet, the train of Lilith's white garments whispered against the floor. Isobel stared as the demon made her way through the parlor doorway, where someone else now stood—a man.

Lilith went around him, her hand, rejuvenated and once more white and flawless, passing across his chest. Smiling, her dark beauty having returned, Lilith glanced over her shoulder at Isobel.

"She would make a nice addition to my ever-growing collection of the lost, don't you think, Gordon?" she said to the man. "Kill her. And then, before she comes to, before she awakens and realizes what has become of her, I want you to place her in my old quarters. I think you know where I mean."

With that, Lilith disappeared around the corner, leaving Isobel with a man she had seen earlier that night. It was the very same man whose face she'd unmasked in the Baltimore cemetery where Poe lay buried.

Isobel pushed herself to her feet, bits of mirror glass that had stuck to her legs and dress tumbling to the floor around her.

Quickly he drew forth one of the two swords he wore on his belt.

The wink of silver flashed cold as he aimed the blade straight at her.

33
Mad Trist

In addition to being without the white scarf, Reynolds no longer had his cloak or hat. In place of his usual solid black clothing, he wore dark brown ash-smudged trousers, leather boots, and a ragged gray waistcoat buttoned over a loose long-sleeved shirt. Garments from another time.

His dark, slicked-back hair gleamed in the subdued light of the foyer chandelier. Its violet glow cast hard shadows across his already stern and unsmiling face. His eyes, black and dead, remained fixed on her.

"So," Isobel said, her gaze darting from him to the blade he held pointed at her chest, "Gordon, huh? I guess that's as good a name as any for a snake and a coward."

"Snakes are cunning creatures," said Reynolds. Or Gordon—whoever he was. "And not so much cowards as they are conspirators."

She watched him as he swept the blade through the air in a clean and threatening stroke that made her flinch and caused the thin strip of metal to sing.

Her eyes met with his again as a thousand questions scrolled through her head at lightning speed. Chief among them was how he'd played her so well from the beginning of all this. Though it seemed now as if he'd played everyone, all his supposed "friends," including Poe.

Why? To what end? To serve what purpose?

If he'd been Lilith's pawn all this time, then why had he ever entered Isobel's world to seek her out and "warn" her about what was happening? Why had he fought against the Nocs and helped her along? If Varen was what Lilith had wanted from the very beginning, if he was what she'd *needed*, then why had he involved Isobel at all?

None of it added up.

However, it had not been lost on Isobel that Lilith had not called him "Reynolds."

Of course, Isobel had always suspected it was not his real name. But why had he needed to conceal his true identity? Why hide behind a mask and cloak?

"She doesn't know about you, does she?" Isobel asked. "The *other* you, I mean."

Lowering the cutlass, Reynolds aimed the blade toward the floor and, thrusting it downward, embedded the sword between the boards. There, the tarnished hilt swayed as he took several steps backward into the foyer hallway. Drawing the second blade from its sheath, he gestured with it to the first.

"Pick it up," he said.

Isobel's hands balled into fists at her side, a knee-jerk reaction to his command. "No."

"You'll pick it up," he said, assuming a stance of defense, his knees bent, blade aimed at her once again, his free arm behind him, held level with his chest, "or you won't. Either way, we fight."

"I don't want to fight you," Isobel said. And it was the truth, though mostly because she had seen him do battle with these swords before. He'd moved like a column of flame, flicking to and fro, a graceful and deadly figure.

Considering that Isobel had never so much as touched a *real* weapon in her life, she didn't think the contest would be a fair one. She stood no chance against him, and they both knew it.

"Clearly," he said, "you do wish to fight me. That, you've already shown. I am simply in a better position, I think, to accept your challenge. At least my back is no longer turned. Now take your weapon."

His answer, infuriating, sent a fresh wave of heat through her veins while also reminding her that Reynolds wasn't big on caring about what was fair. Or right. Only for whatever happened to fit with his own agenda. Whatever *that* happened to be.

"You're calling *me* a backstabber?" she spat.

"I am finished talking."

"Well, I'm not!" Isobel shouted.

"On your guard," he warned. "I strike on the count of five."

Though her palms itched to grab the sword—the only means she could see to protect herself—the last thing Isobel wanted to do was give in to his demand. She'd had more than her fill of doing what he told her. Following his orders without questioning him, believing him when he'd said they were friends—that had all brought her here, to this moment. This time, though, she would not be so gullible as to play into his hands.

"Tell me why you're doing this," she said.

"I am doing this," he growled, "because I have been given the order to kill and am bound to obey. It was not specified, however, that I should not first provide you with the means to defend yourself. That is my own kindness. Now draw!"

"*Kindness?*" Isobel railed.

"*One!*"

She glared at him, and her eyes darted again to the sword still stuck in the floorboards. Now she *wanted* to pick it up.

He was doing it again, she thought. *He's finding your buttons and he's pushing them. Don't do it, don't be his puppet.*

"Two."

Her gaze returned to that of her opponent.

"Three," he said, his face emotionless.

But what had she heard in his voice just now? Had there been a slight catch in that single syllable, or had she imagined it?

"I—I don't know how to fight," she said, stalling.

"You don't have to know!" And now *he* was yelling. "If you paid attention to a single thing about this world, then you would know already what to do. You'd have acted. Four!"

Though Isobel understood nothing of Reynolds—of Gordon—or his motives or who or what he was or what he was after, she had learned enough about him to recognize when there was something more slithering beneath the surface of his words and actions than he was willing to let on.

"And you could have killed me by now if you'd wanted," Isobel said. "So why haven't you?"

"Don't make me." His voice had dropped to a whisper, low and full of warning. He was nervous too, she thought, but about what? Could it be he'd been *allowing* her to stall?

He nodded at the sword embedded in the floor, which had only just stopped swaying.

"I will," he said, and Isobel knew that he meant it.

This was all part of the game, she thought, all part of his charade. If Lilith told him to do something, he had to do it. Or else risk . . . what?

Deciding that she'd had enough of unanswered questions, that it was time for the truth, Isobel hurried forward and grabbed the sword. She pulled it from between the floorboards with both hands and reluctantly raised the blade toward him as she struck her own fight stance.

Though it might have been the pattern of light sliding over him as he moved back, Isobel thought she saw him smile, his eyes gleaming with some dark triumph she couldn't name.

"Begin!" he shouted.

Isobel lunged at him and knocked his sword aside with her own.

His arm followed the movement of his blade, letting her know he'd allowed her to make the connection. Isobel didn't doubt it.

Backing away from her, crossing one leg behind the other, he let her swipe at him again, then easily deflected her advance. Isobel lunged again and again, and each time, he sent her blade aside with his own.

The fuse of fury he'd lit within her grew shorter and shorter with each of her rebounded attacks. He was making fun of her, she thought. He was doing this on purpose to mock her, trying to make her feel weak and stupid.

Well, she wasn't. She had made it this far, hadn't she?

Isobel continued her onslaught, but he repelled her blows one after the other, and their swords continued to clank and clack as they wound their way around the foyer.

He had yet to attack her in return, but she knew better than to think it wasn't coming.

Already losing her breath, Isobel paused and scampered, out of weapon's reach.

Over his shoulder, she caught sight of the painting with the ship just in time to watch the black-water jaws of the ocean open and overtake the battered and ragtag *Grampus*, upending the vessel.

When her eyes returned to Reynolds, though, it was too late to sidestep or use her sword to divert the swing of his own cutlass, the tip of which caught her left shoulder, splitting the skin there in a deep gash.

Isobel hissed, the searing pain of the wound too sharp to elicit a scream.

She raised her free hand to the gash, her fingers coming away scarlet with her blood.

"Your distractions cost you," he said.

Isobel gritted her teeth and, charging forward, swiped at him again. He skittered back, arms spread wide as he narrowly avoided her strike, which slashed across his midsection, slicing a horizontal slit in his waistcoat.

They paused to look at each other, their eyes meeting in mirrored expressions of shock.

"Again," he said, and moved on her, slashing this way and that, slinging blow after blow, forcing her back from him and toward the front door.

Isobel met each of his strokes with a block and a parry, her body moving before she could tell it when or where.

Sword fighting. She was actually *sword fighting*.

The unexplained ability, now seemingly inherent, reminded Isobel of how she had once shared a dance with Pinfeathers at the masquerade ball without knowing how. What had the Noc told her then?

Just let go.

Then she remembered something Reynolds had once told her after pulling her from the sunken grave where the Red Death had nearly buried her alive.

That grave, Reynolds had said, *you could have flown out.*

If that was possible in this world, then so was this.

Isobel raised her sword and rushed him, the heat of her own blood searing her free arm as it ran down to her wrist, where she could feel it soaking into the ribbon. He blocked her, but she whirled, slashing low and quick to nick his leg, tearing the fabric of his trousers just over the knee.

He didn't bleed, but she hadn't expected him to. What had been more rewarding was the look of surprise and momentary confusion that came over his stoic face. For once, she'd actually cracked the Rubik's Cube code of his fortitude and had elicited a response. Flashing a dark smile, she went after him again. Once more, their swords traded back and forth, clanking loudly, and this time, *she* was the one forcing *him* back, driving him through the narrow hall she knew opened into the kitchen.

Once they were through the narrow bottleneck squeeze of the hallway, though, Isobel paused in her onslaught, startled and bewildered to find that they were not in a kitchen at all but outside, on a long and wide stone balcony.

Fierce winds gusted around them, coming first from one direction and then another, whipping Isobel's hair into a frenzy, tugging the skirts of her black dress this way and that. The pink ribbon fluttered in her peripheral vision.

To her left, a line of stone faces carved into the side of the house watched the storm with indifferent eyes. *Green men,* Isobel thought, remembering them from the day she had seen the protector gargoyles on the facades of the houses in Varen's neighborhood.

On her other side, a row of stone columns supported the floor above.

Through them, she saw a streak of lightning slice the sky in two, the ultraviolet spear of light illuminating the crooked line of black rock cliffs below that overlooked a white and rolling sea.

And there, standing on the brink of the farthest bluff . . .

"Varen!" Isobel shouted.

Forgetting her fight with Reynolds, Isobel lowered her sword and rushed to the balcony's edge.

"Var—!"

Her cry was cut short by Reynolds, who had caught her from behind. Hooking her around the waist with one strong arm, he held the blade of his sword to her throat with the other.

"I told you that you cannot reach him this way," he hissed in her ear. Isobel wrenched her elbow up and then jammed it into his stomach. He took the blow with a grunt but did not release her.

"Let me go!" she shrieked.

"You don't understand," he said.

"No!" she yelled. "*You* don't understand!"

Taking the hilt of her sword between both hands, Isobel plunged the tip downward straight in and through the bridge of his foot.

He released her at once. Isobel stumbled away from him and farther down the stone walkway.

"Do not go to him!" he shouted after her, yanking the blade free from his foot. "Isobel, you must listen to me."

"I am *done* listening to you!" she screamed at him.

He limped after her, though his gait seemed to grow steadier with every footfall.

It made Isobel think about what had happened to him at the Grim Facade, when the Red Death had turned Reynolds's own blades against him, running him through with both. Even though Isobel had been sure he was dead, Reynolds had remained unconscious for only a few seconds and then awoke to yank the swords out of his own chest.

The memory reminded her there was nothing she could do to stop him.

But perhaps, she thought, glancing at the sightless eyes of one of the nearby green men, there was a way to distract him, to keep him busy while she found a way to the cliffs, to Varen.

Isobel went to the wall and placed her hand on one of the stone men's faces. She pictured his eyes blinking in her mind, and it was no more than a split second before they did.

"Stop," Reynolds said, still making his way toward her. "What are you doing?"

"Fight," Isobel whispered to the stone man, who immediately began to twist his head from side to side, causing the stone around him to crumple and fall away in chunks, revealing strong shoulders and a muscled torso, as though the rest of his body had merely been trapped within the wall. "Fight in my place," she said.

Isobel did not wait to see what would happen when the gargoyle freed himself completely from the stone. Instead she hurried down to the next green man, and the next, whispering the same word to each of them. She looked back only when she reached the end of the balcony and a short set of stone steps, which led up to a massive and windowless wooden door marked with a large shield-shaped family crest.

The golems, free from the wall, which now bore a row of body-shaped craters, surrounded Reynolds.

Each of them, seven in total, held either a club or a spear clenched in gritty fists. Some of them even bent down to pick up the larger stone chunks of fallen wall.

Dropping her sword, Isobel kicked it across the balcony floor in Reynolds's direction before at last turning back to the door. She pressed down on the lever handle and pushed against the wood, face-to-face with the coat of arms, which bore in its center a pair of outspread bird's wings, in the middle of which blazed the scrolling word USHER.

Isobel rushed into an open and dimly lit hallway. Whirling, she shoved the door shut behind her. It banged into place, its echo reverberating around her, ricocheting into the high vaulted ceiling.

Even through the thick layers of stone and wood, Isobel could still hear Reynolds shouting her name, calling out to her just before the sharp and unrelenting barrage of clanking and crashing ensued.

But it was already too late.

She wasn't listening anymore.

34
The Edge of Reason

Isobel slowed her steps. She spun in a quick circle, taking in her surroundings.

The hallway was too long and the ceiling too high to belong to Varen's house.

Scanning the walls, she could find no windows.

Old-fashioned threadbare tapestries depicting medieval knights, nobles, and ladies hung in their place over the decorative purple-and-gold-papered walls.

A plush Persian carpet runner ran the length of the floor beneath her feet, while tall curio cabinets full of strange artifacts like gold scarabs, Egyptian ankhs, and bleached animal skulls lined the walls on either side of her.

Long hallway tables holding stacks of ancient books sat outside several sets of closed double doors along with heavy high-backed chairs, the arms of which bore the carved images of crouching sphinxes.

Golden candelabra shaped like women in flowing gowns adorned the walls, the low and steady light they offered between their outstretched hands providing minimal relief from the darkness that saturated everything.

Somehow she'd been transported somewhere else, to some type of antiquated mansion or castle.

Disoriented, she thought about making another door like she had in the garden. Picturing the cliffs in her mind's eyes, with Varen standing on the verge of the jutting precipice, she held one hand out in front of her. The ends of her blood-stained ribbon dangled loose from her outstretched wrist.

She waited, but nothing happened.

Isobel held her arm steady, willing a door to materialize, like it had for Reynolds in the woodlands, like it had for her on the floor of the warehouse during the Grim Facade. There was no response to her intention, though, not even a ripple in the air. Her hand, as well as the space before her, remained empty.

She glanced around again and noticed that there, at the end of the hall, one of the walls ended at a staircase.

She ran toward it, and as she sprinted down the passage, the eyes of the figures in the tapestries followed. In her peripheral vision, she saw the heads of the faceless candelabra women turn to watch her pass. Isobel ignored their stares, placing a hand on the grand banister of the staircase, the polished wood shining liquid black in the low gleam of the flickering tapers.

Hesitating for only an instant, already knowing she had no other choice, that she couldn't go back the way she'd come, Isobel took the steps, rushing to the short landing and then up and around the second flight to the level above. As long as she kept moving, she thought as she climbed, as long as Varen stayed foremost in her mind, she would reach him no matter which direction she went. The dreamworld would take her there. She had to believe that.

And if she couldn't find a way down to the cliffs yet, at least she might be able to locate a vantage point—a window or balcony from which she could spot Varen again and try to get his attention.

When she reached the next floor, Isobel hurried into the center of another hall, similar to the one she'd left below. She paused, though, when she heard the sound of low and muffled voices emanating from behind one of the many gigantic ebony pairs of double doors.

At first she could make out only mumbling, then one of the two male voices within grew louder, more discernible.

"Not hear it? Yes, I hear it, and have heard it," the voice hissed, anxious and frantic. "Long—long—long—many minutes, many hours, many days, have I heard it—yet I dared not—oh, pity me, miserable wretch that I am!—I dared not—I dared not speak! We have put her living in the tomb!"

Isobel stepped nearer to the door, straining to catch the torrent of strange words.

"Said I not that my senses were acute?" the voice continued. "I now tell you that I heard her first feeble movements in the hollow coffin. I heard them—many, many days ago— yet I dared not—I dared not speak! And now—tonight— Ethelred—ha! ha!—the breaking of the hermit's door, and the death-cry of the dragon, and the clangor of the shield!—say, rather, the rending of her coffin, and the grating of the iron hinges of her prison, and her struggles within the coppered archway of the vault! Oh whither shall I fly? Will she not be here anon?"

Isobel scanned the surface of the door wildly, wondering who was behind it. She crept even closer and, turning her head to one side, listened hard, her ear hovering over the lacquered wood.

"Is she not hurrying to upbraid me for my haste?" the man's voice wailed. "Have I not heard her footstep on the stair? Do I not distinguish that heavy and horrible beating of her heart? Madman!" the voice shrieked suddenly. "Madman! I tell you that she now stands without the door!"

Isobel sprang back from the doors in shock. Whoever they were, they had known she was there. They had heard her on the stairs, but how?

Shuddering, the doors knocked in their frames before suddenly flying apart with a deafening bang, thrown open by a gust of tempest wind that now surged against her.

The empty room within, reversed like the foyer and parlor had been, was one Isobel knew. Varen's . . .

Except for the two solid black windows, everything else was just as she remembered.

One of the windows, the one through which she and Varen had once fled together, had been flung wide.

The driving wind howled through the casement in an unceasing drone, gusting through the room and past Isobel, moaning as it entered the hall behind her.

Looking up, she noticed a thin crack running vertically

all the way across the ceiling and down the wall, separating the room into two and disappearing into the floor. As she stepped over the threshold, she glanced around to find herself alone, with no indication that anyone had been in the room a moment before. But then whose voices had she heard?

Varen's neatly made bed sat against one wall beneath the chandelier with the electric candles. Their flame-shape bulbs sputtered, trying to stay lit. The nonworking gas fireplace still held Varen's assortment of glass bottles and dried and dusty reddish-purple roses. In one corner, Isobel saw Varen's small television and modest collection of video games.

His books lined the shelves of his bookcase in perfect order.

The closet where she'd once been forced to hide stood open, its sliding door folded back to reveal the empty hanging bars.

As Isobel moved farther in, the plaster overhead began to crumble along the crack and fall like pebbles. She pressed forward, drawn to the open window, through which she could hear the crashing of nearby waves. She stopped in front of the open sash and peered out into the desolate expanse of the dreamworld.

There, in the distance, on the cliff's ledge, stood a dark and solemn figure, his black hair windswept and wild.

She had waited so long to find him. . . .

Isobel pulled herself into the window frame. Straddling the ledge, she was about to climb out onto the top metal platform of the fire escape when a low feminine voice made her pause.

"You do surprise me."

Already knowing who she would find, Isobel dared not look.

"I do not as yet know how you passed through the boundary between our worlds," the voice continued. "And I certainly did not expect you would come this far. But I am impressed by your resolve."

Reluctantly, Isobel glanced over her shoulder to the figure who stood in the doorway — Lilith.

Her face, again beautiful and covered by sheer veils, held a serene expression as she watched Isobel steadily with two large and unblinking eyes.

"Pity, though, to think that you came all this way and have endured so much for nothing," she said. "Because I can promise that he will not go with you."

"You don't know him."

"I do," she said, "far better than you ever could. Well enough to know that he is at home here."

"*This* is not his home!" Isobel spat. "*You* are not his home."

"I think he would beg to differ."

"I know what you've done — or what you tried to do," Isobel said. "The things you showed him about me . . . and what you must have been telling him all this time. You may think he believes you, but he doesn't."

"Why tell him anything when he is perfectly capable of witnessing everything for himself?"

"I don't care what you say," Isobel snapped, and pulled herself through the window and onto the fire escape.

"When he sees me," she went on, her voice steady with certainty, "when he sees that I came for him, that I kept my promise, he'll know the truth."

"Go then," Lilith said, the corners of her lips turning up in a mocking smile. "We both know I can't stop you."

Isobel wasted no more words, and she did not look back again as she climbed down the fire escape. Reaching the last rung of the metal ladder, she dropped down to where the rocks flattened. All around stood the countless ruins of ancient stone structures, the sills of their hollow casement windows filled with ash.

Isobel swung around to face the cliffs. Even though she wanted to call out to him, she knew he wouldn't be able to hear her over the din of the roaring waves or the hiss of the whipping winds.

With his back to her, Isobel could just make out the image of the white bird that blazed on the back of his long black coat.

As she approached the place where the rocks extended outward over the churning waters, the bluff tapering like a pointed finger, Isobel slowed.

Though he had not yet turned around, she thought she could sense that he knew someone was there, drawing closer. His shoulders seemed to grow more rigid. Hanging at his sides, his hands tensed, fingers twitching as though they wanted to become fists.

He didn't know it was her, she thought. He only needed to see her, to look at her, to touch her and know she was real and really here, and then everything would be different.

"Varen!" she called.

Still, he did not look her way, and she began to wonder if this was just another trick, another twisting of her mind. Then she reminded herself that Pinfeathers was gone now, dead, if you could call it that, and there was no one left to assume Varen's image in his stead.

Isobel ventured out carefully onto the overhang, her feet crunching over the craggy terrain that was growing ever narrower. She came to where he stood staring out across the ash-white waters, less than a foot from the cliff's edge, stopping only when she reached his side.

Far below, the waves leaped at the rocks, hungrily licking at the flat face of the cliff.

When and where had she witnessed this moment before?

The wind surged stronger still, growing more and more agitated, the gales lashing at them, lifting Isobel's hair in a maddening dance.

She peered up at him, and as she did, his gaze at last turned to meet hers. His eyes, red rimmed and sunken, bore into her.

She would have given anything for the blackness within them to slip away. But it was a stranger who stood before her now, one who seemed to regard her as a stranger too.

She wanted to touch him, to throw her arms around him—but something held her back. Maybe it was the fear that her arms would pass right through him, that she would have come all this way only to find a ghost after all.

As though he'd been able to read her thoughts, he slowly

angled toward her. He raised his hands and held his palms out to her.

Isobel lifted her own hands to mirror his.

He pressed their palms together, his fingers folding down to lace through hers.

She felt a rush of warmth course through her, a relief as pure and sweet as spring rain.

He was real. *This* was real. She had found him. She could touch him. She could feel him. Finally they were together. Finally, *finally*, they could forget this wasted world and go home.

"I knew it wasn't true," she whispered. "I knew you wouldn't stop believing."

He drew her close.

Leaning into him, she felt him press his lips to her forehead in a kiss. As he spoke, the cool metal of his lip ring grazed her skin, causing a shudder to ripple through her.

"*You . . .*"

His voice, low and breathy, reverberated through her, down to the thin soles of her slippers.

"You think you're different," he said.

She felt his hands tighten around hers, gripping hard, *too* hard.

A streak of violet lightning split the sky, striking close behind them.

The house, Isobel thought. It had been struck. She could hear it cracking apart. She looked for only a brief moment, long enough to watch it split open.

"But you're not," Varen said, calling her attention back to him.

Isobel winced, her own hands surrendering under the suddenly crushing pressure of his hold.

A face she did not recognize stared down at her, one twisted with anger—with *hate.*

"You," he scarcely more than breathed, "are just like every. Body. Else."

He moved so fast. Before she could register his words or the fact that she had once spoken them to him herself, he jerked her to one side.

Isobel felt her feet part from the rocks.

Weightlessness took hold of her as she swung out and over the ledge of the cliff.

As he let her go.

The wind whistled its high and lonely song in her ears.

She fell away into the oblivion of the storm until she could no longer see the cliff—could no longer see him.

Only the slip of the pink ribbon as it unraveled from her wrist, floating up and away from her and out of sight forever.

35
The Sleeper

She saw him sitting alone in the far corner of the small and darkened room.

Slumped in one of the many greenish-blue upholstered chairs, dressed in sweatpants and one of his rumpled school uniform shirts, her little brother sat with his head propped against the wall. He clutched the skull headphones she had given him for Christmas between limp hands, and the tiny LCD screen of his iPod glowed in one slack fist. His shaggy and slightly greasy hair hung like a lampshade over his closed eyelids.

At first sight of him, an inexplicable gush of relief flooded through her.

Isobel started toward him but stopped the instant she realized she didn't know where she was. Or how she'd gotten here. Wherever here happened to be.

The room itself was nondescript, with plain industrial carpeting. Generic landscape paintings hung on smooth turquoise walls. A soda machine hummed in one corner. Next to it, a refrigerator stood beside a long countertop, its surface clear and clean except for a large coffeemaker, a bowl of assorted sugar packets, and two stacks of Styrofoam cups.

Isobel frowned, still unable to piece together enough clues to name her surroundings.

Hearing the sound of approaching footsteps, she glanced behind her. Through a narrow doorway, she saw a simple hall bathed in the glow of bright fluorescent lights, the white linoleum floors shining. The swishing sound of movement grew louder, and a man in blue scrubs passed by at a brisk walk, a clipboard tucked under one arm.

His uniform made her realize that this must be a hospital.

But why would she and her brother be in a hospital waiting room?

Confused and suddenly afraid, Isobel crossed to where Danny sat.

"Danny?"

He did not stir.

With the way he was sitting, his neck crooked awkwardly to one side, she didn't think he could really be asleep. But as she drew closer, she saw that his breathing came in slow and even intervals, his chest expanding and falling in a steady rhythm. Standing this close, she could also see the faint purple half-moons underlining his eyes—tired eyes that darted back and forth beneath their lids.

She knew that their rapid movement meant that he had to be . . . dreaming?

Isobel stopped and scanned her surroundings again, her alarm growing twofold.

Because she now knew that Danny wasn't the one who was dreaming. *She* was.

She had to be. It was the only explanation.

All the elements were there. Or rather, she corrected her-self, *not* there.

Not knowing where she was or where she'd come from. Having no recollection of the previous moment, no where or how that she could connect to—only the faint remembrance that something like this had happened to her once before. Forever ago, it seemed. And yet she could not recall that moment either.

Isobel dug deep in her memory, excavating for an image or a word, for anything at all. But nothing surfaced.

She began frantically scouring the walls for a clock, some-thing to prove her theory, and it did not take her long to spot one mounted on the far wall.

She stared hard at it, waiting for it to change its mind about the time or start spinning and, in so doing, give itself away.

The hands of the clock didn't budge, though. Just like one of Danny's video games, they seemed to hold time in pause.

But she *knew* she had to be asleep. There could be no other explanation for the weirdness she felt. For the gaping hole in her memory.

Only when Isobel saw the minute hand slide forward a fraction of an inch did she give up her scrutiny and look back down at her brother.

If this wasn't a dream, then what the hell was it?

"Danny," she whispered.

He didn't wake.

"Danny!"

When her voice rose, she heard the sound of a static pop and a fizzle directly overhead.

Her attention snapped to the TV suspended above them by a black metal armature. It flickered. Then, once the interference cleared, the screen returned to normal, casting a wan glow over the room.

A man behind a desk, dressed in a suit and tie, grinned in front of the camera. His thick eyebrows rose to his hairline as he spoke. Beside him, a blond woman with neatly molded, almost plasticized hair seemed to be practicing the art of listening, her head tilted in his direction, a polite smile in place, her hands folded in front of her.

"—news for all you Ravens fans out there," Isobel heard him say, catching the tail end of his sentence. "Though Baltimore put up a good fight in last night's game, the Ravens took a fierce beating from hard-hitting rivals the Pittsburgh Steelers, losing out on a chance to play in this year's Super Bowl."

The woman broke from her stiff Newscaster Barbie pose and turned to address the camera. "That's right, Rick. This morning it seems as if the whole city is smarting from last night's grim hour of defeat. Joining us now from the stadium is Steve Crenshaw. Steve?"

Isobel scowled at the television as the camera shot switched to a street view.

"*Baltimore?*" she whispered to herself.

A tingling dread crept over her as the jabber of the

television faded once more into background noise. A split second later, she could feel something rising through the shallow pool of her recent memory, a dark and terrible secret, one that held in it the answer to why they were there.

Isobel wheeled on her brother and reached out to jostle him.

"Danny! Wake u—"

Her hands swept cleanly through him, and she jerked back.

Her brother stirred, though he did not wake, his face scrunching before smoothing out again.

Astral, she thought. She was projecting outside her body— which meant that she wasn't dreaming after all. This was all real, the room and the brightly lit hall and Danny and the TV.

Someone new entered the room. A woman, dressed all in blue, like the man Isobel had seen in the hall.

"Danny?" she called out to Isobel's brother.

He opened his eyes with a start and focused on the woman, who moved quickly toward them.

The nurse's young face, already strained with concern, tightened as she opened her mouth to speak again. She drew nearer, passing straight through Isobel without even blinking.

"Danny, you need to come with me right now, okay?"

"Why?" Danny asked, his voice raspy from sleep. "What's happening? Did the cops find the guy who brought my sister here?"

Isobel glanced back at the nurse, anxious for her answer. It was now clear that the reason they were there revolved around Isobel. Someone had brought her here. Which could only mean . . .

"Listen," the nurse said, "you need to come with me right now. Your parents need you with them."

"What is it?" Danny demanded, and stood, letting the headphones and iPod drop out of his lap and onto the floor. "What's wrong? What's happening with my sister?"

"They're taking her to the ICU. Your mom and dad are wait—"

Danny's face crumpled. "No, they're not taking her there!" he shouted. "She was fine. I just saw her and she was fine!"

"Danny—"

The nurse reached for him, but he jerked his arm away and skittered around her, running past Isobel and through the open doorway.

Hurrying after, the nurse continued to call out to him.

Isobel began to follow but stopped suddenly when a glimmer of light erupted in the space right in front of her, like the glint of a shining object. It drew her attention downward. There, extending outward from her center, she saw it—the silver cord. It wavered, fluttering in and out of existence, as though struggling to remain intact.

When it glimmered into sight again, visible for longer than an instant, Isobel reached out and touched her fingertips to the ethereal strand. Suddenly, in a whir of movement and a haze of images, she was somewhere else—another room in the hospital. One filled with doctors and harried nurses, all of them wearing clean blue medical masks.

They stood gathered around a long table. Whoever was lying on the cold metal surface, Isobel could see only her bare feet, which poked out from the huddle of medical personnel.

"Clear!" she heard someone shout, followed by a harsh slamming sound.

The light inside the room grew instantly brighter around her. Intense enough to smudge away the walls and the cabinets and the swinging doors that flapped like shutters in the wind as nurses came and went. Clean and white, blindingly bright, it erased everything but those two limp feet, the table, and those who stood closest to it.

Already knowing what she would find—*who* she would find—in the center of their frenzy, Isobel slowly rounded the table. All the while, the nurses and doctors remained oblivious to her dual presence, taking turns applying instruments, their frantic movements reminding her of swarming ants.

Peering between the shoulders of two of the medical personnel, Isobel did not think the battered and bruised girl on the table looked much like her. And yet she knew by the thin scratch on her cheek that it could be no one else.

Isobel lifted a hand to her face but felt no trace of the scratch. Yet she remembered in an instant how it had gotten there.

Pinfeathers . . .

The Noc's image was the first to spring forth from behind the previously locked door. Then came the memory of the rose garden and the chaos that had transpired there. From there, her thoughts reeled backward in fast rewind, and she recalled being in the graveyard where Poe was buried, and that *that* place had been the reason she'd come here, to Baltimore.

The tone of the heart monitor continued to sound its long and unceasing note, making it harder to think.

"Clear!" someone shouted again.

The doctor shocked her again, and Isobel saw her body convulse.

The sight made her wonder whether she wanted to continue remembering, and yet she knew she was dying. Or was she already dead? How? What had brought her here, to this point of destruction?

"We've lost her," she heard someone announce.

Lost.

She'd been searching for something she'd lost. No, she recalled. Not something. Some*one*.

A vision of a pale face and black eyes flashed through her mind.

"Varen," she whispered. Of course. She'd come all this way to find him, to face Reynolds in the graveyard, and to bring him home. But then, if she was here, where was he?

Had she been able to bring him back? She wasn't sure. She couldn't delve that deep.

Isobel looked up, distracted from her thoughts when she saw the nurses beginning to unhook the equipment from her lifeless form on the table.

She looked down at her astral body, searching for any sign of the silver cord, but now she could barely see the outline of her astral figure either. It was as if she was fading out, like a ghost.

But it couldn't end like this, she thought. She had to know what had happened to him. At the very least, she had to know if she'd been able to bring him home. She couldn't leave, she couldn't go anywhere until she knew for sure.

"Stop," she said to the man who'd begun to unroll a smooth, clean white sheet over her body.

"Stop!" she shouted again, and this time, as the lights above him and the equipment around him stuttered and fizzled, he did.

Isobel took her chance. She closed her eyes, using the split second of bought time to imagine the silver cord back into existence.

But it was too late, she was slipping backward, falling away. Dissolving. She opened her eyes to see the world whir into an indefinite blur.

The snap came like a punch to her gut.

Then her eyes flew open for a second time—her real eyes. She gasped, sucking in air as though she'd been drowning. She looked up and saw the sheet poised above her head and knew she was back in her body. Raising an arm, she pushed away the hands that held the white sheet just over her face.

The pain in her body came first, an intense surge of fire that raged like lava through her veins.

But it could not compare with what followed after.

A wail rose up from her depths. It left her as an inhuman cry.

Finally, she remembered everything.

Epilogue

He walked into the rose garden, passing from the woodlands through the open doorway.

With slow steps, Varen made his way toward the silent fountain.

Beneath his boots, bits of broken Noc and scattered shards popped and crumbled. All around, the fragments lay strewn like smashed artifacts.

Pieces of me, he thought.

He paused for a moment to glance down at the broken face that lay like a discarded mask amid the ash, petals, and ruin. Through the familiar hole in the creature's cheek, he could see straight through to the marble floor.

Looking away, he passed on but stopped midstep when the sole of his boot encountered a shard that refused to collapse.

He glanced down again, catching the spark of silver that flashed from within the bed of ash and bruised petals.

Bending, Varen retrieved from the rubble a small charm, one shaped like a butterfly.

He realized the trinket was a watch only after pressing his thumb to the wings. Snapping apart, they revealed a trio of spinning black hands within.

He could tell the charm was real and not a dream when it didn't dissolve into ash at his command. Ironic, he thought as he turned it over in his fingers, that something like this could have found its way here. Butterflies represented freedom and hope, life and peace. Things that couldn't survive or remain undistorted in this realm, no matter what form they took.

They were things that no longer existed within him, either.

She, *Isobel*, must have brought it with her.

At the thought of her name, a tightness gripped his chest.

He clutched the watch hard in his fist, determined to destroy it, to prove that it couldn't be real. That she hadn't come here because of him, for him.

That he hadn't done what he knew he had.

The watch remained solid in his fist, the metal burning cold against his palm while, around him, the roses clinging to the dome began to quiver.

All at once, they gave a unanimous shudder, and with a sound like the rush of brittle leaves, they began to shrivel and die. The decay spread before him in a wave, as though wrought by an invisible fire.

Ash rained down around him.

He opened his palm and saw that the watch remained. Still there. Still real.

Varen looked up at the figure that stood atop the fountain.

With a howl of rage, he made it burst apart.

He fell to his knees amid the wreckage and floating dust. Crumpling into himself, he released a choking sob, knowing that he, too, belonged to the ruin.

Acknowledgments

I would like to begin by thanking my incredible editor, Namrata Tripathi, who has believed in Isobel and Varen's story from page one and who helped me navigate through multiple drafts of *Enshadowed*. Thank you for your abounding patience and for your willingness to walk with me through the woodlands, even when my Nocs came out from hiding.

A special and heartfelt thank-you to Emma Ledbetter, whose insight, keen powers of perception, and extra attention to this novel proved invaluable.

My spectacular agent, Tracey Adams, has my immense gratitude for being more than my superhero through my first sequel-writing adventure. A huge thank-you as well goes to Josh Adams and to all the awesome folks at Adams Literary.

Much appreciation also goes to my copy editors, Valerie Shea and Jeannie Ng. I do not know how you do the things you do, but you do them so well—all while making my work shine in the process. Thank you for lending me your polish.

I would also like to extend gratitude to my friends at Atheneum and Simon & Schuster for their expertise and for all of the hard work that goes into preparing my book for the shelf.

That I have constructed a second novel is both humbling and heartening. I have come a long way as a writer, and I owe so very much of my continued growth and success to my friends, including fellow writer April Joye Cannon, who stood by as my trusty beta reader, taking chapters as they came, reading multiple drafts, and telling me what was up, yo. April, you're a godsend and a true friend.

I am also indebted to Megan Evans and Nick Passafiume, who were always ready to lend an ear, to read and share their thoughts. Thank you to Jeannine Buhse, who acted as my soundingboard whenever I hit a speed bump; to Greta Smith, whose sensible input sent me back to the fountain; to Jackie Marrs, for being all kinds of fabulous; to Jennifer O'Loughlin, whose encouragement was integral to the process; to Jackie Wisman, for the use of his office; and to Joyce McDonald, my role model and mentor.

Thank you as well to Michael Luka, (aka Freddie Joe), for teaching me how to pick a lock. Because of you, I believe I am now slightly cooler than I was before. Thanks also to my dear friend Susan Luka, for her counsel and support.

During the late stages of writing this book, I was somehow lucky enough to stumble into the midst of some of the best writing buddies one could ever ask for. Their encouragement and advice continues to boost me to new levels. Thank you, Collyn Justus, for the Quills Coffee writing dates and for being so gosh darn hysterical; Bill Wolfe, Kurt Hampe, Katie McGarry, Colette Ballard, and Bethany Griffin, for inviting me to join in the antics and for making me a better writer every time we meet.

As was the case with *Nevermore*, research played a vital role in the crafting of this novel. I would like to again extend my thanks to the Poe Society of Baltimore; to the curator of the Poe House, Jeff Jerome; to Mary Jo Rodney; to the staff at Westminster Hall; and to the staff at the Poe Museum in Richmond, Virginia. Thank you also to Jeff Savoye, for letting me pick his brain in a certain Baltimore cemetery on Halloween night. Additional thanks goes to the mysterious Poe Toaster (wherever you may be), for creating a legacy, for inspiring the character of Reynolds, and for making history.

Through the writing of *Nevermore* and *Enshadowed*, cheerleading has become one of my favorite sports, and though I can't pull off a back tuck, I am fortunate enough to know a few gals who can. Thanks to Chelsea Winburn, Callie Lynn Gartman, and Carly Howcroft for answering all my questions about the particulars. Cheer on, ladies!

I owe thanks as well to my good friend Jenny Haskell, for providing inspiration and for correcting me about orthodontics tools — I mean, instruments — and to Ellen Haskell, who was kind enough to share many fascinating facts pertaining to the figure of Lilith.

From the depths of my heart, I would like to shout a big thank-you to Nick Davenport. Your support has meant more than you will ever know.

I would like to thank God, my writing partner and the coauthor of all my achievements, and also my family, who have provided tremendous support. A million thanks go to my mother, especially for being a constant source of guidance and encouragement, not only with my writing, but with life. I am an artist because of you. Thanks for the acting, writing, drawing, painting, dancing, you-name-it lessons.

Lastly, I would like to express my boundless appreciation and gratitude to my readers and fans and to the booksellers and librarians who usher my stories into their hands. Thank you for reading and for following me into the shadowy regions of my dreamworlds. You allow me to do what I love most.